The Wild in her Eyes

Karina Giörtz

Published by Never Did Point North Publishing, 2019.

Editing by Jaclyn DeVore @ Devore Editorial
www.devoreeditorial.com
Cover by Regina Wamba ~ Creator of Awesome Things
www.ReginaWamba.com
www.MaeIDesign.com
Final Proofing by Barb Piper

For the misfits ~ the world needs more of us.

Jaclyn —
I can't begin to express how much I have loved taking this journey with you, or how grateful I am for all you poured into this story to help me bring it to life ♡
Looking forward to our next writing adventure! ♡
luv,
Kaia ♡

My hope...

"A moment of consciousness among unconscious thought. And the courage to change it."

~ K

And so begins a different sort of 'Once Upon A Time'...

Chapter One

WRONGS TO BE RIGHTED

The damp earth gave way under her feet and her palms landed in the brush and dirt to catch her. Rather than stop to find her footing, she dug in her fingers and clawed herself forward until her feet found the ground again beneath her. She stumbled breathless through the dark and willed her eyes to adjust to the black of night but feared what they might find there.

Nothing ahead could be worse than what I left behind, she thought. She held tight to this naïve thought. All her seventeen years may have been sheltered and filled with lavish luxuries like those only her father's kind of wealth could provide, but she'd seen the chasm between the world her parents had created and the one beyond their fancy colonial home, built on a hill overlooking the heart of her hometown, or the extravagant parties and her exceptional schooling. She'd always been grateful to live life on her side of the divide, free of financial strain and societal struggles, far removed from the filth and unsavory sort that roamed the streets at night, begging for a handout they'd only have squandered away again come morning. Always, until tonight. There would be no going back. Her survival depended on traveling deeper into this dark night, uprooting herself from all that she knew was the only way to stay alive. Beyond that, nothing was certain anymore.

As the heels of her boots stuck in the mud and her dress dragged along the ground, catching on brambles and ripping to shreds, whispers of nightmares still ahead hissed in her ears. She clutched at the branches that scraped her skin and she pulled herself onward. She was sure that by now he most certainly knew she was gone. There was no telling how quickly he would discover how she'd successfully escaped.

She pulled the worn wool coat tighter around her to insulate against the cold chill sweeping through the forest. A thick woven belt replaced most of the coat's buttons, lost from years of use. She wrapped the sides of the long, rough material so it overlapped across her stomach and then retied the belt tighter without slowing down. She kept moving forward, but her thoughts drifted back to the woman who'd wrapped her in this coat. She and the woman, her housekeeper, had exchanged every article of clothing they both wore that night. She'd shed her gown of rose-colored satin and hand-stitched details, along with her polished white boots, and put on an olive day dress and shoes with hole-riddled soles and frayed black laces, one thicker than the other. She might have been stripped of her past tonight, but it was the other woman who'd paid the greatest price. She had sacrificed her future.

The wind burned her skin raw as tears smeared her cheeks. She hardly noticed the painful friction her hands caused as she swiped at her face. Somewhere in the distance she heard the howl of dogs. Her breath caught in her throat at the sound of the hounds, as bloodthirsty as their owner. She knew they were tracking her. She had prepared for this moment. Her shaky hands moved for the pocket sewn into the side of the dress as she silently begged her thundering heart to quiet, certain the dogs could hear the panic pounding in her chest. Her fingers searched the linen pouch until they closed over the cold, slick, raw beef and flung it far out to the right of her. She didn't wait to hear it land. A cold sweat rushed down the crease of her back as her eyes stayed locked on the night sky and her legs kept running over the uneven terrain. Follow the North Star, she remembered. It would lead her to the water.

The creek was small and shallow enough to wade across, but the current was strong enough to cut the scent of her trail. It was a better way to outsmart the hounds than the meat she'd used to distract them. It would buy her time, but not much of it.

Her own panting rushed in her ears as she struggled for breath. Her lungs cinched from the icy air. Adrenaline pumped through her in almost unbearable surges of energy, making it difficult to control her body's movements. The sounds of water lapping over the rocks along the shore went unheard until she held her breath to listen for the dogs again. Relief tingled through her in waves as she parted the brush with her arms and turned her slender body sideways to pass through. She was almost there now. Almost free. Just a few more feet and she'd be in the creek, washing away her trail and making herself invisible to the night and the monsters hiding within it—those on this side of the water, at least.

The sandy bank of the small river was softer than she'd expected and so she stumbled. Her hands landed under her and shards of small rocks dug deep into her palms, slicing her soft skin. She swallowed the pain and let it land in the pit of her stomach with all the rest of her accumulated hurt. The whole of it twisted in her gut like knives through her abdomen. Teeth gritted, she locked her jaw and forced down all that threatened to overtake her, until the numbness spread and she could feel nothing—nothing except the cold of the water rushing alongside her calves, then moving up around her thighs, until she passed the deepest point of the creek and waded through the dark, waist-high water. It silently coaxed her body to sync with the current and disappear forever in the flow of the creek. She was tempted to surrender and be free of this night and all the terrors that would live inside her mind forever after. Her eyes closed. She let her ankle give way to the current's force. Until she heard it. Her housekeeper's voice rang in her ears, an echo of words lingering inside her. *"You make this right. Whatever wrong comes of this night, you go out there, and you live, and you make it right."*

The sole of her boot kicked hard into the rocky ground beneath her, sending a dull ache through her heel. It felt good. It felt alive. In that pain she knew there would be no giving in to the current tonight. Not ever. Not when the cost of her freedom had been paid by another. She owed it to her housekeeper, to her father, and to herself to stay alive, to keep moving, to make things right, no matter how long it took.

The water began to sway around her, gliding past the curve of her body as if it understood somehow that it would not claim her. Her passage grew easier with every inch that moved her closer to the opposite shore. The cold slipped down her hips and past her knees until it pooled only around her ankles. She felt the squish of water inside her boots as they found dry land. She'd imagined herself collapsing from exhaustion as a false sense of security settled over her after crossing the creek, but she felt neither tired nor weak as she placed one foot in front of the other on the bank, with her shoulders straight, chest out, and head high. There would be no trace left for the dogs to find. There would be no trace left of her at all.

By morning, she'd traveled miles from home. How many, she couldn't say for sure, but she'd kept moving until the orange glow of dawn began to creep up along the horizon. Only when she knew for certain day was upon her did she finally allow her body to rest. Curled up along the curve of a fallen tree trunk, she slept nestled in the leaves and soft moss, hidden away behind the brush and overgrowth that had long ago welcomed their fallen friend back home to the earth from which they'd all grown.

When she awoke, the sun sat high in the sky and the growl of her own stomach reminded her how many hours had passed since her last meal. Even as her hollow insides whined in discomfort, her appetite remained absent. Still, she knew she'd need her strength. And so, her body sore and weak, she began to search for viable sustenance. It took some time and foraging, but the forest supplied well, offering up a fair share of wild blackberries and a handful of mushrooms she recognized from hikes with her father. Those adventures with him seemed an eternity ago now. On the rare occasion he'd been in town to do so, they'd spend the day exploring the woods behind their home, wandering together, basking in the midday sun, and enjoying whatever treats they'd stumbled upon on their walk. Her father had always been good at finding treasured morsels among the weeds and forest debris. His years of travel had taught him much, and so he'd seen to it that she too learned to tell the poison from the berry, the edible from the deadly. It had been all in good fun once upon a time. Now she could hardly bear the pain of dwelling on the memories beyond the details she needed to remember to survive.

Before long, her stomach quieted and she returned to her journey, following paths walked only by hooves and padded paws before her.

She navigated by the sun during the day and let the stars guide her at night, slept and ate only when her body demanded it, and kept far from the bounds of civilization. As the days passed, her blistered feet became bruised and bloody. She left rusty red marks in the dirt with her every step, the evidence of her pain oozing through the holes in her battered shoes. All but one of her fingernails had ripped off at the nailbed—nine casualties of clawing her way through the wild terrain and fending for food and building fires on the coldest nights. Keeping to the woods had sheltered her from rain and sun, but it had done little to preserve her overall appearance. Her dress was filthy and torn. The exposed parts of her body had suffered cuts and scrapes after repeated lashings from wayward tree limbs and debris, which was carried on a whipping wind that left her cheeks and lips burned and raw.

She tripped on a long, knobby root of an ancient oak and let out a hoarse yelp from falling face first and realized the absence of her voice. Startled, she touched her throat. The rough calluses from her own hand against her tender skin caught her off guard a second time. She didn't recognize her own body anymore. Slowly, she climbed back to her feet and steadied herself against the tree whose roots had thwarted her.

There, standing tall and staring blankly at the horizon, her new body and reborn spirit glimpsed their new fate. The silence of the woods, which had been like an invisible veil keeping her secluded during her journey, lifted. Beyond the trees lay a vast, green valley. And it was filled with life, human life. She relished the buzzing of voices and bodies hard at work. She looked closer. The people she saw below were members of a traveling circus.

She'd heard stories, of course, about the freaks who ran with the circus. Scoundrels always on the hunt for their next schemes. Shameless women willing to do depraved things too lurid to even contemplate. Tales of two-headed men and bearded ladies, creatures so deformed and unnatural that the devil himself had a hand in creating them. These stories had been meant to scare her away, to encourage her to keep her distance from the likes of those who sought out the open road, the shows, the tents, and the paths that led from sordid pasts to torrid futures. The tales had always worked, but none quite as well as that of the one-eyed man her mother had called the Human Snake, who hypnotized his audience into submission, leaving them in his control forever after, none of them ever the wiser of the terrible acts he had them perform while in their trance.

Fear of the unknown had held her curiosities at bay. But now the unknown was all she had, and it would take more than scary stories to frighten her away after all she'd experienced. Besides, she couldn't help but notice that the circus people were laughing and working together. Some were even singing! She failed to sense any wickedness, especially after she'd learned that real beasts could hide in her own home. It was unlikely, she decided, that truly evil people would display their traits for the world to marvel at—and charge an entry fee to do so.

Her feet moved ever faster as she gained momentum down the hill, her only focus on reaching the circus camp. Beyond that, she had few plans and nothing to offer. No one seemed to take notice, at first, of the stranger in their midst. Then, one by one, eyes strayed from their tasks and toward her. Motions grew slower, conversations stopped, and the quiet slowly set in. Her footsteps, thudding over grass and gravel, grew louder with each step. She squared her shoulders and lifted the crown of her head skyward as she felt the heat of a hundred stares following her every move. Still, she remained focused, staring straight ahead at her goal: the carriage, nearest the engine, flagged with the brightest red banner and marked in bold yellow lettering. *Brooks and Bennet Circus—Come One, Come All.*

She was inches from reaching for the handle when the door swung open, seemingly of its own accord, and a rail-thin man nearly seven feet tall strolled out. "What the blazes has got you all tongue-tied all of a sudden? I can hear your peace and quiet all the way in here!" He laughed to himself, then stopped when he spotted her. "Oh. I see." For the first time in her life she had to wonder what, exactly, he was looking at as he stood before her, his head tilting sideways toward his slumped left shoulder to get a better angle.

Any other time, she'd have known exactly what he was looking at. Golden hair pinned up in the front, with long, tight curls flowing down her back. Naturally rosy cheeks highlighting a flawless complexion and bright green eyes sparkling under the sunlight. Her whole life she'd never left her room unless she was impeccably dressed. This was most certainly not the case today as she stood there in her housekeeper's rags. Nevertheless, she held her head high and waited patiently while the man assessed her. His tan skin bore scars all around his arms, visible where the sleeves of his shirt had been rolled up. His clothes fit awkwardly due to his height, and the only item that looked entirely in place was the blue linen cap he wore. It hid what was left of his graying hair. Laugh lines were well worn into his leathery skin. The silver shadow of hair reaching around his mouth and down his neck, proof he hadn't shaved in at least a day or two, wasn't able to hide how his thin mouth twitched at the corners, always threatening to break into a smile.

Then, a sadness darkened his narrow blue eyes as he reached one lanky arm up to stroke his stubbled jaw. "You have a name then, love?" he asked with a tenderness that surprised her.

She cleared her throat, remembering the absence of her voice. It took several attempts, but she found the words she needed. Her answer rattled on a long, desperate breath she feared would suffocate her if she didn't release it.

"Annis, sir. Annis Josephine Watson."

She breathed in. Her chest felt light. Her heart beat steadily. And just like that, five simple words had brought her back to life.

Chapter Two

COME ONE COME ALL

"I need a job, sir," Annis said, her voice getting stronger with every syllable.

"I imagine you do," he said, nodding at her pitiful appearance. "Imagine you could also do with a bit of water." He pulled the canteen he wore strapped over his left shoulder up over his head and handed it to her. "Go on then, have it," he insisted when she didn't take it. "Only just refilled it, so there's plenty."

Annis was torn. She'd gone without a drink for so long, she hardly remembered what thirst felt like. Though she knew her body was desperate for fluids, her less rational thoughts forbade her from accepting such a gift so easily. Kindness aside, he was a stranger and her trust in people was sparse these days. Everyone had an agenda. No one gave anything for nothing. Not even water. Not when she so clearly needed it. It would be too easy to use against her later.

"I'm alright, thank you," she said, pushing the canteen away. Maybe the days alone with her overwrought mind and terrorized thoughts had made her paranoid, but she couldn't chance it. Anything she received from here on out, she would earn. There would be no risk of blackmail or unpaid debts left for someone to collect on. "I'm not looking for handouts. I want work."

The man shook his head, his eyes narrowed as though he were attempting to sort out his own thoughts about her but was coming up short. "What you *need* is water. You take it, you see to yourself, and then we'll talk about your wants, understood?"

Annis opened her mouth to argue a second time but was met with a silent warning in the man's steely glare she understood she'd do well to heed.

"How much?" she asked, strength waning from her voice even as she set to strike her own terms for the exchange. Her mind, ever alert, took note of her body's evident betrayal and cursed herself for her weakness. "For the water. How much will it cost?" She hadn't a penny to her name, but at least the number would set her debt before she accumulated it.

"You've only just shown up and you're already a right pain in my arse, you know that?" the man said with a snort, rubbing his forehead with his thumb and index finger, a move she knew all too well from her mother, who had never hesitated to let Annis know when she was cuing the next migraine with what she called Annis's insipid conversations and foolish behavior. "We don't charge for water here, love. It's not the sort of business we're in. You want to pay me, you come see the show. I'll charge you any night of the week for that."

"But," her mouth hung open, her arguments running thin. With little left to counter with, she ran her tongue over her lower lip, stalling for time. She felt the sandpaper skin of her own mouth. Her hand went up to touch it, only to find it was not only rough and cracked, but dry as the desert in the midday sun. Not even her tongue held moisture anymore. At last, she surrendered to his offer, taking the canteen and moving it up to her lips without another word.

She drank. Cold water flooded her throat, awakening everything within, sending an icy rush through her chest and down to her belly. Gulp after gulp, the liquid moved through her. Within moments she'd emptied the entire canteen, leaving her more aware of her thirst than she'd been before even tasting a sip.

The man smiled oddly at her, reminding Annis of the way she used to peer at baby chicks when they first hatched out in the hen house. They were awkward and strange looking at first, but curious and sweet all the same. She couldn't decide if she took offense to his expression or not. He took the canteen from her before she came to a conclusion either way. "We'll get more. Just let it settle for a moment or it'll turn your stomach."

She nodded, wiping the spilled water from where it had dribbled down to her chin. "About the job," she began again, determined to make a case for herself.

"You ever done any work like this?" he asked.

She began to say an adamant yes, but then reconsidered the lie. "I've performed." She tried to hide her shaking hands by pulling the loose strands of hair away from her face and back over her shoulder. She regretted the move at once. The man raised his brows to meet the rim of his blue cap. The line of his mouth pulled in toward the center and stopped just short of a frown at the sight of her now fully exposed face, which she knew was likely covered in dirt and blood.

"How old are you?" he asked, his eyes narrow.

"Twenty, sir," she said, swallowing. Though lying had never come easily to her, this wasn't the first lie she'd told the man. Somehow the first one had come naturally. The words just came out of her mouth without forethought. Maybe they were my last remaining truth, she thought.

At last he smirked, lifting his brows and straightening his shoulders. "Well, we can pretend I believe that." He chuckled softly. "Come along, then." He gave her a nod and began to walk past her toward the workers who'd resumed their tasks. Some of them tended to animals, others flitted about with an abundance of props and costumes nearly flowing from their grasps as they flew past. The bulk of the crew carried on setting up the circus tent.

"Wait. Are you giving me a job?" she asked, almost afraid to believe her good fortune. "You're letting me stay? Just like that?"

"It's the circus, love. No one comes to stay except me and Babe, but you can come along for the ride as long as you wish and get off when you've had enough." He glanced back at her over his shoulder, winking. "You say you've performed?"

"Yes. Yes, sir." Her stride was half the length of his and her tired legs fought to keep his pace. "I've been a dancer from the time I was four, sir." He stopped abruptly and Annis nearly collided with him. He turned to face her.

"Before this goes any further, we need to clear something up, love," he said.

Annis braced herself for his next words. She knew it had been too easy. There would be strings attached to the job. Her mind began to race through all the despicable deeds she'd be forced to participate in. Thievery. Fraud. The imaginary list grew longer as she considered the ways in which one could be forced to collude in schemes of lawless greed and deceit.

"It's Hugh," he said, catching her completely off guard with the simplicity of his words. "Not sir. Not mister." His tone was calm but stern, with a slight emphasis on the labels he eschewed. "Just Hugh. Or Poppy, when you get comfortable." He tilted his head, brows furrowed, but his eyes still twinkled. "Are we clear?"

She nodded. And then she shook her head. She decided it was likely she was delirious from exhaustion, delusional from dehydration, and just plain slow from being starved, but she was also certain that nothing was clear. He was the ringmaster, was he not? Calling him "sir" seemed more appropriate, given his role, than simply Hugh or, God forbid, Poppy. "I'm sorry?" was all she could say.

"That car there," he explained, pointing his long, bony finger to where they'd just met. "It's got my name on it right along with Babe's. Not because this is our business but because it's our family. Our home." He hunched down closer to her and spoke more softly. "We never set out to run a circus, love. We ran away, and the circus found us. Same as you. Same as everyone you see here. You want to work here, you're welcome to any job that needs doing. You'll have your cut of the night's take every show you're here for, same as everyone else. And we all get an equal share. Even me. Even Babe. And we don't get called fussy things like *sir*. Or *mister*. Not me. Definitely not Babe." Annis began to nod her head, still not fully comprehending this unexpected turn in her newfound salvation but eager to please in order to keep it.

"Alright, then," he said, smiling. "Onward." He turned, stretching his fist out to lead the way straight into the nearest huddle of people, who were all working together to string up the massive tarp of the tent and preparing to mount it over the poles that were already in place. Annis gaped at the sight of men and women of all ages and colors, working together as equals, tackling tasks she imagined must be done in complete unison.

"They'll just be a minute," Hugh said, glancing back and forth between her and the workers, amusement dancing in his eyes at her state of awe. And though her gaze stayed with the display before her, her mind engaged in a grand game of ping pong, thoughts flying back and forth between the men and women at work and the strange but kind man standing beside her. What must he be thinking of her and the pitiful state she was in, the obvious lies she had told? He had to have had some thoughts about those. And, given his clear skills of observation, they likely weren't far off. Surely, he'd deduced she was a runaway. He probably wondered if she was hiding from the law. If so, what did he imagine her guilty of? Stealing? Most likely. How many crimes could she really have pursued successfully beyond petty theft? Nothing about her frail and bedraggled body suggested she was physically capable of causing harm to anything larger than a garden snake. Or what about arson? Maybe he thought her to be some sort of firebug. That could even have been the reason he'd let her stay. A knack for playing with flames would probably come in handy around the circus. Alas, the longer she entertained the notion, the more she reconsidered what he was truly looking at when he saw her. Long wispy hair, hardly suitable for being around open flames. Her pasty, pale skin now bore marks that could only imply a massacre of sorts had taken place. But even underneath the dried blood and layers of dirt, the softness of her skin still gave evidence of a girl who, until quite recently, had never suffered more than a needle prick, let alone a burn.

More obvious than anything else, she thought, was her cowardice. The meek way in which she carried herself, light footed and hesitant in her every move. If she was perfectly honest with herself, Annis knew no one would ever count her as a scoundrel. She was running, certainly, but not because she'd sought out trouble. That the trouble had sought her would be clear to anyone.

She dared a sideways glance in Hugh's direction. He was polite enough to pretend not to notice, even if the slight twitch at the corner of his mouth gave him away. Whatever he thought of her, it couldn't be all bad. More importantly, she was starting to think all the bad she'd thought about him, and the likes of those who found themselves drawn to the circus, couldn't be all true either. If there was even a kernel of truth to any of it at all. Her gaze shifted back toward the scene unfolding before her and she finally registered what Hugh had said.

"Just a minute," she echoed his last words dryly, her mind still stuck somewhere between disbelief and a growing acceptance that anything was possible as she took in the scene before her. "Who am I to doubt anything?" Annis wondered to herself. As if on cue, the tent rose from the ground on someone's count of three and began to glide smoothly over its skeleton of poles and beams. Within a matter of moments, the entire structure was secure and Annis was standing in front of a magnificent display of bright red and yellow stripes. Thick golden trim marked the seams of the canvas and matching tassels dangled at each point of the structure. Scarlet flags marked the highest peaks, each flapping in the breeze.

"Wow," she breathed. She hadn't yet noticed the crowd forming around her, composed of people eager to meet the newcomer.

"Annis," Hugh said. When she didn't react, he said it a second time. "Annis?"

This time she registered the sound of her name and her cheeks reddened. "Oh." Now that she was facing everyone, she saw just how much the differences between them spanned the spectrum. Men and women, young and old. Some freakishly tall, others surprisingly small. Women with short hair. Men with long. Large men. Some made up of muscle, some not. The only thing they all had in common was that there was something entirely unexpected in each of them.

Whether he was unaware of her momentary shock or had expected such a reaction, Hugh never let on. He simply carried on as though everything were normal. Perhaps such a scene would be less surprising to young women who had led less sheltered lives.

Nodding to his left at the person nearest to him, Hugh began, "Annis, this is Babe. She's the Bennet of Brooks and Bennet Circus." Hugh grinned and reached out to embrace a stout, jolly looking man with a massive beard and long curly, blond hair that was tied together in a loose, thick braid draped over his shoulder. Babe wore flowing garments that resembled a dress and reached his ankles. He took Annis's hand and curtsied. "Annis, you adorable tulip. I just want to hug and kiss you. May I?"

"Oh, okay," Annis said as Babe squeezed her into a rib-crushing hug that brought her to tears—not from pain, but from the emotional overwhelm at the display of such affection from a complete stranger.

"You'll be safe here, Tulip," Babe whispered, cheek pressed to her ear. "Don't you worry about a thing. Babe'll get you washed up and patched up in no time," he promised in a voice that sounded neither masculine nor feminine, and which Annis could only describe as maternal.

She sighed, melting into the tight embrace, and allowed herself just a moment of peace before untangling herself from his welcoming arms. "Thank you," Annis mumbled as she stepped back.

"I know Babe will be fussing over you just as soon as she gets you out of here," Annis heard a woman's voice say from somewhere in the center of the crowd that now formed a nearly complete circle around where she stood. Annis was too focused on Babe being referred to as *she* to identify the speaker right away. When she did, she noticed the woman was older than Hugh and Babe, with smooth dark skin that reminded Annis of her father's morning coffee. The woman wore her black hair in tight twists that snaked the sides of her head until they met to form a knotted bun. Never had Annis met a woman who commanded such presence. She spoke in a rough, brash voice, with both hands fisted and set high on her waist. "When she sets you free, you come find Momma T. I do all the cookin' 'round here, and you, girl, look like you ain't eaten in days."

It was mostly true. Annis had eaten, though what she'd consumed could barely qualify as food. "Thank you, ma'a—" She stopped mid-word when Hugh shook his head at her, one brow arched, indicating she ought to know better by now. "—Momma

T," she corrected with a meek smile at the woman who, unlike Babe, seemed to house no motherly bone in her body. Annis thought it was a stretch even to call Momma T friendly, with her squared shoulders, thin lips, and heavy-lidded eyes.

"Don't you worry none," a chipper voice said from Annis's lower left. "Momma T's only scary 'til you taste her beans and cornbread." Annis's eyes followed her ears until they landed on a man with messy, walnut-colored hair poking out in all directions beneath his frayed gray cap. He came up just below her hip, though he looked slightly older than she was. His sprite-like eyes met hers. He smiled like he knew exactly what she'd been thinking and had maybe even been waiting for her to finish her thought before he carried on. "Her food is where she keeps her heart. You'll see." He grinned, reaching his hand out to her. "Name's Sawyer. Most folks call me Sawyer Smalls, or Smalls for short." He paused, his eyes twinkling with delight at his own joke. "See what I did there?"

Annis nodded, unsure if it was in good taste to laugh. Instead, she took his hand and shook it politely. "Annis. It's lovely to meet you." His grasp was stronger than she'd expected.

"Give it a week," he said. "Then you'll know better." He winked, releasing her hand. This time, she let out a spontaneous giggle.

"Right, then," Hugh chimed in impatiently, placing both hands on his hips and giving a disapproving glare around the circle, which had lost some of its order due to the recent introductions. "If I'd known you'd all turn this into a bloody pre-show production, I'd have just called out everyone's name in passing and pointed." A rash of amused muttering erupted from the crowd, but they obliged his implied request for order and lined up shoulder to shoulder.

Once they were settled, he continued. "Alright, we haven't got all day to do this, so I'll go 'round. I'll say your name and you raise your hand, smile, curtsy, or do a ruddy headstand, for all I care. Just identify yourself and then let me move it along."

He reached his long arm out and took Annis's shoulder. "Come stand here, love," he said, directing her to an overturned bucket on the ground nearby. "Get up high so you can see everyone." Annis did as she was told, and Hugh began rattling off names. They were claimed, one by one, by someone in the crowd.

"Mabel. Maude."

There was a brief interlude for Annis to spot them. She noticed they not only had identical raven hair and alabaster skin, but also their hips were fused together below the waist so that one twin was always on the left and the other always on the right. They wore a garment made from two conjoined dresses that were tailored for their needs. Both women waved, smiling as they welcomed her.

"Margaret. Oscar."

A woman and man, both nearly as round as Hugh was tall, stepped forward ever so slightly, and the man's protruding belly bumped into the woman in front of him, making her laugh as she jumped forward to keep from falling.

"And that there's Bess. She's our tightrope walker. Everyone's always trying to make her fall, see. Just for fun, of course. 'Cause it can't be done," Hugh said before quickly continuing his roll call before the crowd lost all order again. By the time he finished, Annis had met trapeze artists Della and Leo; Homer, who could juggle anything from plates to balls of fire; Floyd, an albino man in his seventies; August, who claimed to be the strongest man alive; and Caroline, a red-haired woman with an unusual capacity to bend and contort herself. Caroline really did do a headstand to introduce herself, except she'd taken Hugh's invitation literally and, once in an inverted position, bent her feet back until she was actually standing on her own head. Annis met Francis and Will, who did the heavy lifting for Brooks and Bennet. They were on the run from the authorities for their many thieving transgressions. Then there was Lila, Etta, and Viola, a lovely singing trio who were all sisters born to a slave mother and privileged father, both of whom had been executed for their affair. By the time Hugh stopped spouting off names, Annis was dizzy from the volume of information, as well as the oddity of it all.

She was about to ask if there was a place where she could perhaps get another drink of water and a brief moment of solitude to gather her wits when Babe said, "Wait! She hasn't met Sequoyah. Where is that boy, anyway? Now that I'm thinking about it, I don't recall seeing him at all today." Babe seemed worried as she looked past the group to scan the valley beyond.

"Something spooked the horses last night. He took off after them," said Will, the younger and burlier of the two tag-along thieves. "He'll turn up, Babe. Don't you worry. He always does."

Hugh wrapped his arm over Babe's shoulders, curling his wrist around her neck and leaning down to tell her, softly, "He's right, you know. Sequoyah knows what he's doing. You go on and get Annis settled and I'm sure he'll turn up just as soon as you stop looking."

Babe sighed, her shoulders sagging. "That boy's going to have his name on my every last worry line by the time I'm old and wrinkled." She took another deep breath and shook loose her broad shoulders. A timid smile returned to her face, restoring the kindness to it that Annis was already used to from her. *Her.* The female pronoun for Babe seemed equal parts odd and appropriate.

"Alright, Tulip. How about we start with getting you a drink of water? You must be absolutely parched," Babe said. She smiled, but Annis noticed her eyes held a dim of worry as she carried on without so much as expecting a response. "And then let's see if we can find the real girl hiding under all of this dirt and distress." Annis was tempted to tell her the real girl would never be found, no matter how much Babe scrubbed the tarnished shell in which she lived now, but she held her tongue and simply nodded.

Babe glanced over her shoulder, scanning the stragglers. Will was only just turning away when she called out to him, "Will, be a dear and fill the tub in my tent, would you?"

Will stopped on a dime and tipped his head in her direction. "I'm on it, Babe." He was back in motion before finishing his sentence and disappeared behind a cluster of circus equipment Annis couldn't begin to identify.

While everyone else went back to work preparing for that night's show, Annis followed Babe with shaky steps as her adrenaline released its final surges. Annis's mind still lagged from trying to process her new surroundings and the lovely, strange, extraordinary people who occupied them. She kept her head down as she walked behind Babe, forcing herself to keep her eyes on the only familiar sight in her vicinity: the dirt beneath her feet. When they'd arrived at a small tent that extended out from one of the train's cars, the swish of fabric drew her attention back upward. Babe held back a bundle of violet satin that served as a door and used her free hand to gesture for Annis to step inside.

Inside the tent, lanterns hung from a multitude of hooks attached to every pole, support beam, and other available structure in sight. A different colored satin sheet adorned each wall in a delightful rainbow of deepest plum, light rose, earthy sage, and cornflower blue. Standing in the center of the tent was a vanity, complete with a large mirror and basin filled with clear water and fresh wash rags. Beautiful gowns of silk and lace were strung up from one corner to another like dancing maidens standing shoulder to shoulder in a fabulous kick line. Annis felt dreamy as she looked around Babe's colorful oasis, filled with all the riches she'd likely collected on her travels. Handmade quilts hung draped over a rustic wooden bench, strange paintings and sculptures like nothing Annis had ever seen before were scattered about, some leaning against furniture, some displayed from hooks nailed into the tent poles. Quiet music hummed in the background and everywhere her eyes touched she saw color. Babe seemed to have an affinity for flowers. The small space was littered with vases, small and large, some luxurious crystal, some no more than an empty can that was once used for beans. Each one was filled with a different collection of wildflowers, all at varying stages of their life cycle. While some were freshly picked, with tight cusps still waiting to bloom, others had long since seen their days of blossoming and been left to live in glory forever, dried and dead, though still perfectly intact. Together they all emitted the loveliest potpourri, which wrapped Annis in the sweetest symphony of scents. However, she was certain she must really be dreaming, or maybe hallucinating—which was certainly possible, considering her exhaustion and dehydration—when her gaze landed on a hammock, in which sat a very large, striped cat. Though she'd never seen one before, Annis was certain it was a tiger. She had seen many a house cat—and this was no house cat.

"Magnificent, isn't he?" Babe said, admiration shining from her eyes as she looked at the giant feline. "Can you believe someone thought it wise to keep him chained in a cage? A beautiful creature like this?" She shook her head and furrowed her brow.

"He's not..." Annis paused, not wanting to say anything offensive to Babe, who had been nothing but kind despite Annis's suspicious, sudden arrival and unkempt appearance. "...Dangerous?" She wasn't sure why she was asking. Massive though he was, he was also majestic. He carried a sage wisdom in his aura that left Annis feeling more drawn to him than fearful.

"Basileus? Dangerous?" Babe laughed heartily. "Not in the least. I think you'll find most creatures, big and small, will respond according to how you treat them. You show them respect, they'll respect you in return. You love them, honor them, care for them, and the loyalty returned to you will abound."

"Basileus," Annis whispered his name, the feel of it on her tongue making her smile. It was unlike any name she'd heard before. "What does it mean?"

"It's means 'king' in Greek," Babe answered. "Suits him, don't you think?"

"Very much," she agreed, still unable to take her eyes off the tiger who seemed unperturbed by their intrusion.

"Of course, you'd never have known by the sight of him when we first found him," Babe said, reminiscing out loud. "His coat was dull and matted with bare spots where the shackles had rubbed him raw and bloody. Skin and bones, he was. Refused to eat in the state they kept him in. Hugh wasn't sure it'd be humane to keep him going, the way he was. Said he was too far gone. Had given up. But then," she paused, touching Annis lightly on the arm to draw her attention. "His eyes. They told us. He'd seen things. Terrible things. All the worst the world had to offer..." she trailed off. "But," she continued, "he was still there. Alive. On fire. Wild with an unbridled courage, as though he knew they'd done all they could to him, and he'd survived anyway."

"He hadn't given up," Annis whispered.

"Never." Babe gave her a bittersweet smile. "The wild ones never do." She began to turn away but Annis stopped her by touching her arm, grazing ever so lightly with her fingertips, surprised she'd been bold enough to reach out at all.

"Babe?"

"Yes, Tulip." It wasn't a question. "Your eyes tell it too," she said.

A warm wave of gratitude swept through Annis. She knew Babe would never ask to know the worst of what Annis had seen before finding herself here in this unexpected oasis of salvation. Annis, who'd spent her first life an invisible bystander, a mere shadow hidden in the tapestries of life, had come back a girl who could be seen, a girl whose eyes told stories she hoped her mouth would never have to repeat. Maybe it would be the death of them, or maybe those stories would live on, trapped inside her. All she knew for now was that they wouldn't stop her from having hope anymore. There would be new life after the old. And in this one, she would do more than simply serve as a lovely backdrop in someone else's story.

"Why don't you have a seat right here," Babe said, indicating with her hand that Annis should sit at the vanity. "We can start by undoing the mess in your hair while we wait for Will to finish preparing the tub." Annis did as she was told while Babe turned away to fetch the water she had promised.

The vanity chair was made of a soft, comfortable, purple velvet. Annis struggled to keep her eyes open. "You just relax and let me take care of things," Babe said, seeing Annis's efforts to stay awake as she placed a full glass in front of her. But Annis was unable to surrender to her exhaustion, no matter how heavy her lids or how achy her body. Her mind, still wired for survival, would not allow it.

She clung to conscious thought but let her eyes rest, dropping their lids halfway. A sliver of light was all her mind needed to illuminate her rambling trains of thought about tigers and bearded men in dresses, about sisters whose two bodies lived as one, about men who were unusually tall and others who were unusually tiny, about strong men and large men, about women who'd been shunned by society for being something other than timid or chaste or white. What did those supposed virtues matter if you could command a crowd? If you could dance across a tightrope, certain you would never fall? If you could sing or fly or bend beyond the fear of breaking?

Annis was told all her life that she had lived in the presence of greatness, of remarkable and important people. After meeting this band of circus misfits who inspired awe and wonder wherever they went, however, she questioned affixing such grand labels to the people she had known before. What had they ever offered the world besides judgement, snobbery, and division? Rare had a been a kind word, yet they were all quick to point out differences as unacceptable flaws of inferior folks. Never once had she witnessed a welcome quite like the one that she'd received here. A stranger, unannounced with nothing to offer would never have been invited in by any of those men and women she'd known before. Annis saw nothing great or remarkable in that.

Mind ablaze with exciting new truths, her squinting gaze slipped along the lanterns near the opening of the tent just as Will was lifting the corner of a satin sheet to poke his scruffy, red-haired head inside.

"Tub's filled, Babe. You ready for it?" The sound of his voice brought her mind back into the present.

"I do believe we are," Babe answered, placing a handful of pins onto the vanity in front of Annis, who reached up to touch her hair.

"You untangled it?" she asked, combing her fingers through the long, wavy strands. Only this morning she'd been certain she would have to cut the mass of matted knots from it.

"We'll give it a good wash and it'll be soft and shiny again in no time," Babe assured her, gently squeezing Annis by the shoulders and helping her out of the velvet chair. "You'll find a dressing gown just inside there." Babe oriented Annis's shoulders in the direction of the train car attached to the tent. "Give Will a minute to set everything up in here and then you can come back for your bath."

Annis started toward the car to get undressed, then hesitated. "Am I really going to take a bath with Babe in the tent?" she wondered to herself. "Am I going to let a man help me wash?" Dress or otherwise, Annis was convinced that underneath it all he wasn't really a she at all. He felt like one, though, and maybe that was enough to accept him as such. As if Babe could sense her concerns, she added, "I'll be waiting outside myself. Give me a shout when you're under the suds and I'll be in to help with whatever you need." Annis nodded, grateful to her. Her. Babe was a her, whether Annis could form the right thoughts to explain it to herself or not.

The train car door, unlike every other part of the tent, was hard and heavy, made of solid wood with a metal frame. For a moment, Annis struggled to garner the strength to close it. Her first instinct was to ask for help. Her second, much stronger impulse denied that instinct. Taking a deep breath, she squeezed her fists as tightly as she could, channeling every last bit of strength she had in her, and then, with both hands, she pushed, sliding the door back into place. It had barely shut behind Annis when she heard the squeaking tires of a wagon rolling into the tent. Then she heard wooden slats sliding over each other in a smooth motion, followed by a light thump and water splashing. Will was preparing the bath water.

She closed her eyes and took a breath, inhaling the scent of lavender and peppermint, both of which had been freshly picked and placed in small vases on a table near the door. The car itself was hardly furnished. Aside from the table, there was a small bench along one side and a makeshift curtain hung across the corner to create a space for dressing.

As she made her way to the dressing corner, her feet felt light —not numb or tingly, but as though the weight of her soul wasn't fully tethered to her body. *Maybe it hasn't settled on living over dying just yet,* she thought. *Or maybe it's starting to return after abandoning me in that river. Or maybe it's detached itself and will never fully fall back into place. Light footsteps—that's all I'm capable of anymore.*

She untied the belt of her coat as she pondered the meaning of her bodily sensations, surprised that the lightness of her feet concerned her more than the emptiness of her stomach. Her fingertips slid gingerly over the dress's buttons, undoing each as she went until she felt the rough linen begin to glide from her skin and down her body. Stepping out of the heavy skirt, Annis reached for the dressing gown suspended from a hook an arm's length away. The gown was soft against her, which she relished after the harsh conditions of recent days. She hung her clothes on the same hook and then, opening the door just a crack, she checked that Will had left the tent before making her way back inside to take her bath.

Chapter Three
THE RIDER

After she emerged from having her bath, Annis's skin felt smooth and soft except for the parts now scabbed and calloused by the days spent wandering the wilderness. Stepping out of Babe's tent, taking in the sunlight and fresh air, Annis reveled in her new, fresh self. She now wore a pair of purple trousers, a flashy red corset, and a short-sleeved white bodice, all freshly laundered and gifted to her by Babe who'd insisted her previous ensemble was no longer fit for wearing and thus would not be leaving her car on Annis's body ever again. Annis had been more than happy to agree with her in order to shed the last layers of her past as she prepared to embrace her new future.

More important than the clothes she wore, though, were her light, wavy locks that fell loose past her shoulders. Babe, unlike Annis's mother, had refused to do more than brush Annis's blonde hair. Once confined to being pinned snug against her scalp and curled into perfect ringlets, her hair had been set free by Babe, who insisted the wind would know best what to do with it. She was right. Now it shone gold in the sunlight and lifted on the breeze.

Babe had told her exactly where to find Momma T and a proper meal, and yet Annis wandered aimlessly, her arms light at her sides and her hair floating out behind her. She took in all of the circus sights as she walked. To her left was the train, composed of a mismatched collection of patchwork carts, many pieced together from scrap metal and reclaimed lumber, then adorned with unexpected details like stained glass windows and wildly colored doors. Babe had told her all about the day she and Hugh had acquired the engine ("sheer luck alone," she'd said) while she'd been washing Annis's hair. She'd gone on about how it put an end to the years they'd spent traveling the country in a horse and carriage caravan and Annis had soaked herself in the stories much like her bath, allowing a temporary escape from reality. From the stories Annis learned Hugh and Babe had continued to add carts based on need and ability, creating a small but mighty train that had as much character as the passengers themselves.

To her right, Annis noticed a great deal had changed since her arrival. While she'd soaked in the suds, everyone else had worked to complete and secure the circus tent. It was hard to imagine the dazzling tent not standing there an hour ago, and harder still to believe it would no longer stand there tomorrow. Making her way around the massive structure, Annis passed by dainty Bess rehearsing her number on a tightrope rigged only a few feet above the ground. Bess moved over the rope—backwards and forwards and even jumping in pirouettes—as gracefully as if she were dancing on solid ground. Annis continued to meander around camp with her mouth agape, in awe of the gifted group that now surrounded her. She listened as the three singing sisters all warmed up their vocal chords, creating a rainbow of sound in which each voice echoed brighter than the one preceding it.

Then the sound of many hooves thundering toward her snapped her out of her listening trance. A herd of at least a half-dozen mustangs ran straight for the tent's opening, each one a different color, some painted in two or three. From snowy white to charcoal black, and every shade of brown, from creamy blonde to warm chestnut, the rich array coated their stunning muscular bodies in a velvety coat that shimmered in the sunlight. Their long manes and tails flowed behind them. A rider atop a pitch-black horse galloped in behind the herd. He used no reins or saddle.

Annis broke into a run to catch up with them.

A wall of thick, hot air hit her as soon as she stepped inside the tent and reminded her that summer was coming. It seemed odd, the recognition of season, the return of time. She realized she'd expected to find all had passed faster in her absence. And she had felt absent, secluded in the woods, in a universe all to herself. It felt to her as though the world could have elapsed into another year or another decade entirely. It hadn't. The earth had spun at the same speed it always had even though Annis's experience of time had warped while in isolation.

Though the horses had settled in the tent, the dust had not. It tickled her nose, causing her to sneeze. She froze. The tent wasn't nearly as empty as Annis had expected and she wasn't ready for any more attention today. She noticed Hugh, Will, and Francis arranging the rows of benches for the audience later that night. Nearby, Caroline's bright red hair drew Annis's attention. She watched as Caroline bent over backward and curled into a human hoop, through which Homer tossed knives and caught them as they arced back around to him. In the midst of all this, no one noticed her sneeze. Annis sighed with relief and continued deeper into the tent's interior.

Still sniffling from the sneeze, Annis twitched her nose back and forth, trying to help ease the introduction of new scents that seemed to multiply the longer she stood inside the tent. The sun-baked earth at her feet. Stale popcorn and sweets. Fresh hay, and an unfamiliar musk she assumed came from the horses, who now stood at the center of the ring.

Some pawed at the ground while others paced. One even dropped into the dirt and rolled around until his white coat turned a dark shade of grey. Its sheer delight and the carefree ways in which it moved, with complete disregard to cleanliness or propriety, were contagious and Annis giggled at the sight. She'd read books about horses from the time she was old enough to read and daydreamed about meeting one, but she had never been allowed to visit with them, let alone to learn how to ride, even though her father had kept a stable at the edge of their property. Only ballet had been deemed an appropriate pastime, according to Annis's mother, who'd loathed dirt and animals alike.

The herd parted down the middle to make a path for the rider, now on his feet. The young man, with skin tinted red by his ancestors and kissed golden by the sun, wore his long black tresses braided in some small sections and falling loose in others, with feathers and beads twisted throughout. Mischief rested on his dark lips as he took in the herd around him. He took his steps slowly and with great care to respect the space of each animal he passed. He engaged with each of them along the way. A tender palm moving down the forehead, a firm pat on the neck, a scratch above the withers. Quiet whispers and unspoken greetings as he exchanged small bursts of breath in keeping with the horse's natural means of communicating.

Though she understood the implications of staring at a young man, a young native man, no less, Annis found it impossible to avert her eyes. Of all the displays of human talent around her, Annis found the subtle ways in which this man and his horses communicated the most impressive. A tap at one's side, Annis noticed, meant move along. A stroke down another's muzzle prompted the horse to follow him. Curiosity goaded her to approach the rider, to enter into the sacred circle he shared with those mustangs.

"Sequoyah," Hugh called out, breaking Annis's focus from the horses and their rider. She watched the handsome stranger straighten his stance and peek above the herd that still surrounded him.

"I'm in trouble, aren't I?" he said, a quiet laugh rumbling behind his words.

Hugh tried to hide a grin. "Just go tell her you're back, would ya?"

Sequoyah nodded, still laughing. "Someone really ought to tell her I'm not eight anymore."

"It would break her heart and you know it!" Hugh yelled after him. "Who is she going to fuss over when she realizes you're not her little boy anymore?" Sequoyah didn't respond but hurried from the tent in search of Babe.

Meanwhile, the work of setting up benches continued.

"I don't know," Francis muttered just loud enough to be heard, hoisting up a thick slab of wood and dropping it down onto several stumps to create more seating. "Babe's got Annis now. I think someone could let it slip Sequoyah grew up a few years back. Even if she missed it."

Will laughed. "She'd never accept it. Besides, I don't think Annis is going to need her all that long. Bit of sleep, and some proper food, I have a feeling we'll be seeing a completely different girl come morning." He nodded at Francis to pick up the next slab and they bent down in unison. "Might be time to consider getting Babe a puppy, Hugh."

"Right, so Basileus can eat it. Great idea, Will."

Annis's mouth folded into a smile, amused by Hugh's candor. A puppy and a tiger likely weren't the most ideal combination where pets were concerned.

Conscious of not drawing any unwanted attention, Annis quietly began to tiptoe her way back toward the opening of the tent when she took note of shuffling feet moving behind her. Her mind instantly alert, she scanned the area until she saw Floyd, the elderly man whose pale complexion reminded her of powdered sugar and whose pink eyes made it hard to look away even as they bore into her.

She felt suddenly desperate for an escape. He's harmless, she reminded herself. Whatever his appearance might have suggested to her, he had done nothing to deserve her fear or judgement and she did her best to hide every trace of her discomfort as he approached.

Mustering a smile, she watched as he came to a standstill before her. He wore a strange expression. His eyes, though locked on her, were staring straight through her, as though he could see things others couldn't. The oddest part was, Annis thought, the way his mouth barely moved while he muttered under his breath, as though speaking in tongues. Without saying an audible word to Annis directly, he took her hand and turned her palm upright. He then stroked it gently with the rough tips of his fingers and placed a small, black stone at the center of it. He folded her fingers around it as his pink eyes turned red. Annis felt his gaze become present.

"For protection," he wheezed, struggling for his voice, "so he can't find you."

His attention drifted as quickly as it had come, and his feet resumed their shuffle away from Annis, who stood frozen by fear. "How had he known?" she wondered to herself. "He couldn't have. It simply isn't possible."

She opened her hand to peer down at the stone he'd given her. Part of her wanted to throw it as far and as hard as she could. The other part wanted to believe it could offer her what he'd promised. *Protection.* She shook her head, letting her hand fall at her side. Her fingers uncurled until the small stone rolled from her grasp and into the dirt at her feet. It wasn't real. The old man was grasping at straws, speculating about her past, probably like all the others were. Annis closed her eyes and forced her thoughts to believe the words she was feeding them. She was safe. No one knew. And the old man was just that, an old man, and likely a senile one, at that.

Annis gave up all efforts of being quiet as she hurried out of the tent, desperate for fresh air and the freedom of open sky overhead. Her heart raced in her chest as dirt and gravel crunched under the soles of her new boots. Even once outside, she found it hard to breathe. Still, she kept moving aimlessly through camp, yearning for distance from the encounter with Floyd.

"Whoa, there! Slow down, girl. You almost missed my tent," Momma T said as she walked straight toward Annis, bringing her to an abrupt halt. She wiped her hands clean on her apron and said, "Cornbread is golden brown and piping hot. Fresh churned butter will melt the second the two touch. It'll never taste any better than it does right now." When Annis didn't react, Momma T waved her closer, taking a few more steps in her direction.

"Girl, you look like you've seen a ghost," she said, frowning. "Now, I don't know what it is that's got you spooked but I can guarantee you, there ain't nothin' in camp to be scared of. And everythin' outside of camp is too scared to come in and find out." She smirked.

Annis couldn't help but grin back at her. She knew Momma T was right. She'd heard the harsh words people used to describe those who traveled with the circus. Coldhearted misfits touched in the head. The sort who'd toss you off the train just as soon as they'd throw you in a lion pen. Now she regretted ever believing a single one of them because Annis was sure these people had just kept her from dying in the wilderness, even though she was a complete stranger to them.

"It's just...I don't think I can be who people think I am," Annis said.

Momma T crossed her arms, her brow furrowed in concern. "And who do you think people believe you to be?"

"Someone who can be saved," she whispered, hardly able to bear the words.

Momma T nodded slowly, her stern mouth growing tender on her rigid face as she stepped in closer. She draped one arm around Annis's shoulders, her hand curling in around Annis's neck as she tucked her head down to touch their foreheads together. "I'm gonna tell you a secret. We're all beyond saving. But we still found our salvation the second we set foot inside this circus and saw our broken, battered souls mirrored back to us in every face already inside. Here, the rest of the world doesn't get to decide who you are or what you should be. The tarnished, the shunned, can rise to reach the spotlight and do so to roaring applause. The very people who would not approve of you, who foolishly believe they can break you, wind up in awe of you. That's the power of the circus. That's the freedom you find when you no longer allow yourself to be demeaned or attacked by the small-minded standards of an easily frightened society. Being saved, being worthy of saving, no longer looks the same." Her dark brown eyes rested on Annis's for a long time. "It's not us who's wrong. It's you. You'll see."

Then Momma T released Annis from her steady grip and gave her a nudge with one bony elbow and added, "Come on, cornbread won't stay warm forever and I have to get another batch going before showtime." Annis's stomach growled as if on cue. She clutched her belly and turned red with embarrassment.

"Hunger ain't nothing to feel shame for," Momma T said sternly, gesturing for her to hurry up. "Turning down perfectly good food? Now that's another story." Annis didn't argue and fell into step beside Momma T as they made their way into the large emerald colored tent that served as a dining hall. Beyond the massive green tarp was a makeshift kitchen, complete with serving station. Annis could hardly believe her eyes as she took it all in.

"It smells divine," Annis said, inhaling deeply through her nose and sighing to exhale. She couldn't remember the last real food she'd eaten. You don't tend to savor things you don't know are the last you'll have, she thought, and you don't tend to know they're the last you'll have until it's too late.

"It better smell heavenly," Momma T said, "because I must have said about a hundred 'Oh, Lord Jesuses' when I damn near burned my hand off making it."

Annis's eyes widened and a chuckle rose in her throat. She wondered if she'd ever get used to hearing the things that came out of Momma T's mouth. She hoped not.

After a few spins around her makeshift kitchen, Momma T handed Annis a meal large enough to feed ten people and sent her to the nearest table in the attached dining area to begin her feast.

The space wasn't big, but it was well utilized, with banquet style tables and benches lined up in neat rows. Annis counted four in all. She passed the first table, dragging her fingertips over the surface. The wood was worn smooth. Patches of emerald paint still clung to the panels in the places Annis imagined the table saw less wear, down the center mostly, tiny remnants suggesting the tables once matched the tent. The benches were built in a similar fashion, mostly thick slabs of wood lined up and bolted down onto thick, solid legs. But where the tables held small sentiments of green, the benches had once been painted white.

Annis walked until she found herself at the center of an otherwise empty dining hall and took her seat. "Dig in," Momma T called out, her back already turned as she headed out to the fire with a fresh batch of cornbread ready to bake. "There's plenty more for seconds."

"Thank you," Annis said, still taking in the feast plated before her. Her mouth watered. She felt overwhelmed by the choice of what to eat first.

"I'd start with the cornbread." Annis glanced up at the sound of another voice, one she recognized.

"Hi, Sawyer." She smiled, pleased to have remembered his name.

He nodded, climbing up onto the bench across from her. "Take a big chunk and swipe it straight through the beans. You'll never taste anything better."

"If you knew what I've been eating recently, you'd know anything would taste better," she said, but still took his advice. She wasn't sorry she did. The cornbread was perfectly crisp on the outside but soft to the touch. Annis gripped the small piece with both hands and pulled it apart, a fresh burst of steam erupting from the wonderfully fluffy inside. Even before she tasted it, she could smell the sweet scent of honey and corn. Dutifully following Sawyer's orders, she took the smaller of two halves and slid it straight through the beans, watching it soak in all the gravy before carefully guiding the cornbread back to her mouth. Sweet and savory flavor erupted in waves of comfort inside her mouth and slowly spread to her entire being. It was absolutely divine.

Sauce dripped down her chin as she took another bite, and then another, before she could muster humming a sound of contentment.

Sawyer grinned. "Told ya."

"What, you think this is a full-service establishment now?" Momma T said, placing another meal on the table for Sawyer.

"If you're willing to make it one," he teased, going straight for his own square of cornbread. "Thank you, Momma."

"Yeah, yeah," she mumbled under her breath, already on to buttering another pan for her next batch of cornbread.

Sawyer leaned in closer so that only Annis could hear and whispered, "Don't let her fool ya. She serves everyone that sets foot in here. Trying to help yourself to something from her kitchen will get you chased outta here with a wooden spoon." Then he looked up, over Annis's shoulder. "Just ask Sequoyah. He knows all about that," Sawyer said, and then laughed.

"What's that?" Sequoyah asked, walking toward their table. Annis had been oblivious that he had entered, but she could now feel him move in closer beside her with an overwhelming sense of awareness. She couldn't bring herself to look, worried she'd again be unable to turn her gaze away from him.

"Momma and her spoon," Sawyer answered him, chuckling as he picked up his fork and tucked into his meal with more fervor than one would expect from someone not much bigger than the pile of food on his plate. Sequoyah laughed. It was a smooth, deep sound, hearty and unencumbered. The sound was so genuine, so strangely familiar, and yet so thrillingly new that it made Annis's stomach flip with excitement.

"I never was good at following rules," he admitted. "That spoon has left a mark across the back of my hand more than once." He lowered himself onto the seat beside Annis and she felt her chest tighten. Then he turned toward her, his hand outstretched. Even out of the corner of her eye, she could see him smiling at her. It was enough to flush her skin hot pink. "You must be Annis," he said, clearly oblivious to her current condition. She could feel the sweat pooling in her palms.

"Hi," she said at last, moving her head in his direction ever so slightly and running her hand up and down her thigh to dry it on the cotton of her trousers. "It's a pleasure to meet you." Her gaze inched upward until her eyes met with his as her palm landed in his waiting grip. She felt his fingers wrap around her hand, sending a warm tingle down her arm and into the pit of her stomach, filling it so that she forgot about her hunger.

Mesmerized by the sheer beauty of his face and the endless kindness spilling from his dark eyes down onto her, she stared at him. His own gaze never wavered from hers until Sawyer cleared his throat, erasing the magic of their unspoken moment. But it had been magic. Annis was as certain of that as she was of the truth that she understood the instant they had averted their eyes. She and Sequoyah could never do more than share the magic of that moment. It could never be more than that. More would only lead to a target on his back. And no one else would die on her account.

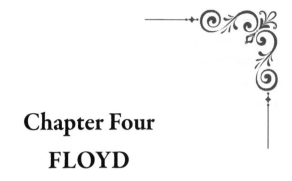

Chapter Four
FLOYD

"**B**abe know you're back yet?" Momma asked, walking over with another plate of food in her hands. "You're lucky she had Annis here to look after or she'd have had time to put together another search party to go out after you again."

Sequoyah took the meal and nodded graciously. "Poppy already got on me for worrying her." Annis watched as he broke what she had already accepted as circus tradition by skipping the cornbread and going straight for the greens. "It's not like I wanted to be out there chasing down horses before the sun cracked the horizon. And if it hadn't been for those men shooting off their rifles in the black of night, I wouldn't have been either."

Annis felt her blood run cold. Her feet and ankles turned to lead and her knees to jelly while every instinct screamed for her to run. She'd never felt more betrayed by her own body.

"What men with rifles?" she asked, unable to hide the fear in her voice as she watched Momma T saunter off, envious of her ability to simply move as she pleased.

Sawyer, much like Momma, hardly seemed bothered by the news of gunmen. "Oh, who knows? But they turn up every few stops we make. Some uptight bully and his bully friends who get together and try to scare the freaks out of town before we get too settled in." He laughed harshly. "As if we'd ever want to stay. Never seen a place yet I'd give up the train tracks for."

The thumping of her heart slipped slowly out of her throat and back down into her chest, where it gradually began to calm itself back into its regular rhythm. "That's it? They're just random? And they just make a lot of noise to try to scare you? They never do anything?"

Sequoyah placed his fork back on the table beside his plate and turned toward her. Annis was unsure whether she appreciated having his undivided attention, or whether it was appropriate for him to have hers. Nevertheless, he most certainly did.

"They've tried in the past," he admitted, a sadness swelling in his eyes. His most beautiful eyes, Annis thought. "But we're always stronger than they expect, and now far more prepared. There's no sneaking up on us. We've taken great measures to keep everyone here safe, Annis. I promise." She liked the way he said it. *Annis*. Before she could revel in her enjoyment for too long, the somber line of his mouth gave way to a curl at the corner and he smirked. "Also, we have Homer. Something about a man tossing large knives about and catching them, occasionally with his mouth, tends to frighten even the most arrogant of men."

"Throwing around those fireballs he's got usually does it too," Sawyer added, grinning from ear to ear. There was something endearing about Sawyer, though Annis had to keep considering whether she was letting his short stature influence her opinions of him. Maybe there was some part of her that thought him adorable simply for being small. She dreaded to think it was possible, and so every so often when he spoke, she imagined a man she once knew. She pictured the grumpiest, most mature-looking man she'd ever met who worked at the butcher shop her mother had frequented all throughout Annis's childhood. After this experiment, she realized with great relief it was simply Sawyer's uncanny way of telling things as he saw them and the ever-present echo of snark in his voice that she was becoming genuinely fond of.

"What about you?" Sawyer asked, catching Annis off guard. No one had prompted any direct questions of her since she'd been there, aside from her name and age, and even those had come with a certain expectation that she would be less than truthful in answering. Sawyer Smalls, however, did not strike her as the sort to simply accept vagueness in response to his curiosities.

"What do you mean?" she asked, picking at a medley of vegetables on her plate, some of which she wasn't sure she recognized. She was certain he'd notice she was stalling but she had no choice. She couldn't dare give up more information than absolutely necessary. Moving forward, she was determined to stray as little from the truth as possible, but it wouldn't be easy to toe the line between honesty and lies when there was so little truth to tell and so much to keep secret.

"What do I mean?" he asked, sounding incredulous. "I mean, Homer juggles flames in his hands. Sequoyah comes galloping into the ring on a herd of horses, war cry and all. And me? Well, I think it's pretty clear where my entertainment value lies." He pointed the prongs of her fork at her. "So, what about you? I know you look pretty damn normal on the outside, but you can't be entirely ordinary to wind up here. You've gotta have something that makes you stand out. Some sort of talent. Something you plan to contribute. What is it?" Despite the badgering nature of his questions, Annis felt it hard to hold them against him when they were delivered with such sincere interest.

"I look ordinary because I was," she said simply, lifting her eyes from the food on her plate to meet his across from her. "Who I am now, what I have to offer...I don't know. Perhaps very little."

"Not possible." Sequoyah's quiet confidence reached her ears and her heart at the same time. Why everyone here continued to believe in her, she could not fathom. But she was slowly starting to think that just maybe they had reason to.

"How can you be sure? You know nothing about me," she said quietly, not daring to look at him this time.

"I know enough." His tone was quiet but certain.

"Probably got an earful from Babe about you as soon as he got back," Sawyer teased. "But he's not wrong. You've got something, kid. And I, for one, can't wait to find out what it is." Then he took a determined stab at his last sliver of greens and dove it straight into his waiting mouth.

"You're close to Babe?" Annis asked, suddenly uneasy. Babe had a way of lifting veils without being invited in. Though Annis had been grateful for the unspoken exchange they shared earlier, she hadn't considered that Babe might put into words the things she'd concluded about her.

Sequoyah shot a look in Sawyer's direction that Annis couldn't interpret as anything other than unpleasant. Then he stood from his seat, clearing his plate as he went.

"They raised me. Her and Hugh," he explained casually, his attention primarily on the empty plate in his hands. Annis had to wonder if it was a tactic meant to keep his gaze directed at anything but her. "But don't go thinking that means Babe is a river letting everything flow through her. She's the safest place to let your secrets land. They go in and never come out." He smiled, glancing over at her at last, but it was laced with a sadness Annis couldn't place. "What I know, I saw for myself. Didn't take more than a moment to see." Then he turned to Sawyer, still picking at what little was left of his food. "You gonna spend all evening on that? Come on, we got work to finish before the crowd shows."

"You go ahead. I'll find you when I'm done," Sawyer said, waving him on.

Annis got the distinct feeling this wasn't at all the answer Sequoyah had hoped for, but he left with no choice but to accept it. He gave a nod in her direction and then took his dishes to the tub filled with suds near where Momma T was busy at work.

Silence set in as Annis and Sawyer sat together, just the two of them again. Uncomfortable with the quiet space between them and the thoughts that threatened to fill it, Annis searched her surroundings for a new topic of conversation. Then, her eyes landed on Floyd, who sat alone on the other end of the tent and was clearly talking to himself. Chills ran down her spine even as she tried to push the memories of her encounter with him from her mind. She moved her gaze back to Sawyer, who went about eating his dinner without a worry in the world.

"Floyd," she started, unsure of how to ask what she needed to know. "What...what will he be doing in the show tonight?"

Sawyer stopped short of taking another bite. "Floyd doesn't have an act," he said, giving no indication that he meant to expound on his answer.

Still, Annis pressed for more. "Then what does he do here?"

Sawyer sighed, slowly turning to glance over his shoulder at the old man still sitting hunched over his plate. His food sat untouched as he muttered words no one else could hear. "Floyd is special," he began, crossing his arms over his chest. He sat back from the table with his eyebrows furrowed. His customary smirk missing from his face. "Where most of us are physically unique, Floyd has the unfortunate predicament of also having an altered mind."

"I'm sorry?" Annis didn't follow.

"You see him," Sawyer said, watching her watch Floyd, who sat in the distance behind him. "Alone. It's how he always is. Because he's already got too many voices in his own head to take on anymore."

"So, he's mad," Annis concluded. She wasn't sure if this made her feel more at ease about what he'd said to her earlier or not.

"He hears voices," Sawyer corrected. Annis could hardly see a difference, but Sawyer went on before she could say so. "Poppy says he has a gift, same as everyone. But, as with most of us, the world just wasn't ready for it. It scared them, and so they tried to snuff it out of him. Only it didn't work. After years of being locked away, of having doctors experiment on his brain and torture him, the gift became a curse."

"I don't understand," Annis admitted.

"They broke him," Sawyer said, sadness darkening his blue eyes. "Flooded his mind until he drowned inside it, unable to surface above the noise." He shook his head, staring down at the table. "Whether he escaped or whether they deemed him too feeble to be of concern to anyone, no one really knows. Babe found him wandering in a field of sunflowers six years ago, talking to them, still wearing his hospital gown. She brought him home and he's been here ever since, still lost inside his own head and unable to get out."

"So, when he talks to others, it's just nonsense?" Annis asked, on the verge of having her fears erased.

Sawyer looked up to meet her gaze with narrowed eyes. "He doesn't."

"He doesn't what?"

"Talk to others. He can't even see us, let alone hear anything outside of the noise in his head. Only reason we know what we do is 'cause of Hugh going into town that night and asking around about him. Didn't want to just take him away if it meant leaving people behind who might miss him. Needless to say, he found stories a plenty, but not a single person sorry to see the old man go." His gaze traveled back to Floyd once more. "He's lost. He'll never find his way back out to us." He shrugged, slowly returning his attention to the remains of his dinner. "Truthfully, I'm not sure he'd even want to."

Annis frowned. "But he talked to me. Earlier, inside the big tent. He looked me right in the eyes and spoke."

Sawyer shook his head. "Not possible. Trust me, we've all tried to reach him. He's not able to come out."

She'd been tired, of course, and still trying to recover from intense dehydration when Floyd had approached her and given her the stone. Maybe her mind had been playing tricks on her, taunting her with what she feared most. It wasn't entirely unbelievable that Floyd had never really spoken to her. And yet she couldn't shake the sense she hadn't imagined anything, and that Floyd was closer to the surface than anyone knew.

She looked at Sawyer, tempted to press the issue more, but then thought better of it when she noticed the thin line of his mouth still unwilling to curve back into its usual smirk. Determined to turn things around with him, she forced herself to stay silent—but it wasn't long before her wandering mind stumbled upon a new nagging curiosity desperate to be answered. Before she could stop them, the words found their way to the forefront and out of her mouth.

"Hugh and Babe. They're...Sequoyah's parents?" It made sense, given the comments about Babe's inability to accept that Sequoyah had grown into a man and her particularly high levels of anxiety where his well-being was concerned. Annis had written it off as part of her maternal flare. She hadn't been far off, except apparently Babe's maternal feeling was more specific to the fact she considered Sequoyah her son.

Sawyer nodded, grin slowly returning to his face. "You just loaded with questions this evening, aren't you?" He placed his fork onto his now empty plate and Annis took note of her own still being nearly full. She'd stopped eating some time ago. "But, to answer, yes, they are. Closest thing he's got anyway. Been with them since he was little. Babe'll mother anyone who lets her, but with him it's more because he really did need a mother when she came along."

"But what about his family. His tribe?" Annis didn't know much about Indigenous peoples and what she'd heard, she was more convinced than ever, probably had little to no truth to it.

"You're looking at it. The tribe of misfits." Then, he added, "There's our chief now." He pointed over Annis's shoulder toward the opening of the tent. She hardly had to move her gaze to see him. Given his height, Hugh was easy to spot.

"If you're finished up there, I could use a few more hands on Millie and Edi. Francis is having a hell of a time trying to get their gear on. Edi keeps snatching everything and tossing it, making Francis fetch like a well-trained dog. It's been fun to watch but we really do need to get things done now."

Sawyer chortled and climbed to his feet, and then up onto the table. "You seriously asking me to help dress an elephant?"

"Not asking you to do it alone," Hugh countered, clearly serious about his request. "Grab Sequoyah on your way over. You can ride on his shoulders. That ought to help you reach."

"I mean, that's offensive. But I can see where it might work." Sawyer jumped from the table, grabbed up his empty dishes, and headed toward Hugh. After dropping his plate with Momma, Sawyer patted Hugh's arm in passing while Hugh stayed to eat the large helping of dinner that he'd just received from Momma T.

"You look like you could use some company," Hugh said kindly, inviting himself to sit with Annis. She didn't mind one bit.

"I didn't know you had elephants," she said, wondering what other animals Hugh and Babe might have collected to complement their quirky tribe of misfits, as Sawyer had called them.

"We don't so much have them as we seem to be stuck with them," he grumbled, though even when he tried, Hugh was hardly

grumpy or stern. "If only our income were as big as Babe's heart."
He chuckled softly. "Seems to always measure up somehow,
though, and saying no to Babe has never been a talent of mine."

"I don't know," Annis said as she picked up her fork again. Her
appetite had slowly returned now that the butterflies had left along
with Sequoyah, who seemed to be directly responsible for them. "I
think your heart may be part of the problem in your ongoing collection here too."

He laughed. "You know, it's not polite to call a man out for his
faults when you're reaping the benefits of his shortcomings."

She smiled sheepishly. "I didn't realize generosity was an unde-
sirable quality."

"Only when you're in the habit of giving more than you've got."
His laugh quieted down to a subtle chuckling as he began to dig into his heaping helping of red beans and ham. "But then I've always
believed in maintaining a vacuum. Keeping the safe empty is a sure-
fire way of getting it filled."

Annis nodded, taking a bite. "Better to live with the flow of the
river than build your life inside a puddle."

Hugh stopped short of letting his fork meet his mouth and
smiled. "Precisely."

Hunger took the forefront as both focused on their meal. A
quiet comfort surrounded the unlikely pair. Annis could hardly believe she'd only just met Hugh a few hours ago. Being near him felt
like being near family.

"Does everyone call you Poppy?" she asked suddenly. "Or is it
just Sequoyah?"

Dabbing his mouth with the corner of a coarse, linen napkin,
he sat back from the table a bit, taking her in as though she'd said a
great deal more than the two simple questions she'd posed.

"He was the first," he answered after a moment of contempla-
tion. "But it caught on rather quickly." He placed his napkin back

on the table and folded his long arms loosely in his lap. "Why do you ask?"

This time it was her turn to hesitate in answering. Why had she asked?

"Sequoyah said you raised him. You and Babe." Annis felt her fingertips tingle from knotting her hands so tightly. She began to fidget with her own napkin just to get the blood circulating again. "And I guess it just helped me make sense of it all."

"What's that?"

"Being around you both. There's just something so familiar about the way you've treated me. The way you've cared for me. And now I understand. It's because you're parents. You treat me like parents would treat their own."

She felt her skin flush hot and cold, waging a war against itself whether to react with humiliation or to go numb from the pain that came with saying those words out loud. Hugh and Babe were parents. But they weren't hers. No matter how much kindness they bestowed upon her, she was grown. She'd been raised. The job was done. She would have no more parents to turn to in her life because she required no more parenting. And because those who'd done the job were gone now.

"I meant what I said earlier, love. This is our family. And we may only call one of you lot our son, but we call everyone here ours. And that includes you now."

Annis gulped to clear the lump in her throat but it bobbed back into place every time she tried to force it down. "Thank you," she whispered.

"Think nothing of it, love." He stretched one arm out across the table until his hand reached hers, cupping it gently. He held her hand as he continued eating and both of them finished their dinner in a warm silence.

By the time they were clearing their plates and taking them back to the suds station, a whole new party of people had shown up for Momma's cooking. Afraid she might get tangled up in the crowd pouring in, Annis stayed close to Hugh, whose wide strides led him through the mess of people in no time at all.

It wasn't until they were both outside that he noticed she was still right behind him. "You plan on being back here all night, then?" he asked.

Annis briefly considered the question before she replied with one of her own. "Is that a viable option?"

Hugh chuckled again. Annis was beginning to suspect this was a standard response of his. "If you plan on sticking with me for the evening, perhaps it will improve your scenery to walk beside me." No sooner had he said the words was he hooking his fingers around her elbow and tugging her up to walk on his right. "Left eye's no good," he explained. "Won't be able to see you there. Liable to knock you out and not even know it."

"Good to know," Annis said, making a mental note to steer clear of his left side at all times. The man did have a habit of excessive gesturing and gesticulating, and so it really could be quite dangerous given she came even with his elbow.

"So, this your way of telling me your aspirations here include taking over as ringleader one day?" he asked. Annis half-believed he was being serious.

"Me? Commanding the crowds? Quite unlikely," she said, skipping over the rocks and ropes still strewn about from assembling the tent. Every time Annis looked at the tent, she was certain it was larger than the last time she'd seen it. Its bright, inviting colors and high peaks like turrets on a castle gave way gracefully to the wind every time a breeze moved through. She admired the way it conformed to its surroundings yet remained sturdy.

"You don't think you have what it takes?" Hugh challenged her, leading the way inside after tying up the tarp to keep the entrance open.

"Oh, I know I don't." Annis had never been good at commanding attention. "I can make a good assistant, though. Or some sort of background person in an existing number," she offered. She was thinking out loud, mostly. After being offered a job, she'd put off the task of having to come up with an act. "I'm trained in ballet. Maybe I could do a little dancing in the background while the sisters sing. Or I could mimic Bess on the ground like a sort of shadow. I've seen part of her routine and I think I could learn it."

Hugh shook his head. "Absolutely not."

The finality in his statement caught her off guard. It was the most authoritative thing she'd heard him say.

"Oh," she said, taken aback. "Maybe it'd be best to just put me to work with Francis and Will, then. I know I don't look strong, but I can do more than I seem capable of. I swear. If I set my mind to it, I'll learn my way, Hugh."

He slowed down, gradually coming to a complete stop right at the center of the main ring of the three in their arena. Once he was still, he dropped his chin and lowered his gaze until Annis could see his face. He wore a serious expression, but there was no sign of the harsh chill she'd expected after his last words.

"Annis," he said calmly, "I have a sense about people. Always have. I can see things in them, things most people can't. Do you know what I see when I look at you?"

She didn't dare consider the possibilities. "A scared runaway who hasn't a clue of the way of the world?" she suggested and averted her eyes from his.

"A phoenix," he corrected her, ignoring her interpretation. "I see a girl life set on fire but couldn't burn. A girl whose fight was stronger than the flame. A girl who conquered the blaze who, when the smoke cleared, simply stepped from the ashes and carried on."

Annis felt his eyes on her but she couldn't bring herself to meet them.

"Now, love, does that sound to you like the sort of girl I would let fade away in the shadows of another? Does it sound to you like that would even be possible?"

She raised her chin and lifted her gaze slowly. "But I'm not really her, Hugh."

"Yes, you are."

Then he turned on his heel and walked away, leaving her there at the center of the ring as though she were the star of the show.

Chapter Five
THE DANCE

"Show me something," Hugh's voice rang out from the otherwise empty audience seating.

"What?" Annis heard the tremble in her voice. She felt furious to think something as simple as being on stage could scare her. There's nothing left to be frightened of, she scolded herself. She'd seen the worst. This was not it.

"A dance. A trick. A secret talent. Anything you'd like."

She'd have liked very much to show him her backside as she marched out of the ring, but she fought the urge to flee. She wasn't a child anymore. This was no time for a tantrum, and pouting would get her nothing but a poor reputation.

"I'm waiting," Hugh reminded her when she still stood there, minutes later, with her eyes closed.

"I'm getting to it!" she snapped, letting her frustration and anger at being forced to perform on the spot to take root and fuel her. She took a breath. Another one. Deeper. Longer. The third breath she held in, and then slowly let it out. On the exhale, she raised both arms above her head and, keeping her eyes closed, began to dance. In that moment she allowed the ballet she'd spent years studying to collide with every emotion she'd denied herself since that night in the river. How many days had passed since? She'd lost track. Seven? Maybe more? It seemed an eternity ago now, she thought. A different life entirely. Every feeling flooded her, the heart crushing pain of her grief, the raging anger of betrayal and the gut-wrenching loss of faith all flowed out through her limbs. She kept rhythm with the manic pounding of her own heart.

Tears streaked her face as she spun in a perfect pirouette, over and over again until all the images inside her head blurred and she became too dizzy to remain upright. Even as she crashed to the ground, her body folding like a ragdoll, she kept moving, crawling, reaching, climbing back to her feet, all part of this dramatic dance performed to the music of her heartache—music no one could ever hear unless she showed them. Unless she played it for them with her dancing body, the way she did now.

The tide of her hurt began to wash away, and her movements shrank into subtler motions, signaling the end was near. Gliding down onto her knees, with her hands reaching for the sky, she dropped her head between her shoulder blades, arched her back, and finished to roaring applause. She wondered where everyone had come from. The last time she'd looked at Hugh, he'd been alone. Now he was surrounded by at least a dozen other faces she recognized, faces that bore a distinct expression of excitement and unexpected pride.

"There she is," Hugh called out over the clapping. "There's the brazen girl I knew was hiding inside." He stepped toward her. "Don't you feel better now, having let her out to peek at the world a bit?"

Annis's eyes were like saucers and her mouth stuck in a single line. The all too familiar feeling of having temporarily left her body returned, only it was different this time. She hadn't been escaping life. She'd been escaping the numbness, breaking free of the self-made prison of her pain, and it had been liberating. But now the moment had passed, leaving her to feel disconnected somehow as she remained hanging in limbo, unsure of how to fully return to the safe confines of herself without returning to the prison as well. Hugh was right about one thing: It was freeing to dance that way. Freeing in an utterly terrifying way. She'd turned herself inside out, allowed all of her vulnerabilities to be wrung from her. And now there would be no reeling them back in —not when half of the circus had witnessed it all.

"Why did you make them all watch?" she hissed, arms crossing over her chest as though she could shield her heart from their knowing eyes.

Hugh shrugged. "Didn't. They were just passing by, getting ready for tonight, and stopped." He leaned in close. "If that's not a girl who's got the makings of a future ringleader, I don't know what is." Not bothering to wait for an answer, he straightened up to his full height. "Right then. Now we've got that sorted out, let's get on with it. You and me's still got a lot of work to do before the good people of Jackson start to arrive." Hugh started walking toward the tent's exit. Annis glanced over her shoulder only to catch the last of her surprise audience dispersing, and then she turned back toward Hugh, who was already nearly halfway through the small ring to her left.

"All's well in hell tonight," she grumbled under her breath as she hurried to catch up. It was an expression she'd heard from her housekeeper anytime things were going about as bad as they could be. She'd never repeated it until now. Annis spent the next hour half running from one place to the next to keep in step with Hugh's long legs. It seemed as ringleader, he had a hand in nearly every aspect of the show. Helping set up props, feeding animals and occasionally approving last minute additions to an act or two. Annis found it all terribly fascinating, even if it did keep her on the move so much that she felt it hard to catch her breath at times. Then, before she knew it, the tent was full. People were cheering and the show had finally begun. Annis sat on the sidelines to watch the event unfold. Hugh burst onto the scene to open the show and drew everyone in with his booming, charismatic voice. Annis had never felt so riveted as by the way he weaved fantastical tales of all the circus-goers were about to behold. Her state of awe grew stronger as the people she'd met earlier that day stepped into the ring to perform. Each act revealed sides of the performers she'd not recognized in them before.

Their diverse talents often had nothing to do with the ways in which they were so extraordinarily different from the society's norms. Oscar and Margaret were notable at first sight for their exceptional size, but their costumes alone intrigued beyond those first impressions. Oscar was dressed to the nines and looked dashing in his sleek black tailcoat and top hat, while Margaret looked divine in a scarlet gown of chiffon and lace, with her strawberry blonde locks swept up in an elegant braid that encircled her head like a crown.

Annis watched in anticipation as they took the ring, wondering just what they would deliver. Oscar stood at the center, under a single spotlight, his hand held out to the dark where Margaret stood hidden in the shadows. Then the soft tones of a waltz began to play, bringing a statuesque Oscar to life. With a graceful twirl into his arms, Margaret joined him. Together they began to glide around the ring as if moving on air. Every move, every step, in perfect rhythm, flawlessly in tune with each other and the music.

The spotlight traced their dance, a beautiful tale of love and hope with every step. Every so often, when they moved closest to the audience, Annis caught the expressions of those watching, briefly lit up by the spotlight. Their faces all reflected the same captivation that Annis felt.

Oscar's powerful command of the floor as he guided his partner. The grace and tenderness with which Margaret responded. The abounding love that flowed between them, expressed more loudly and more clearly than Annis had ever heard between two people who hadn't so much as whispered a single word.

As the song began to wind down, the couple moved back toward the center. The final chords played as Oscar dipped Margaret for a dramatic kiss just before the lights went out and silence struck. Annis clapped with an enthusiasm equal to that of the audience as the couple hurried past her out of the ring, making room for the next performer.

It was Sawyer. While he might have seemed an obvious choice for circus clown at first glance, he did all but draw a laugh as he came onto the scene with two large lions at his command. The tent fell silent as people watched Sawyer Smalls take on the most royal of savanna beasts. Sawyer and the lions bowed to each other before the ferocious looking cats took turns jumping through hoops, rolling over, prancing around the ring, and, for the grand finale, opening their jaws as wide as possible for Sawyer to stick his head in between their massive fangs. What began as horrified gasps from the crowd erupted into explosive applause as Sawyer retrieved his head, completely unharmed.

As she stood in the shadows watching her new colleagues perform, Annis witnessed more talent and skill than she ever had in her entire life.

It wasn't until Babe appeared in the ring that Annis felt nervous. She held her breath, fearing how the audience would respond to her. Babe had traded her flowing robes for a magnificent gown of sage green silk. Her hair was curled and pulled into an updo and flowers nestled around her head like a tiara. Now she looked like a bearded woman rather than a man in a dress. The enigma of Babe left Annis worried she might be too much for some of the audience to comprehend, and that their confusion would distract them from her performance, or worse yet, the fear of being faced with something unknown would trigger emotions of anger or even hate.

And perhaps they would have felt all of those things, had it not been for the way Babe played the harp. No sooner had Babe taken a seat at her instrument and strummed the first note that every hushed comment, hissed insult, and rude question subsided. The crowd's confusion vanished. There was no man or woman. There was simply music, music that stirred emotions, which spilled over as tears that were free to express their truth. Just like Babe. And then it was over. Babe was gone. All anyone remembered was the way she'd made them feel. Unlike the others, there was no immediate applause for her. Too raw were the audience's emotions to react. Annis craned her neck, trying to see why people weren't clapping, just before a thunderous ovation overthrew the quiet and lasted longer than any before it.

Eventually, a new calm settled over the audience and Annis thought for a moment the show had come to an end. Then a familiar pounding of hooves drew her attention to the back of the tent. The team of horses bounded in, galloping from ring to ring, with Sequoyah mounted on the same jet-black stallion Annis had seen him on earlier. This time, though, there was no sign of the gentle mannered man she'd met. He'd been replaced by a warrior who chanted and howled at the top of his lungs as he raced his horses in and out of the rings. War paint decorated his body as well as the horses, who seemed to move in complete unison. Sequoyah began to jump from one horse to another. He hung from their sides. He stood on their backs. He somersaulted off their rear ends. No matter what he did, they kept picking up speed, entirely unfazed by his movements—much unlike the people of the crowd, who were coming out of their seats and cheering and screaming for more. It was the grandest finale Annis could ever have imagined. She felt a rush of adrenaline from watching Sequoyah in action. One look at the audience around her confirmed she wasn't alone in her experience.

Hugh and Babe most definitely understood how to please a crowd. If Hugh had seen in each of his performers the heights they could reach even when they'd shown up to his circus no different from her—broken, lost, and unacceptable by society's strict standards—then perhaps he was right about her too. Maybe she really could create an act of her own. She imagined how she might cast magic upon the audience to captivate them long enough to see something that made them feel as enchanted as everyone else had made them feel tonight. At the very least, she was willing to find out if she could.

"So, what did you think, love?" Hugh asked, his sly grin creeping over his thin mouth as if to say he already knew the answer.

"I've never seen anything like it," she said. Her breath and her thoughts were tied together, racing and struggling to find some equilibrium within her again after watching the whirlwind of vibrant life unfurl before her for the last two hours. While she'd been watching, it had seemed like she'd spent an eternity inside a timeless space of impossible possibilities. Now it felt as though everything had passed in a matter of seconds, like a flash of magic she couldn't wait to see again. One taste was all she'd needed to realize she'd been starving for that magic all along.

Hugh laughed. "Well, I think we all expected that much, at least." One arm swung out toward her, shielding the back of her shoulders and smoothly ushering her out of the way as two elephants, both adorned in delicate headgear and silk blankets, passed by them. The elephants moved with more grace than Annis thought possible. They could easily maneuver a china shop better than she. "Any other insight?" Hugh continued. "Critique from a fresh set of eyes is nothing to plunder away. Give me your thoughts, love. Raw. Honest. Brutal. I can take it."

Annis couldn't tell if he was being serious anymore. "My thoughts? I'm not sure I've any left." She tripped over a stray piece of rope and nearly tumbled face first to meet it. Hugh snatched her elbow just in time.

"No thoughts. No coordination." He chuckled. "Perhaps it's time to call it a day then, love. Get a proper rest from all the adventure you've seen as of late." He turned over his shoulder, scanning the area with his bright blue eyes. "Maude! Mabel!" he called, getting the twins' attentions. "You girls think Annis could bunk with you tonight? Just until we sort out a more permanent space for her?"

Both women clapped in unison. "We'd love to have her," chirped Maude. Or was it Mabel? Annis couldn't tell them apart. Reaching a level of exhaustion at which being polite in her inner dialogue ceased to matter, Annis decided it seemed easier to refer to them as the left one and the right one. Regardless of the name of the talkative one, both twins swooped in with their arms outstretched until Annis was within their grasp. Huddled at the center of both women in an embrace that reminded her of a hug but wasn't, Annis was accompanied from the tent and toward the train cars that surrounded their camp.

During the show, Annis nearly forgot that the twins shared the same torso. Edi and Millie, the two elephant divas who'd given Francis a run for his money earlier, were part of a four-sister act alongside Mabel and Maude. Each woman spent her portion of the act interacting only with her elephant and standing in such a way that created the illusion Mabel and Maude were standing back-to-back instead of attached. Now their conjoined nature was undeniable to Annis, but in the most welcoming way. Being fully cocooned at the center of their twinship was a warm, inviting place to be, especially as the exhaustion spread and turned Annis's legs to lead. She began to drag her feet rather than lift them with each step. Mabel and Maude sensed her weight growing heavier and fully supported her elbows as the three continued to their destination.

The cart was cozy, just like both women. Each twin, however, had her own hand in the decor, proving that they could be as opposite as they were identical. Each side of their sweet and humble home had been claimed by one twin and furnished to her specific likings, down to the color of her designated wall.

"Mabel's always had a fondness for green," Maude muttered in Annis's ear. "Ghastly color, if you ask me, but she didn't. Clearly."

"Maude would hardly know *ghastly* if it jumped in her face and kissed her," her sister countered. "How else do you explain those window treatments?"

Annis glanced back and forth over her shoulders in time to catch both sisters smirking. They'd been teasing. It did make Annis wonder, though, if these two ever had serious fights. She thought it must be unbearable to be furious with someone and be unable to stomp from the room without them. She also took note of how frustrating it would be to be the mirror image of someone you were angry at. And they were absolute mirror images. If they hadn't been stuck always on one side of the other, it would be impossible to tell them apart. She knew she'd likely forget which was which come morning. She giggled at the silliness of her thoughts and realized sleep was necessary and imminent. "Perhaps a full tour, complete with taste discussions shall wait until morning?" Mabel suggested, as though reading Annis's mind.

"Probably best. Poor dear can hardly keep her eyes open," her sister agreed. They began to move again, Annis still between them. "It's not much, I'm afraid," Maude went on, "but it's quite comfortable. Or so we've been told. Our sister Maeve stays here when she visits. Always seems quite pleased with the accommodations."

"Sure, that's what she enjoys," Mabel said with a wink and a giggle.

"I think she's also rather fond of August," Maude explained to a silent, somewhat dumbstruck Annis as the three moved toward the small seating area in the far-right corner.

Placing Annis down in the center of the cushions, both sisters began to clear most of the throw pillows that had accumulated there and, before long, a reasonably sized sleeping space revealed itself. Annis clutched the last of the pillows to her, slid it under the side of her head, and sunk down. Her body melted into the soft surface. She felt a blanket being pulled tenderly over her worn body only seconds before she felt nothing at all. Sleep had finally come for her and, this time, she surrendered.

Chapter Six

MABEL AND MAUDE

When Annis awoke, pitch black drenched everything. Panic struck within her when she was unable to place herself. After several deep breaths, she calmed long enough to remember that stumbling upon the Brooks and Bennet Circus hadn't been a dream. It had all really happened.

Sitting up carefully, she placed her feet on the ground beneath her makeshift bunk in the corner of Maude and Mabel's train car, feeling the vibration of the moving train. The sensation coursed its way up through her soles and into her calves, tingling almost to the point of discomfort. Still, Annis kept her feet in place, thoroughly pleased with the ability to feel connected to the world around her again. She was regaining her presence and feeling more and more at home in her own skin. There was comfort in the sense of home that came no longer from some outside source, from some house-shaped structure. Now, home was inside of her. And it was a place no one could ever rip from her.

"Annis?" a voice whispered in the dark. "Annis, is that you?"

"Sorry," Annis mumbled under her breath. "Did I wake you?" Now that her eyes had begun to adjust to the dark, she was able to make out an outline of one of the sisters, sitting half-upright, half-attached to the other sleeping sibling.

"Not at all," the voice said with a hushed and airy lightness. "I don't sleep nearly as much as everyone else around here. I find my dreaming is a great deal more enjoyable when I'm awake to do it." She fluffed her pillow into a more upright position. "But I noticed a figure sitting across from me when I turned my head and thought I better check and be sure it was you."

"Who else could it be?" The train was in motion, after all. It seemed unlikely they'd have any surprise visitors in the middle of the night here.

The woman across from her swirled her hand dismissively. Annis sincerely wished she'd identify herself. It was maddening not knowing which of the twins she was speaking to, mostly because she was disappointed in herself for being unable to tell on her own. Surely there were distinguishing markers between the two, telltale signs that spoke to their individuality and made it possible for others to tell them apart. If they existed, though, Annis had yet to discover them.

"You wouldn't believe the stories if I told them to you," the unidentified twin carried on with a quiet giggle. "But Francis does make regular visits. Claims it's a problem with sleepwalking, but he only ever seems to wind up in here when it happens. And I don't reckon I believe he makes it through five cars in his sleep, as much as I'm certain he draws his motivation from coming in here in hopes of watching Maude dream about him."

So this was Mabel, on the right, Annis noted.

"He's in love with her, see," Mabel went on. "And I know she feels the same way 'bout him. It's why she keeps him at bay, hoping he'll give up. Move on."

"But... why?" Annis didn't understand. If they both cared for one another, why fight it?

"Same old story. Thinks he deserves better. Wants him to have a sort of normal he could never have with her. With us." Though she delivered the words in the same chipper tone, seamlessly transitioning from the lighthearted parts to the heartbreaking ones, Annis heard the briefest of hesitations, a struggle to take in the breath that gave away the truth behind her seemingly carefree demeanor. Her heart was just as broken as her sister's.

"I've lived an entire life of normal. It's not anything anyone should hold out for. All the pretty perfection is nothing but a façade. Truth is, everything that's preened and polished is likely rotting on the inside. I, for one, hope I never have to endure any sort of normal ever again." She'd meant it to sound encouraging, but the cold, bitter tone of her voice was anything but. "Sorry," she mumbled for the second time since this conversation had begun.

"No need," Mabel assured her. "As for normal, you needn't worry about that here. Won't find any of that rubbish around these parts, that much I can promise you." She giggled again. It was catching. The surge of a giggle bubbling up in Annis's own throat startled her and she gasped loudly at its release, covering her mouth just as fast as it happened. She hoped desperately it hadn't woken Maude, who, by some miracle, seemed to have slept through their entire interaction thus far. She supposed the twins had learned to tune out a great deal of sounds and movement because they were physically attached to another human being. No matter how close, or how dearly loved, Annis imagined there would be times they would simply want to be alone with their own thoughts.

"Mabel?" Annis asked, "how long has it been since you brought me here to sleep?" The longer she was awake, the more she realized all that had to have transpired for the circus to have packed up and be traveling the tracks now. She felt certain she'd slept for days, if not weeks, given her state of exhaustion. There was no telling just how much of life she'd missed, or how far she'd traveled since the time she'd last seen her surroundings. The thought made her heart leap. Distance. The promise of a lasting escape. It was almost too much to hope for.

Mabel turned her head toward the window behind her. Lifting the corner of what Annis remembered to be maroon and yellow curtains, Mabel assessed the state of the night beyond. Annis could make out the rise and fall of Mabel's shoulders as they bounced with a noncommittal shrug before she abandoned her post at the window and turned back to face her.

"Eight hours. Nine, tops. Sun's just about to breach the horizon."

Impossible, Annis thought. "Are you certain you don't mean days?" Annis sat up straighter, a growing desire swirling at the pit of her stomach to peek through the window and see the sun for herself. "I feel as though I've missed a week to sleeping. How long have we been traveling?"

Mabel gave another lazy shrug of her shoulders before she answered. "Four hours or so. Break down's always faster than the set up. You'll see. Next stop, you'll get to experience the entire cycle. Then you'll be wishing you could sleep through half of it, just wait." She gave another carefree laugh, this one louder than the last.

"I think I prefer your approach to resting, actually. Dreaming while awake." Sleep had lost its appeal to Annis. She disliked the way it left her with her guard down, unaware of all that went on in the world as soon as her eyelids were shut. Annis had learned the hard way just how much the world kept busy while she rested. How many lies could be spun in her absence. It was a lesson she had no intention of repeating.

"Well, in any event, we really ought to stretch out again, let our bodies breathe. Won't be long and all around will be up and at 'em, and we'll have no choice but to join in. Too many laughs to pass up on, even for the best of dreams." Mabel didn't wait for Annis to answer before she fluffed her pillow once more and adjusted into a horizontal position.

After a few more seconds of letting the hum of the train buzz through her soles and up her calves, Annis pivoted her legs back into her bed. Tucking herself snuggly under the covers, she let her head sink deep into the pillows while she gazed up at where she knew the ceiling to be. It was still too dark to make out the details of her surroundings, but it was all the same to Annis as she stared upward, seeing neither darkness nor the red wooden panels she knew lined the inside of the sisters' roof. Instead, she saw images of her own design. *Horses. Beautiful horses, galloping over rolling hills of green as she rode atop a red-and-white paint in their midst. The sky, the bluest blue, hung above her and the wind tangled up her hair. And then the scenery changed. The rolling hills flattened, and the horses slowed. Riding up beside her was Sequoyah, smiling.*

Startled, Annis blinked until her vision blurred and the fantasy disappeared. She hadn't meant for him to be a part of it, but her mind had made other plans. Tugging at the blanket until it came up to her chin, she scooted her body down into the mattress, uncomfortable with her own desires and the complications they could cause her.

She wouldn't wind up like Francis, lost in a love she could never receive nor release. She would stop these irrational thoughts and their consequent emotions. She'd choose to be numb, instead. Numb was preferable to the pain that would inevitably follow having a childish infatuation with a young man who most likely would never give her a second thought. And, for his sake, even more than for her own, she hoped he wouldn't.

Indulging in fantasies having lost its appeal, Annis stared blankly into the dark of the cabin and focused her mind solely on the sounds of the train as it skirted along the tracks. She studied the clinks, squeals, and occasional thuds to identify their patterns and origins. Before long, sleep came for her a second time.

A burst of light cut through her lids and instinct made her turn her head away before she was fully awake. "Rise and shine, sleepyhead!" Mabel's voice rang out. Annis realized, quite pleased with herself, that even in her half-awake state she'd easily recognized the chirping tones as belonging to Mabel rather than Maude.

"Has it been a week this time?' Annis asked, rubbing her eyes with the palms of her hands. Mabel laughed.

"Not quite. Still the same Tuesday from the last time we spoke, I'm afraid." Tuesday. Annis had lost count of days during her time traveling on foot. Tuesday would mark ten days since she'd left. It didn't seem nearly long enough. Ten days had passed in the blink of an eye, and she'd hardly accomplished anything. Until now. Now, things were really moving forward. She could get back to tracking the days of the week again.

"Where are we headed?" she asked, sitting up to find that Mabel and Maude were already moving around the small cabin, both fully clothed. Maude braided Mabel's hair while the latter went about fixing the seam on the side of their full skirt.

"Next stop is Dallas, Texas," Maude replied. "Ever been?" Annis shook her head, though she wasn't entirely sure whether Maude had been serious or not.

"Oh, it's lively. You'll like it," Mabel went on, eyes wide with excitement. "Caroline's from there. She's got loads of stories. Knows all the best places."

Annis swung her legs over the side of her bed, the buzzing of the moving train beneath her feet already becoming a source of comfort for her. "I'm not sure I'm ready for lively. To be honest, I quite like keeping out of the way. There's less trouble in it."

Mabel giggled. "Also less fun."

Maude elbowed Mabel's side and scowled. "You're awful, you are. Always trying to get people to go along with your crazy ideas." She turned toward Annis, her index finger stabbing at the air. "You've got the right idea, Annis. Camp is plenty lively as it is. And has the benefit of being free of any hateful individuals who might want to tarnish our good time simply for the sake of pointing out the obvious."

"You mean like how we're attached at the hip and Sawyer's a fully-grown man the size of a small child?" Mabel said.

"Yeah. Precisely. See, even without them we've got you to fill in."

The sisters snickered at their own silliness and Annis couldn't help but smirk at the sight of them. There was something sort of wonderful about the way they not only embraced their oddities, but also had a laugh at themselves—or, rather, had a laugh at the thought of those who couldn't comprehend what really made the sisters unique. The twins being conjoined wasn't what set them apart from the average members of society. Annis realized what made them special was the unhesitating kindness and graciousness they extended to others, without expecting anything in return.

"What do you suppose they'd say about me?" Annis asked, and instantly wished she hadn't. There was nothing physically remarkable about her, no obvious difference to point out. She was perfectly bland to look at, no more unique to the eye than a blade of grass.

Maude, however, seemed oblivious to this as she answered. "I don't suppose at all. I'm quite convinced they'd say you must be mental. Or even possessed, perhaps. All that outward innocence always holds the darkest evil within." She grinned. "Haven't you heard?"

"It would also explain your being tangled up with our lot," Mabel added.

Annis took in their words, allowing theories of innocence and evil to sink in alongside the prospect of being insane. She supposed there was a kernel of truth to all of what they said. At first, it made her uncomfortable. She had assumed they'd said in jest, facetiously poking fun at the small minds of others. But, at the heart of it, they'd stabbed at the core of Annis's secret. All of her innocence *was* hiding a darkness, one wrapped in an unhealable heartache. Then, glancing back and forth between the sisters and their quiet expressions, an unspoken understanding transpired between the threesome and Annis saw clearly the web they'd spun. They hadn't been pulling at strings or making up stories. They were fully aware of the seedling of truth sprouting their theories. She wasn't evil. But after what she'd seen the night she escaped, she'd never be fully sane again.

The honest brilliance of their playful theories made Annis erupt with an explosive laugh from the pit of her stomach. It barreled through her, spilling out in uncontainable waves that shook her core until it hurt. So loud was her laughter that it drew the attention of several of their neighbors, who wandered into the sisters' car to investigate the noise. Annis didn't care. It was the most alive, most carefree, she'd felt in as long as she could remember, and she was determined to hold onto the feeling for as long as she possibly could.

"Well, well, well. Look whose marble shell finally cracked," Sawyer said, looking delighted as he climbed up onto the built-in nightstand and had a seat. Following right behind him was August, Caroline, and Homer, entering from the opposite end of the car.

"I don't recall this part of the train ever being so chipper first thing in the morning," Caroline said over Annis's laughter, sliding her rear end onto the twins' wide cot until her back rested against the wall and her legs stretched out before her. Annis tried taking several calming breaths to quell her raucous howl, but only managed to bring it down to a giggle. Tears streamed down her face, which continued to contort at the mercy of her escaping emotions. Through her giggling, Annis noticed that though the cabin had seemed cozy with just the twins and herself, with seven people it seemed rather suffocating. No one else seemed bothered by it.

With little room to move about, the twins took their seat beside Annis, both still having a good chuckle themselves, while Homer took his place beside Caroline. August remained the only one standing, his massiveness nearly filling the car wall-to-wall and floor-to-ceiling. Just looking at him, Annis doubled over again in another laughing fit. There was something ridiculous about how he could make an entire train car feel like a sardine can.

"Why do I suddenly get the feeling the joke has shifted in my direction?" he grumbled, his arm reaching his hand to the ceiling to steady himself as the train took a narrow curve around a bend. This made Annis laugh harder. Somewhere in the back of her mind she heard engrained warnings about how succumbing to a laughing fit in the company of others wasn't proper behavior.

"Who cares? She's laughing," Sawyer said, pointing at her as he chortled. "It's a good sign she's stronger than she looks and stranger than we thought."

August cocked his left brow, the side of his mouth hitching up after it. "You didn't think she was strange from the get-go?" he quipped, and Annis howled, louder still. This time, she was joined by the others. It shook the walls and echoed its way up and down the train until, at last, the train slowed and so did Annis's inexhaustible giggling.

"Oh," Annis gasped. "Air."

"Yes," Mabel agreed, rubbing her cheeks, which were taut from all the laughing. "And we're about to have plenty of it."

When the train stopped, everyone in the car jolted forward. The others were well accustomed to the motion, but Annis was not.

She nearly toppled into Maude and Mabel's lap beside her. August reached out one colossal hand and caught her by the back of her shirt just before she fell. "Bet you don't think I'm so funny looking now, do ya?" he teased, pulling her back into her seat with ease.

"Thank you." She grinned, remembering what the twins had said about their sister, Maeve. He might not have been her particular cup of tea, but she could certainly see the appeal where August was concerned.

Everyone was soon on their feet and shuffling out of the car. Annis was last to exit, with nerves and excitement tap dancing at the pit of her stomach. Outside, the unloading and rebuilding ritual was already taking place. Canvas tents were attached to train cars. Animal wagons were being rolled from the trolleys. Large wooden masts were being carried off and placed in the center of their new, temporary home. The circus had officially arrived in Texas.

"How do I help?" she asked, hurrying to keep up with the twins. They moved with more speed and grace using all four of their legs than she could muster on her more traditional pair.

"Just follow along and we'll put you to work," Maude shouted over her shoulder, ducking immediately after to avoid being hit with several rolls of canvas that August was carrying past them.

Annis maneuvered the site, which was quickly turning into an obstacle course, as best she could until they reached the elephants' quarters. Unlike many of the other animals' residences, these were a permanent fixture of the train. Two men Annis had seen only in passing were busy dropping the large ramp to the elephants' car. "Wait until you meet our girls," Mabel said, bursting with pride. "They're absolutely breathtaking."

"Yeah. When they're not making you want to rip your own hair out, they're just dandy," one of the two men said.

"You haven't had hair since before we met you, Charlie," Maude teased.

He grinned, pointing at the fellow to his left, who was a great deal younger than himself. His long, shaggy, straw-like hair was second in prominence only to his striking blue eyes, which were alive with curiosity and mischief. "Was talking about Goldilocks, here," Charlie said. "My personal experience with the hair pulling is more witness-based than as a participant."

"Goldilocks," Annis hissed, hoping only Mabel could hear. "Is that really what people call him?" After the last twenty-four hours, she could hardly rule out the possibility.

However, her whispers were louder than planned.

"Sadly, yes," the golden-haired boy answered, hand outstretched to meet hers. "Though I prefer Jacob if it's all the same to you."

She nodded, taking his hand. "Annis. And I think I can manage that."

"Careful of the promises you make," Charlie warned playfully. "I think you'll find Goldilocks to be lot more fitting as time goes on."

Mabel leaned in, ensuring her whispers were exclusively directed at Annis's ear. "It's true. Actually forgot his name was Jacob until he just said it." She shrugged, brushing off the oversight, and carried on with her sister up the ramp. Annis offered an awkward smile at Jacob and Charlie before she followed the twins inside.

It was dark, with sunlight only spilling inside in patches through the small windows on either side of their enclosure. Annis blinked multiple times in an attempt to adjust her eyes to the dimness and stumbled over unidentifiable debris. "What's the story with Goldilocks, then?" she asked, her eyes slowly coming into focus. She was curious to hear how he'd wound up in the Brooks and Bennet collection and why on earth Goldilocks was a better suited name for him than Jacob.

"Some rubbish about bears and porridge," Mabel answered, hardly paying attention. "I don't really remember the details. Was never one of my favorites."

Maude stopped fussing with the buckets she'd been busy filling with a variety of fruits and turned toward her sister, glaring at her. "You can't be serious."

Mabel, however, remained oblivious. "What?"

"She wasn't asking about the fairy tale, you twit. She was asking about the boy."

Mabel looked at Annis, surprise brightening her face. "Oh." She let out a giggle. "Sorry. Let me start over," she said, thoughtfully tapping her chin with her finger. "Goldilocks. What's his tale then, Maude? You remember better than I do."

Maude rolled her eyes and turned away, investing her interest back into preparing breakfast for her beloved elephants. "I'm not telling that story and you damn well know why," she huffed. The back of her head nearly disappeared inside a large trunk, from which she emerged with multiple flakes of hay seconds later.

Mabel seemed temporarily dumbfounded, then a flash of recognition lit up her eyes. "Oh. Right. He's here because of me."

"You?" Annis asked, crinkling her nose. Keeping up with Mabel and her hopscotch way of thinking was something she would need more practice with before she'd be able to take it in stride the way Maude did. Maude always followed along, no matter how scattered or how unexpected a turn Mabel's mind took. "How?"

She shrugged, bending at the waist to pick up a broom and a shovel that had fallen from their hooks during travel. "It's all Harris's fault, really. Have you met Harris?"

Annis shook her head, though she thought she'd heard the name before.

"Well, Harris—though, to be honest, I don't believe that's his real name either...It's actually something strange and hard to pronounce. Hugh tried, but grew tired of it and started calling him 'Harris' instead. Not sure why. His real name starts with a P, best I can recall." Annis was feeling dizzy from the story already and she'd only just learned a man's name—or rather, what his name was not.

"In any event, he answers to Harris now, so that's what we call him. Harris. Sometimes we call him Your Royal Highness, but that's only when we're being prats and want to have a laugh. Harris is a bit of royalty, see. Illegitimate child of some foreign king in some land I've never heard of. It's why I question the entire story, to be honest. But he claims he's a sort of prince even if they won't claim him, and so we do. On occasion."

"Good God," her sister interrupted. "Would you get to point already? It'll be halfway to lunch by the time you finish telling your tale and we haven't even had a proper breakfast, let alone served one to the girls." She thrust the buckets she'd filled toward her sister. "Think we can at least walk and talk while you do carry on?"

"Certainly." Mabel nodded, smiling brightly. "Now, where was I? Right. His Royal Harris. Anyway, the only entourage His Highness stumbled into our midst with was an odd assortment of monkeys."

That's when it clicked for Annis. She'd seen Harris perform last night. It was a sensational number featuring him and his monkeys swinging together from the ceiling, hanging onto everything from ropes to long drapes. Annis had held her breathe while they all jumped and spun about. Mabel seemed oblivious to Annis being briefly distracted by her own recollection. When Annis tuned back in, the story was still pushing onward at full-force.

"...Each of them cheekier than the next. Worst of all is Jacob. That's right. There's a monkey with the same name. Well, one night, as we're breaking down and loading up, that sneaky little monkey runs off. Maude and I were the first to notice, being as our elephant car is right next to theirs, so I start shouting for Jacob to get his little arse into the car where he belongs. It was dark out, mind you. I couldn't see much but for the stars above and the outline of trees on the horizon, so I just hollered orders out into the night until that little rebel came running back to climb onto Maude's shoulder to be escorted back home." She stopped, giving her sister a hand with the morning feeding at last. "Next morning, Goldilocks was sitting in Momma T's tent, having breakfast with everyone else. Apparently, he'd been walking the tracks the night before, wandering across the country looking for work. When I'd demanded he get himself aboard the train, he'd been all too happy to oblige. Been with us ever since." She tipped her head back and forth between both shoulders.

"But..." Annis was still catching up. "Why do they call him Goldilocks?"

Mabel laughed as though it were obvious. "Couldn't very well call him Jacob, like the monkey."

"Right. Of course."

"Hasn't been all bad. He's a good worker. And he's awfully pretty to look at, don't you think?"

"Huh?" Annis wasn't entirely sure what she thought of anything at that moment, let alone of the boy who couldn't keep his perfectly sound name for the sake of not being confused with the monkey. "Oh. Yeah. He's alright," she agreed once she'd registered the question. "Not nearly as impressive as these two, though," she said. Awe filled her from the base of her belly and gave way to overwhelm at the sight of Edi and Millie. Annis found them thrilling during their performance the night before. Standing there in the intimate setting of their small quarters while they peacefully crunched away at their morning meal was absolutely mesmerizing.

"They are quite splendid," Maude agreed, running her hand tenderly up and down the side of Edi's massive torso. "Who cares about pretty boys when you have elephants?" She smirked, eyes cast sideways at her sister.

"Never said I didn't prefer the elephant," Mabel muttered. "Merely trying to point out the silver lining to my inadvertent act of inviting a vagabond to join the circus."

"Oh, well in that case, yes, he's lovely," Maude mused, clearly humoring her sister. "However, he may not be entirely to Annis's tastes."

"What?" Annis had only just mustered enough nerve to reach out and pat Edi's trunk, but was already sweeping back her hand in a hurry, feeling caught in some act of mischief she hadn't been aware she'd participated in.

"You know something I don't? How is that always possible? I'm never away from you. We're always in the same place, living through all the same experiences!" Mabel cried.

"It's possible because you're always talking and I'm always listening. And, more importantly," Maude said, pausing to let her gaze drift toward Annis. She winked. "I'm always watching."

"Go on, then," Mabel urged. "Tell us what you saw."

"Or don't," Annis offered, hoping she'd choose the latter.

Maude let out a laugh of sheer delight. Either because she knew it would torture her sister not knowing what she did or because it would torture Annis wondering whether or not she'd say what she knew. Not that Annis could say for sure what it was Maude thought she had seen, but she had an eerie sense it involved a certain someone who looked almost unbearably handsome riding a horse. And she was positive she wanted no word of it uttered out loud, ever.

A sly grin crept over Maude's mouth. "Oh, alright. I'll let you keep your secrets. But only because it'll make Mabel crazier by not telling than it would do you to tell." She then hooked an arm over Mabel's shoulders and added, "But if the time comes around you want a certain someone to know, you just say the word and I'll be sure to let Mabel here use her blow horn of a mouth the get the message out."

"You're a terrible sister. You know that, don't you?" Mabel scowled, though it was hardly believable and Annis had to work harder than usual to suppress her laughter as she listened to their banter.

"I'm a splendid sister, Mabel. I see you for all your fabulous faults and I love you not despite them, but because of."

Mabel turned her nose up, pouting. "Only because they make you look like the brilliant one."

"And what's not to love about that?" Maude said with a delighted laugh. Maybe it was some byproduct of their physical connection, unlikely though it did seem, but one never did appear to be able to laugh without the other no matter how set against it they might have been at the start. And so, it was no surprise to Annis or Maude when Mabel began cackling loudly right alongside her sister, even if the joke was entirely at her expense.

It took Hugh slipping his head in through the open doors to get them to calm down and get serious again.

"Will we be seeing the likes of you out here by daylight at all today? Or are you planning to wait until after sunset when all the work is complete?" he asked, not trying too hard to conceal his own amusement at the sight of them giggling away beside the elephants, who, in their own way, seemed pleased to be provided with entertainment over breakfast.

"Is that a possibility?" Maude inquired, hiccupping.

"Not in the slightest." Hugh chuckled, shaking his head until his gaze landed on Annis. "My apologies, Annis. I've left you in the hands of the worst sort of influence around here. Please, allow me to rectify my mistake," he teased the twins even as he kept his eyes on Annis.

"Good luck," Maude chirped mockingly as Hugh began to lead Annis from the elephant cart.

Mabel snorted. "Being a good influence isn't exactly a desirable trait around these parts."

"Maybe you should pair her up with Sequoyah," Annis heard Maude holler after them. Her cheeks burned red just at the mention of his name. Thankfully, Hugh seemed to be oblivious to her blushing.

Chapter Seven
SEQUOYAH

"Indeed. Sequoyah's not a bad suggestion," Hugh said. "He does tend to be less prone to leading the shenanigans, though he's never much for putting up a fight where joining them is concerned." Hugh held out his arm, gesturing for Annis to take the lead as they began to funnel their way through the unfolding chaos of setting up the tent.

"What about Caroline?" Annis asked, eager to move his point of interest to someone else. Anyone other than Sequoyah, really, she thought. "I spent some time with her this morning. She was just lovely. Very helpful and informative." Indeed, Caroline had shared a great deal of lessons with Annis where barely-there costumes were concerned, along with the art of keeping all the essentials covered up even when in the most compromising positions. These were lessons Annis hoped never to have to use, but which she found potentially valuable nonetheless.

"Absolutely not," Hugh replied, aghast at her suggestion. "I can't count the times she's been right there at the forefront of some insane act she and Homer cooked up together. I let you go with Caroline and she'll have you spinning from the ceiling upside down, holding you by your toes while she dangles from a rope and her crazy husband goes about tossing flaming daggers around your pretty little head."

"Be quite the number though, wouldn't it?" Annis quipped, entertained and probably not nearly terrified enough at the thought.

Hugh's brow furrowed. "I see what Sawyer meant now about your shell cracking. You going to be one of the reckless ones then, love?"

Annis thought it over as they walked before she answered. "Not reckless. Fearless."

"There's a difference then?" he asked, the rigid lines of his stern expression already melting into curiosity.

"Reckless implies I'll be careless. Stupid, even, with myself or others. Running blindly off the edge and paying no mind to the consequences. Fearless just means I'll be willing to leap even if the drop is steep, because I've already survived falling and I'm willing to risk it again for my chance to fly. One is calculated risk. The other is not. I'd say they're very different, wouldn't you?" She glanced up the side of Hugh's long body, trying to make out his face, but the sun shone on it just so as to obscure his expression.

"I was afraid you'd say that," he muttered, but his arms swung freely as he walked. Annis had learned the day before this swinging motion was a good sign where Hugh's mood was concerned.

"So, Caroline?" she tried a second time.

"No. Not today. And if you ask me that again, I'm going to start to question your reckless versus fearless argument." He turned abruptly, cutting through the animal tent that was already set up and accommodating a variety of furry, four-legged creatures including everything from lions to monkeys. "I'm still sticking you with Sequoyah. Won't be permanent though, so don't get too settled in. I think we best have you bounce around a bit, see what truly sparks your interest. Find where you fit best before we start setting long-term goals where your act in this circus is concerned."

"You're the boss," Annis said, and then sighed.

"You're not still on about not having an act, are ya?" he asked, pausing mid-step to look at her.

Actually, Annis hadn't been concerned about that since she'd seen last night's performances. If Sawyer could command a lion to behave as though it were an innocent house cat, surely there was something hidden in her that was just as unexpected as seeing a two-foot-tall man as the leader among a pride of lions. Her stray sigh was an expression of her displeasure about having to spend the day with a man she'd promised herself, several times over the course of her particularly early morning, she'd stay very far away from—for his safety as much as for her own. But she could hardly admit this to Hugh.

In lieu of telling an outright lie, she shrugged and said, "It's not that. Just feeling a bit overwhelmed, that's all." This was mostly true. These uninvited feelings she was having for Sequoyah were certainly overwhelming.

"You'll do real well with Sequoyah, then, love," he said, resuming his march. "Between these high-strung horses and Babe's worrying, he's had plenty of practice keeping everyone's hysterics to a manageable level." This time, in the shade of the canvas, Annis could see Hugh's grin clear as day.

"I think I'd like to take offense to that," she mumbled dryly.

"But?"

"But that hardly seems appropriate when it's so spot on."

Hugh laughed, slowly coming to a stop. They'd arrived at a temporary horse corral. At first, Sequoyah was nowhere to be seen. Annis allowed herself a tiny exhale of momentary relief, and then nearly choked on it when two of the paints parted just beyond the makeshift fence to reveal Sequoyah standing right in front of her, looking as beautiful as ever.

Hugh gave her a good slap between the shoulder blades to unblock her airway. "It's the dust," he said. "Happens to me all the time."

If only dust were the source of her troubles. "Uh-huh." She cleared her throat before gulping down the remnants of a cough and forced herself to meet Sequoyah's gaze. As soon as she did, she had to fight the urge to look away. The way his dark eyes bored into her made her want to scream from their intensity. She knew instantly the insanity of her believing she could hide herself from him. No one had ever looked at her and seen her more thoroughly than he was doing at that moment.

"Hey, Poppy," Sequoyah said as he greeted his father, though his eyes stayed locked on Annis. "Making the rounds already? That mean Momma T's started serving breakfast?"

"Last I checked she was still searching for her favorite griddle. No hotcakes until she finds it." Hugh shook his head. "And, truthfully, I have a bad feeling the pan she's looking for was used on some very unsavory monkey business and got left behind back in Missouri."

Annis was tempted to ask if he meant monkey business in a literal sense but then decided it was best not to find out. Sequoyah seemed to know exactly what sort of monkey business Hugh meant and, judging by the way he pulled his face into a long grimace, he wasn't eager to revisit the memory.

"Not sure I want breakfast now," he said dryly. "Thanks for that."

"Oh, you're about to thank me double," Hugh said, clapping a hand to his shoulder. "I've brought you a present. Or, a loaner, really. Annis is yours for the day. Teach her something, would you?"

Sequoyah smirked, resting both forearms over the top board of the corral, his wrists crossed, hands hanging lazily out in front of him. "I'm sure she's learned plenty from hanging around the twins."

Hugh shook his head, slowly turning away to carry on with his duties as ringmaster and father figure to all. "Teach her something else. Something she can take pride in knowing," he called over this shoulder.

"Well, that narrows it down quite a bit." Sequoyah let out a quiet laugh, tipping his head slightly to the left where Annis stood in front of him, still separated by the wooden slats of the corral. "How about we start with finding out what you already know?"

Annis, tongue-tied, gave a helpless shrug, crossing her arms over her chest as though they could somehow shield her from his curiosities. Sequoyah crinkled his forehead and his eyes narrowed, their spark ever-present. "You don't know what you already know? I'm going to be honest with you, Annis. That's not very promising." She let out a snort that surprised them both, her arms falling loose at her sides again as she did.

"No, I suppose it's not." She was well aware the amusement dancing over his face was at her expense, but she could hardly take offense when he smiled at her. He stood up taller, pulling his arms back from the wood until only his hands caught on it, fingers wrapping around the front of it. "Maybe it's best if you just follow along with me for a bit, watch how we work around here, see if it triggers anything. Hopefully you'll remember some of the things you already know you don't currently know you know. You know?"

Annis grinned, nervously shifting from one foot to other, pacing in place. "I think I do."

He gestured for her to join him in the corral, and Annis found a renewed appreciation for the trousers Babe had dressed her in the day before. Climbing fences was a cinch when she wasn't wearing a skirt.

As soon as her boots hit the ground again, Sequoyah began moving. He weaved through the herd as though the path he traveled already existed. Annis watched in awe, hesitant to follow.

"I thought we agreed you would be coming along?" he asked, looking over his shoulder for her.

"They...they won't mind?" While striking to look at, the horses also intimidated her, especially now that she was standing so close and right in the middle of their terrain.

Sequoyah's expression seemed to settle on a permanent perplexity whenever he looked at her. "Are you planning to throw rocks at them?"

"No." Annis found it to be a horrible thought.

"Having thoughts about pulling their tails?"

"Of course not!" Annis was nothing short of appalled at the mere suggestion. As if she could ever do any harm to anyone, let alone an animal.

He smiled, and she understood he'd never been serious. "Then I don't think they'll mind one bit."

"Do you suppose you'll ever tire of teasing me?" she asked, though she was focused on conveying her utmost regard for each horse as she passed by, smiling and bowing her head gently. Maybe it was silly but every time their eyes met hers, she sensed that the horses understood her demonstrations of respect. Meanwhile, Sequoyah was showing her far less grace. He was laughing at her yet again.

"It's hard to say, but I get the sense you'll be having a go at me soon enough. And," he winked at her, setting free a slew of butterflies in her abdomen, "I promise to be a good sport about it when you do."

She nodded, trying her best to suppress the smile that threatened to expose the immense pleasure this gave her. She felt like they were making up their own secret rules to a friendship only between them. "That sounds fair enough." One more step and she was finally beside him. "In the meantime, if it's all the same to you, I'd really like to get on with the learning bit of my morning, so we can get on to the working part, and then, hopefully, the breakfast part. Which I'm still happy to partake of, fully able to pretend the previously discussed monkey business was merely an impressionistic sort of expression regarding Momma T's griddle for the sake of hope where hotcakes are concerned." She also hoped he hadn't noticed she was rambling.

"For the sake of hope," he repeated, taking far more care with her words than she'd have expected. "That's probably the best reason to do anything."

She took a moment to reconsider what she'd said just to be sure he wasn't poking fun at her again and she'd missed it. No. She really was being uncommonly profound and brilliant as of late. She assumed her recent entanglements with life and death were to blame. Mabel's talk of silver linings popped into her head and she thought she was beginning to understand the value in seeking those.

"Yes," she finally agreed. "I think it is."

"Well, then, for the sake of hope and the possibility of hotcakes, I present to you our fearless leader, Catori." He reached his hand up to pat the face of a paint horse marked in striking black and white.

"Catori," Annis whispered, trying out the name, letting it move over her mouth. It was the most unusual she'd ever heard. "It's a lovely name. Does it mean anything?"

"Means 'spirit.' And she certainly has plenty of that," Sequoyah said, his hand moving up and curling under the horse's mane to scratch a place Catori seemed to appreciate.

"She? You mean to tell me the leader is a girl?"

Sequoyah nodded, surprise and delight mixing on his face. "It's common among horses to look to a strong mare to lead them." He dropped his hand slightly away from Catori's long neck. The mare nudged him, encouraging him to return his attention to the spot where she had enjoyed being massaged. He chuckled and obliged. "You expected it to be Shilah, the stallion."

"I did," she admitted. She wondered to herself why she had thought that

Watching Catori, it wasn't hard to believe she was the one who the other horses sought to guide them, to protect them. Though far from the largest among the herd, she was solid muscle. Her broad, sturdy hooves were built for every terrain. Her eyes conveyed wisdom and deep understanding. In that moment, Annis saw how the animals here were no different from the people. Basileus was not an exception. He was the rule. He, like the rest of them, met a tacit requirement Hugh and Babe had for every member of their crew: the hard-earned courage of experience.

"Animals don't share the same ideas about men and women that humans do," Sequoyah explained softly. "And I think they do better for it." Annis had to agree. She'd known all her life that the person of greatest strength and dignity in her small world was also the one shunned into silence and treated most like dirt. Though Annis had always respected her housekeeper, she now feared her own complicit guilt for having accepted the actions of others as normal because that person was a woman. And she wasn't white.

"Why do you think we do it?" she asked. An ache arose in her chest the more she dwelled on the faulty notions she'd been taught about how some people were simply born superior. It was a question she'd never thought to ask before because, girl or not, she'd been born into a wealthy, white family.

Sequoyah's way of giving his attention all around and yet never breaking his eyes from her intensified as he gave up patting the mare's neck and tuned in entirely to Annis. "Fear."

"Fear," Annis repeated. Her nerves nearly swallowed the word as she said it. *Fear.* She stared back at him, the gentlest of souls standing before her, and remembered the previous night. She recalled how his was the act that brought the entire audience to a standing ovation. He'd entered the tent howling a war cry that could send chills down the spine of even the bravest of men. He'd looked wild and unpredictable, and portrayed every bit the raw savage some believed his people to be, that they believed *him* to be. And then he'd shown them the truth. Yes, he was different from them, but he was no one to fear. He'd been kind and gracious, showing nothing but respect to every soul he'd encountered in the ring, be it human or horse. His joy for life had rung out loud and clear in his laughter and the passion in his heart had played wildly in his dance as he'd moved to the thundering rhythm of the herd's pounding hooves. No, Sequoyah was no one to fear. He was someone to be admired.

"I think I've remembered what I already know," she said, her voice hoarse.

"What's that?" His dark eyes brightened with interest.

"No one person here is defined by whether they were born a boy or a girl, the color of their skin, or any physical part of them at all. They are measured only in their passion, their talent, their commitment to their craft, and their inexhaustible ability to love without condition or limitation." She held her chin a little higher. "I'm honored to count myself among you and am hopeful that I may someday measure up as an equal in all the ways that matter here."

Sequoyah smiled, dropping his gaze to avert hers for the first time since she'd showed up to join him this morning. He shook his head, chuckling quietly to himself before slowly lifting his eyes toward her again. "You may already have learned everything you need to know after all, Annis," he said, his smooth, dark voice bringing her nearly as much joy as the words he spoke. "I'm not sure you can learn anything more important than that from me."

Annis doubted that was true. In fact, she was almost certain the greatest lessons still ahead for her would come directly from him.

"You're not giving up on being my teacher already, are you?" she teased, particularly delighted at finally finding herself in a position to do so. "At the very least, you could teach me about the horses. How you care for them. What they eat. Where everyone enjoys a good scratch. You know, the important stuff."

He grinned. "True. No one knows the good places to scratch better than I do." He turned halfway on his heel, preparing to dive back into the sea of horses that still surrounded them. "Come on, then. Best start with Shilah. He's the jealous sort, so if anyone around here is about to get extra attention, it'd better be him."

"I'll keep that in mind," she said, making a mental note as she followed him. This time she kept a better pace as they weaved through the horses to reach the black stallion who was kept in a separate corral.

"While you're at it, you may also want to remember that Catori will snatch food right from your fingers. And possibly your mouth, if it's something she really likes. Atsila, the red mare to your left, despises water. She'll treat a puddle as a lake and she'll leap to clear it, so be sure to keep out of her way if ever you find yourself around her and water of any kind."

Annis's head swiveled back and forth, finding each horse and then matching each new detail about them in her mind. She secured these specifics in a sacred new space in her memory.

Sequoyah rattled off at least ten more facts about several other horses in the few steps they took to reach the second paddock. Annis was grateful for each one he shared, feeling for the first time since she'd arrived that she was on her way to being useful around here. If her part only ever entailed assisting Atsila with her fear of water or rubbing ointment on Gola's sensitive skin to keep the sun from burning her muzzle, she would feel she was doing something of worth with her life.

"Why does Shilah have to be over here all alone?" she asked as they climbed into his enclosure, which was sized for only one horse.

"Gola's body is giving off misleading signals right now," he said.

"What sort of misleading signals?"

He coaxed the stallion away from his hay and over toward the two of them. "The sort where it's telling Shilah it's time to make a foal when, really, it means to say, 'No way, brother. No more babies. Sequoyah said so.'"

Annis laughed. "Oh. Those sorts of signals. I can see why he would get confused and need some time to himself to sort it all out."

"Yes." He began to glide his hand down the side of the horse's neck and up over his withers, moving alongside him. "Besides, a little solitude every now and again is good for the soul."

Annis remembered a not so distant past in which she would have argued against this, convinced time spent alone was the worst sort of torture. Being alone meant feeling forgotten and unloved. Abandoned, even. Now she understood better. It hadn't been the time alone she'd found to be so detrimental, but rather the course of events that had led to her seclusion. And, more importantly, her time traveling through the woods on her own had convinced her that solitude could instill strength, independence, and clear-headedness. It was never to be underestimated, just as keeping company and relying on others could never be overestimated, again. No, the only true value lay in what she could provide for herself. Nothing else could be counted on.

"Did you always know you wanted to work with horses? That this would be your act one day?" she asked, reaching out a tentative hand toward Shilah, who welcomed the attention.

Her questions gave Sequoyah pause and she wondered if she'd said something wrong. She was about to plead with him to forget she'd ever asked when he opened his mouth and began to speak slowly. "Horses are the only part of my life that survived the before and reached the after. In a way, they're all I have left of who I was. They're the only thing that still ties me to my family, the family I was born into. Every time I walk out here to talk to, to care for, and to meet the horses, eye to eye, I see my family. I talk to my parents. I care for my people. I walk with my tribe." He moved his palm from the horse to his heart, then back again. "This isn't work. It's just part of who I am. A part I never want to forget. As for the act, the tricks aren't in the theatrics with the horses. It's in the art of taking what the audience is prepared to see and then showing them what you want them to believe. And yes, from the time I was old enough to understand Poppy's power of changing perceptions, this was what I wanted him to use it on. This is the truth I wanted to show people." He waited, letting Annis sift through all he had just shared with her. After a stretch of quiet, he asked, "What's yours?"

"My truth?" She'd known he would ask. She'd hoped he wouldn't but, deep down, she'd known he'd want to know. "I'm not sure I have one anymore."

The corner of his mouth turned up, but before it could reach into a full smile, he turned away, moving around the back of the horse and out of her sight. "I'm not sure you had one before."

Her defenses sparked. She followed him, moving around Shilah with ease. "And how would you know? You've only just met me. You have no idea the person I was before I showed up here."

If she'd meant for him to be flustered by her demanding tones, she'd failed. He was hardly bothered at all. "Do you?" he asked, his tone even.

"Do I what?" Her hands landed in small fists on her waist, frustration building within her. Everyone's constant curiosities were wearing on her, forcing her to look within and examine the strategically buried parts of her soul. Hadn't they understood she'd suppressed them for a reason? Of course they had, she realized. It's why they insisted on prodding and poking, crumbling away her walls to get to what she'd hidden behind them.

"Do you know who you were before you showed up here?" he asked, this time leaving no room for misunderstanding.

"Yes. I know exactly who I was before I showed up here. I know even better now than I did while I was still her."

He nodded. "Looking back gives a much different perspective, doesn't it?"

"Yes, it does."

"What ties you to her now?"

"Nothing." She'd answered without thinking, without knowing if it was true or just what she wanted to believe.

"Nothing?"

"Nothing that I'd like to hold tight to," she amended. "My story's not like yours, Sequoyah," she said with a heavy sigh. "I don't have a past I want to carry with me into the future." She shuddered. Her past was the very thing that jeopardized her future. The farther she kept them apart, the more she could enjoy of the present. "What I lost, I left by choice." Even if it hardly felt like a choice, she knew that's what it had been. She could have chosen to stay. But she didn't. "And the only connection I care to keep I've already secured in a way that can never be taken." She vowed to carry the name Annis as her own for the rest of her life. "And it's a connection I don't want to share. With anyone," she finished, quietly but firmly. Sequoyah didn't question her further.

They worked well together through the morning, keeping to the basics of communication as he showed her all the ins and outs of the horses' care. Then, when all were tended to and lazily chewing their hay, they left the horse corral and moved on to find Sawyer. "Need any help this morning?" Sequoyah offered when they found him.

Sawyer shook his head. "Goldilocks beat you to it. We just finished up. Heading for Momma's now. You two comin'?"

Momma T's food tent sounded as good as heaven to Annis. Her stomach had been rumbling away for the past hour. She'd gone out of her way to hide the sound from Sequoyah, though a few times she suspected he'd heard it.

"Any word on whether she found her griddle?" Sequoyah asked Sawyer as the three fell into step alongside each other.

"Never heard word it was missing…" And then Sawyer made a face. "Wait, not the monkey griddle?" he asked, making the connection.

"Am I going to need to know what the monkey griddle was used for?" Annis asked. "It sounds like it might ruin breakfast, and I'm starving, but this griddle and the monkey situation keeps coming up. So, do I need to know? Or shall I blindly forge ahead and eat my hotcakes when they're served?"

"Blindly forge ahead!" Sawyer said, nodding fiercely. "Believe me, it's what I'd do if only I had the option."

"He's right," Sequoyah agreed. "Besides, for all we know Poppy was right, and the griddle is gone for good. Just because it was her favorite for frying hotcakes doesn't mean it was her only."

Annis considered this for a moment. "Alright. I'm going to go with that. Bring on the hotcakes!" Both men laughed, and everyone picked up their pace. Momma T's was just a few feet away and the scent wafting toward them was nothing short of delectable.

Chapter Eight

HOMER'S SUPERPOWER

Momma T's small tent was the liveliest place Annis had been so far that day. Their party of three grew by four members when they took seats at a long table with Homer, Caroline, Mabel, and Maude. Maude sent a sly grin in Annis's direction as soon as she sat down, followed by a wink that was easy to interpret and impossible to miss.

"What was that about?" Sequoyah asked.

"Just Maude being Maude. You know how she is." Annis shrugged.

"I do," he replied, grinning. "Nice to see you're keeping up with things around here already if you've got her pegged after just one night."

"Pretty sure I've got Mabel all sorted out too," Annis said. She was pleased to see her ability to read others was improving. "Still working on everyone else though. Sawyer's not going to take much longer, and I got a pretty good read on Caroline and Homer this morning. But you," she pointed her fork at him thoughtfully. "I sense you will be more challenging than the rest."

"Why's that?" He took her fork from her grasp, stabbed a piece of fluffy hotcake with it, and stuck it back in her hand. Her mouth twitched but she kept the smile at bay.

"Because you want it that way."

A brief smirk swept over Sequoyah's mouth and for a moment she thought he'd counter her again. Instead, he turned toward Homer, who sat next to him, and began chatting about the show that night and the sort of crowd they were expecting. Annis didn't mind. In fact, she was delighted. Him not saying anything had been all the answer she needed to know she was right. And being right, for a change, felt good, especially when the feeling was combined with the taste of Momma T's hotcakes and honey. Everyone had looked at her funny when she'd refused the maple syrup, but honey had been the way she'd eaten them when her housekeeper had made them. It felt wrong to stray from that. Maybe there were some ties to her old life she wanted to preserve, after all.

"You know, if you're in the mood for a little more adventure," Caroline began, "I've got some new ideas for our act that could use a third person."

Annis twisted her mouth back and forth, contemplating Caroline's idea. A flutter at the pit of her stomach urged her to jump on the opportunity, but the echo of Hugh's words in her ears squashed the thrill. "I can't. I'm not allowed." She shoved another bite into her mouth. "Hugh said."

Caroline blew a loud raspberry, spraying spit all over her own face. She laughed at herself. "Poppy's always such a killjoy." She shook her head, still chuckling. "He's not wrong, though. Homer and I've had some pretty close calls with our schemes. Probably best not to risk your life and limbs until we know if we like you or not," she teased.

Annis paused, a forkful of hotcake hovering within inches of her mouth. "So, if you invite me to join a number in, say, a month or so..."

Caroline shrugged. "Likely not a good sign." Then she grinned. "I wouldn't worry too much, though. I'm digging this rebel attitude of yours already. Honey on hotcakes. That says a lot about a person."

"Oh, yeah?"

"Yeah," Homer chimed in. "It belies an absence of common sense and complete disregard for the basic need for it."

Annis wasn't sure what to make of his statement. It wasn't until the entire table began to chuckle and snort that she understood it was just another joke at her expense. She was also beginning to gather the compliment in it. They all poked fun at each other a lot, so including her in the fun was their way of making her feel part of the group. It wasn't the most conventional way to include someone, and definitely no way she'd ever been welcomed by new friends in the past, but she appreciated it nonetheless.

"Makes perfect sense, then," she said, finally committing to the bite dangling at the end of her fork.

"What's that?" Homer asked, clearly eager to hear how she'd respond.

"Why you'd invite me to join your act. Obviously, lack of common sense and complete disregard for any need for it would be required to participate, judging by the two of you, anyway."

More laughter ensued, confirming what she'd suspected. They liked her. They accepted her as part of the crew, no matter how new she was or how little they knew of her. She was one of them now.

"What's your Brooks and Bennet story, anyway?" she asked, realizing she hadn't yet heard any Homer tales. There were no obvious, visible, physical anomalies about him. "I mean, Caroline clearly has some sort of rubber spine, but what makes you so superhuman you felt a need to run away to the circus? And don't tell me it's your skill for juggling because I've got Hugh's grand scheme of things all figured out. Juggling is the thing you want people to see. What's the other thing? The thing they see that confuses them and hides you?"

All eyes turned toward him, as though they'd never heard the tale for themselves. "Yeah, tell us why you're superhuman, Homer," Sawyer egged him on.

Homer slowly chewed his last bite, and then set down his fork as he swallowed. He slowly wiped his mouth with his napkin before finally clearing his throat. "Alright, then. I will." He directed a smirk at Sawyer before winking briefly across the table where Caroline sat. She blushed in response. Annis thought it extraordinarily romantic to see a couple who'd clearly been in love for quite some time still be able to act as though they were only just on the cusp of their romance.

"My superhuman power is... I can't see."

"What?" *Surely he was joking.* "Of course you can see," Annis said. "You catch flying, flaming things. You have to be able to see to do that."

"You'd think so, wouldn't you?" He chuckled. For the first time, Annis noticed his gaze didn't catch on anything. "Not the case though, as it turns out."

"You're messing with me," Annis insisted. "Right? Another joke? Another poke at gullible Annis?" she turned toward Sequoyah, and then Sawyer, who smirked and shook his head. "A bit of tragic irony in it when you realize one of the most beautiful women on earth is married to a blind man."

Annis still refused to accept it and turned to Caroline, who, even if she were in on the joke, would be first to give it away.

"No joke, Annis. He's blind as a bat, he is." Her mouth curved tenderly as she looked at him. "Just makes the adventure that much more entertaining."

"And terrifying!" Annis said, thinking of the knives Homer tossed around Caroline's body. "How do you do it? How do you catch things you can't see?" she asked.

Homer squared his shoulders, sitting up straighter, using his hands to gesture as he spoke. "There's more to it than just watching the objects go up and down. You might say I'm a better juggler for not being able to rely on vision alone. I have to calculate the time it takes for each piece to rise and fall, estimate the strength it takes to launch it up to where I want it, and sense the air move like wind around the object as it flies up and falls back down. I've learned to become aware of countless details most people would never learn because they rely only on their eyes, completely disregarding all their other senses." His hands dropped carefully into his lap as he finished. "I promise you, Annis. I've never taken a risk I wasn't confident I could overcome. Not where Caroline's well-being is concerned. And, as much as she likes to tease, we rarely include others in our act for the very reason that its success depends on our working together, in complete unison. And that we do exceptionally well. In fact, I'd like to think it's my real superhuman power." He smiled, and it was enough to make Mabel coo at her end of the table.

"You're making every woman at the table blush, Homer," Sawyer grunted.

"Thank you for telling me," Homer mused. "I'd assumed, but it's always nice to hear it confirmed."

The laughter started all over again.

After breakfast, everyone moved a bit more slowly with their bellies filled. "What do we do next?" Annis asked, holding one hand to her stomach and stretching the other over her head to try to make more room within for her breakfast to settle. She'd indulged. But she'd enjoyed every last bite so much that she'd asked Momma for an extra helping of hotcakes, which she'd folded into a napkin and neatly stored in her pocket for later.

"We make our rounds, see what still needs doing and who needs help," Sawyer answered. "Nothing around here ever runs as seamlessly as it ought to. There's always one thing or another that goes awry and changes up the usual routine."

"It's my favorite part, though," Sequoyah said. "Doing the thing you weren't planning on doing. Keeps things interesting."

"You would think that," Sawyer groused, less impressed with the unexpected tasks that always came their way. "Obviously, you've never been two feet tall while trying to place a tiara on an elephant." That had happened just yesterday, Annis recalled. In hindsight, she was sorry she'd missed it.

Sequoyah laughed. "You think it's any easier at six feet than at two? Those four feet don't make much difference when you measure it up against an elephant, my friend."

Sawyer grimaced. "I maintain my argument. No one made you stand on anyone's shoulders."

"Not true. When you couldn't reach, we got August. And, yeah, I had to climb up on his shoulders. And it worked. And everyone laughed until they cried. Don't remember anyone finding the sight of you standing on my back to be all that amusing."

Sawyer was hardly convinced.

But Annis was onto other things. "Meanwhile, what about me? I didn't get to climb onto anyone's shoulders and I most definitely did not get to dress up any elephants in tiaras. If anyone should feel bad for anyone right now, it's clearly me."

Sawyer was baffled into silence.

"I'm sorry, we're being so inconsiderate," Sequoyah said, sounding almost sincere. His expression, however, faltered. "Please, tell me how we can make it up to you, Annis?"

While it was clear to Annis that he was not being at all serious, she was content to take him by his words over his meaning. "Well, you can start by swearing to never, ever leave me out of all the most ridiculous fun ever again."

"Done. I swear." He nudged Sawyer, who still hadn't said a word, aside from some grumbling under his breath. "We both do, don't we, Sawyer?"

"Uh-huh." Apparently, he couldn't be bothered to even pretend to take her seriously. Not that she blamed him. She could hardly take herself seriously. If it weren't for Sequoyah's willingness to play along, she'd never have found the courage to make such silly demands for no reason other than her own amusement.

"And second," she paused, thinking. "You can scour the site for the most obnoxious, most dreadful, most unexpected task to pop up today, and then let me do it."

This Sawyer jumped on. "Done!" He grabbed Sequoyah's arm, tugging him forward. "Come on. Let's start at the monkey cart." Annis instantly regretted her request.

Her regret lifted, however, shortly after arriving at their destination. Though she'd feared the worst, what she encountered was nothing short of spectacular.

His Royal Harris, as she had no choice but to call him—silently, inside her own head, where Harris would never hear her—was frantically running in circles, taking it in turns to scream for help and then curse in a hoarse whisper until his face turned an explosive shade of puce. After a brief inhale, he resumed hollering. People were starting to gather around him on all sides, looking eager to help but clueless about how. There appeared to be no obvious problem outside of Harris's clear distress.

"What's wrong?" Sawyer was the first to reach him in a moment of relative calm, when Harris had cycled back to the uttering of hellacious swear words, some of which were completely new to Annis.

"That rat bastard!" Harris hissed, pointing an angry finger up toward the roof of the train. "He stole Babe's brooch. And now he won't give it back!" He lunged forward, as though he were prepared to fly up there and tackle the tiny—and most adorable, in Annis's opinion—monkey who'd come to a brief halt, only to start running again at the sight of Harris.

"Maybe if you just ignore him for a minute, he'll lose interest in the game and just come down on his own," Sequoyah offered. Annis knew nothing of monkeys, but this one did remind her an awful lot of Benji, her neighbor's cheeky little grandson, and that particular tactic had worked on him more than once.

"Can't do that," Harris said through gritted teeth. "Every time he sits still for even a second, that little cretin tries to eat it!"

Sawyer's eyes lit up. "Let him!"

"I beg your pardon?" Babe came bounding forward through the crowd. "That brooch was my grandmother's. Few things mean more to me than people, Sawyer, but at this very moment, that brooch is outranking you!" Meanwhile, the monkey, who Annis guessed was the other Jacob, settled down on his haunches and opened his mouth wide. Annis admired the gold brooch's Victorian style, with a diamond-haloed emerald at its center, even as Jacob was poised to swallow it. This time, an entire Brooks and Bennet army went after him, which sent him running again.

"I'm saying," Sawyer raised his voice to be heard over all the commotion, "let him eat it and then catch him."

"And then what? Wait until it passes through him?" Babe looked horrified.

Sawyer, on the other hand, was so pleased with his idea that he could barely contain himself, bobbing slightly at the knees, rubbing his palms together as he spoke and grinning from ear to ear with delight. "Exactly. I've even got a person all lined up for the job of retrieving the brooch after. Annis can wait for him to poo and then search through it for the brooch when he does. Every time he does. Until she finds it." He glanced over his shoulder and up to meet her eyes, a satisfied smugness radiating from him. "You said you wanted the most obnoxious, most dreadful, most unexpected task. Well, I do believe we've found it."

Annis let out a nervous giggle. "You're not serious."

"No, he's not," Babe cut in sternly.

"I was, actually," Sawyer corrected, slowly deflating from his gleeful high. "What's wrong with my plan?"

"You mean other than the part where my grandmother's brooch ends up buried in monkey poo? Oh, nothing, Sawyer, nothing at all." Babe took off, following the handful of people still trying to catch Jacob or, at the very least, convince him to give up the brooch.

"Just wait. Whether they like my plan or not, odds are still good the monkey eats it. So, don't go thinking you're in the clear yet," Sawyer taunted Annis as the two of them, along with Sequoyah, hurried to catch up with Babe and everyone else.

"I suppose I'll just have to make sure that doesn't happen, then, won't I?" Annis said, though she had no clue how she might go about convincing Jacob not to eat Babe's brooch, but committed to the plan, anyway. She had no intention of ever sifting through monkey poo on a disgusting treasure hunt. "And, for the record, what you're suggesting I do is not in any way similar to having to place a dainty crown on the head of a brilliant elephant. I don't care whose shoulders you had to stand on, the levels of humiliation are simply beyond compare."

"She's getting feistier," Sawyer mumbled to Sequoyah, who walked on to his left. "Have you noticed?"

Sequoyah nodded. "It's a good thing."

Annis sped up and feigned exuberant interest in Jacob just to keep them both from seeing her face glow as red as the monkey's little vest.

By now, Jacob had given up running the length of the train and was busy hopping from one object to the next, using everything from the shutters above the windows to Harris's head as a temporary landing while heading for solid ground. This meant bad news for the chase. As soon as his little feet touched down, he'd be free to run wherever he chose. There'd be no hope of catching him. Annis watched as Jacob gave one sly glance over his shoulder, and instantly recognized the expression on his happy little monkey face. He really was no different from Benji, her neighbor's grandson. The recognition sparked something in Annis's mind. She had a plan.

"Ooooh, Jaaaacob," she called to the monkey in a sing-song tone. "Look what I have here for yooooou." Annis drew out the last syllable as she pulled from her pocket the now crumbled bits of hotcake she'd saved from breakfast. "Would you like to have this? Smell how yummy it is." She held it out to him a little further, watching him lean in for a better whiff. His little hands began to fidget while his nose and mouth moved wildly at the scent.

Everyone watched, holding their breath and holding completely still, waiting to see if Jacob would take the breakfast bait.

"Don't do it," Sawyer whispered. Annis shot him her sternest of glares.

"I think he's going to," Sequoyah said, his voice hushed to match Sawyer's.

Annis said nothing. She didn't dare to make a sound, worried it might startle Jacob and set him off running again.

Her worries were for naught. Within seconds, he'd dropped the brooch where he stood and launched himself at her. He landed on her arm and clutched her hand with his, wrapping his feet around her wrist while he devoured her leftovers.

"Tulip, you're my absolute favorite person," Babe said, picking up her heirloom and then smothering Annis in a hug so enthusiastic that Jacob bolted. When she released Annis again and dropped a glare on Sawyer, she spoke silent volumes. "You, not so much, Smalls."

"Yeah, yeah." He waved his hand, dismissing her distaste with him. "I'm sure it'll shift next time one of your rollers winds up under the train car and you need someone to crawl under and get it."

"I could do that," Annis piped up, corners of her mouth fighting to stretch upward.

"See?" Babe said. "That's how someone truly helpful sounds. They don't make suggestions about heirlooms and monkey poo."

"Alright, alright," Sawyer finally conceded with a grumble. "But if you'd heard the previous conversation, you'd have been a great deal more supportive of my monkey poo plan!"

"I doubt that very much," Babe huffed. She then kissed the top of Annis's head and pinched Sequoyah's cheek before she sauntered off to join Hugh, who was clearly ready to put this morning's newest batch of monkey business behind him.

"Thank you," Harris said, still looking frazzled as he joined their threesome. Jacob sat, perfectly well behaved, on his shoulder once more. "I hate monkeys. I really do."

"Then why do you work with them?" Annis asked, baffled by his confession.

"Because they're also the only part of my life I can make sense of," he muttered, shaking his head. "And," he added, a small smile returning to his face, "they're also the most fun I've ever had."

Annis thought of the sight of them all, swinging around the circus tent as though they were jumping vines in the heart of a jungle. She smiled. "Yes, I imagine they are."

As Harris returned to his duties, Annis turned to Sawyer. "Can we call it a truce, then? I admit that I was silly to make demands I clearly didn't fully understand, and you agree to stop trying to find the most torturous task for me to do?"

"It doesn't sound like nearly as much fun, but sure," Sawyer agreed. "I can move forward from here knowing you saw reason and I was right. Even if you didn't have to stick your girly little fingers into any poo."

"Thank you," she said with a laugh. "I can't tell you how much I appreciate that."

"Now, then, if we're all done playing games," said Sequoyah, ever the voice of reason, "perhaps we can get back to doing something a little more productive?"

"I don't know what you're talking about," Annis insisted innocently. "I feel as though I've been very productive recently. I saved a brooch from a monkey. I'm practically a hero. How much more productive would you like me to be?"

He shook his head and grinned. Even Sawyer couldn't argue with that.

There were still plenty of tasks left to do before showtime and soon the trio was back at work. They bathed the horses—several had gotten carried away rolling in the dust after breakfast—and built a variety of temporary structures all meant to contain the furrier members of Brooks and Bennet in a roomier, more comfortable setting than their train cars provided them. By lunchtime, it was all they could do to pick up a sandwich and keep going, working as they ate. It wasn't until the sun slowly began setting on the horizon that Annis found she had time to catch her breath and collect her trailing thoughts.

She sat in complete silence at the long, crowded dinner table while all around her people laughed and talked, mostly about the night that lay ahead. Some of the amusement, of course, came from Sawyer's animated retelling of the brooch and the monkey incident. As it turned out, news didn't travel nearly as fast as Annis had expected and there were several people who had not yet heard the escapades of Jacob the monkey featuring Babe's brooch and Annis's leftover hotcake. Among them was Goldilocks. Annis noticed a slight chug at his jaw every time he heard the monkey's name.

She assumed he felt some bitterness about the fact the monkey had won the name game, leaving him to move forward in life known by the same name as a fair-haired fairy tale character with a knack for breaking in and stealing porridge from a family of bears. She could certainly see how he might feel slighted.

"You're dirty," Maude said to Annis, interrupting her silent observations. Maude's lip curled in a sneer, but her eyes were smiling. She bumped her hip to Homer's shoulder, nudging him to move over so she and Mabel could have a seat across from Annis. Homer obliged and slid closer to his wife, never breaking their conversation about recent attempts to juggle a combination of flaming rings and pointed daggers while Caroline, suspended by her mouth, formed a hoop with her body for Homer to throw his array of weapons through. Neither of them seemed to mind being mashed together so closely that they appeared nearly as attached as Maude and Mabel.

"I've been doing dirty things," Annis answered when the sisters were finally seated and ready to eat.

"Yeah, I can imagine," Maude murmured, casting a suggestive glance toward Sequoyah, who, thankfully, was busy being entertained by Homer and his inexplicable skill of avoiding self-mutilation or manslaughter on a regular basis.

"You're terrible," Annis scolded, tossing a green bean over the table at her. "I was doing actual dirty things. With dirt!"

"Oh, God," Mabel gasped, a mixture of pity and horror wrapped into her outburst. "Why?"

"Because I was helping with the mustangs today. Do you know horses literally take dirt baths? Which then become mud baths after you give them an actual bath with soap and water. It was quite the mess."

Maude shrugged and picked up the green bean, which had landed right beside her plate, and ate it. "Elephants don't do that."

"Don't get me started on what elephants do and don't do," Sawyer snarled from three seats down.

"Are you really still on about that?" Mabel asked. "I don't see how it was any worse than that time you thought it'd be a good idea to join Homer and Caroline in their act."

"Yeah, well, had I known he'd wind up tossing me, I'd hardly have volunteered."

"What else would I have done? Tossing things is what I do," Homer said, matter-of-fact. "Especially things most people wouldn't toss."

"Most people definitely wouldn't toss you," Maude agreed, nodding at Sawyer. "Unless it was out on your arse."

The laughter nearly drowned out Sawyer's grumbling. "When did today become torture Sawyer day?"

"Right around the time you started volunteering other people to dig through monkey poo," Mabel chirped.

"Oh, yes," Maude concurred, swiping a gleeful tear from her eye. "We heard about that."

"Really, Sawyer," Mabel chided. "I'd have expected better from you."

"Sorry," he said with a careless shrug that suggested the opposite of his words. "Monkey poo was the best I could do on a moment's notice. But if you can ever get one of your girls to swallow something of value, elephant poo would be a much grander prank next go around."

Annis made a disgusted face. "I don't think I'll be falling for that again." She pointed an accusatory green bean at Sawyer. "Besides, I thought we had a truce!"

"What, you think you're the last person to ever run off and join the circus? There'll be a new newbie soon enough." He smirked, snatched the bean from her fingers, and popped it into his mouth.

"You know, I thought you were so nice when I first met you," she said, shaking her head as she examined the food still left on her plate. She'd already eaten more than half of her helping and wasn't close to feeling sated yet.

He winked at her, his expression drenched in mischief. "I told you you'd know better."

He had.

"You said it'd take a week," she reminded him.

"That was when I thought you were sweet and naïve and needed that long." He tipped his head to the side and back. "Now I know better."

Annis grinned. "Fair enough." The raucous noise lulled as Annis saw Hugh and Babe join their table.

"We really don't require near this much attention when we join a party," Babe mused, having a seat beside Annis, who found herself scooting closer to Sequoyah and unexpectedly touching his thigh with hers. Even less expected was the way he stayed in place, keeping their legs close enough to touch. She told herself he must be used to close dining quarters, but part of her hoped desperately it wasn't true.

"Also, it makes Poppy here very suspicious," Babe added, making her best attempt at sounding and looking stern, but failing on both counts.

"Think we're scheming over dinner?" Sequoyah asked, leaning forward to have a better view of his parents down the table.

"Personally, I prefer to do my scheming at night, when there's peace and quiet and no one around to interrupt my thoughts," Mabel said with a pointed glare at her sister, who ignored her entirely.

"I'm more of a spur-of-the-moment schemer," Sawyer said, stabbing a chunk of potato with his fork. "You never know when the monkey poo will strike, you know?"

Annis laughed, but she did her best to muffle the sound behind her napkin. She wasn't sure if Babe was prepared to find the brooch incident humorous just yet.

"Well, at least you all admit it," Hugh said with a sigh, picking up his silverware and examining his plate of roasted pork, potatoes, and green beans. "You're all schemers."

Sequoyah slid his empty plate to the center of the table and rested his elbows on the cleared space in front of him. "...Says the master schemer."

Hugh said nothing at first. Wholly dedicated to his dinner, he took several bites and chewed thoroughly as everyone else watched in silence, waiting for his response.

At last, he paused, his hand and fork beside his plate. "You don't expect an argument from me, do you?"

"It's not the scheming he minds," Babe chimed in, with her attention on her food as she stacked the perfect bite upon the prongs of her fork. "It's the being left out of it."

"You should have just said, Poppy," Homer said, far too excited, in Annis's opinion, for a man whose schemes usually involved blind juggling of deadly weapons and small humans. "I was just telling August I want to try standing on his shoulders for tossing daggers. What do you think?"

"I think you don't know how high you toss your damn daggers. Or where the ceiling is. Or how tall August is. Or how close you'll be to the ceiling once you're standing on his shoulders. And I think I'd rather not have you slice holes into the top of my tent, which would undoubtedly be part of the learning curve." Hugh turned his head slightly, moving his gaze to Bess. "You're next. What crazy ideas are you cooking?"

Bess cast a furtive glance around the table as though she were hoping someone would interrupt and steal her spotlight. When no one did, she pursed her lips briefly and then began speaking. "I don't know if I would call it crazy, really." Sawyer let out a snort. Bess shot him a glare that pierced as one of Homer's daggers might. "Maude and I have been talking. What if we had Millie and Edi hold a rope with their trunks, standing on opposite ends of the ring, and I could walk across it from one elephant to the other? That'd be pretty brilliant wouldn't it?"

Hugh swallowed his previous bite. "I think maybe you don't know the meaning of the word brilliant." He cleared his throat. "I'm well aware we've all convinced ourselves you can tread wherever you choose and never lose your footing, but I reckon even *you* couldn't make it across what would likely become a game of tug-o-war between two elephants the second you hand each cow a rope to hold onto. They're elephants, Bess. And moody ones at that." His eyes moved over each person sitting around the table. "Come on, someone's gotta have an idea I can say yes to." He paused, hovering on Sawyer, and then shook his head and mumbled, "Never mind," before moving along to his son, who instantly held up his hands in surrender to indicate he had nothing to offer.

"Annis, love, give me something good."

Annis could feel the pressure of every eyeball staring back at her and was certain the heat of a hundred spotlights couldn't be hotter.

"Well, alright then," she said, clearing her throat and sitting up taller. "But, remember, you asked for it." Though what had he asked for, exactly? A wild idea crazy enough to compete with all the other outrageous ideas at this table, but not so crazy that Hugh would shut it down. An idea that could actually work. But Annis had nothing. Not a single thought, crazy or sane. Which was a good thing because, truth be told, she could no longer be certain of the difference.

And then it struck her. One thought. Properly suited for a lunatic and yet brilliantly sound.

"I noticed last night there were some stragglers who wouldn't leave when the show was over. I got to thinking that probably holds everyone up when you're trying to break down and load up and there are still people who don't feel the urge to leave."

Hugh nodded. "I'm listening."

"So, what if, at the end of each show, I stroll into the tent, walking through the rows of seating with Basileus attached to a thin silk lead. I could wear my hair in braids and put on a sweet white dress and just mosey along as though I'm walking around with my puppy. In fact, I should say something of the sort as I go by. I'd look certifiable. People'd be terrified. I don't think anyone would stick around."

Babe nearly choked on her dinner. Hugh just grinned in silence, still studying Annis long after she finished talking. No one else said anything. After what felt to Annis like a small eternity, Hugh pointed his fork at her and gave her a nod of approval before returning his attention to his food. "Good girl. That was a proper crazy idea, love," he murmured, arranging his green beans in a heap before he stabbed them with the tines. "I've got bigger plans for you than scaring off the stragglers, though, so this one will have to be on hold a bit."

Her mouth quirked. She was equally pleased as she was curious. The more she learned of everyone here and their various, at times inexplicable, talents, the more she wanted to know what she would be doing when the day came that she received an official act of her own.

She wiped her mouth one last time, and then crumpled her napkin, placing it beside her empty plate. "Figured you'd say something like that." She sighed. "If I'm not going to be the secret finale after the finale, I suppose I better get back to helping Sequoyah finish up for the proper finale, which really is all the finale anyone should ever need, though I do see why people find it hard to leave after they've seen it," she finished, realizing too late that she'd babbled on with everyone listening.

Sawyer, of course, was least forgiving. "Should we take offense to your obvious favoritism where our acts is concerned, or should we just assume your bias is directed more at the performer than the performance itself?"

"We should not take offense," Maude said, settling the matter. "It's clearly performer bias."

Hugh's brow shot up to meet his hairline while Babe's eyes lit up. Annis, on the other hand, felt the heat in her cheeks reach a new record high and wished desperately for a monkey with a stolen brooch to come along and save her. Even the thought of digging through poo was more bearable than this.

"Am I to assume from this silence that this revelation comes as a surprise to some?" Homer said. "Should I also add that even a blind man can tell that the bias is entirely mutual?"

Annis felt her eyes dart toward Sequoyah before she could remind them of the pact she'd just made to stare down at the ground for all eternity now that he knew about her silly infatuation with him.

"I could have handled that part myself, Homer," Sequoyah said with an ear-to-ear grin as his eyes met hers. "But thanks just the same. At least now we'll know exactly what you're all talking about even after we leave." He stood up and held his hand out to her. "Come on. We have a finale to prepare for and these folks have at least an hour of gossip to cram into about fifteen minutes or so."

Hesitation swarmed at the pit of her stomach, making her nauseated, and her heart and mind battled over the direction her hand was to move next. Neither considered her body, which decided without them.

All ill feelings faded the instant her palm landed in his.

Chapter Nine
A NEW BABY

Neither Annis nor Sequoyah said anything as they walked, nor did they release each other's hands. Annis tried not to make any attempts to decipher the meaning of either, but she found it impossible not to question both from every angle imaginable. By the time they reached the horses, she was so buried in her thoughts that she didn't notice they had come to a stop. A playful pinch at her waist startled her back to the present.

"Sorry," she mumbled, dropping Sequoyah's hand and stepping back.

"For what?" Sequoyah looked at her curiously.

"I'm not really sure what comes next," she said. The fierceness she'd begun to find since joining Brooks and Bennet faded from her voice.

He shrugged, leaning back against the wooden slats of the horse corral behind him. "The horses need brushed off one last time, then we paint them. Won't take long."

Her eyes narrowed, confused by the change in topic. Had he really misunderstood her? "I wasn't talking about tasks for the show."

His mouth curved gently on one side, giving proof of his beautiful smile even if it was only half visible. "I know, Annis," he said, his voice the same deep, tender tone she had heard him whisper to the horses. "Whatever this is that's happening between us, it's okay to just let it be. It doesn't have to be figured out tonight. So, let's stick with taking things one step at a time. Starting with the horses." He rolled his eyes upward, where Catori was busy nibbling on his hair. Annis giggled despite her nerves. What he was saying made sense, and yet something nagged at her. Something he wasn't saying.

"You're letting me down easy," she whispered, trying her best to appear as if it mattered little either way, though even as the words passed her lips, she found it hard to keep smiling.

"Letting you down easy?" He laughed quietly though he hardly sounded amused. "I'm not the one who needs time, Annis. You are. I know you didn't just walk out of some fairy tale and straight here to us two days ago. Something happened that made you run. Something bad. Something you haven't even begun to heal from. And you're in no frame of mind right now to take on anything else, even if it's good." He tilted his head, tugging his hair away from Catori's muzzle. "Even if it's us." He stood up, moving toward her. When she didn't evade him, he took both her hands in his. "Find yourself, Annis. And then find me."

Her eyes stayed glued on their hands and how they fit together, on the tender way his fingers stroked the back of her hand. Could it really be possible she'd found something so beautiful in the rubble of her life's most tragic turns?

She lifted her gaze, slowly, to meet the warmth of his. "Can I brush Catori?"

She felt him squeeze her hands one last time and then release them. He turned away and got to work. "I'd prefer it, to be honest. My hair could use a break from her teeth." Annis laughed, falling into step behind him as though the last few minutes of her life had never happened, and nothing had changed. And yet, everything was different now.

They worked together efficiently in quiet harmony, with the occasional exchanged murmurs as they finished their preparations. By the time they joined the others at the main tent, the audience was jammed into the stands and Hugh was already at the center of the ring.

This time, the show flew by and she was soon sending Sequoyah and the mustangs out to perform the finale. She held her breath as she watched him, flying from horse to horse, releasing blood-curdling howls into the night and bringing the audience to their feet with applause and loud whoops of enthusiasm. To the crowd he revealed the rawest parts of his nature, the gentle warrior within who would lie down his life for another, and who thus had a weapon more powerful than anyone expected: his heart.

She was standing there, clutching her hands to her chest, when she felt another presence move in beside her.

"The greatest joy of my life," Babe said with her gaze on the man she called her son.

"You don't sound joyful," Annis observed. And then it dawned on her that she could be the reason.

"Whatever it was that brought you to us, Tulip," she said quietly, her eyes never wavering from Sequoyah, who was introducing each horse in turn to the audience. "Will it take you away again?"

Annis felt a lump form in her throat. It hardened like a rock as she considered Babe's question. "It could." She turned toward her, desperate for her to understand even if Annis could never explain. "But I never want it to."

Babe's full focus shifted to her at last. "Then I suppose we'll have to do whatever it takes to make sure it never does."

Annis felt her chest swell. Babe wrapped an arm around Annis's waist to bring her in closer and smacked a loud kiss on her cheek. And then Babe slipped away as quietly as she'd appeared, leaving behind only the grace she bestowed so easily on others—and, Annis was certain, the traces of sticky red lipstick on her cheek. She didn't mind. Being branded by Babe's affections was a far cry from the attempts others had made to claim her in the past and, unlike those, Annis was happy to be counted by Babe as one of her own.

The thunder of hooves drew Annis's attention back to the ring. The herd was now galloping toward her as they exited to roaring applause, with Sequoyah bringing up the rear and standing on Shilah's back. Annis was about to follow them out to the animal tent when Hugh caught her, hooking one arm around her shoulders and turning her abruptly to the left, leading her away from Sequoyah and the horses.

"Day two," he buzzed, clearly still feeling the energy of having recently performed. "Tell me, then, what did you think?"

He'd asked her that very question the night before. A small eternity seemed to have transpired over twenty-four hours. Last night felt like a different lifetime. She sucked in a sharp breath of air. She'd been going through a lot of those lately, lifetimes. How many more would there be for her?

"Honest opinion?" she asked, repeating his words from last night back to him to be sure he knew that she had taken in every detail of her first day with Brooks and Bennet. And there'd been much to learn. Most of it, unexpected gems she knew she never would have found elsewhere, like the way the spotlights of a circus tent had impressed upon her the beauty of diversity and adversity.

"Yes. Honest opinion," he confirmed. "Come on, love. I can take it."

"Brace yourself," she teased. "I don't think you'll see this coming."

He laughed. "Maybe I better sit for this, then."

"Yes. Perhaps you should, if for no other reason than I wouldn't mind being eye-to-eye with you when I tell you what I have to say."

He chuckled some more but obliged, pulling over a stack of empty crates and taking a seat across from her. "Go on, then. I'm ready."

"Alright." She took a deep inhale, and then exhaled her words in one breath. "I think you're the smartest man I've ever known, Hugh Brooks."

"And why would you think something foolish like that?" he asked. She could see his mouth twitch with delight at her statement, but he held the smile at bay.

"Because," she shrugged, failing to conjure the words to describe what she felt. Maybe there were no words for it. Maybe that was all part of his magic—to transcend past people's innate need for thought and reach them straight at their core, in their hearts, where they could understand the things their minds didn't yet have a language for. It's what he was doing for her. Even as she understood this, she also knew the words would come if only she let them, because her heart already knew what they were.

"You're changing people, making them better," she said softly. "Healing our broken thoughts and mending our broken spirits. And you let us all believe we're doing it ourselves."

"You are doing it yourselves," he said, tipping his head toward the ring behind her, glowing in gold from the dim light of the lanterns. "All I do is give you all a place to do it."

She shook her head. "You're being modest." She grinned. "Humble Hugh. That's what I should call you. Forget Poppy. Definitely forget *sir*." She giggled, remembering how dumbfounded she had been when he refused the title. She understood now. It did seem silly to call him that. It was far too formal for a man who didn't know the first thing about maintaining any sort of hierarchies for himself or others.

"You will call me no such thing. It'll only confuse people who think I enjoy being the center of attention, seeing as I'm the ringleader and all," he said with a chuckle as he got back to his feet.

"Yeah," Annis said thoughtfully, remembering another thing she'd observed during the show tonight. "How do you do that, anyway? It's like you show up in flashes, just for a second to redirect the audience where you want them to look, preparing them for the next act, and then, just like that, you're gone again. Even when I intentionally tried to focus only on you, I couldn't keep track of you."

"Magic," he said with a wink. Annis got the distinct feeling that would always be the extent of his explanation, no matter how many times she asked.

"I see. Magic Hugh, then," she mused, picking up her pace to keep even with his long strides.

"Unless you want me to start adding adjectives to Annis, I suggest you put a cork in it," he teased in return. "Now then, on to our next business. I have a pretty good idea who to pair you up with next. But before I make my final decision, why don't you tell me what you learned today, love?"

Annis had to think back. Today had started a long time ago and she'd learned loads since then. "I learned about keeping Shilah separate from the herd. I learned what the horses eat, how often, and why it's important to keep them on a steady diet. I learned how to brush and bathe them, how to care for their hooves. Oh, and I learned about their likes and dislikes. Fascinating, really. How animals have personalities, same as humans. And relationships. Oh, and how their judgement is far better than ours. Well, mine anyway." She paused when they rounded a corner and she realized they were heading farther away from the tent and all the work left to be done tonight. "Shouldn't I be doing something more to help? I could come find you when everything is loaded up and ready to go and give you a full report then. Probably a longer one than I could give you now, since I've only set up and not broke down before."

He shook his head, smiling as they moved onward toward the train cars. "No need. We're staying another night. Big turnout today, sold out before everyone in town got their tickets. Doesn't happen often, but when it does we make sure to run the show again." He slowed down a bit, looking over his shoulder to see if she was keeping up.

"Oh. Alright." She still felt strange about leaving all the work to the others, so she sped up her account of the day in hopes of getting back before everything was finished. "Let's see. When I wasn't learning about horses, I learned about cheeky little monkeys and their fondness for shiny things. I learned that Sawyer has a mean streak and that Homer is blind. Might have mentioned that one, by the way. Felt pretty foolish not having been aware the entire time I'd spent with him and Caroline this morning, and then again at lunch."

Hugh shrugged. "I'm sure he felt pretty splendid realizing you never had a clue."

Annis thought this was a point well made.

"Right. Well, even so, if it's all the same to you, I wouldn't mind knowing now if anyone else here is lacking one of their basic senses. For safety reasons, really. If I smell smoke, I might not so say if I think everyone else can smell it too. Or, if someone looks to be running backwards toward the edge of a cliff I'd like to know if they'll hear me when I shout 'stop.' Or, if *I'm* backing toward the edge of a cliff I can't see, I'd like to know the person watching can speak and tell me so. Or, what if someone starts running for it straight on? I'd like to know for certain whether they can see it or not. Actually, I'd probably simply assume that they couldn't. That one'd be pretty clear. Though, maybe more for my safety's sake, I'd rather not find myself volunteering to do something like have daggers thrown in my general direction by a man who can't see where he's throwing."

"Are you finished?"

She took a second to consider her rant. "Yes, I think I am."

"Good. Now mind you, I stopped listening halfway through, so I don't know what you carried on about with cliffs and such. But, in any event, let me assure you that you are perfectly safe, provided you do not volunteer to be part of Homer's target practice."

It wasn't as detailed a confirmation as she'd have liked, but it was sufficient enough to allow her to get back to the task of retelling of all she'd learned that day. "Alright then, where was I? Okay, Homer is blind. Sawyer is mean. Harris? Harris is royalty, and Goldilocks shares his name with a monkey. Not sure how helpful either of those lessons were. And, come to think of it, they came through Mabel and Maude, which in hindsight makes it perfectly clear to me why you chose to take me from the trajectory they had me on and move me onto another."

"I'm glad you can see reason even through all of your rambling," he teased. "Frankly, I'm finding it hard to keep up. Given I've spent many a morning chatting over coffee with Mabel, I think we both know what that means for you."

She felt her lips slip into a sheepish grin. She did indeed know what it meant. Hugh thought she was rambling more than even Mabel could after caffeine. "Sorry. Just feeling incredibly overwhelmed with it all. Letting it all pour out a bit seems to be helping." She shrugged. "Anyway, I think that's all. Horse care. Loads of horse care. That's the most important stuff, the stuff I can use here, right?"

Hugh stopped short. "No. What did you really learn?"

Annis stumbled backward a few steps, both from his sudden stop as well as his unexpected refusal of her answer. She'd told him everything. And there'd been a lot. She'd been busy. Eyes and ears open, taking it all in, focusing on every detail, eager to get it all right. Her mind had been on fire all day, sorting through a million different tasks, observations, and conversations. So many things had happened and been said, especially between her and Sequoyah. He'd taught her more today than she ever could have anticipated.

And then she remembered. She understood the question Hugh was asking her.

He wanted to know what she understood now in words she hadn't known before. Sequoyah and the horses lit up her mind in beautiful, wild, and awe-inspiring flashes. Memories of home and a face she would carry in her mind's eye all her life laced their way through her present thoughts, mingling the old and new, reminding her of what mattered, what was true, and why she'd never seen it before now.

She took a breath, slowed her mind, and let the dust and debris of trivial thoughts settle before she answered a second time. "I learned that most people see first what they fear. And that they're usually wrong about what they think they see."

A satisfied smile swept over his thin lips and he nodded. "Good girl." Then, as if that were all he'd been waiting to hear, he began walking again. "Caroline and Homer," he said. "That's who you'll follow tomorrow. Tonight, you'll stay with Maude and Mabel again, as terrifying a thought as that may be for me. But they offered and the three of you do seem to get on well together."

"Wonderful." She'd missed the sisters today and, oddly enough, craved the comforts of their small cabin in a way she might have craved the four walls of her old bedroom, once upon a time. "Wait, you're letting me spend the day with Caroline and Homer? Just this morning you thought it was the worst idea you'd ever heard."

"That was this morning." He shrugged, picking up the pace even more. "Now it's a brilliant idea."

"Because it's yours?" Annis said, half joking, half certain it made all the difference.

"Because now you're ready to learn what only they can teach you."

"Oh. And what might that be?"

"You'll find that out when you learn it."

She dragged her eyes up from where they'd been glued to the ground, carefully tracking her path in the dark as she raced after Hugh. "Wait, where are we headed right now?" Because they'd passed the sisters ages ago, and their car was near the front of the train, but she and Hugh were nearing the end of it. And she wasn't sure, but she thought Caroline and Homer had a cabin near theirs, given their visit that morning while the train had been in motion.

"I've got something for you back here. Babe found it out on her stroll after dinner." He turned back toward her just long enough for her to see him roll his eyes. "You know how she is. Anyway, she's certain it's yours, so I suppose it must be."

Annis hadn't a clue what it might be. All she possessed when she arrived at Brooks and Bennet were the clothes she had traded for better ones after her bath in Babe's tent.

"Go ahead," Hugh said when they reached the train car designed for animal transport. He held the door for her to go in first. Nerves and excitement furled at the pit of her stomach as she put one timid foot in front of the other. The cart was dark and quiet except for one small lantern hanging in the corner. Straw covered the ground as far as her eyes could see within the dimly lit wagon. And then something moved. And it made a noise. A sad, small whimper came from a little bundle of fur curled up in a nest of its own making in the straw and sawdust that covered the floor.

"Oh," Annis gasped, dropping to her knees right beside the creature. "It's tiny." She leaned her head sideways to try to get a better look. "A puppy?"

"A wolf cub. Babe found the mama dead in the woods. Farmers must have shot her. Of course, soon as she noticed it was a mama, she went looking for the pups. Only found the one." He pointed at the sad little lump of fur as he shook and whined in his sleep. "Babe declared you the keeper, so he's your responsibility. You'll find all you need to make up his bottles in the crates against the wall and Momma will see to it you get scraps every day for him when he gets old enough. The twins'll know what to do if you have any questions but, truth be told, most things are best handled on instinct alone. Trust your heart, love. It's done you well since you've been here. It'll keep you on track." And then, with a nod and a wink, he turned to leave again.

"Wait," she called. "What's his name?"

Hugh glanced down at the newest member of his ongoing collection of broken and lost things and smiled, hope dancing in his eyes. "You tell me."

And she would. Just as soon as she figured it out.

Carefully, she dropped down from her kneeling position until her bottom touched the hay. Crossing her legs, she sat there quietly, unsure of what to do next. After all this little guy had been through, the last thing she wanted to do was frighten him more.

She watched him tighten his small body into a snugger curl, as though he were trying to hide within himself. She understood the feeling all too well. Annis knew the fear that came with the realization that you were all you had left in the world—a world in which you'd gone from feeling untouchable to being the prey of a hunter you had never seen coming. Sadness welled inside her, not for herself but for the pup.

Suddenly, Babe flashed in her mind. Babe in her morning dress, calling Annis "Tulip" and wrapping her up in a hug that overtook all of her terror, if only for a moment. Babe loved harder than anyone she'd ever met and, even in moments when every part of the world seemed to hold only cold, dark, and horrifying disappoint-ment, Babe's embrace could somehow hold all of the world at bay.

The girl Annis was before would never have thought herself ca-pable of that sort of love. It would have been too overbearing, too messy, and far too intrusive. But now she was certain she could give this lost little wolf exactly what he needed because she'd gotten it from Babe first. Now it was simply a matter of paying it forward.

Casting worry and self-doubt aside, Annis reached her hands for the sleeping pup and placed him in her lap. He couldn't be older than a week or two. His eyes were still shut and, while he didn't seem to react to sound, he definitely reacted to her warmth. He pressed himself into her as soon as his body touched hers.

"You poor thing," she whispered softly, bending down to form a cocoon around him with her body and letting her cheek rest against his soft fur. "You're going to be alright now," she promised. "I'm going to make sure of it." She sat balled up with the small cub, rocking gently back and forth as she hummed lullabies she'd heard a lifetime ago, until the car door opened again. It was the twins.

"We heard you got yourself a new baby," Mabel said, her voice hushed as though there really were a sleeping baby in their midst.

"He's precious," Annis sighed. "And I haven't any idea how to take care of him."

"We figured as much," Maude said, already headed for the crates Hugh had pointed to earlier to show Annis where the bottle-feeding supplies were. "Mabel and I have helped Babe raise a baby or two over the years." She stopped short of lifting the lid to shake her head. "You wouldn't believe some of the critters she's come back with after some of her walks. Squirrels. Hedgehogs. Even a skunk once. I thought for sure Hugh was done with her after that one," she laughed. "But you know Hugh. He's just as big of a sap as she is, even if he does have a pretty good bark at times. The bite is useless."

"As was the skunk," Mabel said, scrunching up her nose.

"What happened to it?" Annis asked, wondering if she needed to be on the lookout for skunks.

"Wound up leaving with Pete when he retired a few years back," Mabel answered, and then remembered Annis had no idea who Pete was. "Pete had a knack for swallowing things. Swords. Fireballs. Even the tail end of a snake for a while there. Incredibly talented, but this life just wasn't for him. Only even wound up here because he'd had his heart broken beyond repair. Or so he thought. One stop in Colorado changed his mind pretty good. Next thing you know, he was done with the circus, though thankfully not done with Smelly Jelly the skunk. They had a strange bond, those two." She shook her head. Mabel's inability to comprehend Pete and Smelly Jelly's unusual attachment while standing there, fused hip-to-hip with her sister, made it hard for Annis not to laugh out loud.

"So, every critter Babe finds she pawns off on someone here?" Annis asked, hoping to move the conversation along and not succumb to her amusement, which would require an explanation the twins may not find as funny as she did.

"Not every critter, but most." Maude stood up, holding a bottle in one hand and screwing on the top with the other. "Some wild can't be tamed. We care for them, love them as long as we can, and, when they're strong enough again, we set them free."

Annis peered down at the wolf in her lap. It was hard to believe one day he'd grow to be a dangerous hunter, capable of ripping humans to shreds with his fangs and crushing their bones with his jaw, but it was true. He could grow to be the sort of wild that needed to be released. It was a possibility she had to consider even as she was falling utterly in love with him.

"Babe has a pet tiger," Maude pointed out dryly, clearly sensing Annis's troubles as she handed her the bottle. "But Caroline had to give up the chipmunk she raised. You never know which ones will stay and which will fly. There's no telling ahead of time, so there's no use worrying about it now."

Annis gave Maude a grateful smile, soaking in her words of comfort as she took the bottle from her and carefully offered the pup some milk. After a few missed tries, he started suckling and didn't stop until the bottle was dry. Exhausted from the work of feeding, he sank back into Annis's lap and fell asleep all over again. This time, he didn't shake or whimper.

"Finian," she whispered. "I think that's what I'll call him."

"I like that," Maude said quietly. Sounds like the name of a warrior."

Annis nodded. She'd heard the name in a story a long time ago, but it had stayed with her, as though some part of her heart had always known she'd meet a Finian of her own one day.

"Shall we?" Mabel asked, an eye cast toward the door. "I can hear the comforts of our cabin calling and I, for one, could really do with a good dusting off. All this straw and sawdust is making me itchy." She squirmed and shuddered as she spoke, just in case the words alone weren't convincing enough.

"Can we bring him?" Annis asked, not yet familiar with the baby critter protocol.

"Can't leave him," Mabel said simply.

Reaching a hand down to steady her, Maude helped Annis to her feet without having to disrupt sleeping Finian in her arms.

Mabel stopped at the crate of supplies on the way out. "Best take some of this with us. He'll be hungry again at least two or three times more before the night is over."

A few minutes later, with their arms stretched to capacity with a night's supply of powdered milk and bottles, the three headed back outside. Annis carried Finian snuggly against her body, balancing him and the supplies in her arms. The usual circus commotion had died down to a comfortable rumble of voices and soft laughter.

"Seems strange to be staying," Annis said. She preferred the idea of constant motion. Even if she felt safe where she was, she'd feel even safer if the distance between her future and the threat of her past were growing again.

"I quite like it," Mabel admitted, waving at Oscar and Bess in passing. "Every so often it's nice to end a show and just be done for the night. No worrying about loading up or wondering how long we'll be on the rails until we reach our next destination. To just be, to just enjoy the moment, can be a lovely part of this adventure too."

"I hadn't thought of it that way," Annis said, realizing for the first time that the novelty of circus life could eventually wear thin and that the constant work could become just that: work. It was hard to fathom, given how fulfilled she felt, how much purpose she had found, in only two days of what was really no more than menial tasks.

"You will," Maude said in her characteristic direct but grinning way. "But it won't make you love the nights we move any less," she promised. Annis believed her. It was easy to.

"Oh, Lord," Mabel muttered under her breath, causing Annis's eyes to follow her gaze and see what had drawn her attention. It was Floyd.

"We better get him turned around before he wanders off too far," Maude said, already speeding up and changing course toward where Floyd was on the verge of disappearing in the tree line at the edge of camp.

Annis hesitated for the briefest of moments before she determined it would be wrong not to do for Floyd what everyone here would undoubtedly do for her—what they had *already* done for her—and hurried to catch up with Maude and Mabel, who were several feet ahead of her.

Mabel called out in a sing-song voice, "Floyd! Oh, Floy-yod!" There was no indication he'd heard his name or their rushing footsteps as they closed in on him.

Overloaded with Finian's bottles and struggling to not squish the wolf cub as he nestled into her chest, Annis was fueled by her desperation to keep from dropping all she held. "Floyd!" Annis shouted, surprising herself by the volume of her voice.

It did the trick.

The old albino man came to a standstill, his white hair shining silver in the moonlight and his near-translucent skin took on an almost magical shimmer. Slowly he turned, with his eyes cast down and catching on nothing in particular, and then resumed his usual shuffle across the dirt toward camp.

"That's weird," Mabel mumbled as all three girls watched him go by.

"Really?" Annis scrunched up her face as she watched him move aimlessly, and yet something told her he had intentions set in all he did. "Which part?"

"I think he heard you," Mabel said, her eyes still following the old man.

Annis frowned. "You called his name first."

"Yeah," she said, her eyes widening as she turned to face Annis. "But that was for the sake of habit, not with any sort of expectations I'd see results for my efforts."

"Only person he's ever responded to is Babe," Maude says quietly. "And it was only that first night she found him walking about. She asked him where he was going, and he'd looked at her, said 'home,' and then disappeared behind those burning red eyes again as though he'd never been present at all."

"It's sad," Mabel said, leaning her head on her sister's shoulder as they walked, heading for their car now that Floyd was safely within the perimeter of camp again. "He's always right here, surrounded by all of us, and always alone, too far for anyone to reach him."

"Maybe he's coming back," Annis said thoughtfully, recalling her previous interaction with him and wondering if she should tell the sisters. Sawyer hadn't been at all receptive to her claims.

"It's a lovely thought," Maude said, though Annis understood her meaning. It was lovely, but it wasn't likely.

When they reached their car, it was far from empty. This put an end to any more of Annis's contemplations about Floyd, at least for the time being. Familiar faces from their morning visit filled the space. In addition to those, Annis was pleased to see Sequoyah smiling back at her from the rear corner of the now exceptionally cramped space.

"We were wondering where you girls disappeared to," Sawyer said. "Hope you don't mind we didn't wait for you to show up and invite us in."

"Doesn't seem like the sort of thing we'd mind," Mabel chirped. "Now clear a spot on the bed so Annis can sit and we can get past her to put up these supplies."

"What is all of that?" August asked, craning his neck to see as Annis began placing bottles in a trunk under her bed. "Bottles? Oh, Lord. What sort of orphan did Babe drag home this time?"

Annis smiled, looking down adoringly at the small bundle in her arms. "A wolf." She moved her arms so that everyone could see the pup while still keeping him snuggled against her. "His name is Finian. And I don't know a thing about him beyond that, so all you animal experts speak up, please." She rounded the room and landed on Sawyer. Something about his affinity for lions made him seem like the most appropriate match for her current predicament.

"Completely different beast," he said grinning. "But, I will tell you this. There's nothing quite like being loved by a creature that would just as soon kill you as look at you."

"A comforting bit of insight, thanks," she mumbled, slipping gently back onto the mattress of her makeshift bed. Sequoyah came to sit beside her.

"May I?" he asked, fingers stretched out toward the pup, waiting for permission. She granted it with a nod. "You'll do just fine with him," he said so only she could hear. The others had already moved on in their conversations, ranging from the chipmunk Caroline had raised to the possibility of taking a trip into town the following morning. The latter idea seemed to conjure up a great deal of excitement. But all Annis could think of was Finian, snuggled in her lap.

"You always think the best of me," she said to Sequoyah after a long, contemplative pause. "I'm not sure you're always right, though."

He smirked. "Haven't been wrong yet."

"You've known me for all of two days, you fool." She laughed. "You may yet turn out to be wrong about something you simply have yet to see the results of."

He shook his head, still convinced of his belief that she could always reach the hopes he had for her. "It's not in my nature to be wrong. I say what I see, and I see what I believe."

"Don't you mean you believe what you see?"

He shook his head. "No, I don't." And he left it at that, with no more explanations or discussions. The last of his enigma of a statement rang in her ears and melted into her mind, where it tumbled around with the rest of her thoughts, on hold until she had a moment of quiet to sort through them all.

That moment, however, was hours out of reach as voices grew louder and tales became more animated until everyone, including

Annis and Sequoyah, was in stitches, tears of laughter rolling down their cheeks while little Finian slept peacefully. People came and went, drawn to their carriage by all the raucous noise, though the original group seemed to remain intact despite the comings and goings. Mabel was right. It was nice to stay put for a night and not worry about anything other than enjoying each other's company.

Before long, Finian was awake again, shoving his nose around her stomach in search of his next meal. Determined to learn quickly, Annis insisted on making his bottle on her own.

"I can do it," she announced, reaching under the bed to retrieve the small trunk that held Finian's bottles. "Or," she amended with a little less confidence as she opened the lid and glanced inside, "at least I can figure it out."

Maude—who'd been ready to jump out of her seat to help, which would have resulted in dragging with her a surprised Mabel who was deep in conversation with August—leaned back, one curious eyebrow raised at Annis and her lips cinched at the corner of her mouth. "Alright then, let's see if you've been paying attention."

It turned out to be harder than Annis had anticipated, starting with juggling Finian in one hand while trying to take the rubber nipple off the bottle with the other.

"Sure you don't want any help?" Maude asked, a smug look on her face as she watched Annis continue to struggle.

Annis sighed, accepting imminent surrender. "It would still count as doing it myself if I let you hold Fin, right?"

Maude shrugged. "We can still count it."

Annis reached out and placed Finian gently in Maude's lap, which incidentally also drew Mabel's attention. "Oh, look who we have here," she cooed, picking him up and holding him to her chest. "I just adore how he smells, don't you?" she asked her sister, who crinkled her nose and snorted in response.

Tempted though Annis was to watch what would likely prove to be an entertaining exchange between the twins regarding Finian's scent, or odor, as Maude would likely put it, she forced her focus back to the bottle. Two hands were definitely more favorable than one. This time around, the top came off in seconds.

Next, she drew the bag of powdered milk from the trunk and proceeded to pour it into the bottle almost just as she'd seen Maude do it before. In Annis's case, the powder wasn't so much going inside the bottle as around the outside of it. It took her several attempts and multiple adjustments to the bag and the angle at which she held it, but eventually, she got enough inside. Or, rather, more than enough, leading her to have to pour some back into the bag, which resulted in having too little in the bottle. This game went on for a solid three rounds before Annis finally managed to get the exact right amount into the bottle.

From there, things became easier as she topped off the bottle with water from the pitcher the twins kept on their dresser for washing at night. And then she went to give it a good shake, only to find she hadn't secured the rubber nipple as well as she'd thought, leading her to spray milk around their entire compartment and everyone inside it.

After a good laugh, and a few tears by Annis, Caroline and Sawyer cleaned up the mess while Annis made her final attempt at preparing the bottle.

In the end, her stubbornness won out and, after another near spill and multiple outbursts her mother would have deemed highly unladylike, the job was done. Finian happily nursed his bottle again. Everyone fell silent watching him, fascinated by the simple act of feeding a puppy. Annis had to admit that there was something soothing about the contented way he grunted and how he stretched out his hind legs as he started to drift off near the end of his feeding. He was so small and so helpless, and yet so unaware of either vulnerability as he rested there, curled up against her stomach again, trusting her to care for him and keep him safe. Annis felt like he did once. And until this evening, she'd been certain she'd never allow herself to be lulled into such a false sense of security again. Now, seeing Finian, knowing she would move heaven and earth to protect him, she felt a renewed sense of hope. She considered the possibility that trust was not to be abandoned entirely. Maybe these feelings she was having about him, others were just as capable of, even if those she'd expected it most from in her previous life had not been. It was possible, she though, that she simply hadn't been worthy enough to evoke such feelings of love and protection in them.

"I think Finian here may have the right idea about things," Sawyer said with a loud yawn.

"I hope you're not thinking about curling up in someone's lap for a nap," Maude said flatly.

"I take it you're not offering?" Sawyer responded, matching her tone.

"I am," Homer volunteered loudly. "Come on, then, plenty of room here," he said, patting his thighs with his hands. People laughed, though it was noticeably with less enthusiasm than they'd shown earlier in the night. Everyone was getting sleepy.

"Thanks, brother. But I think I'll pass." Sawyer scooted to the edge of the nightstand he'd been sitting on and prepared to jump off. "But only because Caroline is staring daggers at me, threatening me not to."

Homer laughed, clasping his wife's hand, who chuckled softly and never denied the accusation, making it all the more believable and entertaining. With the quiet hum of dying chuckles still in the air, they made their descent from the bed they'd been sitting on. "Well, if no one's going to be sleeping in my lap, I think I'll go ahead and take it back to my own bed, then."

"I think that's a brilliant idea," Caroline said, leading the way for the both of them as they moved through the small aisle toward the back door, which Annis had learned led to their adjoining car. "Annis, I believe we'll see you first thing in the morning?"

"Hugh's orders," Annis said brightly. She was excited to spend the day with them and, frankly, still a bit on edge about Hugh's sudden change of heart.

"He must really trust you," Homer mused as they walked out.

"He certainly doesn't trust us," Caroline added with a loud laugh, pulling the door shut behind them.

Chapter Ten

THE MAKINGS OF
A FAIRY TALE

The rest of the night passed in a peaceful quiet for Annis, only interrupted by Finian's feedings and the occasional chat with Mabel, who always appeared awake no matter the time. Come morning, Annis felt exhausted and yet completely satisfied about having successfully kept the wolf pup alive through the night.

Even without the usual work of setting up, there was plenty to be done as soon as they stepped outside. Animals needed tending to. Structures needed to be secured where wind and weather had undone the previous day's work. And, of course, there was the task of tending to the basic needs of everyone who lived and breathed the Brooks and Bennet circus.

With Finian left to carry on with his sleep in a sling of burlap handcrafted by Mabel and now tied to Annis's chest, the three girls went about the morning's chores. First, they stopped in to care for Millie and Edi before Mabel and Maude saw to it that Annis found her way to Homer and Caroline.

"Since we don't have animals in our charge, we've got most of our work done already," Caroline explained while Annis followed her through the campsite. "It's simple stuff, really. Polishing the silver, knives, and daggers and such, soaking all the flammables in kerosene, and, of course, checking all the props and equipment to make sure nothing was damaged or strained in the previous show. We may seem crazy, but we put a lot of effort into being safe," she assured Annis, sounding more somber than Annis had heard before.

"What's left to do? What can I help with?" Annis offered, eager to seem useful rather than a burden Hugh had landed them with.

"Some of the costumes need mending. I was going to do that next. Are you any good with a needle and thread?"

She was. Sewing and needlepoint had been deemed ladylike and therefore approved and fully encouraged by Annis's mother. "I can stitch up just about anything," she said. "And I'm neat too. Tight and even stitches were always important to my mother," Annis said without thinking. Mother. She hadn't heard herself say that word since the night she left. The night she'd screamed it at the top of her lungs. Her jaw clenched and her body tensed at the memory.

If Caroline noticed the change in Annis, she didn't show it. "My mother never bothered with tight or even anything," she laughed derisively. "But then I don't suppose that would have aligned much with her life."

Grateful for the distraction, Annis pursued talking about Caroline's mother rather than thinking of her own. "What sort of life?"

"No one's told you?" she asked, looking half-surprised, half-pleased. "I was born and raised in a brothel. *That's* my story."

"Oh." Annis had not anticipated that particular turn in the conversation, but she was getting used to the unexpected around here. "So, you...Your mother..." she stopped, at a loss for words. There simply was no polite way to ask what she wanted to know.

Caroline smirked, obviously sensing Annis's internal struggle. "The answer is yes. To all of your questions. Yes."

Annis felt her curiosity pique. "What was it like?" She'd heard things, of course, but so much of what she'd been told by her parents had proven wrong in recent days that she was willing to accept that this too could have been portrayed with very limited accuracy. Especially having met Caroline, it was hard to associate her with the image Annis's mother had once conjured up for her, which depicted women who were supposed to be quite unlike the woman standing before her. Admittedly, Caroline was hardly the shy type, and the risqué costumes she wore left little to the imagination. But she was also full of grace and strength. She always held her head high and always met others eye-to-eye when she spoke. There was no shame in her, nor did she conduct herself in a way that would warrant any.

Caroline finally came to a stop in front of a long, narrow table set up just outside their car, covered in tools and materials, some of which were shiny metal, while others simply shiny. While an overwhelming sight at first, a second glance showed Annis the simplicity of what lay before her. A work table, shared by Homer and Caroline, displayed everything they needed for their act. One half was covered with things he'd likely toss, and the other with garments she'd likely wear. It made for a dazzling scene, the silver blades and the sparkling costumes. Unlike the cold, unyielding metal on Homer's side, beneath all the silver and gold sequins on Caroline's side was the soft velvet that clung to her body like a second skin every time she stepped into the ring.

"What was it like to grow up in a brothel?" Caroline repeated Annis's question as though she'd never even considered it. "I suppose it wasn't much different from anyone else's life." She dropped her head back, rolling her eyes at her own answer. "I mean, of course it was different than say, your life. I'm guessing, obviously, though I'm doing so confidently," she said. "But, overall, my childhood felt normal to me. Rather boring at times, to be honest. Not much fun to be had when you're the only child around and every grown up only concerns themselves with grown up things, which are the only sort of things happening in a brothel." She paused, leafing through several of her costumes until she found the ones that needed repairing. She handed one over to Annis, who took a seat on the bench that ran along the one side of the table. Once they were both settled with costumes to stitch, Caroline went on. "Don't get me wrong, there were good parts. Mostly between the hours of noon and three o'clock. That's when everyone had time for me. Treated me like a little doll rather than a human girl, but I wasn't bothered by it. There were loads of pretty clothes to wear, always someone around to do my hair or teach me how to paint up my face with all the most fashionable, most taboo colors. You know the sort – colors that drew the eye, that made you stand out rather than blend in and disappear. Then afternoon would grow to early evening and play time would be over. Grown up time would begin. Those were the hours I struggled to pass...Until I became old enough to start to be of use. Not long after that, I decided that life wasn't for me."

Annis was so enamored with Caroline's tale that she hadn't even threaded her needle. Caroline noticed and laughed. "Are you going to be helping me with this or not? I was so looking forward to seeing a proper stitch. Mine are horrid, you know. My only saving grace is the fact every inch of velvet is covered in sequins. All the mess of stitches and loose threads gets completely hidden."

"Sorry," Annis apologized, quickly threading the needle. After a pause, she said, "I keep realizing how utterly unlived my life has been."

Caroline let out a loud snort. "Annis, dear, you're far too comfortable sitting here with me, holding a wolf pup in your lap after having spent the night with Maude, nonsense sleep-talking Mabel, and crazy sleep-stalking Francis for that to be even remotely true."

Annis chuckled. "To be fair, I haven't actually seen Francis show up yet, though I've heard he does make frequent visits."

"Probably scared to come since you're there. Give it time. He'll decide it's not worth you thinking he's sane and start making the rounds again." She watched with great interest as Annis began to sew the seam along the waist, which had split during last night's performance. "You really do have a remarkably steady hand. If Hugh ever stops pecking about you like a mother hen, you should have Homer teach you a thing or two," she said with a wink. "I bet you've got hidden talents you've never even dreamed of."

"Oh, Lord, I do hope so. As far as I know, I haven't got any. And that's not really going to take me very far here, is it?"

Caroline shrugged as though she weren't worried one bit about Annis and her supposed lack of circus talent. "You've got some. Everyone does. Don't think I showed up here ready to bend my body in half, forward and backward."

Annis stopped mid-stitch. She was surprised by this revelation. "Really?"

Caroline nodded. "Honest to God. Couldn't even do a split."

"What made you decide this was what you wanted to do?" Annis asked, picking up her needle work again.

"Must have been here at least three weeks or so, keeping busy, learning, much like you are right now. Then, one day, Hugh sat me down and asked me two simple questions. The answers to those turned out to be the answers to everything."

Annis stared at Caroline with wide eyes. "What were the questions?"

Caroline smiled. Her face took on a dazed expression as though she were traveling back to that moment. "He asked me what I thought people saw when they looked at me. And then, he asked me what I wanted them to see. It's what he asks everyone. He'll ask you too. And, Annis, it'll change your life when he does. Changed mine. And Homer's. Changed all of us."

Annis gulped. Not because she found those two questions to be particularly significant, but because she found she had no answer to either. And that, she felt, was very much significant. And worrisome.

Caroline reached her hand out to pinch Annis's side, bringing her back to the present. "No need to ponder it just yet. Answer will change a hundred times over if you do, and you won't get it right anyway. Not until it's time. And only Hugh ever seems to know when that is."

"Magic Hugh," Annis whispered.

"Indeed, he is," Caroline said with a chuckle.

"Caroline," Annis began, tentatively searching for the words she wanted to use to ask the question she had. She wasn't sure if it was something she was even meant to ask. Maybe it was a personal question too intimate of a topic to discuss. After all, Caroline had not revealed or hinted at it, and she very well could have if she had wanted to.

"Go ahead," Caroline encouraged, almost as if she knew what Annis was about to say.

"What were your answers? To those questions. Or are they secret? Because I'd completely understand if they were. You've already shared so much with me, and I've shared nothing about myself. I just sit here, soaking in everyone's stories without ever contributing. It's rude, come to think of it, to expect everyone to be an open book when I've slammed the covers shut and bound them tighter than tight."

It was Caroline's turn to stare at Annis with wide eyes. She looked as though she might explode, but when she did it was into a burst of giggles. "My, you really do worry an awful lot! And that rambling thing you do...I think you reveal a great deal more than you realize every time you let that mouth of yours run off the rails with a random train of thought you clearly have no control over."

She laughed heartily. "And, for the record, it's not a secret. I'm happy to share what my answers were. My life really is an open book and you're welcome to flip through the pages any time you like. Any lessons you can glean from my experiences, I count as a job well done on my end even if I fumbled my own parts in the story."

Sitting here with Caroline, so strong, so sure of herself, it was hard to envision her fumbling at anything. "I didn't used to ramble," Annis said quietly. "Didn't used to say much at all." She wasn't even sure why that was. Had no one ever listened? Or had she simply never had anything to say?

"I wasn't much of a talker either," Caroline said with a soothing calm in her tone, as though she understood more than Annis was knowingly letting on. "Wasn't exactly what people were looking for from me."

"What do you mean?" Though Annis had an inkling, she knew Caroline would put it into words, into fully formed thoughts she could then understand for herself, because maybe, just maybe, their reasons would be the same.

"You're a pretty girl, Annis," she began, the calmness in her voice laced with a weary sadness. "We're both pretty girls. Pretty girls don't need to do anything else, do they? If you're pretty, you're not expected to do hard work. Or get dirty. Or think. Or be smart. And if you're not smart, or thinking, there's really no point in talking, is there?"

"I suppose not," she kept her eyes down, focused on her needle work, questions mounting inside her mind that she didn't want Caroline to see.

"But that's their mistake, Annis. They're the ones who aren't smart enough to see past the pretty face, beyond the surface. It's not our shortcoming, it's theirs. And it speaks to their faults, not ours. So, don't you let that be your story, Annis. Your story is yours to tell and no one else's."

Annis nodded, appreciating the sentiment. "Is that what your answer was then, to how people saw you?"

Caroline reached into the stack of costumes and pulled out a bright red one with golden flames engulfing the torso. "Well, unfortunately, I think we both know pretty isn't all people see when they look at a girl with my background. Men, women, both see different things. Neither of them are ever right." She threaded a new needle and began to mend a hole that looked large enough for one of Homer's daggers to have sliced through it. She caught Annis watching and shrugged. "Accidents happen. I'd rather the skirt than my thigh, you know?"

She nodded, though she most certainly did not know and preferred to keep it that way.

They worked in silence for a few minutes, both of them moving into a steady rhythm with their stitching, before Caroline went on. "What no one ever tells you is how truly empty you're perceived to be on the inside when you're appreciated only for what's on the outside. And how you start to think it's true. When all the value you believe you possess is tied up in being pretty, it's the most demeaning feeling in the world. There's no value in something you have no control over. I should be no less important, because I was born with a perfectly pointy nose and bright blue eyes, than any other woman born without those traits. Nor should they lack value because they don't meet some standard of beauty no one really understands anyway. So, one day, I grew tired of being limited by what I couldn't change. And I left. And I found Hugh. And he gave me the freedom to be anyone I chose. And so, I walk out there every night and wear the tiny costumes like I used to. I hear the murmurs of admiration from the men and the slanderous words of the women. And then I begin to move my body, the body they are certain they know all about. I show them my grace. My flexibility. My strength. My courage. And, slowly, they forget about the shameful opinions they had tried to brand me with and instead they see someone new. They see *me*, for the first time. And that's who they remember." She smiled, the corners of her mouth curving softly. "The woman I want them to see remains and the woman they believed me to be ceases to exist forever."

Annis ran a finger across the mended seam, checking it for bumps, but her mind was still on Caroline's story. "Hugh's a bloody genius."

"Yes, he bloody well is." She nodded, leaning over to check Annis's work. "As are you with a needle, my friend. That's beautiful work."

Annis took note of her near-perfect stitching. At least she had one skill she knew she could make use of, though she was certain she didn't have the faintest desire to build a life around becoming a seamstress.

"How do you think he became that way?" she asked, folding up the colorful leotard before sifting through the pile for another in need of stitching. "Hugh, I mean."

"If I had to guess, and I do because he won't say, it probably started with being told his whole life he was one way when he knew in his heart that he was another."

Annis understood. "Babe."

"Exactly. We see them together and it seems like the most natural thing in the world, but outside, beyond where our bubble reaches, the world sees them in a completely different light. They skew reality into a story of their own making, turning love ugly, making it unnatural, some even say unforgivably wrong. They see horrible things. Things we know not to be true. Because we have Hugh. And he teaches us how to see ourselves honestly and, more importantly, how to see others." She looked up from her work and Annis followed suit, both of them hearing the sound of approaching footsteps. "You wouldn't know a thing about that though, would you, darling?" she said as Homer came to a stop at the edge of their table.

"Seeing things?" he asked, a crooked grin peering through the dark scruff on his face. "Not really my area of expertise, no."

"Have you always been blind?" Annis asked, hoping he was as welcoming of personal questions as his wife was.

"Indeed, I have," he answered without skipping a beat. She realized it probably wasn't the first time he'd been asked that question.

"Is that why you're so good at faking it?" Annis carried on, letting her curiosities fall off the tip of her tongue and out of her mouth.

Homer laughed. "Faking it? Seeing, you mean?"

"Well, yes," she said, peering back and forth between him and Caroline, who seemed to be exchanging secret glances, though Annis knew that was impossible.

"Not really faking anything," Homer explained, reaching out his hand to pull over a chair he clearly knew was there. "Just happen to be quite comfortable with *not* seeing. And, provided my surroundings stay the same, carrying on with regular things isn't all that different for me than it is for you."

Annis stopped mid-stitch again. "But...Your surroundings change all the time. You're in a new campsite nearly every day."

"True. But all the things that look different to you are not visible to me," Homer explained as he picked up one of his long blades and a rag and slowly began polishing the silver. "Everything I depend on to get around stays the same. Or, rather, becomes the same everywhere we go." He turned his head to indicate the camp beyond their small station. "Every time we set up camp, we do it exactly the same way. Everyone's tents and wagons stay in order, everyone counts their paces making sure the distance between each remains the same. Momma T lines up the tables in the exact same rows every time and the big tent is always the same distance from the main camp, entrance always on the same side, performers flap always on the other, nearest the animal tent, which is always at the far-right corner of camp. Everyone sees to it everything remains where I can find it without struggle or guesswork." He turned back to face them, though his stare was set on nothing in particular as he spoke. "In our car, Caroline sees to it that everything is always where I can find it with ease. She's my eyes in there, in the ring. Wherever we go, she sees for the both of us. She makes the world around me tangible."

Annis fell quiet for a long while after he spoke. She'd never much considered love to be as grand as the sort in fairy tales. Her own parents had been cordial with one another and, while she knew there'd been little romance in their courtship, she'd believed them to be happy together most of her life. Marriage, as she'd known it, was simply an arrangement, one made for the good of all involved. She'd been told from an early age of the boy she'd been meant to marry. His name was William Perrine and his family owned a great deal of orchards back home. He was set to do well in life, according to her mother. Annis had met him, of course, and had even thought he was suited perfectly fine to be her future husband. Now the sentiment seemed ridiculous. Who would marry for the sake of a comfortable life when there was love such as Caroline and Homer shared to be found?

"Biscuits and gravy are done," Sawyer announced in passing. "I can smell them all the way from the animal tent." Before anyone could answer, he was out of sight again, rounding the corner and likely making a beeline for Momma T's.

"Was he running?" Homer asked, chuckling as he set down his dagger, which now sparkled in the sunlight. Annis nodded and then, remembering that was not a suitable response when conversing with a blind man, added, "He was. Momma T's biscuits and gravy must be as good as her hotcakes."

"Not even close," Caroline said, bunching up the material of a skirt that, from her expression, she deemed beyond repair. "But Sawyer has a very unbiased approach where food is concerned. He loves it all, and he wants it every second of every day."

"I think it's 'cause his stomach's small. Can't hold much, so he needs to be fed every few hours," Homer said.

"Mine's not too different," Annis said, clutching her belly, which had been grumbling quietly all morning. "I never should have given my leftovers to Jacob yesterday. It set me back on my food intake the rest of the day," she mused as they all stood and began to head to Momma T's tent.

"It's always the tiny things that eat the most," Caroline said, hooking her arm in Homer's to subtly guide him and help him maneuver the occasional unexpected obstacle along the way: a ladder left behind, probably abandoned for the sake of breakfast, and a few rolled up tarps they'd used to cover equipment overnight. All in all, the path was notably clear, which Annis was taking in now from a new perspective. She'd be more conscious of her surroundings from now on and keep in mind how much Homer depended on things remaining the same to get around.

"I'll have fresh biscuits in just a minute," Momma T hollered as soon as they stepped inside her tent. "Bess and August just got the last of the first batch."

"No rush," Caroline said, trying to set Momma T at ease as she went whipping about her kitchen in a bit of a frenzy. "We'll just go sit with the others until they're ready." She pointed out toward one of the larger tables that still offered plenty of sitting room.

Annis felt her belly do a little flip when she saw Sequoyah, sitting in what she was starting to learn was his usual spot right beside Sawyer. They made an unlikely pair on the surface, but there was no arguing their friendship after having spent time with them both. They balanced each other, took care of one another, and made no bones about calling the other out when necessary. The two of them made perfect sense together.

"How's Finian this morning?" Sequoyah asked as Annis slid into the vacant spot beside him. She tugged at the sling just enough to open it up and give him a peek at the sleeping pup.

"Don't think he has any complaints. Well, until he gets hungry. Then he complains plenty, but he's easy to appease." She smiled, giving the bundle a tender tap with her palm.

"Wait until he starts howling. That'll be loads of fun," Sawyer said, sweeping a large piece of biscuit through a glob of gravy. Annis had never been a big fan of the dish, but she had to admit it smelled delicious.

"I thought they only do that when the moon is full," she said, scanning the rest of the table. Most everyone's plates were drenched in gravy, though some had opted for butter and fruit with their biscuits instead. She had half a mind to ask Momma T if she could have both, but no one else seemed to have made that request, not even Sawyer.

"He's not a werewolf," Caroline teased. "Not that it'll stop him from howling at the moon. It just won't be his only cue."

"Good to know," Annis mumbled, stretching her neck in search of the twins. She'd expected them to be at this table but had found their raven-colored heads nowhere in sight. "Where are Mabel and Maude? Did we miss them?"

Bess appeared quite suddenly from behind a very large cup of coffee she'd been sipping. "They were having a wardrobe disagreement last I saw them. Something about it being Mabel's turn to pick and Maude refusing to wear...How did she put it? 'Gaggy green,' I believe, in public."

"Don't they have a color they both don't loathe?" Annis asked, intrigued by this new predicament.

"Blue," August answered, "but I think Mabel said no on principle. Her day, her color, or something like that." He shook his head, lifting his fork to his mouth for another bite of his breakfast.

Annis was about to ask another trivial question about the twins' trivial argument when Momma T called out, letting them know biscuits were ready.

Annis and Caroline hurried toward her, where a line was already forming.

"I don't know how she does it," Annis muttered. "The sheer amount of food she produces on a daily basis. She must never have time for anything else."

Caroline shrugged. "She doesn't. But cooking is what she loves doing. I think she'd be quite sad if she had extra time to fill and no one to make a meal for."

Annis thought back on the people she'd known in her life before. She couldn't think of a single one who'd had a passion for any one thing so intense that they'd have gladly dedicated every waking hour to it or have considered it a gift even to be able to do so. But here, at Brookes and Bennet, things were different. She was beginning to understand that everyone's set of daily tasks weren't assigned chores so much as they were purposefully chosen activities in services of everyone there pursuing their passions. The work here wasn't divvied up. It was chosen. Or, rather, the work chose. But somehow it all seemed to come together seamlessly, and in such a joyful manner that sometimes it was hard to see how much work was being done in the midst of all the talking and laughter.

Caroline and Annis had moved up to the front of the line and Momma T was serving up full portions for them, as well as a plate for Homer. Both women thanked her graciously, and then, eager to dig in, hurried back to the table.

"Are you planning on going into town?" Sequoyah asked as Annis happily examined the fruit on her plate. Apparently, Momma

T's mission to fatten her up was still in operation, because she'd received double portions of biscuits, one half with gravy and the other with fruit, without even having to ask.

"I don't think so," Annis replied, lifting her gaze slightly toward Caroline and Homer across from her. "You're not going into town, are you?" Neither of them had mentioned the possibility, and Annis was sincerely hoping it meant they had plans to stay in camp. Annis wasn't ready for venturing out just yet. The safety of the circus was far more comforting than the idea of wandering about aimlessly among the public, where she didn't know who might be lurking around the next turn.

"Nothing there I haven't seen before," Caroline said, dismissing the idea.

"Nothing I'm likely to see now," Homer added.

"That's right," Annis said. "Mabel and Maude said this was your old stomping ground, Caroline. They're expecting you to show them all the most exciting places."

"Oh, not to worry. I've drawn up a map for them, marking all the proper highlights, including the music hall and the best place in town for fried chicken. They'll have plenty of fun without me there," Caroline assured her. "Provided, of course, they ever settle on a dress for the day. Or, on second thought, might be more fun if they don't."

"Certainly would be for me," Sawyer said, waggling his brows.

"What about you?" Annis asked Sequoyah.

"I'd prefer they chose a dress," he answered dryly.

Annis stopped, about to take a bite, and grinned. She shook her head at him. "No, silly. I meant about town. Are you going?"

He swung his leg over the side of the bench, straddling it to face her while he spoke. "Nah. Not my kind of crowd."

Her first instinct was to ask what he meant, but she caught herself. It was so easy to forget the differences between them, and yet strangely sad to realize that what held them both apart was the same. Neither felt they'd be safe if they went. Both were targets—he for who he was and she for who she'd been. The various levels of hatefulness and violence people were capable of struck Annis like a brick to her stomach, squelching what remained of her appetite.

She set her fork down and forced a smile. "Only good crowd is in the audience, right?"

He tilted his head, a small grin on his mouth. "You've been hanging around Poppy too much."

She chuckled softly. "Not possible. There's no such thing as too much time spent with Hugh."

"Clearly you weren't ever thirteen and in his care," Sequoyah said, sounding amused. "There were days I couldn't turn my head without finding him standing right behind me at every step."

Annis narrowed her eyes. "Why? What had you done?"

"Why would you ask that? What would I do?" he asked, feigning both shock and innocence.

"I think we both know you did something." Annis maintained her suspicions.

"Fine," he surrendered. "Maybe I did have a knack for wandering off back then. And maybe it did make Babe a little crazy at times."

"For good reason," August grunted. "After that time at the swimming hole, I'm surprised you weren't forced to spend your adolescence chained to her ankle."

"What happened at the swimming hole? What swimming hole?" Annis asked, eyes darting all around the table. No one wanted to offer up the story they all seemed too familiar with.

Sequoyah shot August a look, who shamefully averted his eyes. "Sorry, I forgot we had new ears." He shrugged helplessly. "She blends in too easily."

"Well, I'm not going to blend in right now," Annis said, getting heated. "Not until someone tells me about the swimming hole." She wasn't even sure why she wanted to know, except that it had to do with Sequoyah and that something had happened to him. It was something that scared Babe, and now it was scaring her.

"It was nothing. Just a misunderstanding," Sequoyah reasoned. "One that happened a long time ago, so there's no sense in rehashing it now." He stood up from the table, swiping his empty plate from the wood surface as he went. He marched straight back to Momma T's wash station, where he left his plate and then disappeared outside, through the tent flap.

"I shouldn't have brought it up," August muttered, picking at the last of his breakfast. "It just slipped out."

"He'll get over it," Sawyer assured him, clapping his broad shoulder. "Just needs a good stew and then he'll be back to normal."

Annis sat back and watched as people picked up their plates and left the table until it was just Caroline, Homer, and Sawyer sitting with her.

Annis kept her eyes patiently locked on Sawyer until he broke down.

"You really need to know?"

"I really need to know."

He turned over his shoulder as if to be sure no one else was in earshot before he began to tell the story. "Mind you, this is before I showed up, so all I know is what I've heard. But I heard from plenty, so I'm guessing I know most of what there is to know."

Caroline exhaled loudly. "Lord, Smalls. Are you going to tell the girl before lunch starts or shall I have a go at it for you?"

Sawyer glared at her briefly before he went on. "Sequoyah's always been the exploring sort, I think it's just something he was born with. His ancestors are nomads, he's not one for staying put."

Caroline blew air through her teeth loudly as she rolled her eyes toward the ceiling and he sped things up.

"Anyway, this one morning, right after arriving in a new town, he'd found this swimming hole a little ways from camp. It was spring, so the water was perfect. Crystal clear and not too cold. He ran back to camp and rushed through all his chores so he could hurry up and get back there for a swim before the show. Only problem was, he wasn't the only one thinking about a swim that afternoon. So, when he got there, it was already occupied. By a girl, probably not much older than him." He sighed as though it was putting a strain on him having to tell this story, though Annis still couldn't see much of an issue so far. "Anyway, he scared her, just showing up out of nowhere like he did, and she screamed. Loudly. Her dad showed up with a few other men. They took one look at Sequoyah standing there and all hell broke loose."

"What do you mean?" Annis frowned. Surely, she thought, it wasn't hard to fathom that more than one person had considered going for a swim in the same afternoon.

"I mean...What do you think I mean?" Sawyer said, sounding exasperated. "You think those white men came to answer a young girl's screams for help and didn't jump to all the worst conclusions when they saw Sequoyah standing there? Frozen in place, just as stunned by her screams as she'd been by the sight of him? They didn't see the same man we do, Annis. They saw an Indian. A savage. A threat. And believe me, they treated him as such. As worse. If Hugh hadn't sent August looking for him when he did, I don't think we'd be sitting here telling the tale the same way. They'd have killed him. And not mercifully." His grim expression told her just how unmercifully he thought they might have been. It was enough to send Annis's mind on a trail of its own, trying to fully fathom what could have happened to Sequoyah that day. The men would have tortured him. Made an example of the sort of punishment one could expect if one ever dared come near their women, especially when colored in anything other than a pristine pale shade of white.

Slowly, Annis began to understand. "That's why Babe worries so much about him. Because she's scared of what could have happened that day."

Sawyer nodded, folding his napkin over and over until it became the tiniest of squares. "I think it was the first time she became undeniably aware of the prejudice and murderous hate some people harbor for the son she loves more than anything. Made her see that what his family faced wasn't an act of cruelty she could bury in the past. This would haunt him through his future. Maybe the rest of his life." He looked up. "It's a scary thing to face, let alone live with day after day."

Annis didn't dare look up from her hands, which were folded in her lap. She'd insisted on this, practically forced him to share what Sequoyah had wanted to spare her from, and now she understood why. It didn't change things between them, though, in the way he likely expected. The truth was, it was yet another way in which their fates were aligned, even in the most opposite of ways. They would both spend their lives being hunted—she for who she was and he for who he wasn't.

"He'll be angry you told me," she said somberly, feeling guilty for the rift she'd likely cause between them. Even if they recovered quickly, it wasn't fair of her to put Sawyer in that position.

"No, he won't," Sawyer said, tossing the napkin onto his plate. "Not telling you was never about shutting you out, Annis. It was about shutting down the flood of history that comes with digging it up, before he drowns in it." He stood to leave. "He walks lightly because he's strong, not because his load is light. Sometimes the two are all too easy to confuse." It was the last he said before he exited the tent, leaving Annis with Caroline and Homer.

"I keep doing that," she scolded herself, muttering under her breath and pounding the table with a frustrated thud.

"What's that? Wanting to know people?" Caroline asked, reaching her hand out to cup Annis's fist and squeeze it gently. "Looking closely? Caring so much that you want to see the darkness even when it's scary?" She squeezed again, prompting Annis to look up. "You better not stop either." Caroline's eyes lit up and her mouth drew into a smirk that meant business, even if it was kind. "Promise, Annis. Promise you won't stop doing those things."

Annis choked down the tears she felt welling in her throat and nodded. "I promise," she whispered hoarsely. She cleared her throat and then repeated the words, this time more firmly. "I promise I won't stop."

"Atta girl." Caroline swept back, coming even with Homer, who, up until now, had taken everything in without saying a word.

"Now then, if that matter's all settled," he began, shifting around in his seat and placing both elbows on the table in front of him. "Why does the dark always have to be scary? What's so splendid about this light that you lot are always thinking it's the better of the two? The easier? The safer? Doesn't light sting your eyes? Can't it burn your skin when it's so bright that it's hot? Fire. Fire is light, is it not? Fire can ravage an entire forest in the blink of an eye. You know what doesn't? Darkness. Darkness is still. It's peaceful. And, contrary to popular belief, entirely harmless."

Caroline touched her mouth with her hand as though she were trying to wipe away her amusement. "Apologies, my love. Poor choice of words," she said.

"He's right, though," Annis said thoughtfully. "Isn't he? There really isn't reason to fear the dark. We only fear what we think it's hiding."

"A-ha!" Homer said, stabbing the air with his finger in triumph. "I've won one over. Hugh better watch out. I may be just as wise as he is."

At this, both women began to laugh hysterically.

"Alright, alright." He waved his hands up and down trying to calm them again. "Now that we've lightened the mood a bit, how about we get out of here and have a little fun of our own today?"

Both Caroline and Annis were more than happy to oblige Homer's request. Within the hour, all three of them were lying together in a large makeshift hammock of spare canvas tarp hanging from two trees in the forest just beyond the railroad tracks.

"Do you do this often?" Annis asked, marveling at the way the sun danced between the tall trees, casting leaf-shaped shadows all around her.

"Whenever the opportunity arises," Caroline said, who'd landed the middle spot but was snuggling into Homer as they swung gently side to side. "How's Finian liking it?" she asked, tipping her head back to get a look at the wolf pup sitting on Annis's chest.

"I think he's enjoying it," Annis said, stroking his soft fur with one hand and bracing him with her palm of the other. He was getting stronger already. It wouldn't be much longer until his eyes opened, and he'd begin running around. Then the real fun would begin. "I think you should be teaching me something," she said, thinking of the night before when Hugh had first brought her to meet Fin. He'd had questions about her day, questions she assumed he'd ask again tonight. "Something more than you've already taught me," she continued. "Don't get me wrong, I think that bit about darkness not being scary will be right up Hugh's alley when he asks me what I learned today, but he doesn't ever seem to like my first answer, so I'd rather have options. Plus, as much as he seems to dismiss the idea, I should actually learn the basic skills required to work around here. I wouldn't mind knowing the ins and outs of your act, just the same."

Homer chuckled. "Hugh getting inside your head, is he?"

"He's not in yours?" Annis asked, finding it hard to believe anyone could escape the impression their ringleader had so prominently left upon her.

He shrugged. "No room."

"I'm all he thinks about," Caroline said with an air of haughtiness, before she cracked and grinned from ear to ear.

"No need to pretend you're joking, love," Homer teased. "We both know it's true."

She nuzzled the side of his neck as he leaned over and kissed her forehead. Annis found them fascinating. They were so kind, so loving, and yet so honest and candid and full of humor about things she used to believe were in poor taste to joke about, like his blindness. But then no one treated Homer's lack of sight as a handicap. It was his superpower, after all.

"How'd you do it then?" Annis asked after several minutes of thought. "How'd you decide on your act? How did you learn it, you know, without Hugh in your head?"

"I didn't say he's never been in it," Homer said, stretching his free arm out overhead and kicking his foot lightly off the ground to swing their hammock. "Once upon a time, he was teaching me the same lessons he's teaching you, Annis. And, when my time came to answer his questions, this was the result. To be seen as daring, not disabled."

"But it couldn't have been easy. I mean, I have perfect vision and there's no way I could do what you do."

Homer nodded. "There's certainly a degree of effort involved. It takes dedication. Loads of trial and error. Perfecting the pitch, learning how long it takes for each flip and then properly pacing the count. Caroline's always been a huge help with that. There are always misses and poor catches along the way, though." He held out his hand for her to see. It was covered in scars left by burns and blades.

Annis gasped at the sight. "Didn't that hurt?"

"Of course," Homer said, tucking his hand back behind his head. "But loads of things in life hurt. And all hurt heals."

Annis wasn't sure she believed that was true, but for the sake of honoring his tale she didn't argue. "What about Caroline?" she asked, nudging the dainty woman beside her who seemed to be dozing right through this conversation. "Weren't you ever scared? In the beginning, when he was still learning?"

"I'm always scared," Caroline admitted. "Scared I'll screw up. That my judgement will be wrong, and he'll get hurt."

It wasn't at all the answer Annis had expected, though she noticed Homer wasn't at all surprised. In fact, he curled his arm more tightly around Caroline, whispering words of comfort in his wife's ear.

"You're never scared...For yourself?" Annis wasn't sure why she was harping on it, but she wanted to know.

Caroline reached up for the hand Homer had tucked behind his head, hiding the painful remnants of their tribulations along the path to perfecting their act. "These aren't his errors. They're mine. They're the times I miscalculated. The moments I wasn't in the right place at the right time. These marks were all meant for me, yet not a single one is on my body." Caroline traced the scars tenderly with her fingertips. "I'm never scared for me," she whispered. "I've never had reason to be."

Annis laid her head back, feelings of awe rising into her throat and building pressure in her eyes. She'd never known anyone as certain of another human being as they were of each other. "How did you two fall in love?" she asked. Her voice was timid but her need to know was stronger than ever.

"It was love at first sight," Homer deadpanned. Both girls let out an unexpected laugh. It was a relief after the heightened emotions that came with their current conversation.

"Was for me," Caroline said, after they'd all settled down again. "First time I saw him, I knew he was mine."

"Was it here? At the circus?"

Caroline let her gaze drift upward to the sky. "It was. After a show. He'd stayed in the audience, waiting."

"What for?" Annis felt her curiosity pique.

"Her," he answered quietly. "She'd walked past me as she went out into the ring. She'd smelled of honey, and her silky long hair had brushed against my arm, giving me chills as she went by. She was talking to herself, muttering under her breath, 'Those who bend can't be broken. Those who fly don't fear the fall.'" He paused, lost in thought. And then he said, "I wanted to fly."

The hand he kept tucked around Caroline's neck moved until he could lazily curl the long strands of her hair around his fingers as he went on. "To think I almost didn't go. Everyone thought it was absurd, a blind man going to see the circus. Everyone thinks it's all about what the eyes see, but I daresay I got a great deal more for my ticket than anyone else did."

Annis caught herself clutching her heart, genuinely touched by the beauty of their romance. "Love at first scent," she said, and then sighed dreamily.

"It's all the rage among blind men," Homer joked. "And, frankly, from what I gather, a great deal more reliable than waging your love on someone's looks. At least if someone smells nice, you can suppose they enjoy a good bath every now and again. And there's really no value too high to be placed on being clean."

Annis felt her eyes widen with surprised delight before she burst into a giggle. She knew someday she'd probably become accustomed to the silly things people said out loud around here, and she already dreaded it. Part of the fun was in never seeing it coming. Which was, of course, how Homer experienced everything.

"Right, then," Caroline mused, her mouth fighting a grin as she watched Annis curl up, still chuckling to herself, and waking Finian as she did. "Anything else you'd like to learn today?"

"No," Annis said, releasing the last of her laughter in a loud hiccup. "I don't think anything you two are teaching me is of any use, anyhow."

"I beg your pardon?" Caroline gasped, pretending to be affronted by the statement.

"It's all fussy romance stuff. Having a partner. Falling in love. It hardly applies to me. And, I'm quite sure, Hugh would prefer it stayed that way."

Caroline looked taken aback. "Why would you say that?"

Annis wiggled her body into a straighter line, just for something to do that would keep her eyes turned away from her companions. "You know."

"Because of Sequoyah," Homer said with certainty. For a man who couldn't see, he never missed a single thing. Or maybe he was so perceptive because he was a man who couldn't see.

"That's ridiculous," Caroline scoffed.

"Is it?" Annis wasn't so sure. "Think about it. He found out about...Whatever there is to find out about us...And turned around and gave me a puppy. Don't get me wrong, I love Finian, but I can't help feeling there's a slight bit of consolation prize happening here. Or, at the very least, a lovely distraction to keep me thinking of things other than his son." She sighed. "Not that I blame him. I wouldn't want me as a potential suitor for anyone I cared about either."

"Why would you say that?" Caroline asked, as though she'd been directly insulted by what Annis said.

"I stumbled out of the woods and into camp two days ago, Caroline. All I had was a name and the clothes on my back. Ripped clothes. Dirty clothes. Ripped and dirty everything. And I may not have seen myself, but I can say with a fair amount of confidence that I was nowhere near presentable, let alone respectable."

Caroline let out a harsh "Ha!" and then she continued, "In two days here, have you met a single person who could qualify as respectable?"

"No," Annis admitted. "But I notice no one else is being courted by Sequoyah either. So, there may well be some correlation between the two points."

"There's not," Homer cut in. "He's not courting anyone because he's not the sort to court a girl he isn't certain about."

"Oh." Annis felt the air deflate from her being.

"Don't go getting all disappointed over nothing," he said with a chuckle. "You're it. Or, you will be when the time comes."

"How do you know?" Annis insisted.

Caroline clapped her hand to her thigh, making a smacking sound. "Have you not listened to anything we've told you today?"

"But that was all about you! It's not got anything to do with me and Sequoyah."

"Or," Homer interjected, fingertip rising skyward preparing to make a point, "maybe it has everything to do with you and Sequoyah and that's why Hugh sent you our way in the first place."

"You can't be serious."

"Not usually," Caroline agreed, bouncing her shoulders playfully. "But in this case, I do believe we are. Aren't we, darling?"

He nodded profusely. "Yes, very much so."

The three of them swung silently back and forth for a while, enjoying the gentle sway of the hammock, the balmy breeze that swept through the branches every so often, and the hum of life that surrounded them with the loveliest music nature had to offer.

Then a rustle in the woods drew Annis's attention and she sprung upright in an instant. "What was that?"

Homer waved his hand lazily. "Movement," he said simply.

Annis understood his meaning. Isolated though they felt, they were hardly alone. Even if it wasn't the sound of an approaching dear or a passing rabbit, they were hardly far enough from camp to assume they were the only people in the vicinity.

Still, despite Homer and Caroline's lacking interest, Annis couldn't settle back into the hammock, with her eyelids lazily shut, as she had before.

Seconds passed. Those turned to minutes, and no suspicious sounds followed the first. Annis was almost ready to abandon her worries when another rustle, several feet down from the first, caught her attention. Her eyes darted between the tree trunks, straining to make out anything other than leaves, branches, or hanging vines. Then Annis caught a dash of blue and a fleeting glimpse of shimmering silver.

"Floyd," she said, giving Caroline a soft nudge. "There, in the trees."

Caroline sighed, eyes still closed, body still nestled to her husband's. "Of course it is," she murmured.

"Shouldn't we do something?" Annis asked, thinking of the sisters and their concern when they'd last seen Floyd headed for the edge of camp.

"No need," Homer assured her. "Floyd is like an old cat. No matter what, he always knows how to find his way home."

"Are you certain?" Annis persisted. "Mabel and Maude seemed quite worried about his wandering off last night."

"Not because of where he might go," Homer explained easily. "But because of what he might encounter. You ought to know better than anyone that you need your wits about you to survive the night out among the wild and the elements. And wits, I'm afraid, Floyd has no longer got."

Annis sat back, her skin against the canvas of the hammock. It was warm and reminded her just how much her life had changed over such a short time. Still, her eyes followed Floyd as best as they could. Something about him made her uneasy. Despite what everyone was telling her about him, she couldn't shake the nagging feeling he wasn't nearly as without his wits as he had everyone believing.

Chapter Eleven
WANTED

That night's show was livelier than the one before. A day of rest had served everyone well. The stands were even more packed, as though everyone from the previous night had come back and brought a friend with them. The seats were filled, and people had to resort to standing. But there was no standing room left. A set of feet occupied every available space. Many of the men even held, on their shoulders, women and children who waved and howled with excitement at everyone who passed by.

Annis stood behind the curtains that separated the ring from the entertainers with her eyes wide and her mouth agape. She could hardly believe how many people she was seeing.

"Tell me honestly," Homer said, coming up beside her. "How many people are out there? Before you answer, keep in mind I get horrible stage fright when loads of people are watching."

Annis looked back and forth between his face and the ever-increasing audience just beyond the curtain. Homer was impossible to read and serious as ever, but he was still Homer and deadpan humor was his favorite, after all.

"Honestly?" Annis took one more look at the crowd, and then closed her eyes, taking in the roar of their anticipation. "Hardly anyone out there. Two, three people maybe. Wait, two more just walked in."

"So, five in total, then." Homer nodded, maintaining his iron-clad expression. "Brilliant. That's just the right amount of people I like to perform in front of."

"Talk about perfect." Annis smirked. Homer's special brand of humor was quickly becoming her favorite form of entertainment.

"Indeed," Homer agreed, at last cracking his own subtle smirk.

"What are you two doing lurking at the curtain? Anything interesting happening out there?" Caroline asked, sidling up to them and peeling back the thick material to peek for herself. "Oh, would you look at that."

"What?" Annis hurried to regain her spot where the sliver of light shone through and all the most important parts of the tent became visible.

"Not every night the local authorities turn up to take in a show," Caroline observed, nodding toward the far left where Annis spotted two men in uniforms.

"What do you suppose they want?" she asked, ignoring the quiver in her own voice. They couldn't be there for her. It wasn't possible.

"They're here for Smalls," Maude chimed in from behind them. "He caused quite the ruckus in town today. Serves him right they followed him home."

"What will they do to him?" Though Annis was instantly worried for her friend, she couldn't help but feel relieved knowing she was still safe, still hidden.

"Oh, I doubt they'll do anything," Maude said, flicking her wrist and dismissing all reasons for concern. "He didn't do anything illegal. Just," she paused to flare her eyes at them for added theatrics, "stirred things up a bit."

"Lord, don't tell me it was anywhere I sent you," Caroline groaned, covering her eyes with her hand and shaking her head as though she were already dreading the answer.

"It was *everywhere* you sent us," Maude replied with a laugh. "And Sawyer was sure to spout your name every chance he got, so probably best you don't go back the next few times we pass through town."

"Which reminds me, your mother said to tell you hi, and, well, never mind what else she said," Mabel said, her words dying slowly in a quiet mutter.

Caroline's body stiffened at the mention of her mother. Her expression hardened, showing a side of Caroline Annis hadn't seen before. "I never mind the things she says," she said coldly, her gaze drifting to Homer, who seemed to purposely be tuning out the conversation by staring blankly toward the back of the tent, where the rest of the crew was causing the usual pre-show commotions.

Sensing the need to change the topic and shift the intensity into a more manageable and lighthearted chatter, Annis blurted, "Should we tell Sawyer they're here for him?"

"Who's here for me?" he asked, strolling over in his usual carefree manner at the sound of his name. Annis found it hard to believe he could really be completely oblivious to the trouble he'd caused. In all likelihood, he just wasn't bothered by it. Or, even more likely, he was pleased with himself.

"The police," Caroline informed him sternly. "Want to tell us what you did so we know how to protect you?"

He shrugged, mischief blazing in his eyes as he fought back a smirk. "Didn't do anything. Was just walking about. Not my fault no one ever looks down."

"Is it your fault then when you don't look up?" Maude said. "You know, to read all the signs which so clearly indicate where you are and are not allowed to just be walking about."

He tossed his hands up, pleading innocence. "Signs are meant to be at eye level. If it's important, they should make sure it's posted where *everyone* can see."

"It's true," Homer added. "It's the same rule I live by where signs are concerned. If I can't see it, I don't have to follow it."

Caroline, trying not to laugh, poked his side with her elbow. "You stay out of this. You're just encouraging him."

"Also," Maude said to Homer, "I don't think they would have minded much if *you'd* walked into their private parlors and dressing rooms. Nor would anyone have felt too put out over you taking in a free performance in the saloon when everyone else had to pay to watch the dancers on stage. Some of those posted rules really don't much apply to you."

"Ah, the silver lining of being a blind man," Homer mused. "Always there, hiding in plain sight, isn't it?"

Annis had to cover her mouth to muffle the laughter.

"Why do you all always look so guilty when I walk up?" Hugh asked, joining the small crowd gathered around the curtain.

"Because you taught us well," Caroline quipped.

"And now I live to regret it," Hugh countered, looming over them. One of his long arms reached around to take the curtain from Annis and Caroline and zipped it shut. "Don't you lot have a show to be ready for? Or did the audience out there escape your attention whilst you were over here rehashing the chaos that followed you home from the city?" He cast a disapproving glance down at Sawyer. "Oh, yes, Smalls. I *heard*."

"Be honest, Poppy," Sawyer said, grinning. "You're not really surprised I became a wanted man in less than the course of an afternoon."

"I suppose some days being wanted is all that matters," Maude teased as she and Mabel began to walk away from the huddle. "Even if you are only wanted by the *law*."

"Alright, alright," Hugh said, waving his hands for Sawyer to stop before he started to deliver his retort. "I'm walking out there in exactly ten seconds. I expect everyone to be ready and to follow on their cues." He stood taller, squaring his shoulders and fixing his top hat. "Annis, love, hand me that cane, would you?" he asked, pointing at a long black cane with a white tip that leaned against a stack of crates behind her.

"Don't you mean wand?" she asked, handing it over to him with a broad smile as she recalled their chat about his mysterious, magical ways, which he'd denied, of course.

He tapped her head with the cane playfully. "Shush." Then he spun on his heal, took a deep breath, and walked out. He proceeded to take the circus arena by storm with his whirlwind of sensationalized speech, his waves of theatrical gestures, and his abounding thunderous energy.

When Annis turned around, all but one of the others had dispersed to busy themselves with last-minute preparations before it was their turn to enter the ring. Homer was still standing beside her, a contented smirk resting on his face as his hands played with a dagger, flipping it over, again and again, and catching it perfectly every time.

"Not making you nervous, am I?" he asked, clearly sensing he'd drawn her attention.

"No." An entirely true statement, she realized, even as she said it. "Oddly enough, I'm completely at ease being within inches of your flying blades."

"Oh, good." He thrust the dagger even higher. "Won't mind if I light it up then, get a little warmed up before I walk out?"

"Personally, no," Annis played along. "But Viola and her sisters are coming this way as we speak, and I have to tell you, their gowns are covered in feathers and look entirely too flammable to be anywhere near you and your warm-ups."

He caught the blade and tucked it carefully into the holster he wore on his belt. "Fair enough. No flames just yet."

Annis watched as all three women scurried past, all looking magnificent in their gowns adorned with beautiful feathers and dyed to match their individual tastes. Viola donned a vibrant fuchsia, Etta a brilliant yellow, and Lila a pristine shade of sky blue. All three briefly greeted Homer and Annis before they slipped through the curtain, taking center stage as their voices rang through the air.

Homer leaned in close until his shoulder tapped hers. "Close your eyes," he whispered.

"What?" Annis was only half listening. She was too busy trying to watch what little she could through the crack in the curtain without being seen.

"Just close them," he insisted. "Trust me."

Annis felt herself tighten up. It was a reminder that she didn't, and would never again, trust anyone. The idea began to run on repeat inside her mind as it had for those days she'd been alone in the woods. Then Homer's hand reached down, fumbling for hers until he found it. He gave it a gentle squeeze, urging her to listen to him. Slowly, the voice in her mind faded. The words stopped and the intention, the vow she'd made to herself to never believe in anyone again, to never trust, became obsolete. Because she did trust Homer. How could anyone not trust him when the woman who loved him most in the world trusted him with her life night after night? And when he, who loved her more deeply than Annis had ever seen anyone be loved before, trusted himself with it, as well? Homer was to be trusted. Annis finally did as he'd requested and closed her eyes.

As soon as she did, she felt herself fill up with the sounds of the sisters singing. Their songs were beautiful, more beautiful even than she'd remembered. The music overwhelmed her as she took it in, undiluted and unencumbered by any visual stimulus. Her body began to melt into itself, releasing every bit of tension until the last of it escaped in an audible sigh. The emotion of every note rang crystal clear through the air and landed on her heart, where she soaked it in and reveled in the bliss of bathing her spirit in such sweet music.

"Welcome to my world," Homer muttered softly, giving her hand one last squeeze before he released it. Annis held her eyes shut through the rest of the acts, allowing her to experience Babe's harp and Oscar's humor in new and deeper ways.

"Your world is lovely," she breathed, hearing the swish of Mabel and Maude's gowns as they passed by, followed by the rhythmic thud of footsteps she knew belonged to her two favorite gentle giants, Edi and Millie.

"Introducing Annis to the magic of sound?" Caroline's voice rang in Annis's ears and her lids flew open.

"It is my specialty," Homer said, bowing slightly.

"One of many," Caroline murmured, leaning in to kiss his cheek. When she pulled back from him, her eyes met Annis's. "Wait until you meet with scent. That one's my favorite," she said with a wink before she sauntered off, calling back, "We're up next, darling."

Annis watched as Caroline flitted about, making final checks on all of their equipment. Only when she was absolutely certain all was as it should be did Annis see Caroline begin to relax, filling what she had left of her time with stretching her body for the upcoming twisting and bending she had in store for it. She flipped forward and backward as the red sequins on her corset danced wildly under the lights. The flashes created a stark contrast with her long ivory legs, which drew the eye as easily as the sparkles did.

"It doesn't bother you," Annis mumbled, half to herself and half in hopes of an answer, "the costumes she wears, knowing what everyone else can see...And you can't?"

She felt Homer shift his weight back and forth between his feet, but she didn't dare look at him, worried she would see him uncomfortable, embarrassed by her stupid questions. Always she had them, and always they seemed to spill out.

"I can see plenty," Homer answered at last. Even in the subtle rumbles of his deep voice, she could tell he was smiling. "And see it better than anyone else. You forget I see through touch. All that skin the rest of the world gets to take in with their eyes? I get to feel it with my hands. Her warmth. Her softness. Who cares what parts of her their gaze sweeps over when it's me who gets to hold her, and truly see her for who she is?"

Annis bumped him with her side. "I think maybe you really could give Hugh a run for his money someday, Homer."

"It's my grand plan." He lifted his finger to his lips. "Don't tell anyone."

"I would never," she promised through her laughter. It was short-lived, however. Homer and Caroline were up. Flying, flaming daggers being thrown through human hoops were no laughing matter.

Even after spending the day with them, learning the ins and outs of the act and watching them rehearse, Annis still found their performance captivating. It was as though the audience contributed a final piece of the act, launching the energy to new heights and pushing Homer and Caroline to give more than even they knew they were capable of.

"Never gets old, does it?" a familiar, deep voice said beside her.

She turned to face Sequoyah and smiled before she even saw him. "You tell me. It's only my third show."

"It's well past my third, and I still find them completely fascinating." He stepped in closer until his arm was brushing hers. She wondered if it was due to the cramped space or just a desire to be near her. She hoped it was the latter.

"I don't think I've seen you since breakfast," she said, attempting to sound as though this had only just occurred to her. The truth was, she'd been looking for him all day and growing increasingly anxious every time she realized how long it had been since their paths had crossed.

"With everyone out and about, there was plenty to do here." He must have heard how put out she sounded because he continued in a much milder tone. "Also, I didn't much want to be seen."

"Because of me." Guilt rushed from the pit of her stomach straight to her face, turning her cheeks a hot red. "I'm really sorry I pried. I shouldn't have done that. Please forgive me."

He shook his head, a sheepish smile slowly surfacing. "You didn't do anything wrong, Annis. I'm the one who blew everything out of proportion."

She disagreed. "You have every right to want to maintain some privacy. Your past is your past. I shouldn't have insisted on dragging it into the present, on somehow having a part of it."

"But that's the thing," he turned toward her, timidly reaching for her hand and tenderly lacing his fingers between hers. "I want you to have a part of it. Because, someday, I'll want you to be a part of everything. And how can I expect you to truly commit to my future if you haven't known my past?"

She swallowed hard, forcing down a new wave of guilt. "I don't see why one has to be tied to the other. Who we were before, whatever happened to us, none of it has to be a part of who we become or part of the life we have moving forward."

He looked taken aback. "You don't really believe that."

She nodded. "I do. You don't need to share things with me, the painful things you'd rather forget, the things you don't want to talk about, whatever the reason. I don't need to know."

"I do," he said with a finality she hadn't expected. "I do need to know. Not today. Not tomorrow. But someday, Annis, I'll need to know. And I'll need you to know, as well. It's the only way this thing between us will ever be real. The only way we'll truly be together, sharing the good and the bad of life. No matter how bad the bad is."

She didn't answer. She couldn't. All she could do was turn her gaze back out to the ring where Caroline was balancing her body in a one-handed handstand on a square wooden block barely larger than her hand. The block was perched atop a metal rod that stood several feet tall. Her lower body curled over like a scorpion, with her toes reaching down to touch the back of her head. Meanwhile, Homer stood to one side of her, throwing daggers straight through the space she'd created by hollowing her back and bending her legs around toward her head. Each knife he threw zipped through the hoop of her body with a loud swish before it landed with a cutting thud into a hand-painted wooden target. The scene was enough to take anyone's breath away.

"Annis." She heard Sequoyah say her name, but she still couldn't bring herself to answer his last request. He wanted to know. Everything. She understood, of course, why it mattered to him. It had, after all, mattered to her only a few short hours ago. She'd been desperate to know what had hurt him, even if she'd known she couldn't take that hurt away. She'd needed to know, just the same. She hadn't even considered why, until he'd spelled it out for her. Until she'd seen, just now, the potential outcome of what he was asking. Caroline and Homer had no secrets, no unshared parts between them, and it showed in everything they did, in every interaction they shared. It was the most beautiful intimacy Annis had ever seen.

At last she turned toward him. "I'll get there," she whispered. "I promise, I'll get there."

He nodded, the gentle curve of his mouth and endless pouring of warmth from his eyes flowing down upon her, telling her all she needed to know. It was enough for him, for now. Because he was gracious beyond reason, it was enough.

The end of Caroline and Homer's act marked the end of Annis's time peeking from behind the curtain. As soon as they swept through, followed by boundless waves of applause, Annis fell into step behind them, lightening their load of props as they hurried to clear the way for the next act.

They were barely outside the tent when Goldilocks strolled over and handed Annis the bundle in his hands. "I believe this is yours," he said. "Was in the elephant cart getting things ready for the girls to come back when I heard him moving about. Figured it must be close to feeding time again."

Annis smiled at him gratefully. "Thanks, Jacob." She slipped back the linens that swaddled Finian and gasped. "His eyes are open!"

"Your little babe is growing up," Caroline joked, leaning in to see for herself. "Won't be long now and he'll be adding his own flare to the constant chaos and commotion around here."

"Won't that be fun?" Homer chided.

"I don't think I'd considered the getting more active phase," Annis admitted, tucking her cheek to cuddle the pup who stretched up to meet her with the top of his head.

Caroline laughed. "Thought he'd stay sweet, cuddly, and contained forever?"

"I can't deny I was perfectly content not thinking beyond the little bundle he showed up as." In any event, Annis thought, those days would soon be over. Now would be as good a time as any to consider the long-term consequences of having a wolf pup. She would have a full-grown wolf. On second thought, maybe she was better off just taking things one day at a time.

In quiet comfort, the threesome made their way back to Caroline and Homer's wagon. Packing up was fast and efficient. They had nearly everything loaded by curtain call, which the pair had to return to the ring for. Annis stayed behind to fuss over Fin, who already seemed to be moving around more, taking in his surroundings with curiosity, and spending a great deal of time studying her. She had a feeling as though he were etching every detail of her face into his mind's eye so he would know her forever.

Standing outside with the cub, enjoying the night sky and the golden glow of the moon, Annis listened for the roar of the crowds from the tent. It wouldn't be long before people dispersed and the work of breaking down would begin. The circus would disappear again, until the next time they came through town.

It was hard for Annis to process. The days seemed to last forever, but then they'd finish in a flash. There were moments when she felt as though she'd spent a lifetime here already, and others when the reality of her past life still crept closely at her heels.

The sound of voices drew Annis attention and she took several steps back, retreating into the shadows of the tent. The police officers she'd seen before the show were still walking around camp, stopping to question the stragglers.

"You there," one of the officers called out and Annis followed his pointed finger to Momma T, who was carrying her empty dish tub back to the train. "Where can we find tiny man? And don't tell me he's not here. It's only when you lot come to town that the freaks start running about."

Momma T stopped. Her expression hardly impressed upon them a desire to help, but she opened her mouth to answer just the same. "Tiny man. Clever." Her head tilted back as she jutted her chin forward toward the tent behind the officers. "Only one of those we got was in the show."

The officer shook his head. "No, I mean, really small. Couldn't be any taller than my niece and she's still in diapers."

Momma smirked and shook her head. "Then you may have your own freaks in town after all. All of ours are accounted for from the moment the show starts until it ends. If you didn't see him in there, he's not one of ours."

Annis didn't know whether to laugh or feel offended on Sawyer's behalf. Of course they'd seen Sawyer. He'd taken center stage for his act, just the same as every other night. He only seemed larger than life when he was defying death by sticking his head between the jaws of a massive lion.

"This is a waste of time," the officer huffed, turning away and dismissing Momma T without a word of thanks. She started walking again, slower this time, as though she meant to keep an eye on the wandering officers for as long as she could.

Two more men in uniforms showed up, this time from the opposite end of camp, as though they'd been making the rounds before the show even ended. Annis drew a silent gasp when she spotted Floyd walking just behind them. It was hard to tell if they were aware of him or not, and harder still to determine if he was aware of them. Not wanting to give up the safety of darkness, Annis drew forward as far as the shadows allowed and squinted, trying her best to make out the situation among the strange threesome coming her way.

Then, before they were close enough for Annis to make out what they were saying, one of the officers turned around. She watched as he spoke to Floyd. A moment later, they parted ways, the officers joining the rest of their party and heading for the camp's exit. Floyd still fumbled about, aimlessly.

Or so she thought.

Within seconds, his shuffling footsteps had led him within in feet of her hiding place.

"Murdered her," he muttered under his breath, eyes blank and cast toward the starlit sky. "Do it again."

Annis felt her body go frigid. She was unable to move, unable to think. She stood there, keeping still in the cover of darkness, as he approached. When they were both in the shadows together, his eyes lowered to meet hers. "There you are," he whispered. Then, as quickly as he had surfaced, his eyes glazed and his words turned inaudible. He began shuffling his feet again, moving past her and back into what remained of the camp.

Panic swelled in her chest, hindering her breath. Crazy or not, Floyd was awake in there. And he knew things, things he couldn't possibly know. Unless someone had told him. But who? Even the police officers hadn't been there for her. They'd been after Smalls.

Except one *had* stopped to talk to Floyd, and then Floyd had come to her.

Murdered her.

The words stilled her racing mind, making it impossible to think or to act.

She wanted to run for help. She wanted to tell someone what she'd seen and heard, but her stilled mind also stalled her instincts. Her frozen state was an act of self-preservation, she realized. It kept her from doing anything rash she wouldn't be able to undo.

Murdered her.

The words played inside her mind over and over. Words she knew she could never tell anyone. Not when the words that had followed were, "do it again."

How long she stood there, feeling made of lead and stone, she couldn't say. It wasn't until life spilled from the tent that life came back to her as well, reminding her that even after what she'd witnessed, she'd not yet ceased to exist. More unknown was left for her to discover, more battles for her to fight. Only time would tell who would be on her side when her fate unfolded.

For now, dwelling on things she could not change served no purpose, and so she welcomed the hustle and bustle sweeping through camp that kept her and everyone else busy until there was nothing but dust and dirt where there once stood an entire circus.

She was on her way to find Maude and Mabel, ready to settle in for the night and do her best to forget what happened with Floyd, when Hugh tracked her down.

"There you are, love," he said, spotting her walking with Bess and August. "Spare a minute?"

"For you?" She tilted her head. "Is it ever really just a minute, Hugh?"

He chuckled. "Fair point." He hooked her arm with his and tipped his head down sideways in her direction her. "Let's walk."

And walk they did—right past the cart she'd been aiming for and instead toward the train's engine.

"Am I being kicked out?" Annis asked, casting a worried eye at the empty tracks ahead.

"Depends," Hugh said, his flat tone giving no indication whether he was serious. "You learn anything today?"

She snorted. "I could write a book on all the things I learned today. But I'm guessing you'd want to skip the chapters on dress mending and silver polishing." She bounced her shoulders thoughtfully. "Knife sharpening likely wouldn't interest you, either, though I suspect you'd begin to find interest in the parts I'd dedicate to being pretty in a way that isn't skin deep and the ways in which we are devalued by being valued only for our most superficial and vanity-based contributions."

He nodded, chuckling softly. "Indeed, I would find that to be of interest, though it would only add to my curiosity. You'd have to deliver more."

"Oh, I could," she maintained, fully confident in the things she had to share with Hugh tonight. "Because I would move on to seeing the world from a blind man's perspective," she paused, waiting for him to react.

"I see Homer's sense of humor has made an impact," he said with a smirk.

Annis grinned and, fully satisfied with herself, carried on. "From there, I would beautifully tie together the perfect harmony that comes to life when the blind man falls in love with the woman who's only ever been appreciated for being pretty."

"This could turn out to be the best book I've ever read." He cocked his brow at her, waiting to hear what else she had in store for him.

"You really are hard to please. Your standards are almost unattainably high" she sighed, "Anyone ever tell you that?"

"Love, I've heard that at least ten times just since the end of the show tonight." He unhooked his arm from hers and placed his palm on her back and guided her toward a large fallen tree trunk alongside the tracks. "Let's have a seat so you can collect your thoughts and really prepare for the grand finale." He wiggled his brow at her, teasing.

Annis did her best to feign a grumble, though she was sure he could tell she was being overly theatrical for his sake. Truth was, she'd been preparing for this part of their evening chat ever since she'd figured out why he'd sent her to spend the day with Caroline and Homer after he'd been opposed to the idea the previous day.

Still, she waited until they both had a seat. They sat in silence and stared out at the night sky for some time, enchanted by the magic of the stars sparkling in the deep blue above them.

When she felt the contentment spread through her until it was seeping out, she took a breath and said, "Trust."

Hugh never turned away from the stars. "Trust?"

"People always think love is the greatest thing they can share with others, but it's not. Trust is."

He gave no indication whether he agreed or not, but she held his attention. "And why is that?"

"Because trust is the only thing which truly grants you connection. Trust is what makes you feel safe enough to let someone in, really in, to your heart, to your inner most thoughts, to your fears. It's not until you can let someone enter into those deep, secret parts of yourself that you are truly no longer alone in the world." She paused to collect her thoughts before she continued. "We can be loved by a million people and still feel lonely. And we can love others as freely as we breathe and still feel as though we're suffocating from the pain of isolation. Love is nice and all, but it's hollow without trust to fill it."

Hugh blinked his eyes at her slowly, conveying a silent approval. Then he stood from the log, giving her shoulder a squeeze in lieu of a verbal goodnight before he finally chose to speak again. When he did, it was simply and straight to the point. "You'll be with Bess tomorrow, love." He pointed a lone finger toward the stars as he walked away. "Trust. It's an awful lot like faith, isn't it? Except one is in humans and the other is in the great mystery of life. Master one, you master both. And loneliness ceases to exist forever."

Annis watched as he made his way back to the train. It wasn't until he disappeared into the shadows that she redirected her eyes toward the night sky. The moon was only a silver sliver of light, but there was still no denying her presence in the sky. Every night, without fail, the moon was there. Maybe Annis's faith could start there. Maybe the moon would be the first thing she chose to believe in and depend upon. She thought it would be a safe, and almost silly effort toward regaining her trust in the great mysteries of life, had it not been for the fact that she knew her faith would grow from there. Faith was but a seed that simply needed to be planted.

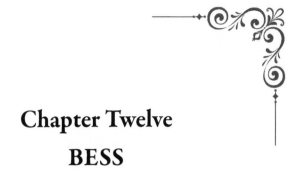

Chapter Twelve
BESS

"Was starting to worry you'd had your fill of the open road already," Maude said when Annis wandered into the cabin just as the train was beginning to move.

"Hardly." Annis plopped down onto her bed, realizing for the first time that night how exhausted she was. She also couldn't help but notice that this was a completely new sort of being depleted. While her days of traveling on foot had already taught her that she'd never been truly tired in her life before then, the heightened levels of physical and emotional emptiness were now being replaced with a new, almost pleasant feeling. A feeling of having given her all. Every last ounce of energy and devotion she possessed, she'd dedicated to her work, and that was more satisfying than she ever would have thought possible.

As Annis laid back on the pillows, Finian's little body began to squirm its way free from the sling across her chest, wiggling out face first, his eyes bright and curious.

"Oh," Annis said with a gasp, sitting straight up again. "I almost forgot. Finian's been widening his horizons through sight this evening."

"Let's have a look, then," Mabel said cheerfully. "Darling baby blues, I bet."

Annis nodded, turning him around in her lap to give the twins a better view. "Will they stay that way, do you think?"

Maude shook her head. "Not likely. Most wolves have dark eyes. Browns, ambers. But, you never know. Won't change over for a few more weeks."

Annis glanced back at Finian, taking in his sweet face, which now had a very different appearance with his opened eyes, big and blue. She wasn't sure why she always asked Maude all of her questions, or why she was never surprised when she in turn had the answers.

"How'd you get to be so smart, anyway?" Annis asked, playing with the pup, rolling him over and scratching his belly. "Is there anything you don't know?"

"Yes," Maude said dryly. "I haven't a clue why Mabel insists on chewing on garlic cloves every night before bed, but I certainly do wish she'd stop." She glared at her sister, who responded by chomping down more dramatically than ever.

"I'll have you know, garlic is very good for you. And I chew it for my health. And yours, incidentally," Mabel scoffed. "You should be thanking me."

"I'll thank you when I don't have to smell you," her sister responded, scrunching up her nose. "Meanwhile, to answer your first question, Annis, books. I got smart because I liked books, and books were aplenty in our home growing up. Mostly because our mother found if she kept my supply heavy, I didn't make silly requests about wanting to go outside. Books brought the outside to me, and so it was enough."

"I didn't like books," Mabel pointed out, though Annis could have guessed this on her own.

"What did you do to keep busy?"

"Same thing she does now," Maude said, eyes cast sideways at her sister. "Daydream and drive me crazy."

"And," Mabel cut in loudly, "I always fancied myself a story-teller, so while Maude was reading, I was writing. Or thinking about writing. That's really what all my daydreams were about, you know. All the grand adventures I wanted to write about."

Annis interest was piqued. "Really? Do you still do it? Write, I mean." Clearly, they all knew she was still exceptionally fond of daydreaming, or nightdreaming while awake. What would that be called? Annis wondered. Wake-dreaming?

"Haven't the time anymore," Mabel admitted. "But I don't miss it because now I have plenty of real stories and far more people to tell them to."

"All these extra people and I still can't get out of being your audience," Maude grumbled. "But, speaking of people who like to tell stories, how was your little chat with Poppy tonight?"

"Good," Annis said, mentally revisiting the talk they'd had. "I haven't had to burden anyone two days in a row yet, so I think I'm learning what I'm supposed to."

"Isn't this your third night in here with us?" Maude asked, cocked brow and a wicked smirk.

"Very funny." Annis tossed a pillow at her, but it hit Mabel instead, who pouted thoroughly for about three seconds before she whipped the pillow around her sister's head, making up for Annis's miscalculations. "I'm only allowed to be around you lot during sleeping hours, what does that tell you?"

"That we're capable of imparting wisdom even under the most inopportune circumstances, like, say, for instance, to a sleeping pupil," Maude countered.

"Oh, please," Mabel sneered. "We hardly ever sleep around here, anyway." The sisters finally settled down and stretched out on their bunk. "Meanwhile, who's your lucky guide tomorrow?"

"Bess." Annis had been thinking about her ever since Hugh mentioned her name the night before. After the last two days, she was beginning to feel as though she understood the genius behind his madness a little better, and it motivated her to try to decipher his intentions. He hadn't chosen Bess at random. There was a method to all of it. Bess had a lesson for her, one that more than likely aligned itself nicely with those she'd already learned.

"You'll have fun with Bess," Mabel said, fluffing her pillow. "She's got a sprite personality. Never takes anything too seriously. Always good for a laugh. And I do mean always."

"Sense of humor bodes well for a girl who's always staring death in the eye," Maude muttered dryly.

"That does seem to a be a common theme around here," Annis said, thinking out loud. "Caroline likes having daggers thrown at her, Sawyer puts his head into a lion's mouth night after night, and Sequoyah jumps from horse to horse while they're all galloping their way through the arena. I'm really starting to wonder if I should be taking advice from anyone here. There are clearly some judgement issues."

"You'll notice Mabel and I did not make that list," Maude said with a haughty smile drawn upon her lips. "The only poor choices we make are in the company we keep."

"Present company excluded, I'm sure," Annis said, eyes wide as she waited for confirmation.

"Sure," Maude agreed with a noncommittal shrug. Annis felt tempted to toss another pillow her way, but her supply was running low and the odds were good that she'd hit Mabel on the way to Maude, and the former might not be as forgiving the second time.

"Ignore her," Mabel said with a dismissive flick of her hand. "If you'd been in town with us today, you'd have known we made far worse choices than you could possibly imagine. Maude's just riding your wave of ignorance as far as it will take her for as long as the tide is out. Soon enough, you'll be there to witness some idiotic thing we do, and there'll be no denying the company we keep is the only decent choice we've managed in recent years."

This time, Maude walloped her with the pillow. "Shut it," she hissed, stifling a laugh. "We had a good thing going. Why'd you have to go and ruin it?"

Mabel threw the pillow back onto Annis's bed. "She never believed you for one second!"

"I tried," Annis offered, "but I was there when Bess pitched Hugh that ridiculous idea of having Edi and Millie hold her tightrope and you were both in on it, so, you know, all hope of believing in your better judgement was essentially lost in that instant."

Maude huffed. "If you recall, neither of us was volunteering to tiptoe across it."

Annis laughed. "Yes. That did make me think more highly of you."

Maude conceded her argument at last by bursting into a fit of giggles loud enough to draw several of their neighbors into their car. And so the nightly shenanigans began all over again.

Come morning, Annis was about as well rested as she'd expected given the late-night visits and the countless times Finian woke her, either for food or out of boredom or loneliness. Despite the lack of sleep, she felt energized and excited for the day. She'd liked Bess from the first time she'd met her, and she was looking forward to getting to know her better.

Even as the train was hissing across the tracks, Annis began to move her way through the cars until she found the one Bess shared with Della and the three sisters. Compared to Mabel and Maude's little cabin, this one had to be considered a mansion. It spanned nearly three times the length and its ceilings reached higher. Annis supposed they needed the room, given there were five of them all sharing the space, and, though three of them were sisters, it was likely none of them had ever found themselves forced to become comfortable with having another human being in their personal space at all hours of the day and night.

"Good morning," Annis called out when no one seemed to take notice of her arrival.

"Annis!" Bess beamed at her briefly before doing a summersault off the top bunk she'd been occupying and landing feet first on the ground, as always. "Poppy said you'd be coming around! You've met all the girls, right?"

All four women looked up from their various morning activities to greet her and she waved back with great enthusiasm. She'd been admiring all of them from a distance the last three nights and was eager to see up close all of their talents today. Even if she was only officially shadowing Bess, she imagined this group wouldn't be much unlike the troupe that included Mabel and Maude in that they continually reconvene throughout the day.

Annis followed Bess to the back of the cabin, where both had a seat on the bench that spread from corner to corner, separated only by the doorway leading to the next car.

"It's not usually this roomy in here," Bess explained. "Most trips we get loaded up with every bit of odds and ends that no one gets around to picking up until the last minute. Having two days in the same spot helped offset some of that chaos. You wait, come see me tomorrow morning and you'll have to dig me out from under layers of costumes and props, and possibly even pieces of tent." She laughed brightly and Annis remembered what Mabel had said about her. She really was a good sport about things.

"Ever think about telling them to get more organized?" Annis suggested.

"And push take off out even farther every night? Nah." She shook her head. "Besides, it's not all bad. You're only used to seeing how us girls live here. We've got it good, because there's less of us, see. The boys are all piled in on top of each other, nothing but bunks and more bunks in their carts. Not that they seem to mind much. All they seem to care about is having a place to stretch and close their eyes. Easy keepers, boys." She laughed again. "Is that your wolf cub?" she asked, apparently noticing for the first time the sling tied to Annis's chest.

"Finian," Annis said, peeling back the material to give her look. "He's just had breakfast, so he won't be all that exciting until after his nap now."

"He's adorable!" Bess exclaimed. "And splendid name choice, Annis."

"Thanks." It wasn't a compliment she'd expected, but she was happy to accept it nonetheless. "How long do you think it'll be before we stop?" The sun had been up for ages already, and passing daylight meant lost hours of work they couldn't make up before nightfall. It also meant waiting for breakfast, and Annis was finding she'd already gotten quite accustomed to Momma T's regular hours of operation. Wouldn't be much longer before her stomach could compete with Sawyer's lions for loudest roar.

"Babe came through earlier," Bess told her, eyes moving toward the window behind Annis, apparently watching the scenery as it passed. "Said we'd be stopped right around breakfast and to see to it that we get Momma set up first, and then get on with chores. Of course, that's just us lot without animals to care for. All those who do are to see to their charges first, everything else second. Part of being responsible for another life. Meeting their needs before any other because they've had to forfeit their abilities to do so for themselves since they're here, in the care of humans."

It was an interesting perspective, and one Annis hadn't considered before. She was relieved to find her instinct had been properly aligned with the animals-first culture where Finian's care was concerned. She'd compromised her own needs and made him her priority from the moment he'd been handed to her. After all, he was helpless. She was not.

"Well, I'm all for helping get Momma T set up," Annis said, tucking the sling in more securely to ensure Finian stayed safe, sound, and asleep, until after they ate. "Though, I've never done it, so I may need a little instruction as we go." Then, worried she might have sounded like more of a chore than a help, she quickly added, "I'm a fast learner though, and strong. Just point me in the right direction and I'll be good to go."

Bess leaned forward, placing her hand on Annis' arm. "You know, I'm really thrilled Poppy picked me today. Especially after that spur of the moment craziness you spun over lunch the other day, I just knew the two of us would get on famously."

Annis sighed an internal breath of relief. She wasn't a bother. "Thank you for saying that."

"Oh, it's more than that," Bess said, her bright eyes locking on Annis's. "I really mean it." Then she laughed again. Annis joined in this time.

"So, tell me, Annis," Bess began after the two settled down, a comfortable quiet spreading between them. "What sort of adventure are you in search of?"

"What do you mean?" Annis wasn't sure she was searching for any adventure. Admittedly, it did seem to have found her, but her initial intentions had simply been to stay alive. Escaping certain death seemed about as grand an adventure as she was hoping for.

"I mean, in life. What do you want? The road is open, the tracks are endless, every door is available. What do you choose?"

Hardly any of those scenarios sounded plausible to Annis. The road was not open, unless it was a one-way street and it was leading in the opposite direction of home with no end in sight. The tracks perhaps seemed endless, but they didn't exactly stray from the course. Doors opening to reveal her wishes coming true were based on fairy tale ideas she ceased to believe in the day all her dreams had turned to nightmares instead.

"I'm not really sure, to be honest," Annis admitted. "Truth is, I'm sort of on a day-to-day track at the moment."

Bess's big brown eyes widened even more. "You're wanted by the law!"

"What?" Annis laughed in surprise. "No, silly. I'm the most pathetically innocent person you would ever hope to meet. I've never even taken an extra candy from my grandmother's candy dish. I'm so good at being good and horribly bad at being bad. The law would have no use for me." Provided the law was honest, Annis added to herself.

Bess twisted her mouth up thoughtfully. "Well, it was worth a shot."

Then it dawned on Annis. "You're trying to figure out my story!"

"I am," Bess admitted with no signs of regret or sheepishness. Her eager face was bursting with curiosity. "Are you going to tell me? You could, you know. I'm a vault. The only one around, incidentally. In case you hadn't noticed, there's not a secret keeper in the whole lot around here. Well, minus Babe, of course, but she's in a secret keeping league all her own."

She had noticed. "No need for secrets when you have trust, right?"

Bess's eyes narrowed as she leaned back against the window. "Ah, I see what you did there." She nodded, grinning. "That's alright. You'll get there. Trust is a hot commodity out there in the big, scary world. Here, in the circus, we have it in abounding quantities. Won't be long, and we'll all be up to our necks in Annis tales, right along with everyone else's." She winked, as if to let Annis know she'd be proving her point sooner than Annis might expect.

Part of her hoped Bess was right. However, before she could contemplate the matter any further, the train began to slow. Then, squealing loudly on the tracks, it came to a stop.

Bess clapped her hands. "Girls, let's get to work."

Della and the sisters were already on their feet and headed for the door. With Viola leading the way and Annis bringing in the caboose, the fivesome made their way outside and straight for Momma T's or, rather, where Momma T's would shortly be.

They were soon met by August and Oscar, followed closely by Goldilocks, Francis, and Will. They all worked side by side to set up the food tent. In under an hour's time, it began to take proper shape. The longer they worked, the more people showed up to help. Before long, the tantalizing scents of Momma T's breakfast filled the air.

Seated with five women and not a single male within earshot of the table for a change, Annis found that the breakfast conversation had a different dynamic than what she'd already grown accustomed to with her usual crew.

"You're looking pale, Della. Are you sure you're feeling alright?" Viola asked the young trapeze artist. Annis guessed Della was probably in her late twenties, like Bess, with heavily freckled skin, bright green eyes, and auburn hair that shone a violent shade of red in the sunlight.

"Haven't been sleeping well," Della answered, approaching her breakfast with a great deal more etiquette than Annis had seen from anyone in a while. Della, she suspected, had come from a life much like her own. The tell-tale signs were there. She placed her napkin in her lap and never slouched or rested an arm on the table. She allowed herself only dainty bites of food and chewed delicately, with her mouth pursed shut and her jaws barely moving as her teeth milled the food back and forth. Her pinky finger lifted every time she had a sip of her tea. "I'm sure I just need a good night's rest and I'll be back in top form," she finished, carefully cutting her slice of ham into tiny pieces.

"Leo?" Bess jumped in on the topic. Leo was Della's trapeze partner. Annis had only met him the one time and knew little about him except that he was close in age to Della, he was handsome, with his olive complexion and jet-black hair, he was tall with a muscular build, and he was skilled in flying through the air and catching himself on a variety of hoops and swings and ropes along the way.

"Why do you always assume everything has to do with him?" Della grumbled, gently stabbing her ham with the prongs of her fork and lifting it to her mouth.

Bess shrugged. "Because it always does."

"It's true," Etta agreed. "Even that time you were on and on about whether or not you wanted to cut your hair, it was really just about Leo making that comment about hating short hair and you wanting to tick him off."

"Are you together, then?" Annis asked. She'd sort of suspected it, given their joint act and all.

Della snorted in disgust. "Absolutely not."

"Don't let her fool you," Lila said, rolling her eyes toward the ceiling. "She's mad about him, just can't admit it."

"And I won't. The man is a complete arse. Most days I think long and hard whether I'd rather fall to my death or let him catch me," Della said with a huff.

"She's just upset because the ring is the only place he *will* catch her," Bess teased.

"Oh." Annis thought she was beginning to understand what the real problem was.

"Two stubborn, pigheaded fools in love," Viola sighed dramatically.

"Which is precisely why we stay apart," Della ended the discussion and so ended the topic of Leo for good—or, at the very least, for breakfast. Annis got the distinct sense it was a constant topic of conversation around these parts.

After the Leo discussion, another about August followed. No one particular woman was tied to him, but they did all seem to share a common admiration for him. By the time they finished gushing over the strongest man alive, they caught sight of Will and Goldilocks clearing their plates and heading out of the tent, presumably to return to work. The discussion of the importance of boys having good hair promptly ensued.

By the time Annis and Bess were making their way toward the tent site, Annis felt as though her head was spinning, caught in a whirlwind of every man's face she'd seen over breakfast.

"You're awfully quiet," Bess noticed. "Why are you so quiet?"

"I'm a bit dizzy," Annis admitted truthfully. "I don't think I'd realized how many men were here until you pointed every single one of them out over breakfast."

Bess shrugged, laughing. "The more the better, right?"

"I suppose." Annis wasn't sure she had an opinion about it. Was there really an increase in benefits when there were more of the male gender? she wondered. Especially when they already outnumbered the female population in camp. Bess and her friends certainly seemed to be pleased with the ratio, even if none of them appeared to be taking advantage of it. "There's something I don't understand, though."

"What's that?"

"You all spent every second of breakfast discussing how lovely all the men are, and yet not a one of you is involved with one. Why is that?" It could hardly be the guys' lack of interest in them, she thought. She'd seen the way August kept sweeping his gaze over

Bess and the way Will continually turned toward Viola, smiling at her every chance he got.

"You heard Della. Some of us are better off steering clear of each other." She giggled. "In my case, I'm best off steering clear of all of them, all the time." She nudged Annis's side with her elbow as they walked. "Doesn't mean I can't appreciate from a distance, though."

"I don't understand. You like them all. But you don't like any of them well enough?" Annis realized she hadn't known many women Bess's age who weren't yet married. Those who hadn't managed to find a husband yet were usually desperate to put an end to their search, in part because their families insisted upon it. An unmarried woman of a certain age was an embarrassment, as though she were somehow unfit or damaged, and so deserved to be marked for life with the shame she brought upon herself and those whose name she carried—and would carry until her death, given she had no husband to gift her with his. The more she thought about it, the more horrifying she found it.

In any event, it seemed now Bess was the one feeling perplexed. "Like them enough for what? Marriage?" She laughed, throwing her head back and slapping her thigh.

"You don't want to get married," Annis concluded.

"I do not," Bess confirmed.

"And, the others..." Annis turned, looking back over her shoulder in the direction they'd just come from. "They feel the same way you do?" This time, Annis was struggling not to sound as though she found the concept absurd. She didn't, really, in her own thoughts, but those weren't always easy to hear when they were being crowded out by all the nonsense people had spewed at her all her life.

"Hard to say," Bess said, tugging at Annis's elbow to redirect their path, taking the long way around the campsite to where Bess usually set up in the back to rehearse. "I don't see Lila ever going down that aisle, though her sisters may, eventually. Della, well, she's obsessed with Leo and he's completely crazy about her. But they're a lot like oil and water. In the end, they just can't seem to mix. Honestly, I think she likes it that way. It's safe."

"How is it safe? What's safe about it?" Annis stopped, stumped. "And safe from what?"

Bess slowed to a stop as well. "Being vulnerable, of course. The temptation to give in, give up your freedom. Risk getting hurt. Risk losing everything, including yourself." She turned and started walking again. "Falling in love with a man she can't have keeps Della safe from all of that."

Annis stumbled, trying to speed up and reach Bess's side again. "But...But what if it's good? What if being vulnerable turns out to be worth it? What if you don't lose anything? What if you have everything to gain?"

Bess smirked, shifting a sideways glance at her before staring straight ahead again. "Yes, spending time with Caroline and Homer will do that."

"Do what?"

"Make you believe in fairy tales." She hooked her arm into Annis's and leaned in until their shoulders knocked with every other step. "Don't get me wrong. I absolutely believe in theirs. I just don't think we all get the same story. Or even a happily ever after. Some of us just get the villain bits and no prince. Or worse, the prince and the villain turn out to be one and the same."

Annis wasn't willing to give up so easily. "Every story has a hero."

Bess nodded. "Yes. And sometimes it turns out to be you. And why not? Why shouldn't we be the heroes of our own stories? I know that's the part I always like best."

As much as she felt as though agreeing with Bess put her on the losing side, she couldn't disagree with her either. The hero was the best part. It just hadn't ever occurred to Annis that she could play it herself. And now, having already been beaten by the villain once, it hardly seemed possible to change the course of her story.

"Right." Bess cut through Annis's mental stewing and brought her back to the present. "We've got work to do and no pretty boys around to do it for us. Come on," she said, pointing at a square wooden box nearly filled to the rim with what Annis assumed were the tools they needed for the job ahead, "you grab that crate there and follow me."

Annis did as she was told and, before long, they were setting up the tightrope. It was a smaller version compared to the one in the ring, of course. The grand one, reserved for the show, would be built inside the tent once it was upright. For now, Annis couldn't help but feel a great deal of pride as she stood back and took in all that they'd accomplished all on their own.

"What now?" Annis asked, looking around for more work to do.

"Now we go help the boys." No sooner had she said it, Bess was marching onward with a stretch of rope wrapped over her shoulder and several tools in each hand.

Annis glanced down at her own hands. She was still holding a hammer in one, so she reached for the bucket of nails with the other and then hurried after Bess.

It felt good, the work they were doing. It was exciting in a new way, as though Annis were discovering her body in a new light and getting reacquainted with it. She was strong. She'd always thought she was, but only strong for a girl, not in comparison to the men she worked alongside here. And, granted, she was nowhere near as well suited for the heavy lifting as, say, August and Francis, who were working only a few feet over from her, but she still managed to hold her own and not require any help to complete her tasks.

It was empowering. It was liberating. Bess's words about freedom began to make sense to her.

"Hold this, would you?" August said suddenly, handing her a stack of boards without looking in her direction. They were so heavy that she nearly fell backward, but she caught herself just in time. "Lord, Annis!" he shouted, realizing his mistake. "I'm so sorry. I thought you were Francis. I swear he was just behind me a minute ago." He began to take back the load, but Annis gripped it tighter.

"Quite alright. I've got it." She nodded toward the board he'd started nailing into the post in an effort to fix the tiered benches meant for the audience that night. Some of the boards had been cracking and bowing so badly, it was just a matter of time before someone fell through.

"You sure?" He seemed to have his doubts.

"Yes." She nodded vigorously. "Very sure." Then, on second thought, she added, "but only if you hurry up already."

August was clearly torn between believing her and determining if she was simply being stubborn. Either way, he appeared to accept that the outcome wouldn't change, and so he hurried on with his task, efficiently shooting the nails into the boards with swift swings of his hammer until, one by one, her load was lightened as each board was put to new use.

"Thank you," Annis said with a sigh when the job was done.

"What are you thanking me for?" he asked, chuckling. "You're the one who was helping me."

"True," Annis agreed. "But you were helping me too. I never would have volunteered to hold those boards because I never had any idea I could. Now, thanks to you, I do." She wiped her hands on her pants, dusting off the sawdust and dirt. "Feel free to throw a stack of wood at me anytime, August." Then she walked away, grinning to herself and feeling filled with the satisfaction of having done the impossible—and having done it by choice. Perhaps there was still time for her to become the hero, after all.

Come lunchtime, she and Bess were sharing a table with Della and Leo, and were soon joined by the twins, and then Sawyer and Sequoyah shortly after.

"Is it just me or are you hungrier than usual?" Mabel asked, staring at Annis while she took bite after bite, barely taking time to breathe. Mabel wasn't wrong. Annis was ravenous from the physical labor she'd done. She also felt free to finally eat a proper meal without her mother's nagging voice reminding her to be ladylike, "Because no man wants to marry a woman who has potential to grow into a hog down the road."

"Bess does all her own lifting of heavy things," Annis mumbled, mouth full. "So I did a lot of lifting of heavy things. And now my stomach is a really empty thing."

"Won't be for long," Mabel pointed out with a raised brow as she slowly began to eat her own lunch.

"I don't recall you ever being fond of anyone telling you to eat less," Maude said to her sister.

"That's because I'm not. And I haven't any desire to limit her intake. I'm simply wondering if perhaps it might behoove her to slow it down," Mabel explained.

The bickering between them carried on like a soothing hum in the background. It was becoming a familiar sound to Annis, and one she realized she looked forward to hearing.

"You two really are lovely," she said, grinning broadly across the table at the two sisters, who were both stunned into silence by her statement.

Meanwhile, Sequoyah was trying hard to contain his chuckling and Sawyer, ever the troublemaker, didn't hesitate to jump right in.

"Did one of those heavy things Bess was lifting drop on your head?" he asked, shaking his own. "I mean, it's the only plausible reason I can conjure up why you might make such poor and inaccurate use of the word 'lovely.'"

"It wasn't inaccurate," Annis corrected. "Wasn't using it on you, was I?"

Bess laughed. "Come on then, Smalls. What are you going to say to that?"

"Don't egg him on," Sequoyah warned. "He'll never stop."

Bess shrugged. "Won't keep me from leaving when I grow bored with him."

"Yes, that is your usual mode of operation, isn't it?" Sawyer said, redirecting his verbal target practice at her. Much as Annis had expected, the attempted stab at Bess never struck. It rolled off into the sound of her echoing laughter. Bess really couldn't fall—not physically, and not in any way at all.

"You must need a nap, Sawyer," Maude said dryly. "Your wit is barely alive today."

He huffed but surrendered all further arguments to his plate of food, which had hardly been touched so far.

"You two coming to help in the ring after lunch?" Sequoyah asked, a hopeful note in his tone.

"Is the tent ready?" Bess asked before Annis could answer.

Sequoyah nodded. "Got the last of it done just before we came this way." He reached for his glass of water and took a long drink. "One of the flags is down, though. Poppy's trying to mend it now. Could probably use your help getting it back up when he's done."

Bess slid her empty plate to the side and propped her elbows up on the table, placing her fingers together in the center as though she were contemplating the best possible way to do this. "The center flag? The one that's been leaning for weeks?"

"That's the one," he confirmed.

"Yeah, I can get up there. Should be easy enough with the center pole right there." She turned to Annis. "Want to make the climb with me?" Her eyes lit up with adrenaline already, but Annis couldn't conjure nearly as much excitement at the thought of scaling a massive wooden pole to the highest point in the tent, and then somehow getting beyond that and reattach a fallen flag. Liberated or not by her own physical strength, she was certain she lacked the balance and grace to pull it off without falling to her death halfway to the top.

"I think I'll pass," she mumbled, doing her best to focus all her efforts on collecting the last few kernels of corn from her plate just so she could avoid looking Bess in the eye.

Sawyer seized the moment, as usual, despite not being previously involved in the conversation. "I think you should do it, Annis. Opportunities like this won't come around again so soon, and you want to learn as much as you can from your day with Bess, don't you? Might as well see if you can get a handle on her ability to maintain her balance under any and all circumstances."

"You're horrible," Annis said, lifting her eyes to stare straight at him. "You know that, don't you? I mean, you're so horrible, I'm starting to wonder if you're trying to knock me off. To get me killed."

He laughed, but it only made her carry on. "You're trying to murder me and not get caught. It's brilliant, but it won't work. I won't be lured to my death by a man who can't even see out the train windows without standing on the nightstand."

Sawyer's mouth, still open in preparation for his next round of comebacks, widened and his jaw dropped nearly to his chest. "Annis. You're getting to be mean." He smirked. "Maybe I'll let you live after all."

"How very gracious of you," Annis replied dryly.

"Yes," Sequoyah agreed, grinning. "We really do appreciate it."

"Meanwhile," Bess said, "are we still convinced climbing the pole will end in certain death or are you willing to take a risk with me?" She flashed Annis a brazen smile. "Don't you want to be the hero who puts the flag back, Annis?"

It was all she'd needed to say to steer Annis toward her next adventure.

Chapter Thirteen
THE STORY

"**S**wear this won't turn out to be the unexpected end of my story?" Annis whispered, staring up at the tent ceiling. She was sorry she'd asked the twins to care for Finian while she went with Bess to tackle the flag problem. He would have provided her an excuse to back out, completely through no fault of her own. After all, who could have blamed her if Fin had been too scared, or too squirmy to hold on to? Not to mention feeding time.

"I swear," Bess said, squeezing her shoulder. "It'll make a wicked good plot twist, though. No one would see it coming," she laughed. "Least of all you, from the looks of it."

Annis felt her entire body shiver, starting at her core and spreading evenly in both directions until her teeth began to clatter. "Maybe I can't do this," she breathed.

"It's just nerves, Annis. You need those. They let you know when you're growing, taking chances, becoming more. If you don't feel the rattle of your teeth between your jaws every now and again, you're not living right. Hell, you're probably not living at all."

The words *reckless* and *fearless* bounced back and forth inside Annis's mind, and the conversation she'd had with Hugh about them ran through her thoughts on loop. The longer she listened to Bess, the harder it was for her to determine which one she was chasing at that moment. Was she being reckless? Taking a stupid chance? Or was this calculated risk without the fear of falling? Because that's what she would be required to do to complete this task: Give up the fear of falling.

"Tell me again how we'll do it," Annis begged.

"Nope," Bess answered. It was the most cheerful rejection Annis had ever received.

"Okay," she muttered, following Bess, who reached up for the first rung drilled into the pole and began to climb.

"Don't look down, Annis," she said for what had to be the hundredth time since talking Annis into this asinine plan. Annis wasn't sure she agreed with Bess's advice. Looking down seemed sensible. How else would she know when she'd reached the point of no return? Or climbed so high that survival was out of the question should she make one mistake and slip?

"I won't look down," she promised, despite her reservations. Annis reminded herself repeatedly that Bess was the height expert, the woman who knew how not to fall. Whatever Bess said, Annis would treat as law and follow to a T. Annis would not look down.

Seven rungs in, and she was still whispering the same words to herself over and over again: "Don't look down, Annis. Don't. Look. Down."

And she didn't. Instead, she kept count.

Eight rungs.

Nine.

Ten.

By the time she reached fifteen it occurred to her that she might have preferred knowing how many there would be in total, so she could track the climb. On the other hand, should the number have been something as terrifying as a hundred or more, she likely wouldn't be at number twenty-four right then, or on any rung at all.

"Just a few more," Bess called back.

"Oh, thank goodness," Annis wheezed. She heard Bess laugh. Bess really did find everything amusing. She also, as it turned out, had a very different definition of how many a few was, compared to Annis. "A few" turned out to be ten more rungs to climb, making the grand number they had scaled thirty-five. Not nearly as horrifying as one hundred, but still frightening all the same.

Annis watched as Bess twisted and turned her body to navigate several ropes near the circus tent ceiling. She then slithered through an opening at the top where the materials of the tent overlapped but were held in place by the weight of the heavy tarps alone. Bess's feet were the last to disappear as she pulled herself through to the other side.

For a moment, Annis felt completely alone in the world. It was as though everything and everyone had disappeared and all that was left was her, clinging to her rung, desperate to stay alive. Then, after what felt like several minutes to Annis, but had likely been only a matter of seconds, Bess reappeared. The world came back along with her. Sticking her head through the opening and reaching her hand down toward Annis, she called, "Grab ahold."

And, knowing a second thought would lead to a third and a fourth thought, all of which would tell her not to do it, Annis emptied her mind and took Bess's hand.

A rush of air swooshed down her body as Bess yanked her upward. As soon as she was outside of the tent, knees weighing into the canvas tarp creating a sort of hammock for her to sit in, a new breeze hit her. This one was warm and pleasant, as was the view.

"I told you not to look down," Bess snapped. Then she laughed, letting Annis know she was only teasing. "Pretty incredible, isn't it?"

"Do you come up here often?" Annis asked, surprised at how commonplace it all seemed to be for Bess.

"How do you think the flag wound up like that in the first place?" She winked. "Don't tell Poppy."

"No wonder he's always suspicious of everyone around here," Annis muttered.

"It's true," Bess agreed. "We give him good reason." She grinned, staring out at the horizon. "You should see it at sunset. It's magical." Her gaze drifted toward the train. "Sitting on top of the cars isn't too shabby a view either. I'll take you up there next."

"I think I'd like that." Annis smiled, taking a long, deep breath in until her chest felt as though it might burst. "I might have liked it even more if we could have started with that. They're considerably lower to the ground, you know."

"I do know," Bess said, her eyes glossy from the wind. "That's why we go big and work our way down. If you work your way up, there's less fun in it. The trip gets comfortable, you lose your nerves. And you need those, remember?"

She did remember, though. She realized she no longer had them. They'd been replaced with something new, something better, something more tremendous and rewarding than anything she'd ever experienced. She liked the nerves. She wanted more of them, especially if they all led to feeling like this. Strong. Rebellious and almost euphoric. Question was, how far would she have to push herself out of her comforts to generate nerves the next time around?

Conversation dwindled between them as they got to work replacing the flag. They secured it better than the previous one for reasons Bess chose to keep to herself. Annis assumed they were related to preventing the flag from falling again the next time Bess attempted whatever act had caused the flag to break in the first place.

As it turned out, once she forgot how high up she was, Annis didn't feel at all out of place working at the very tip of the tent. Not until it was time to make their descent did she find her nerves ready to return—and with a vengeance.

"You looked down, didn't you?" Bess said, matter-of-fact, when she noticed Annis glued to the top rung.

"It was an accident," she hissed. "I went to move my foot down and my eyes just followed automatically."

"Alright. Hold on." As if there were any other option for her.

"What are you going to do?"

Rather than answer, Bess apparently thought it best to show her. Gripping around the outside of Annis's hands, Bess took hold of the rung and then carefully lowered herself down behind Annis to the next one. Instantly Annis's fears jumped from herself to worrying about Bess. "Be careful!" she cried out, feeling Bess's body slip against her back.

"I'm fine, Annis," Bess assured her, moving past Annis and then looking up to meet her terrified eyes, pools of endless white surrounding pupils that swallowed up the irises, making them look entirely black.

"Now what?"

"I'm going to go down," Bess said, already moving toward the ground. "I suggest you do the same."

"But...How?" Panic rose from Annis's chest to her throat, making her hiccup.

"One foot at a time, Annis. Same way you got up. Same way you get anywhere."

"What if I can't?" Surely there was another way down.

"Can't's not really something we do around here. Impossible tasks get done every day, Annis, because people simply have no choice but to do them."

It wasn't at all the answer she'd wanted to hear, though it was exactly the one she's expected. She closed her eyes, trying to shut out the image of the ground a million miles away from her, blurred and possibly shaking, growing more vivid and more horrifying the more she tried to erase it from her mind's eye. Her own thoughts, ruthless in their attempts to destroy her, added scenarios of falling—a slipping hand, a misplaced foot—that all ended with her body broken beyond repair in the dusty dirt below.

Fear was completely taking over, until she nearly lost her footing just standing there, worrying. And then fury stepped in. Fury with herself for getting in this ridiculous situation in the first place. Fury with her stupid instincts to look down when Bess had hammered it into her head not to. Fury with her own cowardice. She'd allowed her fear to spread malicious lies about her fate when she already knew, had already decided once, that death could call for her, but she would not answer. Not yet. Not when there were debts left to be paid and terrible wrongs left to be made right. She could not be defeated. And she would no longer allow herself to be taken in by fear and its laughable lies.

Annis was halfway down before she noticed she'd been moving at all, huffing and puffing along to the angry rant inside her head.

"Giving yourself a good talking to?" Bess called out from below. "It's good. In the end, you are usually the only person you'll listen to. It's the only person any of us listen to." She laughed. "It's a bloody shame we usually don't have a clue what we're talking about."

Annis reached the last three rungs and leapt to the ground, abandoning her climbing efforts. And, because she'd finally got her head straight, she landed firmly on her feet. There was no fall left in her.

"Well done, Annis," Bess said, nodding approvingly. "I knew you'd do it."

"You knew I wouldn't stay up at the top of the pole and die a slow and terrible death because I was too scared to come down? Thanks, I'm glad you knew I could make that judgement call."

Bess hooked Annis's arm with her own and tugged her back out of the ring. "Don't be silly, Annis. We would have to get you down tonight after the show. Tent doesn't stay up longer than that, remember?"

She did now.

Flabbergasted by the realization she'd suffered for naught, and had looked a fool doing it, she could do nothing but sputter nonsense the entire time they walked. Her frustrations with herself and Bess's clear disregard for sharing valuable information Annis could have used amid her harrowing efforts to have her feet meet with the ground again, fumbled back and forth within her mind. Not until they reached the train and headed into Bess's cabin did Annis feel she could start making sense again.

"I can see why you don't value trust a great deal," Annis grumbled, following Bess inside.

"You're saying I'm not trustworthy?" Bess asked, sounding far more amused than offended.

That had been Annis's initial intention, but now that she was thinking about it, she wasn't sure. "I suppose I'd trust you with my life, but I wouldn't trust you to be all that forthcoming with truth you didn't deem to be required information, even if I might prefer to have it, if given the option."

"You know," Bess said, pulling the pins out of her hair and letting the long brown strands spill down her back, "I think I'm okay with that."

"I kind of thought you might be." Annis looked around the otherwise empty cabin. "What are we doing in here? It's hours yet before showtime." She knew this for certain because she was still down one meal for the day. Annis couldn't remember a time she'd been more concerned with eating her fair share in one day but heading back to Momma's for dinner had been on her mind ever since touching down on solid ground again. Following Bess around certainly worked up her appetite.

"We need a change," she said, lifting the lid on a massive trunk and shuffling carelessly through its contents. "Here," she said, tossing a new pair of trousers at Annis. "Wear these."

Annis looked at them, and then down at the ones she already had on. The ones she wore were the same pair she'd received from Babe a few days ago. Annis had seen to it they'd been washed and pressed by those on laundry duty, so there really was no need for a new pair. "What's wrong with the ones I have on?"

"They're too pretty."

"I beg your pardon?" She'd been working in them all day. When had they become too pretty?

"Believe me, for what we're about to go do, you want a pair of trousers you won't want to wear again." Mischief flared in her eyes and Annis knew she was in for it. Again.

"I don't suppose you're going to tell me what that is, are you?" Annis mumbled, already giving in to the inevitable and changing her pants while Bess did the same.

"And ruin the surprise?" she mocked. "Absolutely not!" She threw a pair of boots in Annis's direction. "You'll want these too."

The boots were so crusty and old that Annis couldn't tell where the leather was flaking and where the dirt was coming off in layers. She didn't want to touch them, much less wear them, but if there was even a chance her good shoes could wind up looking like these by the time they were done doing whatever Bess had in store for them, she knew it would behoove her to put them on.

"Brilliant," Bess exclaimed, taking in the sight of Annis's new wardrobe. Brilliant was hardly the word that came to Annis's mind when peering down the length of her body, but she wasn't about to argue, not when Bess had a potentially torturous surprise in store for her. Sensing Annis's apprehensions, she added, "You know, you really don't need to look so frightened. I haven't steered you wrong yet all day."

Annis's mouth flew open to point out the various ways in which Annis had nearly died already, but then thought better of it when she remembered that the other side of feeling scared was feeling more alive than ever.

"Alright then, steer me onward to the next grand adventure," Annis declared, throwing her hand up to her forehead in a dramatic salute that made Bess laugh out loud.

"Oh, it'll be grand, alright." She turned toward the door and began marching. "And away we go!"

Indeed, they went. All the way past the train toward the end of camp, stopping only when they reached the animal tent.

"Bess."

"Yes, Annis?" Her innocent tone impressed Annis.

"Will this adventure involve poo?" Jacob the monkey flashed in her mind and it was all she could do to keep from running in the opposite direction. If she'd thought Sawyer was brash for recommending she dig around in monkey poo in search of a brooch, she was sure she'd have to come up with entirely new descriptive terminology once she discovered what Bess intended for them to do. It did give her some peace of mind, though, knowing Bess was planning to participate herself. Not much peace, of course, given the things Bess was willing to do, but a little.

"I can assure you, poo will be no part of it," Bess said, very seriously. Annis believed her and let out a loud breath of relief.

Inside the animal tent, there was nonstop commotion. Sequoyah was busy running the horses while Sawyer was at the other end rehearsing his act with Roderick and Phryne, two of his lions. Millie and Edi seemed to be on their own for the moment, and neither of them was dressed for the evening, so it was only a matter of time before someone came along to begin the hazardous affair of putting tiaras on them.

There were others in the tent as well, but Annis was too busy staying close to Bess and trying to figure out their mysterious task to pay attention to them.

"Here we are," Bess announced, coming to an abrupt halt in front of the monkey enclosure.

"No!" Annis burst out, hands flying up in protest. "You said no poo!"

"And I meant it," Bess insisted. "We're not here for poo. We're here for demolition!"

"What?" Annis asked, taking in the sight before her. It was reminiscent of her neighbor's tree house, with its mismatched wooden slats for walls and its odd shape that one tends to end up with when working with scraps for building material. Also, it was clear that additions had been made after the original structure was built and there'd been either no measuring tape on hand, or Homer had been the one to craft it all. Somehow, in its chaotic construction, it managed to appear perfectly suited for monkeys.

"This enclosure isn't making the next trip. Goldilocks and Francis already built another, so this one's gotta go. But, I want some of the parts, so we're going to be the ones to break it down."

Annis frowned. "You can't just tell Goldilocks and Francis which parts you want?"

"And let them have all the fun?" This time there was no mockery in her voice. Bess was completely serious.

"How do we do this, exactly?" Annis had never broken anything intentionally. This would be a new experience – one that felt all wrong.

"We use these," Bess said, leaning forward to grab an axe and something that looked like an enormous hammer someone had apparently left there for them. "Which would you like? The blade or the crusher?"

They both sounded destructive and dangerous. "I'll take the crusher. I don't think either of us should trust me to swing around a large knife attached to a long stick."

"Probably shouldn't trust me to either," Bess said, rolling her eyes sideways, and sticking her tongue out. "But that's not going to stop me, is it?"

Annis saw no point in answering Bess's question. Accepting her currently turbulent fate, unchangeable as it was at the moment, she reached for the crusher and waited for Bess to make her next move.

It turned out to be a heavy swing at the enclosure door, splitting it right in half.

"Ooh, that was fun!" she exclaimed, sounding slightly breathless. "Your turn, Annis. Have a go at that wall right there. Let's crack this thing open so we can really get started."

Annis swept her surroundings, hoping for a last chance of escape. When no opportunity to bolt arose, she turned her eyes back at the structure before her and took a tentative step toward it.

"Just...swing at it?"

"It's wonderfully freeing, I tell you. You'll love it." Bess seemed to be beside herself with glee over this new activity.

"Alright," Annis said with a sigh. "Here I go."

Shaking from a new set of nerves that could easily contend with the ones she'd had climbing to the top of the tent, Annis raised her arms, squeezed her eyes shut, and swung blindly at the wall as per Bess's request.

She was expecting the impact to be hard and to jar her body. Instead, she felt herself lunge forward with the weight and momentum of the hammer as it burst straight through the wood, never slowing, never stopping. When she caught herself, she looked up to find a giant hole in the wall, and the handle of her tool sticking out through it, her hand still holding the end of it. "Whoa," she wheezed. She'd never hit anything in her life. She would have to rectify that mistake every chance she got from now on.

"Do we keep taking turns?" she asked, wondering how soon she could have another go at it.

"I think we both have the brains to know better than to swing at each other," Bess said, pointing at the wall Annis had just smashed a hole though. "You stay to the right and I'll work on the left. No meeting in the middle."

"No meeting in the middle," Annis agreed. Chances were good there would be no middle left to speak of anyway, once the sides were demolished.

For the next several minutes, both of them worked steadily, swinging, assessing the damage they'd inflicted, and swinging again. However, once they'd worked their way inside, Bess gave the cue to stop.

"Find something you prefer not to have crushed?" Annis asked, eyeing what was rapidly becoming her favorite new tool.

"Indeed, I did," Bess said, her face lighting up as she stepped through the rubble and toward an array of ropes, all twined to various sizes and attached to the walls in a sort of maze for the previous inhabitants.

"Those aren't nearly long enough for you to traipse across," Annis pointed out.

"Then it's a good thing that's not what I want to do with them," Bess replied with a cheeky smirk. Both women temporarily abandoned their tools of destruction and untangled the maze using only their hands for the job. They worked with an ironclad focus, efficiently taking down the ropes and coiling them up one at a time until all that was left were bare walls and ceiling.

The cycle of smashing and salvaging carried on for the next two hours until only a neat pile of rubble remained where there had once been a monkey enclosure. All of Bess's newfound treasures had been safely placed in a large trunk August had delivered mid-demolition, ready for transport.

By the time they were walking out of the animal tent, they both wore glazed expressions, somewhere between delirious delight and exemplary exhaustion. Their clothes were covered in dust and dirt. Their pants especially had encountered a fair amount of rips and tears from catching and scraping on the materials they encountered during the demolition.

"Thanks for making me change my pants," Annis said, trying to swat off a dark mark that wouldn't budge. Not until she pressed down hard enough to touch her leg did she realize it was likely blood, and hers, since her skin was tender just below.

"Thanks for trusting me." Bess winked. She laughed and wrapped her arm around Annis's shoulders as they walked. "You know, I don't remember the last time I've had this much fun. Thanks for spending the day with me, Annis. I may enjoy being a one-woman act, but it does get lonely from time to time. It's nice having someone along to share in the shenanigans, for a change."

"You can consider me available anytime for those," Annis told her as their hips bumped while they walked, their strides in perfect rhythm.

"Big words, Annis," Bess said. "You sure you don't want to reconsider?" she teased. "You might regret having offered."

"Oh, I have no doubt there'll be plenty of regret. But," she paused as they maneuvered their way around a small group of workers on their way to Momma's tent, "knowing you, it'll be short-lived and superficial because you'll make me tough it out even when things seem unbearable. Which means I'll get to the good parts at the end, and then I'll remember that sticking with you likely means having no regrets in life, ever. Because I'll never have missed out on all the things that scare me most."

"You know, Annis," Bess said with surprising emotion, "I think that might be the kindest thing anyone's ever said to me."

"Be prepared to hear plenty of horrible things down the road to balance it out. In moments of terror and discomfort I can be an absolute beast, and we both know I'll be experiencing both anytime I'm with you."

"You weren't so bad today," Bess pointed out.

"Only because you couldn't hear me from where you were, down below, while I thought I was stuck at the top of the tent, destined to die."

"No," Bess said, shaking her head, "I could." She shrugged. "I've heard worse. From Sawyer, mostly."

Annis found this entirely believable. "He does have a bit of a temper, doesn't he?"

Bess nodded. "Especially where those ruddy elephants are concerned."

"He really does seem to dislike them an awful lot," Annis agreed.

"I think it's size envy, to be honest," Bess mused.

"Oh?" Annis acted surprised. "I was certain it was the tiaras he was jealous of."

There was a brief second of complete silence, the tiniest of interludes in their chatter, and then they burst out laughing and giggled all the way back to Bess's cabin, where they shed their wrecked wardrobes and changed back into more favorable attire. Unlike Annis, who put on the same clothes from before, Bess reemerged from the cabin in a fancy bit of white lace and sequins that fit her body like a second skin and that was accompanied by a light rose-colored tutu, much like the sort Annis had worn for ballet.

"That's just lovely, Bess."

"Thank you," Bess said with a curtsy. "The girls and I all make our own costumes. Part of the fun of sharing the cabin. We all pool together our supplies and help each other with designs."

"That sounds wonderful." Annis wondered if perhaps one day she'd join them.

As they walked, Annis's thoughts drifted toward the future. It seemed like a lifetime ago that she'd allowed herself to daydream about what life had in store for her. But today, she let herself wonder. She knew that wherever the tracks led, the train would follow, and that she would be on it. She had no doubts about this. But, as her days and experiences went on, she began to see how different life could be, even among those who traveled the same tracks.

Perhaps it was silly to consider, but there was such joy in imagining the possibilities that Annis couldn't resist. Where would the tracks lead her? What sort of act would become her life's work? And where would she belong when she found it? Would she remain with the twins? They already felt like sisters to her. Or would she wind up with Bess and the others? Living free, first and foremost, and happy for the companionship of those she enjoyed, but not tied to anyone for longer than she pleased.

Or would the stars align with her deepest desires? Would she fall in love? Trust with her whole heart, and give it to Sequoyah? It was the dream she didn't yet dare to believe in, and she jarred herself back into the present, where she found herself standing directly across from him.

"Hi," he said, sounding pleased to see her.

"Hi," she answered. She silently scolded herself for her timid tone. She'd built structures with her own two hands, climbed to the top of the tent, and destroyed an entire small building that day. Surely, she could muster a bit more gusto when she spoke.

"I don't feel like I've seen you much today," he said quietly, gently taking her hand in his as they walked into Momma's tent together.

Annis's eyes darted around. She searched for Bess, fearing her disapproval or, at the very least, her mockery, if she saw Sequoyah holding Annis's hand. But Bess was already ahead of them, chatting with Momma and Babe.

"It's been a very strange day," she said, letting her palm sink into his as though she could anchor herself with him permanently. It was an inviting thought, and she pushed it from her mind as fast as she could. Inviting or not, ideas like those simply weren't hers to entertain. Not yet, anyway.

"I sensed that when I happened to glance up and see you practically hanging on the flagstaff on top of the tent," he said, his mouth taking on the same quirky grin it always seemed to wear whenever he was talking to her.

"You saw?" She hadn't thought anyone would, though it seemed an odd assumption now. She and Bess had hardly been hidden, standing up on top of the world, perfectly visible to all of camp, and possibly all of the surrounding counties. "It was the most terrifying, most wonderful experience of my life," she breathed. Even just thinking about it still took her breath away. "Bess is such a remarkable woman. I've never known anyone like her. She's not afraid of anything and she's teaching me so much," Annis went on, the words bubbling out of her as her excitement grew.

Only as she felt her own exhilaration rise did she notice Sequoyah becoming more subdued until even the grin she adored so much began to fade.

"What's wrong?" she asked, wondering how his mood had changed so rapidly. "If you're worried we haven't been safe, I swear I thought I might die only once and, as it turned out, I was scared for nothing."

"It's not that," he assured her, leaning in ever so slightly, bringing them closer together. "It's not anything really. I think it's wonderful you're having such a great time. It's amazing to see you this way. It's just..." his words trailed off as though he weren't sure which ones to use.

"What? You can tell me. Whatever it is, you can say it," she promised, anxious to find out what had him looking concerned so that she could find a way to ease his fears.

"It's just... Bess's specialty," he said quietly, tilting his head to meet her eye-to-eye.

"What do you mean?" Annis didn't understand.

He sighed, and then took a deep breath and held it in, squeezing his eyes shut until, at last, he said, or maybe asked, "She's teaching you not to fall."

Annis's mouth opened to respond before she had an answer and she was forced to close it again, without uttering a word.

Patiently, he waited until what he'd said began to make sense to her.

He wasn't asking about literal falling. He was asking about him. About them. About whether she was learning to see the brighter side of flying free and never risking the misstep that was possible when trusting others.

"She's teaching me to fly," Annis whispered. "And it's the grandest feeling I've ever felt. But," she paused, wanting to be sure she made no mistake in her phrasing, "I think I like it so much because I'm not afraid of falling. Not because I know it won't happen, but because I already know where I'll land when I do."

Warmth pooled in his eyes and poured down on her, making Annis's heart swell in her chest.

"Good," he said. Annis suspected the way he kept nodding and swallowing had more to do with wanting to hold in his emotions than not having any words to let out.

"Yes, I think so too," she agreed.

He cleared his throat, breaking his gaze away from hers as though he couldn't bear to be locked in any longer. "I assume you're famished from all this flying?"

"We destroyed the old monkey enclosure," Annis added, her excitement returning again. "Did you see that too?"

He laughed. "So, yes to being famished." He began to lead the way toward food, all the while paying careful attention not to miss any of Annis's retelling of her newest adventures.

As she went on, talking faster and louder by the minute, it struck her how very wonderful it was to have someone to share her new stories with. Someone who truly listened and genuinely wanted to know them. And though the voice was quiet, it was strong enough to answer the question her wandering mind had conjured up only a short while ago. The stars would align, and when they did, her heart would be his. And even the ugliest parts of her past would be powerless to stop the beauty of it.

Chapter Fourteen

A FIRST TASTE OF SPOTLIGHT

Annis had three helpings at dinner that night. She only passed on the fourth because Finian was insisting he was hungrier than she was, and Mabel was refusing to feed him again on account of he'd peed on her lap the last time. She had been kind enough to fix his bottle for him, though. So, with her belly slowly settling, Annis found a quiet spot near the tracks on the other side of the train and fed Finian a proper dinner. Even after just a few hours apart, she'd missed him. He was becoming like an extension of her, always resting right atop her heart. She felt him move when he was awake or vibrate when he'd snore in his sleep, both of which had become comforts. Now, as she watched him wiggling about, growing bigger and stronger by the minute, she realized he wouldn't always be content to stay in the sling. He'd want to run, to explore. And, someday, he'd hear the call of the wild. When the time came, Annis would have to learn to live with his answer.

"There you are, Tulip," Babe said from behind her, the sound of relief clear in her voice. "I've been looking all over for you." She held her long, flowing gown hiked up in her hands as she made her way over the uneven ground of dirt, weeds, and overgrown tree roots, her beard twitching as she muttered under her breath. At last, Babe reached the large rock Annis had claimed as her seat and sat beside her. Annis smirked, noting the disgruntled huffing beside her.

"You realize, of course, I was never gone, yes?"

Babe's nose scrunched and released, her nostrils flaring as though she felt genuinely entitled to be upset but could find no rational reason for it. "You felt gone," she said, her voice still just as stern as her expression.

Annis sighed, and then smiled. She made sure to turn away, so Babe wouldn't see. Most people didn't enjoy seeing the party they were cross with looking so pleased by it. Sliding Finian down to the ground where he could move about more than he could in her lap, she glanced across from her, into the woods. They grew ever darker as the sun continued her descent on the opposite horizon.

"I'm not the sort who's prone to wander, Babe," Annis said softly, sitting up straighter and taking Babe's hand. "I've seen the beasts that go bump in the night and I don't care for more encounters. Unless I'm keeping company with the sort who can ward off evil, I'm staying put, in camp. Where it's safe." Even as she said it, she did wonder if a beast of sorts was hidden there, buried inside Floyd.

Babe's gaze peered back and forth along the tree line, the trees slowly but surely being swallowed by the shadows from within. "If it's all the same to you, I'd still rather you stayed on the other side of the tracks. I know it's silly, but humor me, would you?"

Annis nodded. "I can do that." She leaned in until their shoulders touched. "I'm sorry I worried you."

Babe's arm reached across and pulled her in tighter. "It's only because I've seen the beasts as well, Tulip," she said sadly. Annis felt a pang in her heart because she knew Babe was referring to the beasts who came for Sequoyah. And, even before those, there were the ones who'd killed his family. There were more beasts lurking than any of them dared to imagine. Babe had good reason to want to keep everyone safe and within reach.

"No stray lions or bears tonight on your walk?" Annis asked, attempting to lighten the mood.

"If I'd found any, you'd be taking care of them right now. The only wild I encountered were the flowers. Fierce in their beauty, but harmless all the same," Babe assured her. "How's little Finian doing, then? He seems a completely different pup from the one I found two days ago."

Annis bent down to scoop him up just as he was rolling over onto his back for what seemed like the hundredth time since they'd sat down.

"He's a lot more active since his eyes have opened," she said.

"And who could blame him? Once you catch a glimpse of the world, it's hard not to want to see every last inch of it."

Annis turned to look at the train behind them, and then back toward Babe beside her. "Is that why you do it? The circus, I mean. So you can see all there is to see?"

Babe smiled. "It's certainly one of the advantages. But no, it's not why we do it." She reached into the front of her dress and pulled out a locket that hung from a long chain around her neck. "Here, open it," she said, handing it to Annis.

Annis took the locket. She ran her fingertips gently over it and felt every detail of the engraved rose that bloomed in the center. It looked old, but it was well polished. Then, carefully, she opened it. Inside, she found two pictures. One was a woman who looked a great deal like Babe, only younger, and without any indication of a beard. The other was a man, tall and with familiar looking eyes. Annis noticed the woman was the less feminine-looking of the two.

"Your parents?" she asked, peering back up at Babe.

"My parents," she said softly, taking the locket back and clasping it shut before placing it back over her heart. "I wear this locket every day but haven't seen either one of them since I was fifteen years old. That's when they told me to leave and never come back."

The harshness of their words cut Annis's heart, slicing through it like a hot blade through butter. Babe was the kindest, most loving person she'd ever met. Annis couldn't imagine anyone being so cruel and hateful to her. No, she could imagine it. She could imagine it well. She just didn't want to because it was Babe, and that sort of behavior, that sort of hate, would crush Babe.

"Sometimes our parents aren't the people we wish them to be," Annis offered.

"Spoken by the voice of experience," Babe said, tilting her head sideways to get a better look at Annis's face. Annis turned her head to pay an unnecessary amount of attention to Finian, who was at her feet, attempting to catch his tail between his teeth.

It didn't take Babe long to determine Annis's lack of interest in carrying on about how or when she'd earned such wisdom about parents, and so she went on with her story. "After I left, all I wanted to do was go back. I just always believed, deep in my heart, that they would change their minds. That they would regret what they'd said to me and hope for my return." She patted the locket, which now hung beneath her clothing. "So, for the first few years, I kept going back. And every time, they sent me away. The seventh time I showed up, they refused to open the door. The eighth, I found a small gravestone sitting under my favorite tree with my name one it. And, at last, I understood. I was dead to them."

"Babe," Annis said as she winced, wishing she had comforting words to offer her that could ease the sting of the pain she still felt after all this time.

"Oh, it's alright, Tulip. This was many, many years ago. I've found my peace with it." Her eyes trailed down and straight ahead, following the endless tracks ahead. "But I never could quite give up the desire to return. So, here I am. Still going 'round and 'round in circles, passing through my hometown every so often. Just in case..."

"My heart aches for your parents," Annis said, her gaze following behind Babe's. "They've been loved by you, by the person whose capacity for love reaches far beyond the capabilities of most, and they've deprived themselves of it all this time. They've lost out on so much, Babe. On so much wonderful you."

Babe turned until their eyes met. "Lucky for them, love knows no bounds."

Annis smiled. "Lucky for them, neither do you."

"Lucky for everyone."

Annis laughed. "Indeed." The sound of a drumroll filled the air and both women turned their heads in the direction of the sound.

"Annis, I do believe it's showtime."

They hurried to their feet. Annis struggled for several seconds to hold Finian, who seemed far more interested in acting like an oversized roly-poly bug than being tucked back into his sling, but they finally made their way back around the train and into the camp.

Toward the front of the tent, people were already pouring in, buying tickets and peanuts on their way inside. In the short time that Annis had been sitting just out of bounds of camp, the entire energy had changed. Where before everyone had been focused on preparation, calm and calculated, now the whole place was alive with anticipation, from the audience to the performers. This time before the show began was quickly becoming one of the best parts of Annis's days.

"Can I help you with anything before the show?" Annis asked Babe as they approached the back entrance.

"Francis will already have seen to everything," Babe answered. "Thank you, Tulip." Babe gave one last smile before they parted ways inside the tent. Annis scurried off to find Bess again. Tracking her down turned out to be easy, as she was sitting just inside to the left, having a lively chat with Della and the twins.

"Would you believe he actually said that to me?" Della was asking the girls as Annis walked up.

"We all believe that part, Della," Maude said dryly. "What we struggle with is *your* constant stream of disbelief over the whole thing."

"Really, Della," Mabel added. "Even I'm only mildly entertained by Leo's efforts tonight. The real star of this show is you acting as though the poor misguided soul has never suggested the two of you could be more than just trapeze partners before."

"Ah," Annis had finally caught up to the topic. "The will-they-or-won't-they saga. A brilliant, breathtaking tale which will never truly satisfy because, well, it will never end."

Bess and Maude laughed while Mabel snickered behind her hand.

Della was less amused and resorted to scowling at them all. "Oh, it will end. In fact, it has already ended. No, forget that. It can't end because it never even began!" she said before marching off.

"Did I miss anything of more substance than Della's obsession with hating the way she loves Leo?" Annis asked the remaining group.

"Not much," Mabel said, bouncing her shoulders. "The monkeys got loose from their new enclosure, but they're all caught again. And Sawyer did say something about Roderick the lion having eaten something he shouldn't have, but he was mostly muttering to himself, so I'm not really sure if he meant for anyone to hear that. For all I know, Harris is short a monkey and just doesn't know it yet." Annis stared back at Mabel, baffled by her casual tone.

"Your idea of not much is not at all like mine."

"You also missed out on watching Oscar and August duke it out trying to prove who was really the strongest man alive. In the end, Oscar just sat down on the giant metal thing they were trying to bend and won by default. August refused to acknowledge it, claiming Oscar's tactic disqualified him." Maude said with a smirk. "Now we're all waiting on Hugh to sort it out."

"I'm sure he's thrilled." It was just the sort of thing that would send Hugh grumbling obscenities under his breath as he pretended none of them existed. She'd seen him do it a time or two already, when the maturity levels dropped too low.

"You should have seen him when both boys went running to him, demanding he referee. It was nearly as good a show as watching August and Oscar battle it out in weight versus muscle," Bess said, stretching and lifting up onto her tiptoes to look over the commotion and people backstage and get a clear view of the line up near the curtain. "Oh, Annis. We're up." No sooner had she uttered Annis's name had she grabbed her by the hand and dragged her off.

"What do you need me to do?" Annis asked, realizing this was the first time today they'd even talked about the act itself. Bess's was a one-woman show, after all. Annis hadn't really expected to have a part in it.

"I don't need you to do anything," Bess replied. She flashed her trademark smirk with a fierceness in her eyes. "But I do want you to come out there with me."

"What?" Surely Annis had misunderstood. "You want me to come out where with you? Into the ring?" Annis wasn't ready.

"Absolutely," Bess said, nodding. It was then Annis noticed her hand was still being held captive by Bess's.

"To do what?" She could feel the familiar vibrations of nerves start to spread behind her belly button and her feet began to tingle, as though threatening to go numb and render her useless.

"First, hand that bundle of fur over to Goldilocks," she demanded. Before either Annis or Goldilocks could protest, Bess reached for the sling around Annis's neck and scooped it over her head to hand it over to Goldilocks, who very much seemed at the wrong place at the wrong time. "And second...You're a dancer, right?" Bess said. When Annis didn't react, she added, "Hugh told me."

It would hardly do to deny it now, Annis thought. "I am," she said. "But we haven't even rehearsed. I have no idea what you'll be doing. I can't possibly keep up."

"Then it's a good thing I'll be following you," Bess said, sounding exceptionally pleased with herself and as though the suggestion weren't the horrible proposition destined for failure it was to Annis. Instead, Bess acted as though she'd presented a top-notch plan to top all schemes in the history of the Brooks and Bennet circus. Annis was betting on the first and couldn't bring herself to hope for the latter.

"I think I'll need a bit more instruction prior to being pulled out into the ring by your chicken wire fingers and their tight and twisty grip." Even as she said it, Annis tried to pry Bess's hand from hers to no avail.

"Annis," Bess said with a calm that inexplicably spread to Annis. "I've not let you fall once today, and I've asked you to do task after task you deemed impossible, even potentially deadly. Haven't I earned a bit more confidence from you yet?"

Annis closed her eyes and forced away all rational thought, which was useless when dealing with Bess. "Alright. Tell me the plan, then."

"Plan? What plan?" It took Bess only a second to realize she'd pushed Annis too far this time. "Just kidding. Of course I have a plan. A good plan is the foundation required to keep from falling on your arse under any and all circumstances life brings upon you." Bess delivered this line as though she were reading it from a secret handbook of rules for never falling, as though it were her mantra, her motto, her golden rule. The gravity with which Bess pronounced those words seared them permanently into Annis's mind.

"The plan is simple," Bess continued, stepping up to the curtain and peeling it back a sliver. "When it's our turn, we'll walk out together, both of us climbing to the top and onto the platform. Then, I'll walk out onto the tightrope and do a few basic moves before I cue you. When I do, I want you to take the lead, moving into a variety of ballet positions, whichever you like, and I'll follow out on the tightrope. It'll be fun and the audience will love it because neither they nor I will know which pose we'll be doing next and whether or not I'll be able to do it, see?"

"Sure," Annis said. It sounded easy enough—Annis's part did, at least, as long as she didn't consider the enormous responsibility that came with choosing their moves. She'd have to keep things daring enough to entertain the audience, but still attainable so that she didn't cause Bess to falter. "Do you have a background in classical dance at all?"

Bess shrugged. "How hard could it be?" Annis's eyes and Bess laughed. "I'm just teasing, Annis. I was a dancer all of my previous life. There's nothing you can throw my way I couldn't do in my sleep. Promise." She peeked out into the ring, and then back at Annis. "Ready?"

"Not remotely."

"Perfect."

Seconds later, they were running into the center of the ring to roaring applause. From there, Bess climbed her way up to the top of the tent on the left side of the ring, while Annis made her way up to the platform using the ladder on the right. They found each other again only a few feet from the ceiling, where the tightrope was strung from one end of the ring to the other, separating the girls from each other.

Annis stood still on her platform, waiting while her mind raced in circles attempting to conjure up a proper plan for their spontaneous act. Not until she glanced up to find Bess standing only feet from her out on the tightrope and staring straight at her did it all clicked inside her head, like magic. While she'd been searching Bess's face for some sort of cue, Bess had stared back at Annis, the same clueless expression mingled with a hint of desperate hope. It had been like looking into the mirror.

Annis began to move more deliberately. A curious touch of her cheek. A wave of her fingers, every motion made with a curious awe as though she couldn't believe the reflection she was seeing was truly her. From there, her movements grew bolder, trying out each of her limbs. Soon, she was pirouetting and jumping, delighted by the new reflection she had found in Bess.

Hearing the drumroll, which signaled the end of their act was near, Annis became ever daring, leading Bess into a sequence of moves that ended in a flying leap just as the lights cut out for their dramatic end. The next the audience saw of them, Bess and Annis were both firmly on the ground, hands held high as the spotlight lit them up for their bows.

Seconds later, Bess was dragging Annis back through the curtains, howling with excitement over their success. Annis gasped for air, certain she'd been holding her breath since before they stepped into the ring. Now that it was over, the world around her slowly came back into focus, as did the notion that Annis already wanted to go back out there and do it all over again. One taste of it, one brief moment in the spotlight, feeding off the audience's excitement and being fueled by the waves of adrenaline pounding through her veins, was by far the most exhilarating, most profound lesson of the day.

She was an entertainer. She craved the ring and the way it made the flames within her dance to life. The feeling was unlike anything she'd ever found in all the years she'd been in the ballet. She felt free. She felt powerful.

"Annis!" Bess exclaimed, both hands firmly on her shoulders and shaking Annis with overwhelming enthusiasm. "You were perfection! Absolute perfection! Did you feel it? Did you see how wildly magical you are? How fiercely destined you are to hold the light and cast it on the world around you?" She ceased shaking Annis to squeeze her tightly, hugging her as she began to jump up and down, still squealing with joy over their success.

Meanwhile, Annis was still struggling to catch her breath. Even as Bess's words were slowly seeping into her consciousness, people were coming from all around, clapping her shoulder, tousling her hair, and smacking kisses on every spare patch of her head to congratulate her on her first attempt at showmanship.

The show was only just beginning, and so Annis and Bess had to hustle out of the way, cutting the celebration short as they hurried to assist the others wherever they could. It seemed to Annis this night flew by faster than any other before it.

"I do believe this is yours," Goldilocks mumbled, handing Finian to her. Both of Goldilocks's hands were wrapped around Fin's center, causing his limbs dangle awkwardly. "He soiled the sling," he informed her, frowning. "And my shirt."

"I'm really sorry," Annis offered, though she felt it was hardly enough of an apology. "I can wash it, if you like."

"It's alright. Not the first animal to do that to me." He grimaced, casting his eyes sideways toward Harris. "Hard not to take it personal sometimes."

"Oh, it's definitely not personal," Annis assured him. "He's peed on Mabel and he adores her."

His brow lifted, turning his frown to a more curious expression. Then, after a moment's thought, he grinned. "So, it's a compliment, then."

Annis felt it was a bit of a stretch, but she was happy to go along with the notion that Finian's bodily functions were also a sign of his affections. "It's the only reasonable explanation, really."

Goldilocks laughed. "Well, I appreciate you humoring me."

"Not nearly as much as I appreciate you watching Fin."

He nodded. "Was happy to. Wish I'd been able to see you out there. Heard you and Bess put on quite the show."

"Hard to make Bess walking around on a tightrope look bad," Annis said, feeling a bit silly for all the attention she was getting.

"True. Hard to make her look even better than she always does too. But you still managed, from the sounds of it." Goldilocks reached out and gently pinched the top of Annis's arm. "You're going to have to get better at hearing people say nice things about you. No harm in believing them when they're true." He smiled and then started off in the opposite direction, heading for the now abandoned ring to prepare for breakdown.

With Finian wiggling in her arms, Annis went in search of a new way to contain him. She made a beeline for the horse corral and Sequoyah. "I need help," she pleaded, holding Fin as far away from her shirt as possible. "He's ruined a shirt and his sling in the last two hours."

Sequoyah took one look at the two of them and laughed. "I think I have an idea. Come on." He waved for her to follow, which she did, and happily. Together they rounded the backside of the corral to a stack of hay bales, each draped with several ropes and various horse supplies. Sequoyah examined them all quickly before selecting a sturdy stretch of tarp usually used for feed bags. In only a few quick flips of his hands he'd adjusted it, transforming it into a new sling. He secured it gently over Annis's shoulder and chest. "There. It's not as comfortable as the last one, but it should be more resistant to his messes."

"Thank you. You're a lifesaver, really," she gushed. "I was starting to think I'd be covered in pee from now until he's old enough to use the grass."

"Glad I could help," he began as the pair headed back toward the main tent where most of the commotion was centered on taking down the massive structure. "Though I think you would have managed just fine, if you'd had to. You have a way of working things out for yourself, Annis. You should trust yourself more."

Annis thought about it, considering all she'd taken on and conquered in only the course of a day. "I suppose you're right."

He grinned. "I suppose I am."

"Where are you headed once we get in there?" she asked, secretly hoping they would wind up on the same task for a change. She missed working alongside him.

"To help Will and Francis take down the tiered benches. You?"

She tried to hide her disappointment. "Bess said to meet her at the center of the ring. We're breaking down the tightrope and trapeze tonight."

"See you later?"

"Hope so." She smiled. Even after he turned away and could no longer see her, she kept smiling. And the more she thought about all the reasons she had to do so, the wider her mouth stretched over her face. Life had a funny way of turning itself upside down and right side up all at the same time.

"You've seen a boy," Bess teased as soon as she spotted Annis coming toward her and Della. "I can tell by the moony look in your eyes. Oh, Lord. I know which boy put it there too."

"He's dreamy with jet black hair that runs the length of his muscular back and has a complexion so beautiful it could make you weep," Della said with a dramatic sigh, mocking Annis the same way all the girls had done to each other over breakfast.

Annis grinned sheepishly. "He *is* dreamy, isn't he?"

"No one answer that, or we'll never get any work done!" Bess called out with a laugh.

"For the record," Leo cut in as he joined them, "my answer would not have impaired productivity one bit."

Della rolled her eyes at him, but she smirked as soon as she turned away. Annis caught it from where she was standing and got the distinct feeling Leo was fully aware of Della's expression, too, even without seeing it for himself. He confirmed her suspicions when he called after Della. "I can still see you, you know."

Della spun back around. "Stop looking all the bloody time!"

He grinned with one eyebrow cocked and his head tilted to the left. "Can't help myself."

Della didn't seem to know whether to be furious or delighted, and for several awkward seconds her face switched between utter disgust and complete adoration. Finally, she settled somewhere in the middle, still somewhat perplexed but obviously amused. "You're ridiculous."

"Quite likely," Leo admitted. Annis couldn't deny he was charming. Perhaps he was the water in their incompatible duo—calming, clear, and able to put out any fires feisty Miss Oil might start.

"Annis," Bess summoned her. "Mark my words, boys are a distraction." She nodded at Della who was still holding onto the same silver trapeze hoop she'd been attempting to pack up since Annis's arrival. "Case in point, the trapeze duo over there who's been too busy flirting to pack up a single item while I've managed to load an entire trunk already. Also, it's worth noting you've been held captive by their little saga, unable to move a muscle, too wracked with the anticipation of what will happen next." She shook her head at them, shaming all three for their disgraceful behavior. "Just pitiful, you lot are."

"If I do double the work in half the time, will I be forgiven?" Annis offered. Mockery notwithstanding, she felt it was a fair trade-off.

"We'll see." Despite Bess's attempt at being stern, Annis knew from her eyes that she was already cleared of all wrongdoing.

"I'm not doing double anything," Della announced haughtily. "You're the one doing all the distracting," she said, jabbing Leo in the chest. "If we fall behind tonight, it's on you."

"So like a woman. Always pushing off the blame onto the man. Completely incapable of handling their own load and then trying to relieve themselves of the responsibility."

Della looked as though fire might come out of her mouth if she dared to open it, and Annis, who had sworn to be beguiled by their interactions no longer, now found it impossible to turn away. She knew Leo was in for it now.

"You have some nerve!" she shouted, getting so close to his face that her angry breath made his black hair fly up. "Name even one incident in which I have not carried my weight on this team. Because I can count several in which I've had to carry yours as well, you ignorant, male chauvinist arse!"

"You think every man is a male chauvinist arse. You really think I could have made it through the last three years of my life being bossed around by you, day in and day out, if I was that sort of man?" he hollered right back at her, never giving an inch.

Neither did Della.

"The fact you call yourself a man at all is laughable."

"Della!" One single word he shouted, and yet it resounded like an entire statement, demanding that she desist with her flaring insults this instant.

"Don't you 'Della' me!" She shoved him hard in the chest and spun around on her heel, stomping off in the opposite direction, only stopping when she'd reached Hugh, to whom she stuck like glue for the remainder of the night.

"I suppose that's one way to keep Leo from shouting at her, huh?" Annis said, still amused by Della's antics as she and Bess worked twice as fast at breaking down as they had when setting up. The lure of their cabins and their impending free time was a stronger incentive than the upcoming show had been.

"Della's sneaky when she fights. Plays dirty," Bess said, matter-of-fact. "And always considers it a win if she's had the last word."

"Who doesn't?" Annis said, joking. She couldn't help but let her eyes veer toward Leo every so often. He hadn't said a single word since Della's name. It seemed to Annis that he'd chosen to funnel all of his anger at Della into his work, exerting far more physical effort than was required, making a great deal of noise as he slammed, pelted, and dropped things into place.

Until tonight's display, Annis hadn't seen Della and Leo interact outside of their performance. They were an odd pair not because they seemed an unlikely match, but because they went together too well. In their performance, everything about their interactions seemed effortless. They moved so easily together that it was hard to fathom they were just as skilled at fighting as they were at being in sync with one another. If Annis hadn't witnessed their quarrel, she'd probably refuse to believe it could be true.

As the night went on and work dwindled down to odds and ends, Annis noticed Leo's fury diminish too, until all that was left were his hunched shoulders and slow movements, a pathetic mope he wore for all to see. He topped it off with a spectacular pout on his otherwise flawless face. Meanwhile, Della had done all in her power to steer clear of him.

"Think you'll ever want it?" Annis asked when the last of Bess's equipment was stored away, back on the train. "Love, I mean. Do you think it'll ever be worth the trade-off for you?"

"I'm not sure," Bess admitted, pulling the heavy door shut with a loud bang. "But," she continued, carefully hooking the lock into place and pressing it shut. "If I ever do decide it's what I want, I'll go after it, same as I do everything else. With a bit of nerve and a whole lot of laughter."

"Those are key to all things then, huh?" Annis said. A soft smile curved her lips.

"Yes, those, and one last thing," Bess said, turning to Annis expectantly.

"Never look down."

Bess nodded. "Never look down."

Chapter Fifteen
A JOB TO DO

Tonight, rather than wait for him to find her, Annis took it upon herself to track Hugh down. Part of her hoped taking the initiative would be enough to impress upon him all she'd learned today and that he would simply bid her goodnight without questioning her to the point that her head was swimming with a million different thoughts, each causing a cascade of more thoughts, until she was drowning in wisdom and new perspectives that she wouldn't appreciate until morning, when the sun rose and a fresh, brilliant day was upon her, along with a new and wiser her. At times she still found him daunting. Or, rather, she found his incessant pursuit of the deepest, most intimate pieces of her soul daunting. And tiring.

"Am I interrupting?" she asked, opening the door to Hugh and Babe's car after three solid knocks and a muffled answer to come in. Waiting just inside the door was not just Hugh, but the entire Brooks and Bennet threesome. Foursome, if you included Basileus, the tiger.

"Not at all, Tulip," Babe insisted, ushering Annis in to have a seat. "We were just chatting. Nothing important." She caught Hugh's eye and quickly carried on. "You know, Sequoyah was just saying how beautiful the moon was tonight. I think I'm going to go have a look for myself." She tugged at her son's sleeve. "And by that, I mean you're going to show me."

He laughed. "You don't think you can find the moon on your own?"

"I think you're horrible at picking up on subtle cues. Now, come on. These two have things to discuss," Babe insisted, dragging him toward the door.

"Why can't I ever be part of the discussion?" he mumbled, just as Babe was pulling the door shut behind them.

Hugh waited until the sound of Sequoyah's muttering faded along with his and Babe's footsteps. Then, only when he was sure they were long out of ear shot, Hugh took a seat across from Annis in a chair that seemed custom-made for him. Its tall, slender back was lined in an understated linen and minimally cushioned, except for the padded headrest.

"Have a big day?" he asked, his brows raised and his mouth clearly fighting a smile as he settled in, crossing one leg over the other and resting an elbow on his top knee to lean in toward Annis.

"You could say that," Annis said, making no effort to conceal her own grin.

"Do you plan to say anything else about it, or would you care for me to guess for myself?"

Annis's eyes lit up. "Is that something we could do? Turn things around and have you do all the sorting things out for a change?"

He laughed, but his laughter went as quickly as it had come. "No," he said, rather curtly, though Hugh's best attempts at being stern were still relatively harmless.

"It was worth a shot," Annis said, leaning back in her chair and fully relaxing her body for the first time since she'd crawled out of bed that morning. It felt good. Really good. So good, in fact, she didn't dare close her eyes for fear she might fall asleep if she did.

She felt particularly soothed and had never quite appreciated the feel of velvet cushions so much before.

"So," Hugh said, "what did you learn today, love?"

Her words came without hesitation. "A good plan is the foundation required to keep from falling on your arse under any and all circumstances that life brings upon you." It sounded, Annis realized as she said it, perfectly rehearsed.

Hugh chuckled. "A good lesson indeed. But hardly the one I'm asking about."

"Today was tricky," Annis said, mentally reviewing all she'd taken in. "At first, I thought for sure you sent me to Bess to see the other side of love. To learn that loving yourself is just as valuable as loving someone else. Maybe more so, even."

"A valid viewpoint that I'm sure Bess showed you beautifully," Hugh agreed.

"Yes," Annis said. "But that's not why I was there."

"No?" His eyes twinkled with curiosity and Annis knew she was on the right track.

"No."

"Why then?"

Slowly, Annis pulled herself upright again. "Well, I wondered that too when I started to consider that it's not only about loving ourselves, but also about becoming someone we love. Someone we want to be in our own story. At first, I thought, I wanted to be the hero, that *everyone* would want to be the hero."

Hugh's efforts to hide his pleasure were waning. "Is that who you want to be?"

Annis shook her head. "No, I don't. Even if the hero saves the day, they're still bound by the story. They're capable of fighting evil but not able to change it."

"And who is?"

"The writer." It had taken her the whole afternoon and her chat with Babe to figure this out. "I want to be the writer of my story. Not the hero. Not the princess. I don't want to wait for happily ever after or to accept that someone else decides what that might look like. I want to create it for myself."

"Smart girl, Annis." Hugh smiled. "But that wasn't today's lesson either, was it?"

She locked her eyes on his, smiling back. "No, it wasn't." She folded her hands in her lap. "Didn't learn that until just before I came here."

"Really?" he sounded almost surprised.

"Sort of," she said, tipping her head back and forth. "In a physical sense, I learned it in the most inopportune way earlier this afternoon. But I didn't realize its significance until later."

"Go on then, don't keep me in suspense."

She cleared her throat. Nerves tingled at the pit of her stomach. The pressure of saying what Hugh truly wanted to hear mounted to a peak in her chest, threatening to burst her ribcage.

"Don't look down."

Hugh's nostrils flared, the only motion on his otherwise still face. But it was enough. Annis knew the telltale signs of his suppressed delight.

"Don't look down," she repeated. "Don't look back. Don't look anywhere except where you want to go. Looking anywhere else will only lead to fear, doubts, distractions, and false impressions. The key to writing your story, to keep from falling off the pages of your life, is don't look down."

Hugh sat back in his tall chair, his hands together, palms meeting and lifting two of his fingers in a point, which he tapped thoughtfully to his lips. Pride swelled in his eyes as his mouth gave way to the smile he'd been trying to hide. "Good girl, Annis."

Contentment spread all throughout her body, replacing her previous nerves and anticipation. She didn't know why gaining Hugh's approval meant more to her with every passing day. She knew it was silly, really, because Hugh approved of everyone, just as they were. He asked no questions and made no demands. And yet, seeing him so pleased and knowing she was living up to his expectations of her was enough for her to start believing she could set some expectations of herself beyond just making it through another day.

"So, who's next?" she asked, eager for her next challenge.

"You."

"I beg your pardon?"

"You've got all you need to start, Annis. Now it's time to let it settle. Time to rest your mind and work your hands." He stretched his long legs out before him, twisting his ankles out and making them pop in their sockets. "From now on, the work you do here is up to you. I encourage you to learn as many skills as you can. You never know when they may prove handy or how your act may evolve when the time comes for it. But do so to your own liking, your own interests, and know that you've fully completed the lessons I placed before you. You're ready now to set your own terms. You won't get lost. I promise."

"You were never going to lead me the whole way," Annis said, his intentions finally dawning on her.

"I can only give you the tools to navigate, Annis," he said, his tone dropping deeper as the kindness in it rose higher. "In the end, we all have to choose our own destination and how we want to journey there." He smiled. "Do you trust me, love?"

"I do." There was no question. She'd made an unconsciousness choice the day she arrived to trust him. And, in his way, he'd earned it every day since.

"Then trust that I trust you." He reached out and rested his hand on her knee, shaking it playfully back and forth. "You're ready, love. Go forth and start a storm the world can't help but make a path for." Long after their conversation ended, his parting words stayed with her, swirling inside her mind as though they were forming the funnel that would grow into the tornado he'd called on her to become.

Back in her crowded cabin, Annis let the calming chug of the train lull her out of the loud chatter that surrounded her and into the quiet of her mind, where Hugh's most recent words were the only sound. They shut down even her own internal noise, for once, and brought clarity and concise thoughts, and a new sensation settling within her that she had absolute control of her life.

Over the course of the next several months, life flew by in a blissful blur of adventure. New cities to visit nearly every day. New tasks to learn with every setup and breakdown. Though her time in the ring remained elusive for the time being, Annis didn't miss it. The way it had touched her soul the night Bess had dragged her out there stayed with her, never fading or changing her desires to reach the center of that spotlight. She knew her time would come. And so waiting became easy. The passing days meant more laughter, more friendships, and, of course, more time with Sequoyah. It also meant an old coffee tin she'd gotten from Momma and now kept under her bed, where it continued to fill up with her savings. Hugh remained true to his word and paid out her nightly shares at week's end, same as he did for everyone, whether they had an act or not.

Annis wasn't the only one growing on this adventure. Finian seemed to be gaining weight and height every passing hour and, come December, his wooly thick coat and golden yellow eyes gave every indication he had grown into a full wolf, even if his behavior occasionally belied his youth.

"Fin!" Annis said and then snarled, matching the sound he was making as he tugged relentlessly at one of the tent's ropes that she was trying to fasten back into place after he'd only just yanked it loose. "You're not helping!"

The wolf pup released the rope and sat back on his haunches and waited for her to finish.

"Thank you," she said. Maude had told her that wolves didn't care much for manners, but manners mattered to Annis, so she decided to keep using them.

"I see someone's been in trouble," Sequoyah teased Fin, tousling the fur on the top of his head as he walked by. "Trying to steal things again, you little thief?"

Annis sighed, dropping the end of the rope now that it was securely knotted in place and there was no chance of Fin coming along and running off with it. "You should see the things I've been finding under my bed. He's such a hoarder. I swear he's planning to build his own train car so that he doesn't have to share with three girls anymore."

Sequoyah laughed. "Or maybe he's just not as grown up as he looks and still needs toys to play with."

Annis scowled. "He has toys. He doesn't need to try to eat the tent." She threw her arms up at the red and yellow tarp she'd only just saved from flapping in the wind after Fin had ripped the rope from her hands.

"Fair enough," he agreed, taking her hand as they began to walk. It was a small gesture but one that had become a constant in recent months, and one Annis took great pleasure in. "You know, I think he's bored. Maybe he needs more to do. He needs a job. A place in the world. Just like the rest of us."

"What do you suggest I have him do? Round up the monkeys every night?"

"There's an idea!"

For a moment Annis couldn't tell if he was being serious. She had to crane her neck around to face him as they walked, to see what his eyes were saying.

"Oh, thank goodness." She sighed. "You were joking."

"About the monkeys, yes," he said. "But not about him needing a job. Look at the herd. They all get restless with nothing to do. That's when they start breaking boards or jumping fences. Taking off and causing general mischief. They're smart. They need a good challenge. Fin is no different."

He was right about that much. Finian was smart. Annis was often in awe of the things he sorted out for himself and of the ways he understood her. He was brilliant and, young or not, he needed more than just a few toys to throw around and chew on. Sequoyah was right. Fin needed to use his mind.

"Maybe I can start training him to help me around here. Teach him to fetch tools and hold things without turning it into a game of chase or tug-o-war. It's not much, but it's a start, right?"

"Absolutely!"

Annis wasn't sure if his enthusiasm stemmed from his relentless support of her or if he genuinely believed she was on track to finding a job for Fin, but she appreciated it nonetheless.

"Think you can help me?" Maybe his experience with wolves was limited, but he still knew a great deal more about animals than she did.

"You know I'll do whatever I can," he promised. She felt a tender pressure against her palm as he squeezed her hand. "Come find me after lunch and we'll start with something simple."

"Perfect." She beamed back at him, gratitude and admiration moving through her in abundant waves. She was used to the feeling by now, but it never grew any less enjoyable.

He smiled at her one last time before he released her hand when they parted ways at the horse corral. She continued on until she reached Hugh and Babe's car, where she'd promised to help Babe with the wash. With the constant travel, costumes were worn as often as possible before washing them. When it was time, a few people would see to the laundering for the whole troupe. Today the job had fallen to Annis and Babe.

Annis always welcomed time spent with Babe, no matter what they were doing. Last week, she'd spent hours collecting tiny beads out of the dirt with her after Babe's necklace had burst in the middle of the show. The next day, every little gemstone had been strung up on a new chain by Hugh before finding its way back to gracing Babe's neckline.

"Ooh, I smell something sweet!" Annis declared as she stepped inside Babe's makeshift tent.

"Momma brought us fresh pie," Babe informed her, pointing at the golden, flaky, still-steaming crust that rose from an iron skillet. "Brought us all her linens too."

"Sounds like a fair trade to me," Annis said with a laugh, hurrying over to the pie to get a good whiff. "Is it apple? It smells like apple." Apple was her favorite and she hadn't had it in ages.

"I do believe it is." Babe came to stand beside her. "Shall we start with linens? Or pie?"

Both of them laughed. Obviously, the answer was pie.

Within minutes, they had served themselves up a hearty slice each and walked out into the sunshine with it, finding seats on an array of boxes and an abandoned trunk, which made for surprisingly adequate seating. Even as winter was knocking at their door, traveling south had held the cold at bay, at least during daylight hours. Come nightfall, Annis had started to notice a chill in the air. It made her all the more thankful for the bit of warmth from the sun that graced her skin as they sat there, about to enjoy a perfectly delicious slice of Momma T's apple pie.

Fin circled the area several times before he took his place at Annis's feet. Though he was lying down, he remained perfectly alert. Annis hardly registered his behavior anymore. It was simply part of how they went about their day.

"He's become quite the shadow," Babe said, pointing her fork down in his direction before using it to spear another piece of pie.

"He has," Annis agreed. "Half the time it's almost as though he can anticipate my moves before I make them."

"He looks to you as the leader," she said. "That's good."

Annis made a face. "I'm not so sure that's true. He's always getting himself into trouble lately and I'm definitely not leading him to do it."

"But does he stop when you ask him?"

Annis grinned. "When I growl at him," she said with a laugh. "Sometimes I think we've spent so much time together, neither of us really knows which language we're supposed to be speaking."

"Doesn't make much difference as long as you understand each other," Babe said, her gaze still down on Finian. "And you do understand each other."

Annis nodded. "We do. Sequoyah thinks I should start training him. Give him a job to do."

"He's right." Babe's head turned absentmindedly, and Annis followed her gaze back to the tent where they'd left Basileus. "Even the old man in there needs purpose to thrive."

This was news to Annis. "Basileus serves a purpose?" She cleared her throat nervously and began to add in rapid waves of words, "I mean, clearly he serves a purpose. His presence alone serves inspiration to all, not least of all me. And, I mean, he's king, so, he's ruler of all Brooks and Bennet, in a figurative sense of course, not literal. I wouldn't imply he was literally the ruler of this circus. That would be silly. Oh, Babe, shut me up," she pleaded.

"Tulip, you'd burst if anyone ever forced you to keep those words in. When they rush out like that, you just let 'em pour. No one minds." She shrugged, scooping up a piece of fallen pie filling from her plate. "In fact, I think we all rather enjoy it. You're quite funny when you're not trying to be."

"What about when I am trying to be?" Annis realized this was not the current issue. Babe, however, had brought it up and now she needed to know.

"You're quite humorous all around, Tulip. No need to fret." She chuckled, patting Annis's arm with her free hand while her plate lay on her lap, quivering with her quiet laughter. "But for the sake of staying on point, and to answer your previous question, yes, Basileus does in fact serve a purpose outside of being royalty, and a muse of sorts."

Annis was scared to ask what it was. Her previous bout of disbelief seemed rude enough. She didn't want to add to it by inquiring further. Instead, she waited, desperately hoping Babe would tell her, unprompted.

Apparently, Babe sensed Annis's silent suffering. "I suppose it's eating away at you not knowing what it is." She laughed again. Annis was well aware the laughter was at her expense. "For starters, he guards our home. I know you've never seen him act viciously, but that's because you were invited in and he's had a good sniff of you since. He likes you. Trusts you. Knows you mean no harm. He's not always so mellow, Tulip."

"He's not?" The most effort she'd ever seen the tiger exert was to give a good stretch when he was yawning.

"No." She scanned camp ahead as though she were looking for someone specific, and when she couldn't find them, she went on. "A few weeks before you turned up, we had a stowaway. No one knew. Now, ordinarily, and you know as well as anyone, this wouldn't be a problem around here. We're the welcoming sorts, even if we didn't officially ask you to join us. But this was different. This wasn't someone seeking refuge." Her expression turned bitter and left Annis with a sinking feeling in her stomach.

"What did they want?"

"To hurt us," she said sadly. "Or, as he put it, to do God's will and put a stop to the evil we were spreading around like a deadly disease."

"Us?" Annis didn't understand. "You and Hugh? What evil?" And then, like sand through a sifter, the pieces began to fall into place. "No."

"Oh, yes," Babe insisted. Though her voice was breathy, her words were strong. "And he might have succeeded had it not been for old Basil."

Annis felt a new sort of chill, one that had little to do with the weather. "What happened to him?"

"He got beat up pretty good, but nothing time wouldn't mend." Her eyes looked glossy as she dropped them down to examine her nearly empty plate as though it held a great deal of interest for her. "We took him to the first doctor we could find in the next town we came to. Never saw him again."

They sat in silence after that, both moving bits of pie crust around their plates with their forks but too preoccupied to notice they were doing it.

Annis wrestled with an array of emotions. All the work Hugh did each day to show the world the things that people couldn't seem to see for themselves, and still there was such blindness and hatred. It made her chest ache.

"I'm really glad Basileus is so good at his job," she said at last, when she could no longer bear the silence.

Babe's mouth cracked into small smile. "Me too, Tulip. Me too."

"You said he had more than one?"

Babe's smile spread. "He's also our official taster anytime Momma tries a new recipe. And it's his nightly job to warm the bed before we crawl under the covers. He's very efficient at those, as you might imagine."

Annis welcomed the laughter that bubbled out of her. After it subsided, she focused on Fin, who was watching Annis and Babe's interactions. His eyes and ears were in constant motion, as though he were simultaneously tuning in to countless different things while never taking his attention from her.

"You'd protect me, wouldn't you?" she said, reaching down to scratch under his chin the way he liked.

"He'd do more than that, Tulip," Babe said, watching the two. "He'd kill for you. Anyone ever tried to lay a hand on you, there'd be nothing left. Fin would see to that."

Annis gradually lifted her head, turning her attention back to Babe. When their eyes met, she didn't have to ask the question burning in her mind because the answer was written all over Babe's face. Annis hadn't been chosen at random to foster the wolf pup. Babe had wanted her to have him because she knew all along that he would grow to be her guardian. And they both knew what no one else did. She needed one.

"It's the one job you'll never have to train him for," Babe said, nudging her with her elbow. "Unlike helping us with the wash. He'll need loads of practice and I think we should start right now."

Annis forced a grin, still shaking off the weight of the memories of her past. For some reason she found a twisted sort of comfort in lingering in the dank, dark space that fear and pain provided her. She always needed a taste of it before she could spit it out and move on.

"Better start with the linens," she said, going through the motions of sorting the laundry as she waited to for the flavor of her pain to turn sour and purge itself from her system, at least for the time being. "Momma will need those tonight and they might not dry in time otherwise."

"Suppose you're right," Babe admitted. "We don't need any of these costumes until tomorrow. Far as I know, everyone's set for tonight's show."

Trudging along as though their empty pie plates each weighed several tons, they made their way back to the tent that currently housed not only Babe's extensive wardrobe but also a great deal of dirty laundry.

"Here," Annis said, holding the rope end of a laundry sack out to Fin. "Take this outside, would you?" She laughed at herself for her foolish demand. But then he took the rope between his teeth, gripping it tight and waiting for her to make the next move. Annis stopped laughing. "Really? You're going to do this? Just like that?" But now was not the time to wait for him to learn to respond in English. Instead, accepting her good fortune, she picked up a large wicker basket mounding high with towels and tablecloths, and lead the way outside to the wash buckets and washboards that Francis had already set up for them.

"See if you can make him scrub the stains out of these next, would you, Tulip?" Babe joked, holding a handful of aprons out to her.

"I'm not sure we're ready for that quite yet," she said, a giggle setting in where the darkness of her past had resided before. Light was always stronger than the darkness, and love and laughter were light's greatest sources. These days Annis tended to have plenty of both.

Aside from the occasional quip about wolves doing laundry and other household chores, they worked steadily without much distraction. Before long, Annis and Babe had drawn up clotheslines all around. The clothes and linens formed a maze to get in and out of Babe and Hugh's corner of camp. By the time they finished the laundry, the sun was already setting.

"It's my least favorite part of winter," Babe said watching the bright orange slowly dim. "The days are far too short, the nights far too long."

"You don't like the nights?" It seemed odd to Annis, given most of their days were spent building up to the show, which always took place after dark, no matter what the season.

"I like the nights." Babe lifted an empty basket off the ground to take it back inside. "I just don't like having to do daytime things when it's no longer daytime. And somehow, all the things that need doing never do seem to adjust to fit the hours we have to do them in."

"Hadn't ever thought of that." Annis followed Babe with several empty laundry sacks.

"That's because you have young eyes and can see in the dark," Babe said, and then chuckled. "Some of us older girls aren't so lucky."

"Well, from now on just use my good eyes, then, for the things that need doing," Annis offered. "I mean it. Consider me at your service from now until spring."

Babe gave Annis a squeeze and kissed her cheek, making a loud smacking sound and leaving a bright pink imprint of lips. "I'll hold you to that."

"Please do," Annis insisted. "But for now, I think I'm going to take my good eyes and see what sort of trouble I can get into before supper."

"Make it good," Babe called out after her as she slipped out the door and into oncoming dusk.

Good trouble was easy to come by. Annis knew all too well the best places to find it. So, walking quietly with Fin at her side, she tuned in to all the noises surrounding her, then one by one, began to shut them out, until she'd zeroed in on the voices she was seeking. Smiling with delight before she even reached them, she weaved in and out of the people still wandering about and finishing last-minute tasks before supper and the show that would follow.

"There you lot are," Annis said in her most accusing tone as soon as found them, all huddled around a small fire behind the animal tent.

Each of the seven sets of eyes staring back at her looked startled.

"Oh," Sawyer said, waving his hand and dismissing the threat. "It's just you."

"Why do you always do that?" Mabel asked, still clutching her chest from the fright Annis had caused her.

"Because it's fun. And it's so easy," she teased, dropping down to the ground between Sequoyah Mabel and stretching out her legs to warm her feet by the fire. "What are you trying not to get caught doing right now, anyway?"

"Not doing anything yet," Maude said, rubbing her hands together to generate extra heat between her palms. "Still in the plotting phase."

"Plotting's my favorite," Annis said, looking around at everyone. "What are we plotting?"

"Christmas," Sequoyah told her with a smirk.

"Christmas?" Annis wasn't sure if it was right to feel so disappointed. "What's there to plot about Christmas?"

"Oh, Annis," Sawyer said, shaking his head at her, his eyes glistening with pity as they reflected the fire's flickering flames. "Poor, poor Annis. Circus Christmas isn't like normal Christmas, you sad, silly girl."

"It's not?" Her interest was piqued. "What's so different about it? Are there pranks? Do we hang a tree from the circus tent ceiling? Dress Sawyer up as Santa and have the monkeys pull him on a sleigh? Oh, if we don't then we should!"

Annis could tell from the way Mabel's face lit up that she wholeheartedly agreed.

Sawyer's sour expression showed less enthusiasm. "Why am I always at the center of your most insulting ideas?"

"Why are you always insisting I'm poor, sad, and silly? Think that's a particularly flattering combination?" Annis demanded. "It's not."

"True," he agreed. "And you forgot pitiful. It may go unspoken at times, but I'm always thinking it."

"Children, children," Homer's baritone cut through their arguing. "Can we get back to talking Circus Christmas? The real sort?" Then, he turned toward Annis's general direction. "Though I'd like to revisit that monkey sleigh idea when we have time."

"Harris would never go for it," Goldilocks chimed in.

"Right," Sawyer added grumpily. "The monkeys would be hard to get. They'd be the reason this wouldn't work. Not the part where I said no."

"You always say no," Caroline pointed out. "You never mean it. It's just your starting point."

"It's true," Maude agreed. "If you really meant no when you said no, we'd have far less fond memories of you."

"Also, you wouldn't have that scar on your rear end from when you fell from the trapeze hoop and landed smack on someone's tiara," Sequoyah said, laughing. "Saying no to Della and meaning it would be worth learning, though."

"Wait, that's what happened to Edi's tiara? Your arse?" Mabel sounded downright appalled.

"Don't even start with me. That damn elephant's headdress has been the bane of my existence for months now. Maybe if you didn't leave things lying around, I wouldn't land on them as I'm falling from the sky," he huffed. "Now, about Christmas."

"Yes," Annis said. "I want to know about Christmas. Though I think we'll all want to hear more about the flying-and-falling-on-tiaras story later."

"Not happening," Sawyer said sternly, cutting the air with the back of his hand.

"I'll tell you when he's not around," Sequoyah whispered in Annis's ear, but Sawyer must have caught him leaning in closer to her.

"Is that how` it's going to be then?" he said. "Are none of our stories sacred anymore?"

"What's sacred about stabbing your rear end on a dainty little crown?" Homer asked, barely able to maintain his serious expression.

"Never mind the bit about my rear end," Sawyer snapped. "I'm talking about confidentiality between two friends," he snarled under his breath. "You wouldn't understand. You're married," he sneered.

"I think he meant that to be an insult," Caroline chirped, hardly seeming offended.

"I think someone would be a lot less fussy if we gave him some chocolate," Mabel said, digging around in one of her pockets and retrieving half a cookie she must have saved after lunch. "Here. I was going to have it later tonight, but I think for the sake of our overall well-being you should eat it." She pressed it into Sawyer's hand. "Now."

He looked furious, but he ate the cookie in silence.

"Can I tell it?" Goldilocks asked, looking himself like a child on Christmas morning. "It's my first year not being the new kid, let me tell it. Let me pass on the tradition."

"You have to do it right," Maude said, sounding very serious.

"Yes," Homer agreed, "poem and all."

"Poem?" Annis asked, growing more excited with every passing second. "There's a poem?"

"Of course there's a poem," Mabel assured her, as though it were common knowledge that every Christmas tradition was passed down in the form of poetry.

"Is there an Easter poem?" Annis asked, nearly coming up from where she sat. Her feet jittered around from the anticipation.

"One holiday at a time, kid," Homer chided. "But, yes. There is."

"Oh, Lord," Caroline sighed with a laugh. "Look what you've done. The poor girl is coming out of her skin with excitement. She'll never be able to focus now."

"Yes," Annis insisted, forcing her knees back to the ground. "Yes, I can." She took a breath and calmed herself, nodding at Goldilocks to gesture for him to begin. "Go ahead. You have my undivided attention."

"Alright, here goes," he started, but Maude's quiet coughing stopped him before he got any further.

"He's not standing on one foot, is he?" Homer asked.

"He's not," his wife said, confirming his suspicions. She cast a warning look in Goldilocks's direction. "Go on, you're the one who wanted the job."

He sighed, and Annis wondered if perhaps there were aspects of the task he'd neglected to remember. "Alright, alright," he grumbled, scrambling to his feet. To ensure Homer was aware, he said, "I'm standing, okay? On one foot."

"Hands in a peak over your head?" Homer asked.

Annis watched as Goldilocks, who already had his knee drawn up and foot laid flat against the inside of his thigh, rolled his eyes and lifted his arms over his head to create a sort of triangle top.

"Oh!" Annis called out. "You're a Christmas tree!"

"Obviously," Sawyer mumbled under his breath, but from the sideways glance he cast in Annis's direction she knew he had wanted her to hear him.

"Listen, I'm only doing this once. I'm starting to remember there's a reason I'm not in the show. My balance is lousy and I'm terribly uncoordinated, so this tree bit here, it's not easy," Goldilocks said.

Annis opened her eyes as wide as they would go and stared straight at him, letting him know in no uncertain terms that he had her fully captivated with his impending, possibly once-in-a-lifetime, performance.

With all the attention square on him, Goldilocks took a deep breath, and began to recite,

"Hear ye, oh, hear ye,
'tis my time to be the Christmas tree
To tell you all a tale so true
Of the Circus Christmas big to-do
As the year goes by we come and go
And still they're there at every show
They fill our hearts each single day
They lift our spirits in every way
And though perhaps to them it seems
It's they who get the best of dreams
It's we who get to dream awake
And live the circus life we make
So as December rolls around
And we start coming to new towns
Those of us who have always received
Prepare to give back to those in need
For as it goes with every year
The best of Christmas is the cheer
So we spread it around with a swirl and a swish

Until we've fulfilled each and every Christmas wish."

Then, still in tree form, he took a splendid bow. Annis, still rapt with attention, gave a loud, solo round of applause.

"That was amazing!" she insisted, still utterly confused about what any of it meant, but not daring to admit it in front of Sawyer. "Really splendid!"

"The fun in Circus Christmas, Annis," Homer began to explain, "is that we *all* get to be Santa Claus." Of course the blind man could see her confusion. He saw everything.

"Though no one dresses up," Sawyer clarified before anyone could suggest otherwise.

"No," Caroline said, supporting his statement, sad as it made Annis. "In fact, we don't do anything to draw attention to ourselves at all. We're more like secret elves in the dark of night. We wait until right before we're ready to leave and then we make a hasty run through town, leaving little surprises everywhere we can before we jump on the train and disappear."

"On Christmas Eve?" Annis asked, enthralled with the idea.

"No, the whole month of December," Sequoyah explained. "So, starting tonight."

"And you're only just now telling me?" Annis stared around the circle in disbelief. "Was I not going to be included in Circus Christmas?"

Mabel reached an arm out and hooked it around Annis's shoulders, pulling her in tight for a dramatic hug against her side. "Don't go getting yourself all worked up now. No one gets invited. You either stumble upon it on your own and thus become a member of the Circus Christmas crew, or you go on living your life with normal Christmas. No harm, no foul. Just no Circus Christmas either."

"It's the rules," Sequoyah said with a shrug when Annis turned to him next.

"It's not in the poem," Annis pointed out indignantly, as though this were a major error on their part and should somehow negate their silly don't-tell-Annis rule.

"No need to put it in the poem. Once you hear it, you're already in," Maude said haughtily. Annis suspected she'd had a hand in writing it. "And, more importantly," Maude continued, "do you really think we would have a had our meeting right here, knowing you were coming any second, if we weren't intending for you to find out and be included?"

"Oh," Annis sat back, somewhat stumped and unexpectedly humbled. "Right. Thanks."

"Now that she's all clued in, can we get back to what we were doing?" Sawyer asked. He'd finished his cookie and was no longer mollified into silence. "It's not like we have all night, here."

"Yes," Homer agreed, though Annis found he lacked the flair Sawyer had for obnoxious rudeness. "Where were we? Right, we finished drawing for those absent from the circle. That means Maude and Mabel, you're next to draw."

"Draw what?" Annis whispered to Sequoyah, afraid to derail the meeting again but certain she wanted to know.

"You'll see," he said, nodding at the twins who were leaning forward and reaching into a large tin cup Homer was holding out in their direction.

A second later, they'd retrieved two small pieces of paper and were looking them over. "We got stockings and sweet treats!" Mabel announced half a second later, looking absolutely pleased.

"Who's next?" Homer asked, shaking the cup. Its contents made a dull rattling sound.

"I am," Goldilocks said, standing to draw from the cup. He then read his note aloud. "I've got a Christmas task. It's good. I like those." He grinned and wiggled his brows, looking silly and making Annis giggle into her arm where she was careful to muffle the sound.

Annis watched with quiet anticipation as everyone around the fire took a turn pulling a note from the cup. When her turn came, she held her breath and closed her eyes. Her hand dangled out in the air aimlessly, trying by sheer miracle to meet the cup Homer blindly held out in her direction.

"You've got to be kidding me," Sawyer grunted as several others began to laugh.

Then, sensing her inability to open her eyes and feel with full awareness her excitement, Sequoyah took her hand and gently lead it to its intended destination.

Fumbling inside, Annis felt only two small sheets of paper. Hers and Homer's.

Her fingers felt hot, as though she might singe the paper, from the pressure to pick a Christmas mission she could complete successfully. Deciding there really were no parts of Christmas she didn't enjoy, she gulped down her nerves and grasped a sheet of paper with her fingertips.

She stared at the swirly writing upon the scrap of paper for several seconds, calming her mind long enough to read what was written. "An act of love." She looked to the others. "What does that mean?"

"Means you got the best one," Homer said, smiling. "You get to choose. Only requirement is that it comes from the heart, whatever it is you give or do, and for whomever you choose to be your recipient." He pulled out the last little piece of paper. "Of course, that means that I got the second best."

"What's that?" Annis asked, clearly the only one who didn't already know.

"The gift of believing," he said, carefully placing the empty cup down on the ground beside him. "I get to find a nonbeliever and turn them around. The only reason it's not the very best task is because it can be maddeningly difficult." He chuckled.

"How do you do it? All of this in one day?" Annis asked, slowly grappling with the enormity of the gestures they'd all volunteered to make. "And do we choose a new task every day?"

"No," Caroline explained," what you chose tonight is yours until Christmas." She smiled, stretching her arm down Homer's until she could anchor her hand in his, now that it was free again. "We usually start small. Takes a bit of practice when you haven't done it all year long, but you'll see, once you get going, it gets easier. Your ideas get loftier and the fun only gets grander."

Maude nodded. "Don't get us wrong. It's no simple undertaking. But that's what makes it worth doing."

"Keep in mind, you won't know who you're gifting any more than they'll know who it came from," Mabel went on. "Tonight, after the show, we'll head into town and spread out. Have your gift ready so you can just drop and run. There's never much time and the less you linger, the less likely you are to get caught."

"But how do you choose where to leave your gift?" Annis asked, still not sure it was as easy as they were making it sound.

"It's a lot more random than you might imagine," Mabel answered.

"Once you're in town, some place will call to you more than any other," Caroline assured her. "You'll see. And the more we do it, the more you'll know what to look for. The door missing the wreath. The windows left dark and empty. Homes that seem dreary, broken, or hopeless. Those are the ones you choose."

"So, we just have our show, and then what? Follow the audience home?" Annis was joking, of course.

"Essentially, yes." Sawyer was not. "Usually the easiest way to find town without getting lost our first time out."

"Oh." She frowned, having suddenly very mixed feelings about this. "And Poppy and Babe? They won't have a nervous breakdown between now and Christmas wondering if we'll be shot or arrested for following strangers home in the dark of night?"

"They'll be fine," Sequoyah said.

"Because they don't know," Sawyer added.

"That's part of why we plot in secret," Maude said, pointing out what was now obvious.

"And what makes Circus Christmas a proper shenanigan," Mabel finished.

It did little to appease Annis's internal conundrum. "Just out of curiosity, *has* anyone ever been shot or arrested?"

"No," Homer answered, a little too quickly. "Well, shot *at,* perhaps, but never shot and hit."

"And *nearly* arrested," Sawyer said, raising a hand to indicate himself. "But the coppers never think to look in places they deem too small for hiding." He grinned. "You're pretty tiny yourself. You'll be fine."

"Grand," Annis said.

She felt Sequoyah bump her shoulder with his. "Welcome to Circus Christmas."

Circus Christmas certainly had all the makings of turning Christmas into a circus. And, while she had no idea whatsoever how she was to find a stranger and bestow upon them a random act of love, sitting there, with those she adored most in the world, she could see that somehow it would be possible. And, just maybe, it would be completely lovely—provided no one was shot or arrested.

Chapter Sixteen
EMMELINE

The sky was already pitch-black by the time they all stood huddled together at the train's caboose. The group had grown some since the fire, as Annis had suspected it would. August and Bess were rarely left out of anything they did. Francis was also among the Christmas Crew, as was Momma T. From where they stood, they had a clear view of camp, which was still full of workers breaking down and packing up their circus.

"It feels wrong to leave when the work isn't done," Annis mumbled.

"Our work *will be* done," Maude reminded her. And she was right, they'd all seen to it that they could hurry out and hurry back, at which point they'd be getting everything loaded up in record time. But it was still different for Annis. Without an act, she had no clear-cut work and always bounced from place to place to help wherever she was needed. Her job was never finished until the train was moving along the tracks, headed out of town. So, even though she knew she'd be returning to do a fair share of tasks, she felt as though she were somehow cheating her way out of work.

"Come on," Sawyer grunted. "We don't get going, we won't make it back in time. And I don't know about you lot, but I didn't see anything here that made me want to stay in town on a permanent basis."

No one made any audible responses, but there was a general consensus that Sawyer was right. They all began to move around the back of the train to the other side, where they were officially free of any potential prying eyes.

From there, the road into town was easy to travel. The group kept a safe distance from the townspeople who were heading home for the night, though they'd hardly have noticed the strangers in their midst. They were too enthralled from the circus to be aware of much outside of recounting their favorite moments of the night's show.

Before long, they were coming up on houses. Most were built acres apart, but the little farms promised that town lie not far beyond.

"Are we getting close?" Homer asked, squeezing Caroline's hand.

"I think so," Caroline said.

"I can see the glow of lights ahead," Annis said, still a bit unnerved at the thought of venturing off on her own in uncharted territory. It didn't seem to matter how often she reminded herself of the days and nights she'd spent fending for herself prior to finding Hugh and the family. Somehow, those memories had become a separate life all together and they hardly felt real anymore.

"You'll be fine," Sequoyah promised, taking her hand as they walked. "We'll all be close by. You'll see."

"Also," Sawyer muttered, with a touch of aggravation in his tone, "the girl is traveling with a wolf. I find it highly unlikely she'll be harmed."

Annis knew her four-legged shadow was at her side with every step, though it did continue to escape her that she was no longer the caretaker in their partnership. He'd been so dependent on her in the beginning that some days she still saw him as the same little wolf pup who spent weeks curled up in a sling against her chest. But

Fin was far from that helpless bundle now. And she was no longer the one looking after him. Somewhere along the way, their roles had reversed and Annis had missed it.

"Maybe I shouldn't have brought him," Annis whispered after considering how little Fin knew of the world beyond their traveling camp. "What if he gets frightened? Or runs off?"

"He won't." Sawyer's voice was calmer and kinder than usual. "As long as you stay safe, he stays safe. So, see to it you stay out of trouble and all will be well." He came closer to her and the wolf, patting the back of Fin's head as they walked. "Besides, you couldn't leave him behind even if you wanted to. He'd never allow it."

Annis noticed that the road beneath her felt harder packed than it had closer to camp, and soon the group turned down the main street of what was a grander town square than Annis has expected.

"We meet back here in exactly fifteen minutes," Homer said. No dawdling. No exceptions. If you're delayed by unforeseen circumstances, stay put. We'll come to you."

A wave of nods moved through their small assembly, and then they began to disperse, some in pairs and some solo, until Annis and Sequoyah were the only two remaining.

"You know what you're going to do?" he asked. His own Christmas treat was stowed carefully in a leather satchel over his shoulder, much like a true Santa Clause would carry.

"I have an idea," Annis whispered, though it wasn't nearly as clear or prepared as she'd have liked. She was relying a great deal on inspiration to strike in the moment.

He leaned in and softly kissed her cheek. "Remember, it's supposed to be fun." Then, facing her, he backed away until the shadows swallowed him. She was on her own.

"Right, Annis," she muttered to herself to keep from feeling as alone as she was. "You're going to love this." Nerves swirled at the

pit of her stomach and, though the sensation still made her nauseated, she'd learned to welcome the feeling because it eventually led
to brilliant results, as she'd learned from Bess.

"Come on," she whispered to Fin, though he never needed
prompting. "Let's go find our Christmas mark."

Moving swiftly through the dark, Annis walked along the main
street until she felt pulled to turn right, into a dreary alley that was
made more ominous in the pitch of night. Annis wasn't scared. Instead, she felt determined in her mission, convinced she'd found
the path to the recipient destined for her Christmas cheer.

Her steps slowed until she came to a stop near the end of the
alley.

"What do you think?" she asked Fin. He sat back on his
haunches as though to let her know he also felt they'd arrived.

The brick building was four stories tall, and several of its windows were patched with boards. From where she stood Annis could
see clotheslines filled with laundry that flapped gently in the
evening breeze.

"I think I've an idea," she muttered, approaching the building.
Scanning the walls, she searched for a way to scale them. The drainpipe would have to do, she decided.

"Wait here," Annis told Fin, who accepted the order and lowered himself to the ground to wait for her. She took a deep breath,
reached both hands as high as she could, and clasped the pipe to
pull herself up. The bricks provided reasonable traction under her
shoes. By the time she'd reached the first floor, she'd established
a comfortable rhythm in her movements. When she reached the
rooftop, she swung her legs over the ledge one at a time. There was
no time to catch her breath or appreciate the success of her climb.
She went straight to work. She took down the clothes, folded them
neatly, and placed them in the baskets sitting at the center of the
roof. When she finished, she placed on each stack of laundry a

small bundle of Christmas cookies she'd baked with Momma after supper.

Taking a step back to assess her work, she let out a satisfied sigh. Not bad for her first time. She glanced at the clock tower in the center of town. Only three minutes to spare.

Annis wasted not a second getting back to the drainpipe. Rather than grip it with her bare hands, she looped around it the sling she'd used to carry her Christmas cookies and slid all the way down. As soon as her feet touched the ground, she began running, with Finian right on her heels.

Exhilaration spurred her on as she raced through the alley, heading back the way she came. There was no time to check the clock, so she kept her eyes forward and ran faster and faster until she reached their meeting point, where she crumpled over at the waist and gasped for air. "Did I...make it?" she stammered in between breaths while trying to count the shadowed figures in her midst.

"Not even the last one back," Caroline told Annis, patting her back.

"There they are," Sawyer said, pointing to the left. Even in the dark, there was no mistaking the twins. Their shape, the way they moved, and the constant bickering always made them easy to recognize.

"Would you hurry up?" Annis could hear Maude even from several feet away. "I told you not to wear those shoes!"

"You're just mad because they make me look taller than you," Mabel huffed, clearly struggling for breath and speed.

"You're ridiculous. You can't walk in those heels, and even if you could, it's throwing off the entire balance between us. I feel like I'm being yanked up with every step you take. Worse, it's pulling me backwards, because all you can manage is a speedy hobble when what we need to do is run!"

"Are you mad? I'm not running in heels!" Mabel's indignant tone was enough to make Maude snort in exasperation. When they realized they'd been within earshot of the others for quite some time, neither said any more on the matter.

"Perhaps wardrobe issues can be discussed prior to leaving next time?" Sawyer said, and then smirked. The group seamlessly moved forward as though the twins were the missing link they'd needed to be set into motion.

"I don't want to hear anything about my wardrobe from you, Smalls. You haven't managed to pair up a proper set of socks in weeks," Maude said in his direction.

Sawyer said nothing in response, which Annis took as a silent truce. He'd never accept defeat, but there was little for him to retort with for the moment.

The group carried on, leaving town faster than they'd entered it. They grew increasingly louder as they moved, sensing safety in their isolation.

"You're being awfully quiet," Annis said, noticing Goldilocks glance in her direction for the fourth time in the last few minutes. "Have a hard time with your task?"

"No," he said curtly. He stared down at the ground, a grim expression taking over his face so that he looked nothing like the lighthearted boy they all knew him to be.

"What's wrong?" Sequoyah asked, apparently noticing as well.

Goldilocks came to an abrupt stop, prompting everyone around him to do the same. "The problem is I found this when I was in town." He pulled a piece of paper out of his pocket, unfolding it before he held it out for everyone to see. "I don't know what to make of it. Maybe you could help, *Emmeline*." He glared at Annis. "It is you, isn't it?" he demanded, thrusting the wanted poster directly at her.

"Don't be stupid," Mabel sniped. "Of course it's not her. That says wanted for murder. You think Annis would kill someone? Look at her."

Annis could feel all eyes cast in her direction, burning through her with a curiosity she couldn't bear the weight of. She had no answer for them. She had no words at all. Her throat had closed up the second she'd seen the empty stare of her own eyes cast back at her. She remembered the day the photo was taken. It had been a portrait ordered by her mother as a present for her father's birthday. Annis's mother had nagged the entire time, complaining about everything from her hair to the way her fingers couldn't help but fidget from the nerves of being picked apart.

Her feet felt cold and tingly. Her knees were certain to give out at any moment. Her head felt dizzy, as though a fog had seeped into her brain that made it hard to think, hard to see clearly, and harder still to hear.

Voices were blending together in a whir of sounds, none of which she could understand before they were drowned out by the thunderous beating of her own heart exploding in her ears and obliterating the world around her.

"Annis!" Sequoyah's voice reached her through all the chaos, and she blinked several times, trying to focus on him. "Annis, answer me," he pleaded with her.

"I'm sorry," she wheezed through clenched teeth, stumbling backwards. Her knees buckled. Her hands clasped at dirt and grass as she hit the ground, landing hard on her left hip. She was sure it would hurt later but she felt nothing now, too stunned by the unexpected turn of events to feel anything.

Sequoyah was down in the dirt beside her, holding her hand. His hand was clammy and cold. No. That was hers. Cold beads of sweat ran down her back.

"Annis," he said, ever the calm eye of her unfolding storm. "Talk to me. I don't care what you say, but I need to hear your voice. I need to know you're still there."

"Emmeline," she breathed, the name washing over her the way the cold of the river had the night she'd let her die.

"Is that your name?" he asked softly.

"No," Annis shook her head. "I'm not her." Tears stung her eyes and a wicked lump forced its way into her clenched throat, causing an agonizing pressure she couldn't release. "She's...gone."

Annis felt Mabel take her other hand as she and Maude knelt on the other side of her. "Annis," Maude said quietly. "We need to get you back to camp, alright?" She looked to Sequoyah, who nodded. Gently, he reached both arms around Annis, one under her legs and the other around her torso. Then, ever so tenderly, he lifted her out of the dirt and carried her the remainder of the way back.

Annis closed her eyes to keep the world from spinning.

Murder.

Wanted.

Months had passed. The miles she'd traveled, and still, here she was, closer to being caught in the deadly fangs of her past than ever.

Annis remembered little of their walk home. Upon arriving back in camp, she was whisked straight to their car and told repeatedly not to leave by several people, though the only voice that stood out was Sequoyah's.

As soon as the door shut behind everyone, Annis was on her feet, pacing. Back and forth from one door to the other, stopping at each end just short of turning the handle and making a run for it every time. She couldn't stay, couldn't risk anyone else getting hurt. But then she considered their efforts to bring her back here, to keep her safe. Maybe they could help her. Maybe this didn't have to be the end of it all. But maybe someone else would be asked to pay the same price others had already paid in an attempt to save her.

No. She couldn't risk it.

Her hand twisted the handle before she could have another bout of doubts. She stepped outside and slammed the door shut before Fin could follow. She wouldn't make him live the life of uncertainty and sacrifice that lay ahead for her. Making a sharp left, she cut through to the other side of the tracks, running as fast as she could without looking back, without thinking at all.

Tears ran down her cheeks as she relived the night that she thought she'd put behind her for good. How often would this cycle repeat? How could she prevent this madness from consuming the rest of her life?

Keeping north of town, she watched the stars, relying on them once more to guide the way the farther she got from the train. The terrain was already changing. The thicket of woods made it harder to run. Still, she pushed onward, seeking the shelter of the trees, knowing they would keep her hidden as they had before. The pounding in her ears grew louder as she ran. Maybe her heart would burst right in her chest and put an end to her story all at once—a beautiful, tragic mess tidied up in one swift move.

Then, she felt the familiar motion of another falling into step beside her, merging with her movements seamlessly. Annis didn't have to see to know that it was Finian. Nor could she continue to deny the true source of the endless pounding getting louder every second. She knew what she heard were hooves marking the earth with each thunderous step that Catori took toward her.

"Annis!" Her heart stopped beating all together at the sound of his voice. Her feet followed suit.

"Go back," she yelled, turning to watch as he drew nearer.

"No!" The mare's legs stretched out in front of her, bringing her to a dramatic sliding stop only feet from where Annis stood. Sequoyah leapt from her back and rushed to Annis's side. "What are you doing?" he demanded, shaking her by the shoulders. "We told you to stay in the train car. We told you we would take care of things. Why would you run?" He sounded as helpless as she felt. "What is really going on here, Annis? Is it true? Did you really kill someone?"

"No." She couldn't even believe herself when she said it. How would she ever convince anyone else. "Not directly."

"What does that mean?" He shook his head, frustration and fear twisting his face up in agony.

"It means I knew she would die if I left, I knew he would kill her for helping me escape. We both did..." Annis cried, screaming out into the night and reeling her breath back in with a chest-shattering sob. "But I left anyway." Her knees gave out and she fell into his chest. He caught her and held her tight as she fell apart in the safe confines of his strong arms.

"Please come back with me," he whispered, his mouth pressed to the side of her head to place desperate kisses over her hair. "Please come home. Let us help you."

"No," she blubbered. "You'll all be in danger. I can't let you risk your lives for me. I've already lost one family. I won't lose another."

"That's not a reason, Annis," he refused her. "We can all protect ourselves. Hell, most of us have been hunted ourselves at one point or another. That's why we're all here. And why you belong with us, where we can keep you safe!"

"I'll never be safe," Annis whispered, dreading the sound of her own words and the truth they bore. "Even if I thought you could keep me safe, it's not just one person who's after me anymore. I'm wanted, Sequoyah. Every second I stay is a second that I put everyone at risk. I'd be asking everyone to break the law to let me stay."

"We already do that, Annis," he reminded her. "Or did you forget about our friendly circus fugitives, Francis and Will? Or even Sawyer, for that matter."

"Goldilocks didn't seem too keen on adding another when he found my wanted poster though, did he?" Annis was grasping at straws to keep him from winning this debate. If she lost, she'd give in and go home. From there, the deadly consequences were anybody's guess.

"Goldilocks doesn't care that you're wanted any more than I do. It was lying about who you are that set him off. You should trust us by now, Annis. You should have told us yourself." Unlike Goldilocks, Sequoyah wasn't angry. He was hurt. She understood. He had every reason to be. She'd owed them the truth, but she'd been selfish. Keeping everything in had been easier than sharing it, and choosing easy over right was a mistake that she knew, even as she was making it, would come back to reap its due payment.

"I know," she said, feeling herself crumble internally, her physical body slowly folding in on itself and threatening to surrender. "I just...couldn't." It was a weak answer, but she was weak. She felt broken from all she'd been running from and was now no longer certain she would ever recover, not when he was coming back for her a second time—this time from both sides of the law.

"Please," Sequoyah tried again. "Come back with me. Get on the train. Get cleaned up. We'll make tea. We'll all be there. And you can tell us then. And together we can figure this out."

"There's nothing to figure out." Annis's frustration created tension that reached from her clenched jaws to her back. A dull pounding started inside her head. "I'm wanted for murder, Sequoyah. Not petty theft."

"But you're not guilty!" His voice raised louder than she'd ever heard it.

"It doesn't matter!" Her lungs burned.

"Why not?" he shouted. They were both caught in the chaos of emotion.

"Because he's the law! He killed them, and he'll never get caught because he's the law. He decides who's guilty. And he's decided it's me. This will never go away. I'll never be able to prove my innocence because no one will ever question my guilt. Don't you see? He's cornered me. It was bad enough when I thought it was just him and his men, but now he's gone public. His reach is limitless. It's only a matter of time before he finds me. And I don't want any of you anywhere near me when he does."

"Too bad." Maude's voice startled Annis.

"Because we're in this with you," Mabel continued.

"Where you go," Caroline said.

"We all go," Sawyer, of all people, concluded.

Annis could hardly believe it. They'd all come after her. Even Homer, who must have struggled across the terrain, even being led by his wife. She would have been nearly as blind as he was in this dark. Goldilocks was there, too, along with August, Momma T, and Bess, and they all nodded in agreement with what the others had said aloud.

"But I never gave you a choice," Annis said, guilt swelling in her throat as the words spilled out. "I never told you what you were really opening your lives to when you let me in. It's not right. And dragging you in deeper, it wouldn't be fair to any of you." A lone tear trickled down her already soaked cheeks.

"We're choosing now, Annis," Homer said, stepping forward. "And we're choosing you."

Annis had no words, though a million different thoughts raced inside her head. Questions, mostly. She wondered why they saw such value in her when she'd yet to contribute anything to the circus or the crew she deemed worthy, and why they were so willing to risk their own lives to save hers.

She turned to face the man beside her in search of answers. "Why?"

"Always have." Sequoyah's arm nestled her tight to his side.

"Thank you," she breathed, her throat too swollen to pass much more than air. "You'll never know what this means to me. What you all mean to me."

"I do believe that feeling is mutual," Maude teased with a smirk.

"Now, then, if we've settled the all-of-us-or-none-of-us debate," Sawyer interrupted with a tone gruffer and more characteristic of him, "can we get on with the all of us heading back to the train bit? Because I see no real reason to miss it and be stuck here indefinitely, yeah?"

There was a resounding yes all around, and they began the trek back to the train.

Annis hadn't realized how far she'd run until the time came to walk back. She found herself apologizing repeatedly for putting everyone through the extra hike given the long day they'd all had already. The bulk of her apologies were met with dismissive laughter and obscene gestures, the latter coming primarily from Sawyer.

It wasn't until they all were settled back on the train, chugging peacefully along toward their next stop, did a deeper conversation begin among the group. "Let's have it then," Maude said. They all cradled in their hands fresh cups of chamomile tea, served by Momma T. "The whole story," Maude continued. "I don't care how long, or how far back you have to go. We want the beginning."

"Yes," Mabel agreed with a vigorous nod. "Now we've established you're not going anywhere, you needn't worry about how much time it'll take. Just start, we'll all still be around when you finish."

Annis sipped her tea. The hot golden liquid felt like magic potion going down as it eased her aches and filled her with warmth. "Thing is," she started, "I'm not even sure where the beginning is." She shrugged her shoulders helplessly. Trying to tell a story she'd yet to sort out for herself would prove challenging. "Maybe it was always happening. Maybe the truth was always staring me square in the eyes and I couldn't see it because the lies were told from the time I was born. Maybe longer. I can't say..." she sighed, closing her eyes and sticking a mental needle in the first thought that passed slowly enough to catch. "My father died nearly a year ago. Accident. Or so I'd been told. After all I've witnessed since, I suspect it was nothing short of murder."

"The policeman?" Sequoyah asked, clearly recalling the conversation they'd had earlier in the woods.

She nodded. "A detective. My father's best friend. But I had no idea he'd been involved. Not until six months ago when my mother came home in hysterics after a meeting with my father's attorney. That's when everything changed. All my life the lies were built, and in one single afternoon they all came crashing down." She felt her body go rigid as she numbed herself to the memories about to spill out. "I can still hear it. My mother yelling his name. *William!* Her shrill voice could be heard throughout the entire house. *William!*"

Her eyes closed, and the images of that day flooded her mind like a movie playing out on a silver screen.

Emmeline looked to Annis, who made it a habit never to react when others were fighting. She'd lived a life of being invisible unless spoken to, and she'd mastered her craft beyond error. "Keep your eyes on those green beans, Em. Don't want to have some snapped in half just because you're too busy eavesdropping on conversations which don't concern you," Annis scolded, her gaze never even lifting from her hands as they reached for a bean, snapped off each end, and tossed it into a large black pot already filled with water.

Most days, Emmeline wound up right here in the kitchen beside Annis, begging for any task just to be of help. Ever since her father had passed, life had changed. Where before he'd seen to it that she kept her mind on education, now her mother had claimed it a waste of money and time. She was nearly old enough to marry, and no respectable wife needed to have her head filled with all that rubbish. Instead, her daily activities included private lessons to undo all the lofty ideas her father had allowed all those years, and instead replace them with the proper charm and etiquette required to run a respectable household of her own. For the most part, Emmeline found she was bored out of her wits. Come evening she was all too desperate for more substantial conversations than her tutor deemed tea appropriate, and so she wound up sitting with Annis, who was the only one still welcoming of her ramblings and inquisitive chatter.

"Do you think something's gone wrong with the will?" Emmeline asked. "Mother's been worrying for ages. Told me herself last night she was ready to give Mr. Charleston, her father's lawyer, a good talking to if he didn't start sorting out Father's estate soon."

It had been months since her father's death, and whatever funds had been available in the family account were likely dwindling just from keeping up the essentials.

Mother had been so panicked about the family's well-being that she'd even agreed to marry William, who'd said he felt it his responsibility to see to them now that Emmeline's father was gone. They'd been best friends, after all. He'd said he thought it was only right that he be the one to step in and carry on as head of the family. Her father would have wanted it that way, would have trusted no one else, William had said. It had been strange for Annis at first, watching William move around the house. He sat in her father's chair at the table and drank his sherry in the evenings. So much about them was similar, from their stature to their clothes to their mannerisms, and yet William was so very different from her father. He spoke in harsher tones, lacked in patience and had an intimidating air about him, whereas her father had always been warm and welcoming. But having William around had eased her mother's grief, and so Emmeline had seen to it she found a way to be accepting of the changes, however drastic and hard to swallow they were at times.

"I think you could do a better job with those green beans," Annis said, nodding at the limp green stalk dangling in Emmeline's hand. She'd had yet to snap either end.

"Annis," Emmeline said, and then sighed. "What aren't you telling me?"

"I don't know what you're on about," she said, acting as though she really didn't have a clue. "You know me. I keep my head down and my nose in my own business. And you will do well to do the same."

It was a warning. Annis knew more than she was letting on.

"You're keeping secrets," Emmeline said, doing her best to focus on the job she'd been given. "I feel like there's been a lot of that as of late. I know you all think you're protecting me, but I'm not as weak as I look."

Annis stopped what she was doing. Her stern gaze caught Emmeline as she reached for another green bean. "I've never once believed you to be weak. What I keep from you, I keep to myself to protect us both. Some business is best left to others. We mind ours, they mind theirs. And we all go on in peace together."

It was more cryptic than enlightening, and it only made Emmeline hungrier for the truth. She was tired of always being left in the dark. Her father had never treated her this way, like a child who needn't be bothered with too much information. She couldn't help wondering if forcing her to live in blind faith regarding all the decisions being made around her was just another part of grooming her to be a proper wife. How long would they wait, she wondered, before they married her off? She was still young, but not so young that marriage was out of the question.

"Annis," she started again, her thoughts on an entirely new track. "Is this about my getting married? Has my mother been searching for more suitors? The right sort of families to merge with?" Those things mattered to her mother, whether Emmeline could find value in them or not. And though her future husband had been preselected many moons ago, she also knew her mother would have no qualms about *releasing him from his obligations should she find a better, wealthier, match.*

"Em," Annis answered, her patience clearly dissipating by the second. "You know you're not to be wed until after your eighteenth birthday, your father always insisted on this when he was alive. I have no doubt your mother will see this done even in his death. That much at least, will be honored." She ended her explanation curtly and turned away, taking her pot of beans with her.

Emmeline was about to get up and follow her to the stove when she heard her mother's high-pitched screams echoing through the house again. "He's ruined everything! He's not even here and he's still making my life miserable! Controlling everything, the bastard."

Emmeline opened her mouth to question Annis again, and then thought better of it and ran for the door instead. Best to learn the sort of goings on around here as they were happening.

"Tell me everything the lawyer said," William demanded of her mother as Emmeline followed the voices down the hall and toward the den.

"He said," her mother squeaked, apparently still unable to get ahold of her emotions, "Emmeline is his sole heir. A monthly stipend to cover household costs will continue to be deposited in the family account until the time she turns eighteen, at which point everything will be signed over to her. The business. The fleet. The money. Every last asset. All hers."

"She's still a child. Surely, as her parent you can override this," he insisted.

"No. The will was very clear. She receives her inheritance on her eighteenth birthday and not a day sooner. Unless she marries sooner, in which case she will be counted as an adult and be able to take her place as head of family," her mother recited as though she'd memorized the entire document, word for word.

"Well," William said thoughtfully, "that's going to be a problem."

"Yes," her mother agreed heatedly. "I should say so."

"Sadly, I don't believe you'll be of much assistance in solving this, my dear."

Emmeline turned the corner just as he said it. First, she saw her mother, who seemed both stunned and appalled to see her. Then, at the sound of a metallic click, both women shifted their gaze toward William. His gun was drawn and pointed at Emmeline's mother.

"What are you doing?" her mother asked, sounding too perplexed to be frightened.

The gun went off in response. A single bullet pierced her chest, sending her to her knees. She collapsed to the ground, the look of surprise never leaving her eyes even as they stared ahead, no longer seeing anything at all.

Emmeline stood frozen, unable to make a sound. Out of the corner of her eye she could see Annis come down the hall and stop short. Annis lifted her finger to her lips, motioning for her to keep quiet, as though Emmeline even had a choice.

"I'm sorry you had to see that," William was saying, placing his weapon back in its holster. "However, I think it's important you know from the start the lengths I will go to in order to be paid a debt long overdue."

Emmeline blinked her eyes repeatedly, praying that she'd open them again to see something, anything else. Any sort of nightmare would be welcome compared to the one in which her mother was lying on the floor, dead, shot by her father's best friend, a man that had been like an uncle to her all of her life. A man who now stood only feet from her, nothing stopping him from bestowing her mother's fate upon her as well.

"What...debt-t?" she stammered, stalling for time as if it would help her to understand what had happened, what was still happening.

"You're not that dense, Emmeline," he said, shaking his head and turning his back on her to face the main wall of the den. It was lined with frames, each one holding an image of a ship her family had owned, and many of which they still did. As one of the largest importers in this country, her father's company needed a sizable fleet to keep up the demand of products being sent back and forth between the continents.

She watched as his fingers grazed the frames as he passed them by. "I should have known your father would make you heir. It was, after all, what his father did for him as well. No matter who else deserved it, who else had worked for it, who else had earned it through blood, sweat, and tears, day after day, for thirty long years." He turned back around in a flash. "My father gave his life for this business. He died at sea while your father sat safely in the comforts of this lavish home, reaping all the rewards of my father's hard work. And in return for his service and sacrifice, what did we get? Barely enough savings to make a life."

Emmeline frowned. "My father offered you a job. You could have here with him." She swallowed hard, trying to force down the fear screaming inside her. "Father always said you walked away when it was offered, that you wanted to make your own path, leave your own legacy."

"And I would have, if I'd been given so much as an ounce of support. But no. Every last drop of energy went into Peter, the golden child. The one they'd been preening to take over from the start, the only life that ever mattered." He sneered as though the memories of his best friend, Emmeline's father, left a bitter taste in his mouth. "I had plans, big plans, Emmeline. I was going to be a grander success than your family had ever seen. But when I went to your father for help, for a minor investment in what was sure to garner him double the return, he refused me. Told me it was too great a risk. Said I didn't understand, that I had no head for business and needn't bother trying my hand at it when I'd refused to learn it all the times that he'd tried to teach me."

"*What was it?*" *Emmeline asked, rotely following the protocol of courteous conversation. She was too numb to be afraid anymore and too dazed to understand most of what he was saying.* "*Your dream, your grand plan?*"

"*It was brilliant.*" *He beamed, his arrogance lifting his chest and raising his chin until his gaze swept over her, no longer deeming her worthy of his direct eye contact.* "*An extension, really, of what your family had already built. I wanted to expand their reach, invest in the railroad, start my own company for moving shipments on land.*" *He scowled.* "*But your father, the smart student just barely out of university, deemed it a bad investment. Said the market was going to crash and the railroad industry right along with it.*"

Emmeline bit her lip. Her father hadn't been wrong. The entire country had been struck by financial panic during his first years of running the company. She'd been too young to remember, but she'd heard stories and learned plenty during her studies. Nevertheless, it hardly seemed prudent to point this out to William, nor did he seem to be waiting for her input. His gaze was back on the images of her family's history at sea. His family too, she supposed, wondering if his father was in any of those images. He'd been a captain, one of the first to sign on.

"*I could have been a brain like your father. It would have been easy,*" *he said with such a dismissive air that Emmeline suspected it would have been anything but. Her father and William had never been alike regarding intellect, but he'd always admired his best friend. The stories her father had told her had shined a bright light even on the darker spots in William's past. William had struggled in school but had been a marvelous athlete and an avid huntsman. He'd snubbed his nose at business, but had been keen on finding the next lucrative venture. He'd never been successful, but he'd taken the things he excelled at—physical strength and sharp-shooting—and dedicated his life to serving others in the police force. Her father had made him sound honorable. Now, as she watched him, all she saw was a bitter, jealous man who'd always felt entitled but had never been willing to do the work.*

"You can have the business," Emmeline said, the pieces beginning to fall together for her. "I'll sign anything you want." Whatever he wanted, she would give, if only it would help her escape this nightmare. And escape would be all she could do. After all, who would she run to for help? Annis was the only one left. No one would side with Emmeline, who was still a child in the eyes of the law at barely seventeen, or Annis, a former slave. They couldn't seek justice from the law. William was a local police detective. He was the law. Emmeline was not dense. William had been right about that much. In looks she'd taken after her mother, but her mind was all her father's.

"Oh, believe me, Emmeline. I will have it," he said, a strange new smile on his lips and a flash of wickedness in his dark eyes. "But you heard the stipulations of the will. You're not eighteen. The only way you can give me what's owed to my family is if you marry."

"Marry who?"

"I should think that much would be obvious." He glanced around the room, which seemed to Emmeline to be shrinking with every passing second, making her feel trapped and leaving her straining to breathe. "After all we've been through, who do we have left to turn to in our time of grief...but each other?"

Her stomach turned, bile rising in her throat. She doubled over, retching until her insides hurt, unable to stop herself. And then she straightened her back, despite the pain in all her muscles, and forced her chin up. "No."

"That's not a polite answer, Emmeline," he chided. "A proper lady would know better than to refuse such a life-saving proposal."

"You won't kill me," she hissed through clenched teeth, still tasting the vomit on her tongue. "You kill me, you get nothing. I'm the last

heir. *If I'm gone, everything goes with me. You'll never see so much as a penny."*

His eyes narrowed. "You really are your father's daughter."

She said nothing in return but allowed the words to swell her chest and square her shoulders. She was indeed.

"I think you'll find I have more talents in my skill set than simply pulling a trigger, Emmeline. There are...other ways...of convincing you."

She forced her eyes to meet her mother's dead stare, forced herself to truly see what was before her. William had the makings of a beast who harbored a relentless, tireless, merciless, and unscrupulous hatred.

"If I marry you," she said through gritted teeth, "what happens after you get what you want?"

He shrugged, evil still lurking in his eyes as his mouth spread into a smirk that would make the devil himself shudder in fear. "I can't say. It's never happened before now."

It was then she fully understood. It wasn't simply about gaining all the money he felt was owed to him. William wanted more. He wanted to rip her father of all he'd held dear, of all his greatest and most valued treasures. And that included Emmeline.

William had her in his clutches, and now he'd never let her go.

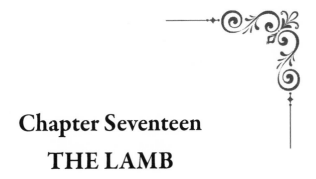

Chapter Seventeen
THE LAMB

"So, Annis," Maude said after listening to her horrid tale, "the real Annis, she was your housekeeper. She helped you escape."

Annis nodded. "I told her I could do it. I could stay and marry him and see to it he didn't harm her. But she refused. Said she owed my father. He'd saved her son years before when some white men accused him of stealing. They'd wanted his life over some missing burlap he'd never even touched. She said my father took a chance by going against everyone, even William, to defend her son. And she would gladly do the same. Risk it all to save me." Annis began to weep. Wiping her cheeks with the palms of her hands, she said, "I begged her to come with me, but she wouldn't hear of it. Someone needed to stay behind to slow him down, to give me a real chance. And that someone was her." She hiccupped. All the crying had shaken up her belly and staggered her breathing. "She'd have done it anyway. Even if it hadn't been for my father helping her son. Annis was the closest person in the whole world to me. She was my mother, sister, and best friend, all in one. I know she'd have done anything for me. Even before that night."

"That's why you took her name," Mabel said softly. "So that a part of her would always stay with you. So that she could live on through you."

Annis sniffed, reaching for what she thought had to be the hundredth tissue. "It was more than that. I needed her as much as I needed to be someone else. The girl I was, Emmeline, she died that night, right alongside everyone else." Annis looked out the window, staring out into the black night. There was nothing to see but her own reflection mirrored back to her in the glass. "That girl was never going to make it on her own. I had to let her die."

Silence swept over the cabin, filling the space between what was thought and what was never to be spoken.

Annis understood the quiet all too well. She'd given everyone too much to think about. Though she wished they'd worry more about their own well-being, she knew them well enough to know the only concern they had was about saving her from William.

"Not quite the Circus Christmas you all had planned, huh?" she joked, desperate to clear the tension, which was so taut it could snap at the flick of a finger, just so she could breathe again.

"Eh." Sawyer shrugged. "We'll have another go at it next year. Besides, Circus Christmas is nothing compared to Circus Chaos."

"What's Circus Chaos?" Annis asked before she could determine she didn't really want to know.

"Circus Chaos is the bountiful hell we unleash on anyone who dares to threaten one of our own," Caroline replied. Her icy tone sent a chill down Annis's spine.

"It's not quite as lovely a notion as Circus Christmas," Homer said, his crooked grin lightening the mood. "But it's a hell of a lot more fun when it gets going."

"I don't want any of you to get in trouble on my behalf," Annis said.

"Oh, we won't," Maude assured her.

"We're just going to start it," Mabel added.

"Stir it up real good," Bess said.

"Until we've got our mark in sight," August growled.

"Then we unleash it," Sawyer said, popping his knuckles as though preparing for a fight.

"Trouble likes us," Homer said, still smirking. "Never comes back for us once it's set free."

Annis wasn't sure whether to laugh or to cry. "I'll never forgive myself if any of you get hurt."

"We know," Sequoyah said, speaking for the first time in ages. He had sat quietly at her side, listening to everything. "We'd never forgive ourselves either."

"I've only got one condition," Goldilocks chimed in, drawing all eyes to where he sat in the far corner.

"Name it," Annis said, waving her hand for him to go on. Whatever he wanted from her to regain his trust she was willing to offer without question.

"You give us your word that there will be no more secrets."

"I promise." She placed her hand over her heart. "There's nothing left of me you haven't seen. This, it's all I am now. But I'm willing to dig through the buried bones of my past anytime you like if there's ever anything else you want to know. You have my word."

Gradually, a new wave of emotions moved through the group. The air felt peaceful and oddly content, given all they'd been through together over the course of the night.

Annis took a deep breath in before allowing it to slip from her lungs along with the residual ache still anchored in her hollowed chest. Being there, surrounded by so much unexpected love, she held out hope the cavernous hole that had once housed her heart would someday mend and find new ways to fill itself.

Resting her head on Sequoyah's shoulder, she opened her mouth to ask the one question still burning on her mind. "What about Poppy and Babe?"

"They'll need to know," Sequoyah said.

"What will they say when they find out?" It was a foolish question she did not expect anyone to answer. How could they know how Poppy and Babe would react when no news quite like this had ever been brought to their front door?

"I imagine they'll say a lot," he said, a touch of amusement in his voice. "You know Poppy. He's never short on words."

Annis felt her mouth involuntarily stretch one corner up, but this was no laughing matter. "You know what I meant."

"They'll say this William fellow had better watch his back," Homer informed her, using a tone similar to Sequoyah's. "Because no one messes with Hugh and Babe's lot and lives to tell about it."

"Also, Babe will cry," Momma T added dryly, from her spot beside the door. She'd been quiet for so long that Annis had assumed she'd drifted off to sleep by now, but it was clear she was as coherent as ever.

"I'll tell them." Sequoyah held her closer as he spoke. "It'll be easier coming from me. They'll have time to digest it all and decide how to proceed before you talk to them."

Annis nodded, slipping deeper into his embrace. Now that everything had spilled out of her at last, she felt drained and exhausted. Sleep was coming for her and she had no fury left within to stop it.

Come morning, she awoke alone in her bed with Finian lying at her feet and the cabin empty but for the twins. They were both still curled under their covers and sound asleep. The train was still moving. Annis remembered they weren't set to stop until later that evening, when they would set up the basics of camp and wait until the following day to prepare for the next show.

She wondered what time it was. She wondered more if Sequoyah had gone to see Poppy and Babe already. Would they seek her out once they knew? Or would they wait for her to come to them when she was ready? She'd never be ready. Whatever calm had held her captive last night had been fleeting and she was right back to feeling anxious today, though the weight of it all had shifted, at least for the time being, and perhaps even for good. She wasn't alone in this anymore, and that felt as comforting as it did terrifying. She couldn't live with any more regret. And she was out of lives if she didn't make it through this one.

"Your thoughts are screaming," Mabel murmured from across the cabin, her eyes still closed. "I can hear them all the way over here and I was sleeping."

"Sorry." Annis pulled her covers up to her chin and rolled onto her side to face Mabel. Quirky as she was, she had a depth in her soul unmatched by anyone Annis had ever met.

"It's alright," she whispered. "'Least now I know what they're on about. Why you can't ever quiet them. Be hard to shut down memories like yours."

"Do you think Poppy will be angry?" Annis hated the thought of disappointing him after all he'd done for her.

"Absolutely," Mabel said, brow scrunched into a stern line. "Murder and blackmail have a way of really getting under his skin."

"I meant with me," Annis said.

Mabel looked surprised. "Angry with you? I don't see why he would be."

"Because I kept it from him." For someone who could read her mind while asleep, Annis found it hard to follow how Mabel needed things spelled out for her while awake.

"Oh, that." Mabel tucked her head into her pillow and closed her eyes again. The corner of her mouth that Annis could still see curved slightly as she whispered, "It's Poppy, Annis. No one keeps anything from him. Not really."

As if to confirm this, there was a quiet knock on the door, and then a crack just large enough for Poppy's hand to reach through.

He hooked his finger in Annis's direction and motioned for her to follow him.

Without saying a word to Mabel, who seemed to be well on her way to drifting back to sleep, Annis slipped out from under her covers, pulled on a dressing gown and headed for the door. Finian was at her heels, as always.

Poppy said nothing as he led the way through two more cabins of sleeping crew members before reaching the one he shared with Babe.

Only once they were inside, with the door shut behind them, did he begin to speak.

"Tea, Annis?" he offered from the kettle still emitting steam at the center of their small table. "Babe only just made it. She's got a bit of toast and jam coming too," he said, nodding toward Babe in her flowery dressing gown, moving about the back end of their cabin.

"No, thank you." Truth be told, she wasn't sure she could stomach more tea after last night. Nor was there room for much else.

"Perhaps you'll change your mind," he said, guiding her to have a seat in one of the three chairs, and then doing the same and pouring himself a cup. his, eyes twinkling with a hint of mischief, and whispered, "At least pretend to want the toast when it comes. You can always feed it to Fin when no one's looking. Babe's in a tizzy already. If she thinks you're not eating, she may take us all to the brink of insanity."

At his words, Annis felt an internal battle between guilt and amusement—guilt because she hated to know she was causing Babe this sort of turmoil and amusement because it was hard not to laugh when Poppy had that look in his eyes.

"Don't do that," she hissed back, forcing her face into a frown worthy of her current predicament. "This is serious!"

"Which is precisely why we should all find ways to have a laugh when we can," he said, stirring honey into his tea before placing his spoon neatly onto the saucer. He then took a sip.

"Please," Annis pleaded with him. "Don't be all Poppy about this. Just come right out and say what you need to say to me. I can take it. What I can't take is having to figure it all out for myself after you spend two hours dropping secret clues in an otherwise meaningless conversation."

Poppy didn't seem to know whether to find her plea funny or insulting. "I shall have you know, love, I've never once in my life engaged in meaningless conversation. I value my words and my breath more than that."

Annis sighed, succumbing to the fact this conversation with Poppy was going to be slow-motion torture but also acknowledging that, in the long run, she would come to appreciate wherever it led. "Let's have a cup of tea then," she said, nodding at the kettle and lifting her cup for him to fill.

He smiled and proceeded with the task of serving her. "I think it's time, Annis."

"For what?" She could conjure a million different answers to that question and hoped with all her might that Poppy would still offer an alternative.

"To talk about your act," he said. "What else?"

Annis nearly choked on her tea, causing Fin to jump up on all four paws and watch her with concern. "I'm sorry?"

"It's time you find your place in the show, love," he reiterated, though she found it no less confusing after hearing it a second time.

"Didn't Sequoyah come and talk to you?" she asked, glancing around the cabin for any sort of sign that they were still having the same conversation.

"First thing this morning," Poppy said, still sipping his tea, calm as ever.

"And there isn't anything you find more pressing to discuss than my act?" She could feel her eyes grow wider with every word.

"Not remotely," he said, sounding more serious this time.

"Poppy," she said, gulping down the bouts of hysterics that seemed to unfurl from her on a moment's notice these days. "Wanted posters with my face on them are currently spreading across the southern states and who knows how far beyond. Do you really think it's wise to put me in the ring? In front of an audience?"

"Best place to hide is always in plain sight, love." He set down his tea cup, making it clink against the porcelain saucer. "Besides, if there are fools grand enough to seek you out for a battle, I think it's high time we show them exactly who they're calling out to war."

"I hardly think they'll be intimidated," she scoffed. "I'm not exactly terrifying. No bulk or muscle to be found here. No flying, flaming daggers or a pride of lions at my command. I'm not even unusual or peculiar enough to be unnerving to look at. I'm just plain. And small, but not oddly small like Sawyer. Just...ordinary small."

Poppy said nothing in response. He just sat back in his chair and watched as Babe came around, placing on the table platters of mounting toast along with three different sorts of jam and a big block of butter.

"I'm out of blueberry," she mumbled. "I'll go see if Momma has some." A second later, she was out the door, her flowing robes billowing behind her as she disappeared in a whoosh.

Alone with Poppy, Annis watched as he reached for a piece of toast, and then slathered it first in butter before adding a heaping dollop of raspberry jam. Her frustrations swelled when she saw him take a large bite and chew it meticulously before he swallowed, only to take another without saying a word. The toast was nearly three-quarters devoured when Annis was certain she couldn't take another second of being steeped in this hellish limbo, where she had no idea which way the conversation was headed, when Poppy finally opened his mouth not to take another bite but to continue their conversation.

"I wonder what it is you think people see, then, when they look at you."

There it was. The question she'd been told he'd ask all those months ago. Back then, she'd been convinced her answer would be different by now. And it was, though her answer had changed not for the better. Six months ago, she'd believed herself to be a survivor. She had no fight in her but at least she could persevere. She'd seen value in this. This morning, sitting here with Poppy, it was clear to her how little she truly had to offer. Her ability to outlive deadly situations were but a blessing to her. Those who got caught up in the net with her had perished.

"Someone timid. Weak. Easily frightened. A lamb," Annis answered, anger coiling at the pit of her stomach. "Someone the bad want to hunt and the good want to save."

Poppy's eyes turned soft with such sadness that Annis knew he saw the lamb in her as well. "And what do you want them to see?"

"Something wild." The words came from her lips before her mind had fully formed them. It was the first time she'd been able to answer that question. As she heard herself say it, she knew she'd gotten it right.

"A beast?"

"No." Her eyes dropped to her side where Finian lay, his attention wholly on her. "A wolf."

"Good girl." He picked up his piece of toast as though that were the end of their talk. "Have a piece. You're hungrier than you think. Trust me."

Brooding, she did as she was told and took a still-warm slice. It smelled divine as she brought it closer to her plate, setting it down to finish it with a proper layer of butter and jam. She decided on strawberry only because it was closest to her. She still couldn't muster up an appetite. Until she took that first bite. Then the ravenous cavern inside her screamed for more. Within seconds she was reaching for her second slice, still chewing the last bite of her first. She gorged herself on toast until five whole slices had found their place inside her stomach. As she leaned back to stretch her core, the comforts of a full belly spread, and she could start to think more clearly again.

"How will you do it?" she asked as Poppy poured more tea, topping off both their cups.

"Do what?"

"Turn me into a wolf."

"I'm not going to do that." He placed the teapot back onto the table and picked up the honey. "You are."

"How?"

"That is entirely up you, love," he said, still sounding no more bothered than before. "You pitched, I approved. You have complete creative control. Go forth. Become a wolf."

"Become a wolf."

"Certainly." He tipped his head toward Fin. "I should think that would be easy given that your source of inspiration is also your own shadow."

Annis bit her lip, holding back the slew of questions she had. She knew not a single one would garner the answers she needed, so she shifted course. "What about...the other thing?"

"What other thing?"

He really did have a knack for being infuriating, she thought.

"The thing with my family. The thing where I'm wanted for murder. That thing."

"I don't think it's a thing," he said, dismissing the topic all together. "That's part of the outside world. We're here. In our own. Until the two do cross, it's of no concern to us."

"But..."

Poppy's demeanor took a more comforting tone as he reached his hand out to cover hers where it lay on the table. "The two will cross, love. I know that. We all do. But fretting about it now won't help us do what needs done to keep you safe." He gave her hand a squeeze and released it. "Create your act. Take your part in the show. And I promise, your enemies will come to fear the wolf in you more than you fear the hate in them."

In the days that followed, Annis spent most of her free time studying Fin. She watched the way he moved, how he took in the world, what pleased him, and what made him cautious. He handled every encounter with such a heightened sense of awareness that Annis was certain he'd never felt the sense of surprise.

By day five, she was starting to think there was no way she could ever find a way to embody all the things that made Fin so acutely tuned in to life and the world around him, least of all, in the form of entertainment.

"You're overthinking it," Sawyer said over lunch on the sixth day. "You're always overthinking everything."

"I'm sorry, I like to be thorough," she snapped, in no mood for his insults.

"You're not being thorough. You're stalling because you're scared. And that's stupid." He jabbed his fork in the air, directly at her, prompting her to shut her mouth before the comebacks came flying out of it. "It's stupid for someone so brilliant to be so scared."

"You don't think I'm brilliant."

"Don't you tell me what I think. What, you believe I'd waste my time on someone who wasn't worth it? You are. Brilliant. And talented. And, when you're not sucking up everyone's time thinking about it, you're quite brave too. So how about you get out of your own damn way, open your mouth, and bloody well ask for the help we're all willing to give you."

Annis stared back at him, dumbfounded, for a good long second while he carried on slurping his tomato soup.

"You know, you're not very nice," she said, when at last her spell of silence wore off. "But your heart is so profoundly good that I always choose to forget."

"I don't hear what I need to hear there, Annis," he grumbled, though his cheeks turned a soft shade of pink, letting on that her words had touched him more than he cared to admit.

"Do you think you could help me create an act?" she asked at last.

"No," he said flatly. "But we'll all help you put it together when you tell us what it is."

"But, that's the thing. I don't know!"

"Really?" Mabel questioned, brows so high they nearly touched her hairline. "No idea? None whatsoever?"

"You don't honestly expect anyone here to believe that, do you?" Maude asked, her head tilted sideways to catch a better view of Annis's face down the bench from her.

"Surely you've some idea the sort of act you'd like to have. I mean, you've been watching us for months," Homer said. "In all that time, you've never imagined yourself out there in the ring?"

"Of course I have," Annis answered without thinking.

"Well, then." From beside her the quiet rumble of Sequoyah's voice reached her ears. "What did you imagine?"

She shook her head, unwilling to say. "It was just silliness. Nothing I ever truly considered."

"Let us consider it, then," Bess said. "Go on, tell us what you cooked up."

"Magic," Annis whispered under her breath, even going to the trouble of sticking a slice of bread into her mouth just as the word was coming out.

"Magic!" Mabel shouted for all the world to hear, or, at the very least, everyone at their table. "She said 'magic'!"

"Oh, I do like that," Caroline said and smiled. "Magic would be very good, indeed."

"We haven't had anything like it since Horace and his illusions act," Maude said, sounding far more excited than Annis had expected from anyone, let alone her. "The man really did know how to make things vanish into thin air."

"Yeah," Sawyer agreed dryly. "Including himself. Anyone ever hear from him after that night he disappeared in his vanishing cabinet at the end of his act?"

"What?" Annis shuddered.

"Relax." Sequoyah laughed. "He ran off with a girl whose father hated him. Eloped. Taking off during the act was only meant to buy them more time."

"He left loads of his old equipment when he took off," Bess said, standing, apparently too energized by this new idea to sit still any longer. "The girls and I have a lot of it in the cabin. Figured someone would make use of it sooner or later."

"Really?" The nerves were starting to get Annis too. Suddenly, her childish daydream was looking more and more like it could possibly become reality. "Does anyone know how to use it?"

"I do," August said. "Used to help Horace set everything up." He turned to the group at large. "She'll need an assistant."

"No." Annis was clear on this one part over everything else. "No assistant. Just me."

"You heard her," Sequoyah said, a triumphant grin marking his handsome face. "Just her. She's all the magic she needs."

"I'll believe that when I see it," Sawyer muttered. But as he stood to walk away, Annis caught his eye and he winked.

"I'll show you, then," she declared, pushing up from the table as well. "Bess! Let's see all the fun you and the girls have been hoarding."

Bess didn't need to be told twice. She was more than happy to lead the way to her cabin, and everyone was more than willing to follow her there. Within the hour, Annis was looking at everything from a vanishing cabinet to transformation cages, and a multitude of parlor tricks she'd been enthralled by as a child. She wouldn't be wasting her time on those. She didn't want to amuse people. She wanted to shake them, unnerve them, and remind them how easy it was to believe what you were seeing even if it wasn't real.

Together, they set to work. They experimented with the equipment, found what worked, what didn't, and what could be improved upon. Annis found new ideas bursting from her lips with every discovery they made among the magician's abandoned treasures. She felt as though each piece were calling to her, asking her to touch it, learn it and put it to use. She found she had and instinct for magic, like she was coming home to a part of herself she'd never even known existed. The magician. No. *The alchemist.*

By sundown, they'd created an entire act. Skeletal though it was, all the makings of Annis's act were there. All she had to do was master her new craft.

Gone was her fear of William and the looming terror of his ongoing hunt for her. Poppy had been right. William was part of the outside world, a world she no longer lived in. Until he found a way to penetrate the veils that kept them separate, she was safe. And when he did, she'd be ready.

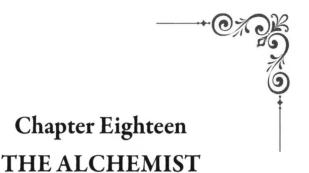

Chapter Eighteen
THE ALCHEMIST

I t was cold outside. Even in the depths of the South, winter could be felt as Christmas drew nearer.

"Tonight's the night," Babe said, walking beside Annis on their way to the tent. "You nervous, Tulip?"

"Yes." Annis repeatedly smoothed out the golden bodice of her of corset before tugging at the waist of her pants, as though she were trying to make more room to breathe. Nothing was wrong with the fit of her costume, though. Every detail, from her elegant black top hat to the shiny points of her shoes, was perfectly tailored to her. Her corset moved like a second skin with her every motion. The smallest intake of air allowed the fabric to give way. Even her trousers, which were black, wide-cut, and ran the entire length of her leg before draping nicely over her matching black boots, had been taken in by Bess to fit her perfectly. Nerves were the only real source of imminent suffocation tonight.

"Good." Babe draped an arm around her waist and tugged her near. "Nerves are the best part. No nerves, no magic. And that goes for every performer, not just the magician sort," she said, pinching Annis's side.

"You sound like Bess."

"That girl knows what she's talking about."

Annis laughed. "I still can't believe I get to follow you into the ring." She'd hoped for a less prominent spot in the lineup, but Poppy had insisted. "Go big or stay backstage" had been his exact words.

"I can't believe it either," she said, sounding suddenly disgruntled. "Do you know how fast I'll have to move these old bones to get myself out of the way and into a good spot to enjoy the show? You better be in for a slow start because I don't want to miss anything."

"It's an act based in illusion, Babe." Annis snorted with a laugh. "I'm hoping you miss *a lot* of things."

Babe chuckled.

The pair walked in quiet comfort until they reached the tent. Babe turned Annis to face her. She swiped the long, unruly strands of blonde hair away from Annis's face before she cradled both her cheeks in the palms of her hands and tilted Annis's head forward to kiss the top of it. "You'll blow them away," she whispered. Then she released Annis and walked inside without turning back. Annis got the distinct feeling she hurried only to hide her tears.

The evening calm she'd encountered outside was nonexistent within the tent walls. Noise and dust filled the air, along with an orchestra of scents, some enticing, some outright assaulting. Annis suspected the monkeys were to blame for the latter. Everyone moved so fast that they were but a blur in Annis's line of vision, zipping in and out of spaces to make last minute preparations before the show. And then she saw him. He was the only stable thing in sight, and a constant she was learning to depend on. Sequoyah.

"Ready?" he asked.

"I think so." Her fingertips stretched at her side, grazing the top of Fin's back. She found herself doing this more and more as the days went on, wanting to be sure he was beside her, drawing a comfort from his presence that she couldn't find anywhere else.

"If it helps, I *know so*," he said, leaning in to kiss her cheek before he moved on to check on the horses.

It did help, tremendously.

From the moment Poppy entered the ring to roaring applause until the second Annis saw Babe taking her bow, the world sped up to a flurry of lights and noise. When she got her cue to go on, Annis's feet felt like lead and her arms stuck to her sides like wooden boards, unable to bend or move. Stage fright left her paralyzed. Then she felt a dainty palm in her lower back, shoving her out into the light without any concern for her feelings.

"Thanks, Smalls," she murmured under her breath, knowing it was him without looking. The lights of the ring blinded her eyes but awakened her heart. The sound of a drumroll echoed the beat in her chest. She felt electrified by the energy taking her over, sparking, zapping, and setting off small fireworks all over her body. Parts of her felt as though they were coming alive for the first time. Pieces of her spirit that had lain dormant all these years, as if they'd known this moment would come—the moment when she would take the stage and bend the audience's beliefs until they saw only what she showed them.

A wild rage burned inside her as she strode toward the center of the ring and lifted her arms into a dramatic V. The drumroll stopped. The magic began.

Annis felt the pressure of a few hundred mesmerized eyes, all watching her with bated breath as she performed her first act of trickery. She started small by transforming multicolored tissues into flowers and making a dove appear out of the black top hat she wore as part of her costume. As even the oohs and aahs died down, she knew she had them too intrigued to even speak in single syllables.

She calculated every step and timed out every breath, choreo-graphing her motions for success. She didn't hesitate when it came time to reach for the chains. the last big illusion before the grand finale.

"I'll require a volunteer," she called out into the crowd. As expected, several hands flew up in an instant. Pretending to be choosy, Annis walked the circle to and fro, carefully examining her options before deciding on practicality. She chose the boy closest to the ring. He couldn't be any more than twelve years old, and he was delighted by her choice.

"It's not a tough job, but it's very, very important," she told him, mimicking Poppy's voice to the best of her abilities.

"Yes, ma'am," the boy replied, his eyes wide and looking com-pletely enthralled with her.

"You'll take this chain here and you'll wrap it all around me. Nice and tight. You don't want me wiggling out now, alright?" She handed him one end and then helped him by twirling into it as he did his best to wrap her in it. When the job was complete, her hands were buried beneath layers of cold metal links and pressed to her sides. She nodded toward the set of locks laid out on a small table. "Now, you'll take those one by one and secure the chain in place. Put them anywhere you like. The goal is to make it impossi-ble for me to escape, understand?"

He nodded, though his excitement appeared to be giving way to anxiety as he began the task of locking her in. In contrast, Annis felt amazing, in control, and entirely in her element, as though the world were at her beck and call, waiting for her next command.

Annis counted clicks. Three locks. Four. Five. She watched the boy grow more fidgety the tighter the chains held her. Six. Seven. Eight. He looked up at her with worry in his big blue eyes. "Are you sure, ma'am?"

She smiled. "Absolutely."

He leaned in close and whispered. "But I haven't the key. And it's not on the table."

She tilted her head in an attempt to meet him at eye level, no longer able to bend at the waist to do so. "That's precisely the point." She winked.

Nine clicks. The job was complete.

"Thank you ever so much," she called out for the crowd to hear. "Now if you'd just be so kind as to help me up these steps." She directed her gaze towards the temporary staircase leading up to a platform yet to be fully revealed.

"Yes, ma'am," the boy answered politely, though he seemed less sure than ever about his actions.

Annis had practiced enough to know she could take the steps easily if she lifted onto the tips of her toes. Within seconds, she was standing at the top. "Lastly, before you go back to your seat, I ask that you do me one more favor and reveal to the audience what you and I have already seen." She arched a brow at the boy, whose eyes were still glued to the scene before him.

"Uh-huh," he stammered, this time forgetting his manners.

Annis watched patiently as he made his descent, and then turned back to the platform. His hands shook so hard that she could see it from where she stood. Then, with one determined yank, he pulled off the curtain that hid her glass tank.

"Just to be sure," she called out as she dipped the tip of her boot into the tank to flip up a splash of water for the audience to see. "Yep, the water is real." she said and laughed. Then, without further ado, she dropped backwards, straight into the pool of water, and sank to the bottom in an instant.

She imagined the audience's panic and anticipation mingling in the air while she was underwater. She pictured them nervously chatting among themselves, wondering if it were possible, if she could really escape the chains in time to save herself from drowning.

Seconds seemed to last forever as Annis held her breath. She calmly took the steps to free herself while she continued to swirl her body in the water to create enough turbulence to keep her actions hidden from the audience's view. One lock, gone. And then two. She released a tiny slip of air when she reached five. With her hands freed from the chains, she worked efficiently until she undid the rest. The second her legs were free, she kicked up to the surface, bursting through the water like a mermaid thrust from the sea. The audience struggled to rein in their cheers long enough to hear what she had planned next.

Wrapping up her wet body in a sparkling golden coat that served mostly for looks, Annis drew the crowd's attention to the ceiling, where a large box hung overhead. As they watched, she gestured for August, who stood by just behind the curtain, to lower it down.

"I know you're probably thinking you've seen everything now," she yelled out over the raucous noise of the crowd. "But trust me, you haven't seen anything yet."

As the newest of mystery boxes graced the ground beside her, Annis pulled back another set of curtains to reveal this was no more a box than the water tank had been a platform. It was a cage, one large enough to hold a beast, like a lion or a tiger. Or a wolf.

She unlatched the door and stepped inside without another word. Then, after pulling it shut, she signaled August to raise her up again. The curtain fell back into place as he did so.

Once hidden inside, Annis slipped into a small trapdoor built into the floor, and then released the false back wall to reveal Finian. Seconds later, August was lowering the cage again to the sound of the same drumroll that opened her act. The cage touched down.

Out of sight, Annis tugged the latch that released the curtains, and she waited.

Silence.

And then hushed mutters of disbelief.

Annis could feel Finian pacing above her. She knocked the floorboards softly. Three times. When she heard the creak of a metal door swinging open, she knew he had recognized his cue.

Annis wished desperately that she could see the audience's faces as they watched the wolf who took her place inside the cage step out into the ring and command the space the same way she had only seconds before.

She'd worked with him tirelessly to perfect this finale. She knew he would circle the ring once left and then once right before walking into the center and taking a bow. He'd hold it. And then he'd dash off to join Sequoyah backstage, where he would wait for her.

Annis, of course, had no choice but to spend the remainder of the show lying beneath the floorboards of her magic cage, which August raised again to make room for the next act, leaving Annis dangling beneath the circus tent's ceiling until show's end.

She didn't mind one bit. She'd learned from Homer to value what she could hear. The stomping feet, the raging applause, the gasps of admiration. She'd done it. She'd turned herself into a wolf, and they'd believe her. The world would never know the lamb again.

The end of the show marked the first time Annis felt truly integrated into the world she'd come to adore over the months she'd lived in it. With an act of her own came new responsibilities, equipment to break down and load up, costumes to care for, and, of course, the continued care of Finian, her grand finale and her closest companion. But added work wasn't the only difference. There was a certain sort of comradery she hadn't been able to share with the performers until now. It was a bond among only those who knew the secret life of a performer. The taste of the air at the center of the ring. The vibrations rising up through the ground from turbulent applause. The way every color's vibrancy multiplied from the abounding energy of the crowd. There was nothing like it. Until you've stood at the center of it all, orchestrating the waves of emotion into your own symphony, you simply couldn't share in the knowledge of what it meant.

"You've come a long way from the girl who wanted to dance in the shadows of someone else's act," Poppy mused, catching up to her before they stepped aboard the train.

"I sense an unspoken 'I told you so' here, Poppy," she teased.

"Good. I'm a man of few words, after all. The less I have to say, the better." Even he seemed to find it hard not to laugh through that statement, boldfaced lie that it was.

"You were right, though," she admitted, the gravity of what he'd said before creeping up on her. "I'm more than I thought I was."

He nodded. "You are." He leaned in until his shoulder bumped hers. "Tell you a secret?"

"Alright."

"You're only just getting started."

She laughed. "I've got an act of my own, a wonderful new world filled with a family I adore, and the most wonderful man who's waiting for me on the other side of growing up. I think I'm far past started, Poppy. I feel like I'm in the homestretch. Just one last curve in the road before I complete a journey I never dreamed I'd take, before I find a happily ever after I hope will last a lifetime."

He smiled, his eyes crinkling at the corners. "I want all that for you, love. All that and so much more. And you'll have it. And then you'll see."

"See what?"

He shrugged. "That you were wrong. And I was right." He gazed wistfully out at the horizon. "Only the beginning, love. Only the beginning." Then, his strides grew longer, and he moved out ahead of her, leaving her alone to ponder his parting words.

Annis felt conflicted as she considered what he'd said. On the one hand, she'd been pushing boundaries from the moment she ran out of her family home six months ago. She'd pushed herself, forced herself to face fears, discomforts, and soul-crushing heartaches, never once allowing a challenge to get the best of her. Now that she'd arrived in a place where all of it was beginning to make sense, where the end of all her struggles seemed so near, she wasn't prepared to accept that she was only just starting to unravel the string that would unwind to be her lifeline. On the other hand, nothing she'd done in the last six months leading up to this moment had been physically hard. Painful, terrifying, and at times paralyzing, yes, but the tasks themselves, the lessons, the chores, Finian and performing, those things, had come naturally to her. In time, it had all taken her from just surviving to soaring. Maybe, just maybe, it was reason enough to believe, she had more in her yet.

"You seem vexed about something," Maude said when Annis joined the twins a few minutes later.

"Can't be," Mabel insisted before Annis could get a word out. "Not possible. Not after tonight's show. There's no room for vexed." She lifted her hand and began counting on her fingers. "There's excited. Giddy. Elated. Let's see, what else? Grateful. There's room for that."

Annis sighed, her face softening. "There certainly is." She plopped herself down onto her bed and pulled a pillow in toward her, hugging it to her chest. "Tonight was incredible. And I have everyone to thank. I may be the new magician in the Brooks and Bennet Circus, but it's you lot who make the real magic happen."

Maude turned to Mabel, frowning. "Told you holding her breath that long under water would make her nutty."

Annis had to resist the temptation to toss her pillow at Maude. Experience had taught her that targets were often missed on a moving train. Maude also had a habit of confiscating items when used as weapons against her, even if she fully deserved the pillow assault.

"I'll have you know, I've never been more clearheaded," she informed them. "But, as you two tend to be displeased with too much ado and appreciation, I'll save it for those who relish it. Like Sawyer."

"There's a person who is never tired of hearing just how wonderful he is," Mabel said. "Probably because his sour attitude makes him less likely to be at the receiving end of such statements very often."

"Yes," Maude agreed. "Save the gushing for Smalls. And bestow some on Goldilocks while you're at it. He needs it more than the rest of us."

"Have you noticed he's been exceptionally pouty as of late?" Mabel asked.

"You know," Annis said, "now that you mention it, I have noticed. I thought it was just around me. He's been a bit short with me ever since that bit about my former life came out."

"He's just cross because you got to decide your new name for yourself and he got saddled with a ridiculous moniker like Goldilocks," Maude said. She chuckled to herself as she undid the ties in her hair and let her long waves drape down her shoulders.

"It is a pretty unfortunate name," Annis agreed, making her bed in preparation for the host of crew members who would soon start piling in. Her bed was usually the first seating space to fill up.

"I think it's a perfectly fine name," Mabel huffed. Annis suspected she'd played a fairly large part in assigning it to him.

"Regardless," Annis said, intent on staying on topic. "Do you think we should talk to him? Find out what's bothering him?"

"I think that's an excellent idea," Maude replied, her head stuck in her nightdress while she waited for Mabel to get caught up with putting her half on. "Let us know what he says when you do." Even muttering through the material, Maude was too easy to understand for Annis to feign confusion or having misheard her.

"Why's it I always land the jobs no one else wants around here? You two have double the mouths, double the comfort—"

"But half the brains," Maude interjected.

"You know that one was insulting to you too," Mabel pointed out, proving that the thinking portion of their twin power wasn't solely provided by Maude after all.

"Still worth it," Maude said with a carefree shrug. Her nightgown was fully in place now, which allowed both women to move their heads and arms with ease again.

"So," Mabel said in a hushed tone. "Have you heard?"

Annis hadn't. "Heard what?"

"Poppy's having posters made," Maude said, much to Mabel's disappointment.

"It was my news, Maude! I asked if she'd heard—obviously if she hadn't, I wanted to tell her," she whined.

"Maybe you could tell me what the posters are of?" Annis offered, hoping to avoid an argument while getting an answer.

Mabel looked at her sister probingly, daring her to spill her news a second time. When Maude remained silent, Mabel's excitement rose again, and her voice dropped back down to a whisper. "Posters of you! New adverts for the show. Our fabulous new act—Annis the Alchemist! That's what they say! Even got a picture of you on it."

Annis remembered posing for it, though Poppy hadn't been specific about what they were to be used for. Posters sounded like a terrible idea.

"Posters with my face on it? Grand," she said. "Aren't there enough of those already up around these parts?"

"I suppose that's the point," Maude said, sounding more serious than usual. "I think he's going to try and speed things up. Cross lines between worlds. Bring the battle to us."

"But why?" The thought made Annis queasy.

"Our territory. Our rules," Mabel said.

"But..." Annis wasn't sure she wanted an answer to the question she was burning to ask next. "What do you think will happen when he finds me here? To him?" William's safety was of little concern to her, but the thought of anyone here staining their souls with the dark mark of murder was enough to make her want to put a bullet in him herself. He was her burden and no one else's.

"No one here's looking to have a poster matching yours, Annis," Maude said dryly, her usual tone of sarcasm returning. "Tempting as it would to be let him fall in with the lions, I don't think it will come to that."

"You're the illusionist, Annis," Mabel said. "Decide the ending you want to have, and then create it. Whether it's real or not will hardly be the issue. Making him believe it, that'll be the only thing that counts. And you, dear girl, had hundreds of people believing at least ten different impossible—no, unbelievable—things tonight. Convincing one man of one thing will hardly even be a challenge for you."

"But make him believe what?"

"That's the fun of it, isn't it?" Maude said. "You get to decide."

Annis wasn't convinced there was fun in any of what they were saying. As she pondered what sort of illusion she might conjure up to free herself of her father's murderous best friend, a quick knock on the door gave way to several people bearing with food and drinks, spilling into the cabin. They brought everything from hot tea to cocktails, the latter of which the likes of Bess and Maude were always happy to partake in when the following morning promised to be a late one, as was the case tonight.

"You were amazing out there," Sequoyah whispered when everyone around them settled into their usual banter-filled conversations, none of which had to do with them. Annis suspected they did this intentionally to allow the two young lovebirds a bit of privacy even amid the madness of a full cabin.

"Because you all made me that way," Annis countered, turning away so he wouldn't see her blush. "Besides, it was all illusion, remember?"

"There was no trickery in the magic I witnessed," he said softly, moving a curl of her hair from her face and tenderly tucking it behind her ear. "You were born for this, Annis."

There was a bittersweet truth in what he'd said. She *had* been born for this, but only after she'd died to release all that came before. The old her, the Emmeline part of her, would've never found her way to the center of a circus ring, let alone to the side of a native man whose gentle hand held so much more now than the curl of her hair.

"How long do you think we'll have until he turns up?" she asked, hoping Sequoyah would know exactly what and who she was talking about.

"Next stop we'll be just two states out from where we found you," he answered without hesitation. "You tell me. How long'd it take you to stumble from your back door into our camp?"

"Days." Annis bit her bottom lip. "And I was on foot, literally stumbling. He'll have far more efficient ways of travel to choose from once he gets word I'm with the circus."

Sequoyah nodded grimly. "I think this could all be over by week's end."

Annis glanced over her shoulder at the wreath the twins had hung on the door. "Sunday is Christmas Eve," she said, trying to hide the sigh that swept through her chest. "First, I screwed up our secret outings my first night out, and now I may be bringing the enemy home for the holidays. If you're right, I'll have properly ruined every last part of Circus Christmas. No one will ever let me join any secret plotting around here ever again."

"I wouldn't count yourself out just yet," he said, his lips quirking. "Takes a special sort of plotter to bring a murder mystery into our midst and leave it here for us to solve."

"Right." She smirked. "Forgot about that." She straightened herself up a bit taller. "I am a master plotter of circus shenanigans if there ever was one."

"Would you stop filling her head with nonsense?" Sawyer had apparently caught the tail end of their conversation. "She gets any more full of herself, she won't fit into the tent."

"Be still, small man-child, or Annis the Alchemist shall make you disappear," Annis boomed dramatically before curling over in giggles. As Sawyer considered a proper retort the cabin's noise rose with the sounds of laughter.

Their fun sustained itself well through the dark blue skies of night and slowly began to dissipate with the orange glow of morning, which sent everyone to bed at last. When the train arrived at its destination later that evening, there was little need to hurry. Nearly all the attention was placed on getting Momma set up for the sake of a proper supper. The animals were cared for and brought out to stretch their legs even as the sun was sliding down the far end of the valley, signaling another night to come. With little to do but wait until morning, the crew busied themselves with building fires, playing music, and dancing, lots of dancing.

The crisp chill in the air, the hot glow of the fire, and a million twinkling stars overhead made for a magical night and, for the first time since their outing to deliver secret Christmas Cheer, it felt like the holidays were truly upon them.

The following day proved harder than Annis had expected. The weather turned, leaving them to do most of their work in the pouring rain and cold winter air. Everyone worked harder and faster than usual, doing all they could to warm up from the inside out. But it was useless. By lunch, Annis was wearing two blankets over her damp clothes. Her teeth chattered as she tried repeatedly to spoon hot soup into her mouth. Between the shivering of her body and the lock in her jaw, it became an increasingly frustrating effort, given how particularly hungry she was and how desperately she yearned to feel the heat of that soup burning its way down her throat into the pit of her being.

"Where have you been?" Annis heard Maude ask, and looked up to see who she was talking to.

"Poppy sent me into town," Goldilocks said, an odd look of guilt on his face as he pulled his soup bowl nearer to him. "Wanted me to hand out those new flyers he made," he said just as he lifted his spoon to his lips.

"Don't suppose you found a matching wanted poster to tack it up next to?" Annis asked, forgetting all about the cold weather. She was too aware of the anxious chill running through her now.

"Thought that might be a bit too obvious," he said dryly. "Though I saw some. Even had his name on them, Detective William Faber. Deems himself your concerned parent now, in case you're wondering."

"Isn't that lovely?" Annis's words dripped in dark sarcasm. "Talk about a lucky girl."

"Parent and would-be killer, that's quite the combination," Sawyer mused. "Though I can't say I'm surprised. Anyone forced to spend a great deal of time with the likes of you would eventually have to walk that very thin line between loving and wanting to kill you." He shrugged. "You have a way about you, Annis. It's grating on the nerves." And then he grinned.

"Thankfully no one here will have that problem, being as they've all had their nerves grated down to numb nubs by you long before I ever came along," she said. She was preparing, at long last, to sip her soup straight from the bowl, as though she were having a large, savory cup of tea.

Sawyer smirked. "Your wit is getting to be quite entertaining, Annis."

"Glad you think so," she replied, giving her bowl another tip. Truth was, she appreciated Sawyer always pushing her buttons. More often than not, he was doing it when she most needed the distraction. Like now, when she could have let her mind unravel at the thought of every possible outcome that could follow from trying to lead William straight to her. Instead, she wound up searching her thoughts for clever ways to insult Smalls. And they did have to be clever. Poor comebacks were frowned upon. He wanted high-quality battles of banter, an even exchange of offensive commentary. Otherwise, he quit bothering.

The day remained in nonstop motion, giving Annis little time to revisit her previous attempts at panic. Come night, and the beginning of a new show, her mind was only on one thing. The performance. And there it stayed in the days that followed. Her thoughts were busied with work, and then derailed by play before they sank into exhausted sleep that was deprived of even her most stubborn nightmares.

Until the third day.

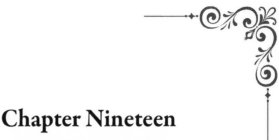

Chapter Nineteen

THE BEGINNING OF THE END

"Coppers are here," August hissed, passing through the back of the tent. "No one do anything crazy. Everyone knows the plan."

"What plan?" Annis said.

"The plan to keep you safe, you dolt," Sawyer said under his breath.

"Oh, right. That plan. It's a good plan. Let's go with that plan," she rambled.

"Annis," Poppy's voice found her in the center of her mental undoing. His calm tone was always steady, even now. "Let's walk, love."

Her eyes cast down, she fell into step beside him, unable to think, and hardly even capable of drawing breath, but she moved one foot in front of the other nonetheless.

"What's the one thing you always do to keep from falling, love?" Poppy whispered.

"Don't look down." She remembered the depth of those words as she heard herself say them. "Don't look down, no matter what."

"That's a good girl." Poppy walked them through the small area behind the curtain, snaking his way through all the performers preparing to go on, all scurrying about with the added anxiety of their impending collision with the local police and the possibility of William attempting to take Annis from their midst.

When he reached the far end of the small space, normally only used for the animals and their keepers, he stopped. Annis stopped along with him.

"Whatever happens tonight, I want you to know two things, love," he began, sounding more serious than Annis had ever heard him. "One, everyone is responsible for their own choices. Everyone. Do not attempt to absolve anyone of that right."

She nodded. Though it was hard to swallow, she understood his meaning. Whatever happened, whoever was hurt, she was not to blame herself.

"And two, I shall see you safe at the end. You have my word on this, love. Whatever you encounter along the way are but steps to get there. You take them. You survive them. You conquer them by any means necessary. You get to the other side of this. You get to the end of it."

She swallowed down the words of doubt bubbling up within her. "I'm scared."

"It's just nerves," he said, winking. "Perfectly normal."

"You find this particular situation to be perfectly normal, do you?" she asked, hardly able to contain the fear threatening to overtake her.

"We're about to open the show. The audience is alive with anticipation. The tent feels hot and sticky, and it smells of peanuts and toffee apples. Seems perfectly normal to me, love." He bent down and kissed the top of her head. "You're an illusionist now, Annis. Tonight, you don't even have to convince them. You only have to plant a small seed of doubt. Everything else will grow from there."

She wanted to ask him what he meant. She wanted to know more. She needed to understand the insight he had that gave him a constant peek into the future that no one else ever seemed privy to. But there was no time. He was being summoned by Harris, who needed assistance with Jacob, as always.

Wringing her hands, she marched off, leaving behind the screaming sounds of Jacob taunting anyone who tried to persuade him to behave. Even with her head held high and her eyes straight ahead, she moved blindly, unable to focus on anything outside of her own thoughts. They were fragments of memories, mostly. Flashes of her old living room. Fleeting images of green beans resting in a pot of water. The gun. Her mother collapsing to the floor. Blood. She remembered expecting to see more of it. She remembered waiting, her gaze morbidly captivated by the small stain on her mother's blouse. Annis had waited for the stain to grow, but her mother had been bleeding out through her back, lying in a puddle no one could see.

"Tulip," Babe called out, reeling Annis's racing thoughts back into the present. "Come and help me with these ties, would you?" Babe was struggling to fasten the silver corset she was wearing over her billowing red gown.

"Of course," Annis agreed, grateful for the distraction.

"If you could just fasten it here at the back, that would be lovely, Tulip," Babe said, spinning around to show Annis exactly where she required her assistance.

"I'll have you all set in a matter of seconds," Annis promised, getting to work on it even as she spoke.

"Thank you, Tulip," Babe said, twisting her wrists the way she did every night to warm them up before she played her harp. Next, Annis knew, she'd begin working each individual finger. Babe's warm up usually mesmerized Annis. Tonight, however, even the soothing, repetitive motions of Babe's ritual couldn't hold Annis's attention for long.

Just as soon as she was finished getting Babe's corset bound tightly and its laces tied in a delicate but secure bow in the back, she could feel her own heart rate begin to pick up again as her breath shortened.

"You're all set," she told Babe, walking around to face her.

"As are you." Babe leaned in closer to her, cradling the side of Annis's face in the palm of her hand. "You remember that story I told you the first day we met, don't you? About Basileus?"

Annis nodded. That story had stayed with her every moment of every day since. "He's a survivor."

"He is," Babe said, nodding softly. "But you don't survive simply by persistence alone, Tulip. To survive, you fight. Sometimes the beast is death itself and at others it's a more tangible enemy. No matter who you encounter in your moments of travesty and devastation, you stand up and you fight." She gave Annis's cheek an encouraging squeeze. "Because you, Tulip, never give up."

Annis smiled through the glistening of tears welling in her eyes. "The wild ones never do," she whispered.

"Never." Babe reached her hand around Annis's neck, bringing her in for an embrace before she released her, never letting on the depths of their conversation to anyone around them. It was better that way. Annis was certain she couldn't take even one more heart-to-heart talk with anyone who owned a piece of hers.

"They're all spread out," Mabel hissed, coming up to stand beside Annis at the curtain. "We've been peeking in on them from the main entrance. All the coppers are in their seats. Trying to blend in with the audience."

"It's working out about as well as it does for Sawyer anytime he tries to fit in with other adults," Maude said with a snort.

"Talk about a *low* blow," Sawyer muttered, never missing out on an opportunity to be in on the joke. "Height jokes are utterly uncreative and ought to be beneath you."

"Like you?" Mabel chirped, and then giggled.

"Joke's on you, Smalls. I was referring to your lack of maturity, not your lack of height." Maude stuck out her tongue at him for good measure.

"I'm not sure any of this is suitable material for jokes, to be honest," Annis said, watching the curtain swish back and forth with the commotion backstage. Its movements revealed a glimpse of the audience every other second or so.

"If we waited for material to be suitable, we'd hardly ever have a good giggle," Maude pointed out. "The joke is *made,* Annis. We *create* the humor, we *choose* to laugh. You know that."

She did. And Maude was right. She had a choice. Always. She could be scared tonight. She could give in to the swell of tears choking her or she could choose to laugh at the utter absurdity of the situation. She, formerly Emmeline, now Annis, was performing in a circus tonight while her father's best friend, her mother's husband, and the overall family murderer, sat in the audience, hoping to arrest her, provided he didn't still have any misguided hopes of marrying her.

Annis couldn't conjure up a more ridiculous tale if she tried.

"You look confused," Mabel said, frowning.

"Just trying to decide which I find more disturbing. The thought of being arrested or being proposed to before the night is done." She grinned, because laughing at the absurdity made her feel strong. He laughter reminded her of her own power to choose, no matter what the circumstances. Whether she laughed or cried would always be up to her.

"Oh, definitely the proposal," Bess jumped in, offering up her most disgusted grimace before falling into soundless laughter beside the others. A few more rounds of obscene humor carried on before the show was upon them, and all that it would bring was set into motion. The first hour of the show passed in what felt to Annis like seconds. And then Annis was stepping out into the ring.

Even before she could see him, she sensed he was there. A heavy feeling in her gut spread through her and a cold chill spilled down her spine. But she refused to entertain not one of her body's betrayals of fear. Instead she devoted all of her energy to her performance.

When the time came for Annis to request an assistant from the audience, she knew how it would turn out. William would relish the thought of making her squirm before the audience, but she would never deliver him the satisfaction. And so, when he stood to volunteer, she offered him the same rehearsed welcome she gave everyone who accepted the challenge.

"It's not a tough job, but don't be fooled. It is very, very important," she told him, her eyes wide and her mouth pursed dramatically. Even as his gaze bore into her, a sneer resting on his thin lips, she allowed herself no flicker of recognition or flash of fear. She simply carried on as though he were no more significant to her than any other volunteer she called into the ring.

With narrow eyes, William went along with her act. He went along with binding her up in the chains she handed to him. When he was nearly finished and closest to her face, he hissed, "You don't really think a little makeup and a silly costume are enough to hide you from me?"

"I think you're confusing this part of the act with another, sir," she said politely. "I won't be vanishing, simply escaping. They sound similar, of course," she smiled. "But they're not."

He pulled his head back and ground his teeth before he said, "Don't care what you call it, you won't be doing either," he growled, snapping the final lock into place.

"Obviously you haven't seen my act before," Annis said before stepping up to the water tank and dropping herself inside.

She'd hoped William would be so startled that he'd run to yank off the curtain keeping her hidden from the audience. She was not disappointed. Keeping her eyes locked on his the entire time, she moved steadily in the water. One by one she undid her restraints until, at last, despite his prophecy, she broke free and burst through the water's surface with a triumphant shout.

By show's end, the police did not surge in from all around or start questioning the crew. As Annis and the others crowded around the small gap between the curtains, it seemed the remaining officers were rather unconvinced they had reason to be there at all.

"Sir," one of the men in uniform said to William. "Perhaps it's best to end the night early. Not waste any more time pursuing this lead. I think it's clear to everyone here that it's simply a matter of coincidence the two young women appear so similar."

"Absolutely not," William insisted, drawing himself up taller and letting his jacket flap open just enough to make visible the badge he kept clipped inside. "There are not two women, deputy. It's her. It's Emmeline, and I will see her taken into custody tonight." Powerless in his rank, the officer stepped back and motioned for the others to go ahead with their original plan.

"Get away from that curtain this instant," Babe hissed when she caught them all. "This is no different from any other night, you hear me? We break down, we load up, and we leave. Same as always. Their business isn't our business until they make it such."

Caroline pointed to the back opening of the tent and the two officers leading the way inside. "I think they're making it such," she said in a hushed voice, clutching tighter to Homer's hand.

"Annis," Sawyer grunted. "We've animals to tend to." And he spun on his heel, marching on toward the lions' cages. The two rarely worked together after the show's end, but Annis understood his cue and followed quickly in his steps. Lions and wolves roaming loose tended to keep outsiders at a distance. And distance was safest for Annis.

"Oh, I'm sorry, did my elbow get you in the face? I didn't see you there. Left eye's no good, you see," Annis heard Poppy say loudly.

"Perhaps your right eye will be of better service then. I'm looking for someone, a girl named Emmeline Sanders. I believe you know her," William's deep voice boomed for everyone to hear.

""I'm sorry, there's no one here by the name of Emmeline Sanders," Poppy answered, matching his volume while still maintaining the same air of obliviousness he'd expressed over accidentally hitting William in the eye. Something Annis was positive, had been purely intentional, poor left eye or not.

"Annis, then," William snarled. "Or do you suppose it's coincidence your illusionist shares a face with my murder suspect and a name with her victim?" he demanded.

"Says here your victim's names were Sarah Lynn Sanders and...Anny?" Annis watched from behind several crates filled with animal props as Poppy read aloud from the wanted poster.

"Anny was all we have on record for her. She grew up a slave and apparently remained on as housekeeper even after she was freed," one of the deputies explained.

"Annis," William insisted. "That's what Emmeline called her. Not Anny. Only one ever called her that was Peter's father. He's the one who would have put it down as such when he gave her as a gift to his son as a wedding present."

The conversation made Annis's stomach turn. She'd known of course, about slavery, how her family had come to add a housekeeper to their family, but it hadn't ever felt to her as callous as William now described the situation. He spoke as if the woman who'd been at Annis's side from the time she was a baby were less than human, something more akin to the teddy bear Annis dragged about with her until it became too ratty and was then thrown away.

"Don't go getting hung up on what they're saying about your Annis. The world likes to give names to all sorts of things and people," Sawyer said under this breath. "They hardly ever get it right though." He nodded toward the lion enclosure where Roderick and Phryne were anxiously pacing about, ready to be moved to a more spacious, private area. "Let's start with them. Finian will be at your heels the whole time, anyway. If that doesn't remind people to give you a fair amount of personal space while you move about, nothing will."

"You know," she said, watching him unhook the latch that kept the lions' door locked. "There are moments my head wants to explode just hearing some of the asinine things you say to push people's buttons,"

"And?" he grunted, reaching inside the enclosure and coaxing Phryne toward him as though she were as intimidating as an average house cat.

"And there are others when my heart swells with gratitude just knowing you're my friend."

He sighed as though he were experiencing physical pain. "Girls." He rolled his eyes. "Here, take one of your lot and start walking her over that way, so I can get Roderick out next." He handed her a rope that served as a leash, which he'd tied around the lioness like a body harness. Annis had seen him do this night after night, but she'd never once been asked to participate by holding onto one of the leads herself.

"Are you sure she won't mind?" Annis asked, feeling anxious.

"You really think I'd go out of my way to save you from your crazy stepfather only to have you get eaten by one of my lions?"

"Suppose not."

He snorted. "No, suppose not."

Annis gripped the rope tightly, though she couldn't help but have mixed feelings about her actions. Part of her couldn't deny it felt wrong trying to ensure she and the lioness could not be separated. Even Finian was careful to keep a wide berth around the two as they began their walk from the tent out to the train's animal cars.

"There, it's her!" William called out as Annis was nearly at the exit. "Stop her!" he demanded of the officers guarding the only way in and out.

"Sir," stammered the one to Annis's left. "The lion?"

"You have a gun," William snarled. "Use it if you must." Even in all his fervor, it was hard for Annis to miss that he was making no efforts of his own to get closer.

"If you even try to reach for your weapon, I promise you Fin will have your arm before you even touch the trigger," Annis warned, pointing at the wolf whose watchful eyes darted about, being sure not to miss a single detail as his charge passed through. "If you want a word with me, simply ask."

The deputy nodded, visibly gulping. "Ma'am, a word?"

"After I get the lion to her car," Annis replied as though she hadn't a care in the world and like this was all business as usual. Then, to prove she was setting the terms of their interactions, she stepped through the opening between both officers and disappeared outside.

As soon as she felt the cold night air hit her face, she heard a scuffle of noises from inside the tent behind her. She kept moving forward, walking toward the end of the train. Phryne's safety was at hand now and she would see to it the lioness was out of harm's way before William decided to put Fin's reflexes to the test himself. If any bullets should fly tonight, Annis would see to it she remained the only target.

"No one believes him," Sawyer said as he caught up to her beside the train, with Roderick in tow on a long lead that allowed him more freedom than some might find comforting while walking alongside a grown lion. "All the other officers are looking at him like he's nuts for still insisting you're Emmeline Sanders, the timid and troubled rich girl who shot her own mother. All they can see is fierce and fancy you, Annis the Alchemist." He chuckled. "To be fair, I'm a little confused myself."

"About which part?"

"The part where this fool believed anyone would ever mistake you for the little waif he wrote you up as. It's his own fault they all think he's crazy now. He should have depicted you more accurately from the start."

Annis handed over Phryne's lead and walked up the ramp to pull open the sliding door to their car. "I don't think he knew how different I'd be now."

Sawyer paused just as he was about to walk inside, looking at her curiously. Then, without saying a word, he smiled, shaking his head as he moved into the dark of the lion's den with both big cats following close behind. A moment later he was out on the ramp beside her again. "Can I ask you something?"

"Anything." She saw no reasons to keep secrets now.

"Your name. The name you chose, I mean. If Annis's only real name on record is Anny...Where did you get Josephine Watson?"

Annis smiled. The name had come to her without a conscious thought. "Jo Watson was a character Annis made up. Every night, she would sit on the side of my bed and tell me stories, the grand adventures Jo had. She couldn't read, see? Not until I could, anyway. Once I learned, she learned, but before, all the years she couldn't, it never stopped her from sharing a bedtime story with me." She turned toward Sawyer. "Before Annis took the part for herself, Josephine Watson was my hero. She was everything I ever wanted to be. She sailed the world on her ship, braved storms, outwitted pirates, and always had a laugh at the scariest and most intense moments of her stories. Didn't matter what she was faced with, she never gave up. She never quit trying until she succeeded."

"Makes sense," Sawyer said, guiding her to step left and avoid a patch of ice that had formed over the course of their show. The temperatures had dropped tremendously in recent days.

"Why no one's ever heard of an Annis Josephine Watson?"

"No." Sawyer shook his head. "Why Annis Josephine Watson is exactly who you turned out to be."

Annis felt a rush of emotions and the lingering pressure of them on her face, weighing down on the bridge of her nose and above her cheekbones. "You're being exceptionally kind to me tonight. Why is that?"

"I'm always kind," he said. "I'm just not nice about it." Then he sped up, taking the lead as they braced themselves for whatever was waiting for them back inside the tent.

Annis could tell as soon as they walked in that even in the short time that they'd been absent, several things had happened. One, the only people remaining in the tent with the police were the handful of faces Annis had grown most familiar with in her time at Brooks and Bennet. The twins, of course, along with Sequoyah. Poppy and Babe were leading the conversation with two of the police officers. Off to the side, pretending to be exceptionally busy with the dagger collection used in Homer's act, were Homer and Caroline, accompanied by Bess, August, and Goldilocks.

The second thing she noted was the energy. Gone was the tension that had made it hard to breathe before. Now, the air had shifted to one of conflict as William's frustration increased. He was trying repeatedly to make his point about the resemblance between his wanted poster and the Annis the Alchemist's circus flyer. And third, though it almost escaped her, was the silence. Aside from the set of voices still carrying on a heated debate about her identity, there wasn't a sound to be heard.

"Where is everyone?" Annis whispered, hoping Sawyer could hear her even while she was faced with the back of his head and the slight distance between them.

"Trust me, they're here," he answered through gritted teeth, making his response nearly invisible to anyone watching.

"Annis," Babe called out once she spotted her. "Come here, Tulip. Help these men clear things up once and for all."

It seemed an odd request, and yet it was a perfectly simple one. She only had to decide which girl she was, which picture depicted the girl she believed herself to be, because they couldn't be one and the same. She knew choosing one meant giving up the other. There would never be room for both.

"Your name?" the deputy asked, sounding official and looking the part. He held a pencil to paper as he waited for her response.

"Annis Josephine Watson." She felt liberated even as she said those three words. Annis Josephine Watson would never inherit her father's empire. She'd never have a great deal of money or be viewed by greater society as a person of importance. She wouldn't have a family history or legacy to carry on. But she would be free.

"Age?" he continued.

"Twenty."

"No, you're not," William spat with rage. "You're seventeen, you lying little brat."

"You will not speak to her that way," Poppy reared up to him, his shoulders squared and his chest raised. "You hear me? She's done nothing to warrant any sort of disrespect from any of you. She's playing along, no matter how far-fetched your accusations. We all are. We're accommodating and answering every question no matter how often you ask it, or how trivial it seems to us. But I will draw the line and put a stop to you right where you stand, you take that tone and resort to name-calling with anyone here again."

The deputy glanced back and forth between William and Poppy, clearly anxious to complete the interrogation. "Um, birthdate?" he asked, his voice several octaves lower, as though he were hoping not to be heard by anyone other than Annis, a feat impossible given the close proximity in which they all stood.

Annis hadn't once considered a birthdate to match her rather sped up age, and so she hesitated to answer.

"December 1," Sequoyah said for her. "Only just celebrated a few weeks ago."

"And the year?"

"This year," Sequoyah answered, as though it were obvious. "That's how I know she's twenty, because we celebrated her twentieth birthday *this year.*"

Annis nodded. "That's right. On December 1. Said so on my cake and everything."

The officer jotted it down without giving it a second thought, whether he truly believed them or just couldn't be bothered to continue dealing with their games was unclear. William, however, remained unconvinced.

"She's lying. They're all lying."

"Sir," the deputy interjected. "I understand how important this matter is to you, but perhaps you're too close to the case. And you're seeing...ghosts." He took the wanted poster from Poppy's hand and held it to Annis's face. Three weeks ago, it had been all the resemblance Goldilocks needed to know they were the same girl. Tonight, she knew they weren't. "Look at them. Really look." The deputy did a double take himself, just to be sure. "The eyes are different. The hair. The mouth. Even the shape of their faces aren't the same. Subtle differences, but sir, differences nonetheless."

"She's wearing makeup. Her hair isn't tied up and back the way as would be proper. And her face is fatter," William countered, curling his lip in disgust, clearly finding the changes she'd made to herself to be less than favorable.

The deputy sighed, unable to sway his stubborn superior.

"For argument's sake, let's say all of those things are possibly to blame for the difference in her appearance," though it was quite obvious he didn't think this to be the case. "Do you honestly believe your stepdaughter wandered into the woods that night, completely out of her mind, mentally unwell as you yourself have accounted to, only to wind up walking across two state lines to run off with the circus? How would she even have survived that? No money. No shelter. No food. No drink. No way to protect herself from the elements, animals, or the sort of riffraff she'd have encountered wandering the rails and desolate paths she'd likely have taken."

"It's a traveling circus," William shouted, adding volume to detract from the missing evidence. "For all we know, they were just outside the city limits that night. Could have picked her up right then and there."

"No," Poppy cut in. "I've shown you our travel register. We weren't anywhere near your state, and only just barely cut the corner of the South on our way northwest when we crossed paths with Annis. What you're suggesting is impossible."

"I don't care what you say," William insisted, his fists balled at his sides as he shook with anger. "I know that this is Emmeline and I will prove it."

"You can't prove what isn't so," Poppy said.

"But I can prove what is," William snarled. "And believe me, I intend to. Starting with a complete search of the train. Somewhere here, hidden among your smoke and mirrors, is the proof I need."

"Sir," one of his officers cut in. "We can't just search without reason."

William contorted his face, but then regained his composure before addressing the crowd. "If anyone here can think of anything they've seen or heard in the time that this young woman has been here that would lead you to believe she's not who she claims to be, step forward. A substantial reward will be paid to the first person who speaks up."

He waited, pleased with his announcement, clearly confident that somewhere among them there was another human being as vile and as easily motivated by greed as he was.

Annis held her breath. She hated herself for even having a sliver of doubt or a hint of fear that someone in her family would turn on her. But the past had proven it possible, and now she stood in limbo, waiting for the future to unfold.

Patience waned from William's face the longer he stood alone at the center of the ring. He shifted back and forth on his feet, rubbing his jaw with the palm of his hand. Annis knew the signs. He was regrouping, coming up with a new tactic. At any moment he would open his mouth and the wait would be over.

And then a quiet shuffle. Feet slowly dragging across the dirt. A sound every member of the Brooks and Bennet Circus knew by heart. Floyd. Quietly muttering under his breath, he approached. The crowd parted out of habit, allowing Floyd passage as they always did for him. The act was instinctual, meant to honor his space in the world because it was all of him that remained. But today, it was more. Because today, the ease at which he moved through their family gave him a direct path to the man trying to tear it apart.

"I knew it," William huffed, vindication spreading in his face. "Tell me what you know, and I promise you will be paid handsomely."

"He can't tell you anything," Poppy began to explain, but William stopped him.

"I'll be the judge of that."

Floyd, creeping ever closer to William, mumbled on, appearing, as usual, entirely unaware. Then he came to a halt. His head slowly tipped upward to gaze upon the man before him. Floyd's eyes widened and Annis's heart stopped. He could see William. There was no doubt in her mind.

"Letter," Floyd said, his voice ringing clearer than ever. "They'll find the letter."

It was all the reason William needed. Taking a step back from Floyd, he addressed the officers. "I want her cabin searched. Better yet, I want everyone's car turned upside down. You find this letter, and you bring it to me," he demanded, his voice booming through the tent.

"You can't be serious," Caroline piped up. "Your men going through all of our belongings is a complete invasion of our privacy. You've no right."

"I'm the law. I have every right to do what I see fit where my quest for justice is concerned," he answered, staring down at her.

"This is outrageous," Babe insisted as William was turning his back to them. "You're abusing your power and defiling all you claim to represent in doing so. This is nothing but a witch hunt, and we, merely easy targets. But I promise you, you won't find what you're looking for. No matter how many laws you break trying to find it."

"I already found what I came for," he said, his back still turned. "Only collecting what I need now to leave with it."

One by one, the officers requested an occupant of every car to accompany them and then marched out to the train with their guides.

Annis stood frozen as Maude and Mabel were among those leading the way outside. She repeatedly told herself there was nothing to fear. Despite the clarity with which Floyd had spoken, there was no letter to be found. There was no letter, period. But, traces of her past were still hidden among the glitter and lace stashed in Babe's traveling trunks. The clothes Annis had arrived in had stayed with the person she'd trusted most that first day here. Giving the clothes to Babe to keep gave Annis some comfort in knowing that what remained of the woman she'd loved so dearly was safe. The relics had been tucked away, but not gone for good. And William would know them. He would recognize the dress after having seen it on the original Annis, who wore it day after day for so many years. He'd also know the coat had once belonged to Annis's mother. He'd be able to prove it through the simple act of revealing a small stitch of red in the lining where it had been mended, which made it no longer suitable for Annis's mother to wear herself.

How long would it be before the officers' search turned from seeking a letter to finding the evidence that would tie Annis to that night and the very people William claimed she'd murdered?

Her heart pounded in her chest and Annis tried her best not to show her nerves as they waited for the police to search the train, but the lump in her throat made it nearly impossible. She attempted to force it down, to will it away, but all it did was make her have to cough, which drew more attention to her.

At first, her eyes sought out Floyd every few seconds. He still stood in the same spot where he'd stopped to meet William. His eyes were empty once again, and his words returned to an inaudible blithering. It wasn't long before he began to wander again, moving about unnoticed by William and the officers, who'd dismissed him as quickly as he'd come and gone. If he'd really been present, it was already becoming hard to believe and harder still to fathom why he'd surfaced for the sheer act of selling her out. He'd been haunting her since she met him. Annis, keen to believe it was her anxious mind taunting her with fears of her past, had dismissed his strange but suspect musings.

At last, all the officers returned, each carrying bundles of papers in their hands. Letters, as it turned out, were abundant among the circus folk.

"We searched the compartments as you requested," said the last of William's men to return. "We found letters, but nothing that suggests this woman is Emmeline, nor anything that leads us to believe there is anyone here connected to the Sanders family in any way."

"Not possible." William spun on his heel, glaring at Annis. He stared her down, as though he could mentally break through her thoughts and retrieve the evidence that he was so desperate to find. "It's here. I know it is," he snarled under his breath.

Annis, not worried about any letter, was stunned to hear the search had been completed without turning up her old belongings. She didn't dare glance in Babe's direction, afraid she'd give away her fears, but even out of the corner of her eye she could see Babe's beard twitching at the corners. Nerves always did this to her.

"No matter," William said after a moment of thought. "I still have what I need most right before me. I'm taking her into custody tonight."

"On what grounds?" The deputy, who'd only just concluded the search and turned up no shred of evidence, appeared not only confused but almost frightened, as though he were starting to wonder if the mentally unwell person that they were seeking wasn't in fact the detective in front of him.

"I don't need grounds. I'm her guardian. She's a minor. If you won't help me on criminal charges, I'll take her home and have her committed for the sake of her own well-being."

Babe stepped out in front of Annis, as if to guard her with her own body. "You're not taking our girl anywhere. You're no guardian. You're a predator. Even if she was the girl you're looking for, which she's not, I'd unleash the furies of hell upon you before I ever let you lay a finger on her."

"Don't you threaten me, you freak," Willian snarled. "I'll have her out of here, and away from the likes of you, if it's the last thing I do."

Annis could see Poppy on the verge of blowing up. She'd never seen his temper tested like this. He possessed more patience than anyone she'd ever met, but William was about to rob him of all he had.

But it was Sequoyah who stepped forward. "I'm sorry," he said in a calm, menacing voice that Annis had never heard come from his mouth. "Which freak, exactly, are you referring to?"

August, Goldilocks, and Homer began moving in around them, accompanied by Bess and Caroline, while Maude and Mabel took a step in to meet Annis at her left. Babe was still glued to her right. Sawyer strolled in last, laughing. "You all should see your faces right now," he said. "It's almost as though you forgot you were still at the circus."

"We're done here," one of the deputy's announced, circling his finger above his head to signal everyone to round up and clear out.

"Good," William agreed smugly, reaching his hand for Annis's arm but coming up short when someone stepped between them. This time, it was one of his own men.

"Sir," the deputy said, quietly but insistently. "You...you can't take her. She's not Emmeline Sanders."

"The hell she's not," William hollered. "I can prove it!"

"You've had your chance," the deputy reminded him. "And you've not succeeded in convincing anyone but yourself that this woman is your stepdaughter." He tilted his head, pity glazing his eyes. "Perhaps it's time to consider that the grief is playing tricks on your mind, showing you what you want to see instead of what is."

"We had a witness step forward," William argued, his voice growing louder with each word.

The deputy turned back to Floyd who'd only just wandered back in, clearly out of sorts and without his wits. "Sir, look at him. He's far from credible."

William refused. Instead, he glared at the lot of them, all standing up for Annis and keeping him from his prey. He had lost, and it was evident to all that it was doing little to diffuse his determination and rather fueling his furious need to get what he wanted, no matter the cost.

"This isn't settled," he snarled, turning away. "Not by a long shot."

"Sir," the deputy said in a warning tone, but William ignored him.

"There'll be other towns, other policemen. Sooner or later, someone will see what I see, and then I'll have my moment of justice, Emmeline. And you? You'll have nothing."

All eyes were on them as they made their way from the tent. Then, time stopped. The earth refused to move. Everything stood still until the sounds of the men moving outside subsided and their world was theirs once more.

Air flooded Annis's lungs like a tidal wave, and it was only then she noticed she'd been holding her breath. Everyone around her flew into action as though they, too, had been frozen, held captive by the anticipation of their impending freedom from William and his threats.

"Load up and let's get moving down those tracks," Poppy's voice boomed overhead. "I have a feeling our friend William isn't nearly as quick to surrender as he'd have us believe. The sooner we get going, the better!"

No one needed to be told twice. In record time, the tent was broken down and put away. Props, tools, and temporary lodging were all packed up as though camp had never existed. When all that remained of their presence was the train sitting stagnant on the tracks, Poppy ordered a headcount as people boarded.

"Where's Smalls?" Poppy demanded, nearing the end of his count. "Step your tiny arse forward so I know you're here." The remaining crowd shifted back and forth, looking over their shoulders, waiting for someone to move toward the center. But no one came.

"He's not here," Annis called out, half hoping he would yell an insult at her from wherever he was, proving he was present but Annis was simply too dimwitted to look down.

But no snort, scoff, or otherwise offensive sounds could be heard. Annis's heart sank.

"He's probably still in the animal car. Roderick was antsy after tonight's rocky ending," Sequoyah said, sounding the voice of reason. One look into his eyes told Annis he was just as unnerved by Sawyer's absence as she was.

Of course, she told herself, it was all in her head. Just a lingering panic causing paranoia after the evening they'd had. Sawyer would turn up in a matter of minutes, and he'd have a grand laugh at their expense when he learned they were actually foolish enough to worry.

"Just to be sure," Poppy said to Sequoyah, pointing his hand toward the end of the train, "go have a look. And drag him back here when you find him." His son nodded, already turning away. "August," Poppy added. "Go with him." Hearing that Poppy felt a need for extra measures did little to ease Annis's already whirring mind.

With August and Sequoyah off in search of Sawyer, the final headcount went smoothly and was completed before any of them returned.

"Annis," Poppy said sternly. "I want you in your cabin with the twins. Lock the doors once you're inside." Annis nodded, biting back the defiant words aching to jump from the tip of her tongue.

She hated the thought of hiding out when those she cared for were left outside and unaccounted for.

"You heard him," Maude muttered, grabbing her sleeve and dragging her along, causing her to stumble backward the entire way, unable to commit to this act of cowardice she was being sentenced to for the sake of her own safety.

"He's alright, don't you think? Smalls? He's just off reminding everyone he's never bothered by any rules. It's just the sort of pigheaded thing he'd do," she rambled, determined to feed her mind whatever rubbish it needed to believe.

"It's Sawyer. He's always alright. It's what he's best at," Maude assured her.

"Well, right after getting into trouble," said, much to Annis's chagrin. "But, then he's always great at getting out of it. So maybe the two are tied."

"I'm sure you're right," Annis said unconvincingly.

The women were a few feet away from their cabin, just seconds from stepping inside, when Fin growled. They stopped in unison. "What do we do?" Annis hissed, her instincts telling her to turn back. But that would only mean more running, and she was done with that. She was ready to face whatever was coming for her.

Maude glanced back and forth between the door and the wolf. "I say we push the door open and let Fin at whatever is behind it."

Mabel nodded with great enthusiasm, though Annis suspected nerves were also to blame for the erratic way her head was bobbing up and down. "I second that."

"William has a gun," Annis whispered. "What if he's standing there, ready to shoot? He'll kill Fin!"

"No way," Maude insisted. "He'll be expecting a person. His aim will be off, and Fin will be too fast for him to correct it."

Annis was sick with the thought, but Fin seemed eager for the job and she had no better ideas than to let him do what wolves did best, go for the kill.

"Alright," she breathed, her gaze moving to the door. "Do it."

It was as though Fin understood perfectly. He watched with a calculating eye as Maude reached for the handle in slow motion, gripping it hard and sliding the door open in one swift swoop at the exact moment that Fin leapt forward, darting inside their cabin, launching himself at whatever was lying in wait.

Annis and the twins waited, ears strained. She expected screams, the sounds of a scuffle, or barking, but none came.

Slowly, huddled together, they took small, hesitant steps toward the door. The closer they got, the more Annis could make out Fin's low but cautious growl. She understood that he didn't know how to proceed. Then they reached the doorway and Annis understood why.

"Sawyer." His name escaped her mouth on a mere breath. "No."

"To be fair," he said, sounding casual despite the gun William held pressed to his temple, "I was right. The bastard was in here, hiding. Hoping to snatch you, I'm assuming." He shrugged. "Unless of course, you were the decoy all along and I was the one he truly wanted. Which is likely, if you think about it."

"Shut up," William snapped, jerking Sawyer by his shoulder with his free hand. "I told you, I'm not here to play your stupid games."

"Let him go," Annis said, surprising even herself with the strength and sheer volume of her demand. "Let him go unharmed and I'll leave with you. Right now. I won't fight you. I won't call for help."

"No!" Mabel gasped.

"She's not going anywhere with anyone," Sawyer cut in with no remnant of his previously carefree attitude. "And she doesn't need to call for help because there's plenty right here. Annis may not fight you. But believe me when I say that we will."

"No one will fight," Annis insisted. "No one will fight because no one will get hurt on my account. Not over money, and that's all this is for. But that family fortune attached to my name is precisely why I'm the only one here he won't harm. Anything happens to me and he loses every chance of ever getting his hands on my inheritance."

"Annis," Maude hissed under her breath. "You can't be serious. He's not just going to take you home and leave you in peace."

"Of course not," Annis said, her eyes filled with hatred as she stared down the man who was killing her but could never put her out of her misery. "He'll lock me up. I'm a murderer, after all. An unstable girl with a broken mind, a threat to herself and others. It'll be prison, or an asylum, but the truth is, it'll be all the same to me. I'm already caged by what he's done, the memories of his terrors haunting me, always with me. The empty stare of my mother as she fell, lifeless, to the floor. My father's death at the docks and wondering if he suffered. Or if it was really as sudden for him as it was for us. And Annis, *my* Annis, who gave her life to save mine. A gift so grand the guilt of it makes it impossible for me to breathe sometimes." She paused, a painful cinching around her lungs as she took in air. "I'll never be free. And I'm done pretending I could be."

"You don't mean that," Mabel whispered, dread pooling in her eyes.

"I do." Annis lowered her gaze to meet Sawyer's, silently pleading with him to give up the fight on her behalf and save himself.

His stare turned cold. His stubborn streak flared, made visible in the way his jaw tightened and his lips pressed together into a thin line that turned white around the edges. Silence spread around the small cabin like humidity, making it uncomfortable to breathe or move.

William seemed to be the only one unbothered. He was biding his time, obviously certain the tide was changing in his favor. Annis was doing all the work for him, convincing the others to step out of his way, to let them walk out together.

"Fine," Sawyer said at last, his defeat ringing in Annis's ears. "If this is what you want."

Slowly, William shifted the barrel of his gun away from Sawyer and toward Annis. "I'm glad to see you're making better choices now, Emmeline," he said with a bite in his words. "Too bad you couldn't see reason the night you left poor Annis alone to die."

"It won't work," she told him, her eyes narrowed and her shoulders squared. "Your lies, your guilt. The evil you spew touches only yourself. Say what you want. Treat me as you wish, but don't for a second think that I see the world as you spin it, that I believe the twisted words you try to wrap me in. I don't. I never will because I've learned far too much truth to ever be blind to it again." She stepped forward, out of the safety she felt standing nestled between the sisters. "We should hurry. They already know Sawyer's missing. Won't be long 'til they come looking here."

William held his gun even with her eyes. She stared straight down the pitch of his barrel and said, "Lead the way."

Turning on her heel, she allowed herself a brief moment of unyielding fear, knowing he was the sort of coward who would shoot her in the back. She swallowed it down and marched onward, never even glancing at the sisters or Sawyer as she bid them a silent adieu.

She had no plan. She'd had one, a small one, but it had run its course the moment William had shifted his weapon from Sawyer to her, and now that she was out of the cabin, alone with him, her friends out of his grasp, her plan was complete. Shame swirled at the pit of her stomach at the small part of her that secretly hoped their paths would cross with the likes of Poppy, or Sequoyah, or anyone who would override her efforts to be selfless and coura-

geous. The greater part of her, however, knew they wouldn't encounter anyone because she saw to it that they took the path least
traveled. They walked the darkened side of the train, hidden in
the shadows while moving in hurried silence along the tracks toward the caboose, which, by now, would be abandoned as everyone
searched for Sawyer.

They were seconds out from being caught, but seconds was all
she needed to clear the train and cross the small opening between
the tracks into the woods beyond. Once they made it past the tree
line, there would be no tracking them. This time, they wouldn't
have Fin to find her. William was as of yet unaware, but the wolf
was with them. Fin trailed several feet behind, keeping a safe distance but never falling so far behind that she was out of his sight.
She could hear the soft pad of paws moving over the ground, nearly inaudible. If it hadn't been for the months that she'd spent ac-
climating herself to the quiet rhythm with which he moved, she'd
never have been able to detect it herself. She found solace in knowing he was with her, walking this last stretch of her journey. She
wasn't alone.

"Hope you don't think you can lead me astray in these woods,"
William huffed, struggling to move over the uneven forest floor in
the dark of night.

"You've been astray since before I ever knew you, William," she
responded calmly. The woods no longer held anything to fear for
her. On the contrary, there was a sense of coming home in wandering deeper into the trees, feeling the soft leaves of young branches
brush against her skin. She tilted her head back, looking at the sky.
Patches of deep blue sprinkled with glittering stars peeked through
the treetops. "But for the sake of our travels, the North Star is just
overhead," she said, pointing at the brightest light amid the fairy-
dusted ceiling of night. "See?"

"I know how to keep direction," he snarled. "Just keep your eyes moving forward and don't try anything stupid."

Annis bit her tongue. The temptation to respond with a slew of insults nearly burst from her lips. Instead, she shifted her focus to Finian, still moving in their shadows, and the sounds of nocturnal life all around them. Despite these noises, she also heard an aching silence. She and William moved swiftly but had not covered so much ground that she wouldn't have heard the commotion when news spread of her departure. But she heard nothing. She told herself it was better this way, better for them not to be panicked and dashing off after her. Better for everyone to just simply accept what was. But her heart failed to feel the comfort in realizing even Sequoyah had given up for good this time this time. He had no choice, of course. Neither of them did. She'd known this from the start and had tried to remind herself of it over and over during the course of their courtship, but she'd failed to heed her own warnings. She'd done the one thing she'd sworn not to. She'd fallen in love with a boy whose future she would never see. Tears stung her eyes, but she refused to give in to the sob striking her chest and suffocating her heart. The one thing she wanted more than anything to offer to Sequoyah was being held captive by the man she detested most in the world—or so he believed.

Annis knew better. What William wanted, he would never get. Annis no longer cared what it cost her. She had nothing left that she couldn't bear to lose. She took a breath, closed her eyes, and stopped. They'd gone far enough.

"What are you doing?" William called out from behind. "Why are we stopping?"

"Because we've no further to go," she answered simply.

"I beg to differ." He moved in closer, pressing the barrel of his gun to her shoulder. She responded by leaning all of her weight against it.

"Do it," she said. "Shoot me."

"What?" Even through his anger, confusion was swimming to the surface.

"Shoot me. I'm all there's left here. No one else around to bully or use to blackmail me. Only us. You and me. And I'm no longer following your orders. So," she paused, slowly turning around to face him, letting the gun slide over her heart. "Let me go or shoot me. But, either way, you're going forward without me."

"Think I won't just swing you over my shoulder and carry you if I need to?" he roared.

"I think you'll try," she said. "But I know you'll fail if you do. I'm not the same girl you remember, William. I'm not the same girl you once could have dragged home with one ferocious glare. I'm not her. Not anymore. And you're to blame. You made me an opponent you can't beat. Don't you see? There's nothing you can take from me I won't willingly give, including my own life. But you can't take the money, can you? Not here. Not tonight. Not ever."

"We'll see about that." He lunged for her, his hands gripping her throat and his gun tumbling to the ground.

"You really think you're ready to die tonight? Think it's that easy? Maybe when death comes in a bullet, fast and painless. But there are other ways to kill you, Emmeline. Ways that could take days to end you. And by then I'll have all I need from you to get what I deserve."

Annis glared back at him, her eyes wide. She refused to let them even blink, not wanting him to mistake any small move as an indication of fear. She felt none. All she knew was the fire burning within her, promising her victory even if it came at the expense of her last breath. She would have it. She would go on her own terms, by her own choice, and William would lose.

Though blood rushed in Annis's ears, drowning out all other sound, she wasn't surprised when William's eyes lit up with shock and he fell forward. And then she saw Fin on William's back, his claws digging into the man's torso and his teeth piercing his shoulder flesh, inches from William's throat. Annis saw fear flash in William's eyes but he quickly recovered, wrestling the wolf from his back. He dropped to the ground and searched for the gun he'd dropped.

"Fin! No!" Annis shouted, knowing she had only seconds to get him to safety before bullets fired. "Go home! Please! Go home, Fin!" But the wolf wouldn't listen and instead launched another attack, tackling William to the ground. Jaws wide, Fin went straight for the man's head. But William was no small man, and he fought well. Too well.

Annis scrambled over the uneven ground, desperate to join the fight and save her friend. Even as fangs flew past her face, she knew Fin would never harm her, would never mistake her for his target. With that trust she reached between them, trying to pry the wolf from the real beast, but it was to no avail. Fin and William continued their battle. The wolf slammed his body into Annis's side to throw her from their fight and out of harm's way.

She screamed, helplessly begging Finian to let go, to release and retreat, but Fin refused. Even as William was gaining ground in their battle, landing a punch to the wolf's hip and making him squeal in pain, Finian continued to tear at him. Annis couldn't bear to stand by. She tackled them a second time, this time throwing herself entirely between them and covering William with her body as much as she could to shield him from the wolf's attack. Fin retreated instantly and began pacing back and forth, anxiously waiting for Annis to clear his path so that he could resume his fight.

William's body felt limp and weak beneath Annis's. For a moment, she wondered if Fin had dealt him wounds that he wouldn't recover from. Slowly, cautiously, she peeled herself up. She held out her hands to ward off the wolf.

"He's not worth it, Fin," she whispered, pleading with him. "He's not worth becoming the evil he is. You're not a killer. You're a hunter. The two are different, Fin. And you mustn't forget. You forget, and the world around you will forget. They'll see a beast. Unless you show them your grace. Your mercy. Your wonderful brave heart. You show them the wolf, Fin. Always show them the wolf."

Gradually, she put more distance between herself and William, who remained a shallow breathing lump on the ground, and moved in Fin's direction until she was kneeling before him, pressing her face to his forehead.

"I know you don't understand, but I don't need saving anymore," she whispered. "I'm not afraid of anything he might do to me. But I'm terrified of what he might do to you. Even if the thing he does to you is die at your efforts. The only way he can hurt me is by hurting you. Please, go home. Be safe." The wolf shuddered under her embrace and she knew in her soul that he understood what she was asking.

Slowly, she straightened up, and together they began to walk, leaving William to rest where he lay. Annis wouldn't be long. Just a few more steps and she would feel confident that Fin was safe, back in the shadows, standing down despite his every instinct to attack.

And then, all at once, noise exploded around her. She heard the sounds of ruffling leaves up ahead as familiar faces became visible, their bodies moving quickly. No one said a word as they marched in unison through the dark, on a mission to retrieve what William had taken.

Behind her, she heard a thud in the dirt, and then another, as William rose to his knees, struggling to gain control of his battered body. Then Fin, growling, barking, and launching himself in front of her, shielded her from something she couldn't see. And she couldn't turn to look. Her wide eyes were glued to Sawyer, who broke from the pack of familiar faces and tumbled himself to the ground, rolling over until he came to a stop behind her.

Annis watched as all the pieces fell together. William's drawn gun. The thunderous crash of a freed bullet, flying straight for Fin. Sawyer, throwing himself in front of it. Sawyer, catching the piece of lead for himself and falling to the ground in a heart wrenching thud. And then the sound of another bullet releasing.

Confusion swarmed Annis as she watched William sink to his knees, a look of surprise still etched in his face like the one her mother had worn when she died. Sounds overwhelmed her senses and everything around her went blank. She couldn't think. She couldn't hear. She could hardly see through the blur of tears shrouding her eyes. Though they were silent to her, the screams coming from her mouth left her lungs burning raw. Her gut twisted and ached with the pull of a hundred knives dragging their way back and forth over her insides.

Sawyer was gone.

Men in blue uniforms were spilling in from all around, centering on William, the man they'd shot and killed. Even as the strength of familiar arms lifted her from the dirt, her body gave way to the pain, her heart drowned in the dull cold ache of death, and her eyes drew only blackness.

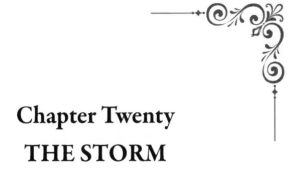

Chapter Twenty
THE STORM

When Annis awoke, it was to the comfort of the sounds of the train humming over the tracks, with the occasional squeak as the rails hugged at a curve and made a tight turn before straightening out again.

For one blissful second, her mind entertained the possibility that she'd just woken up from a terrible dream. That every last horrible second of the past twenty-four hours was only a nightmare. Then the creak in her weary bones and the pain of her bruised flesh made the lie impossible to believe.

"She's waking up," she heard Mabel whisper. Her voice reached Annis as if through a hazy veil, like she was lost in an alternate dimension, able to see across but not reach over. Arms tightened around her waist and it was then she realized that she wasn't lying in her bed alone. There was no need to open her eyes and see who it was. Only one person could steady her heart by filling her with the beat of his own. Sequoyah.

"Go back to sleep," he whispered. "It's still dark out, it'll only feed the pain. Wait for light. We'll face it then."

She wanted to face it now, to soak it all in. The dark. The guilt. The blame. She wanted it all, wanted it to spread, to poison everyone around her. All of those who'd been foolish enough to follow when she'd made it clear she wanted to finish her fight on her own.

They hadn't listened. They hadn't respected her choice, and now, Sawyer was dead. And they were all to blame, herself included. His blood had stained them all, and it would never wash clean. No magic river nor full moon overheard could cleanse them of that burden.

Her body stiffened against his, and though she said nothing, she knew he understood.

"It won't work," he murmured, "you can't separate yourself from me. Can't push me away. Can't be alone. It's too late for that. You're not a half anymore. You're a whole. And I'm part of that whole." His steady embrace drew her in more, until there was no space left between them. She surrendered, and sleep came back for her a second time.

The train was still the next time she awoke. Sequoyah's arms were absent, as were the quiet muttering of Mabel and the snide commentary of her sister. Light streamed in, warming her skin, and she knew, wherever she was, day had arrived there right along with her.

"We need to talk." Poppy's hoarse voice met her from across the cabin. As soon as she heard him, she could feel him.

Her lids were heavy, tears and sleep adding to the struggle of lifting them, or maybe it was her intense yearning for darkness that kept her from wanting to face the day. Or Poppy.

"You're going to have to come back sooner or later, Annis," he said quietly. "Might as well be now when you're still in limbo, aware of the pain but not anchored to it at the bottom of some dark abyss you'll never be able to surface from."

"Maybe I don't want to surface," she whispered with her eyes still shut. She pulled her covers up higher around her face.

"'Want' is not the issue, love," he said sadly. "You *need* to surface. If you don't do it now, I fear Sequoyah will drown pulling you back up. And I won't lose you both."

At last, her lids fluttered open. The sun blinded her, but she welcomed the sting. The physical pain was somehow comforting. It matched what she felt on the inside.

"Sawyer's dead," she said. She needed to hear the words, and she could no longer bear to wait for someone else to say them.

"He is," Poppy confirmed. He tilted his head as he gazed down upon her from where he sat beside her on the bed. His eyes were filled with love, concern, and heartbreak.

"It shouldn't have happened," Annis said through gritted teeth. "He wasn't meant to be there. No one was. I had a plan. I. Had. A. Plan." Pain choked the breath from her lungs, making it impossible to speak.

"I know you did," Poppy said softly, his hand stroking her hair gently. "Sawyer told me."

For the first time since the world had ended in a shocking crash, she felt surprised. "He did?"

Poppy nodded. "He did. He was furious, mind you. Shouting about your madness, your 'stupid selfless courage,' I believe he called it." He smiled, but it was drenched in grief. "Said you'd tried to convince them that you were giving up. Giving in to William and his demands. But he'd seen it."

"Seen what?"

"In your eyes," Poppy's voice was little more than rasp. "Your fight. You hadn't given up. You would never give up." He sighed, breath leaving his body in a ragged shudder that shook his body. "He knew you would never let William win, Annis. And we all knew the only way you could stop him was by taking his only way to get the money. Yourself."

"It was my decision," she insisted, her throat feeling as though it were being twisted up in knots, same as her stomach. "You should have let me make it. Should have honored it."

"Why?"

It was the only question she hadn't expected.

"Why should we have honored your choice to sacrifice yourself?" he asked again.

"Because," she sat up straight, scrambling for words that would convey the conviction she felt deeply within her. "Because I would have been able to see things through without any more loss. Without any more pain. I would have felt relieved knowing everyone else was safe. That William would never succeed in what he set out to do. I wasn't scared, Poppy. I was never scared for myself."

He nodded.

"I know that."

"Then why not let me do it? Why not let me go?"

"Because we were scared," he said softly. "For you. Everything that motivated you, motivated us. You would have given your life to keep us safe. Don't you understand that we would do the same for you?"

She shook her head. "William wasn't after anyone else."

"So, it was your burden to bear alone, then? Being chosen as a target by a greed-consumed madman? I don't think you're entitled to quite that much."

"Poppy," she wrung her hands in her lap, anger fading and making way for the pain she wasn't nearly ready to face. "It should have been me. William should have killed me. Not Sawyer. Never Sawyer."

"I don't think you get to decide that."

"Why not?" she demanded, defiance fueling a new wave of fury.

"Because you're not the one who pulled the trigger, love. Nor are you the one who took the bullet. Both of those choices were made by other people. And I assure you, love, they were choices. There were no tragic accidents last night. It was all orchestrated by conscious will and intentional decision. You want us to honor yours, and yet you find it impossible to honor Sawyer's. And I, darling girl, would choose to honor neither if I could. As fast as we moved through the woods in search of you last night, we held back nothing in our efforts to cross between Sawyer and that bullet. We simply weren't fast enough this time."

Annis took in his words in silence. She remembered now. The wave of people flooding past her as she sat at the center of unfurling chaos. They'd never stopped at her side, they'd gone straight for Sawyer the instant they'd understood what he was doing, because he'd been the first to understand what William's actions would lead to. What they did for her, they'd have done for everyone here. It was the same as she was willing to do for them. They were no different from her. She was no different from Sawyer. The only thing separating them now were split seconds of time she'd had to be saved that he hadn't.

"The police," she said, clearing her throat. "How did they know?"

"They returned before we even knew you'd been taken. Said they found Floyd walking in the dark and thought it best to bring him back. It was only then they noticed William had separated himself from the group and they grew worried that his obsession with you had gotten the best of him after all he'd been through. Shortly after, we found out you were gone too." He sighed heavily, "Of course, they still believe Emmeline Sanders is guilty, but they also still think you to be Annis Watson and not Emmeline Sanders."

"I am Annis Watson."

"I know."

But there was still one person who seemed to think she wasn't. One person whose motives she still didn't understand.

"Floyd," Annis said.

"Hears voices," Poppy reminded her quietly.

"I know," she said, not wanting to argue or accuse anyone after all they'd already suffered. "But there have been moments, strange encounters with him, ever since I arrived. He's spoken to me. Looked me directly in the eye, same as he did William." She paused, the ache of his name on her lips piercing her chest. "I know what I saw. What I heard. It wasn't just rubbish churned out by his dizzying mind."

"Of course not." The words were so matter of fact that Annis was certain she'd misunderstood. "Floyd hears voices," he said again, slower this time, as though he wanted to be sure Annis followed along with their meaning, "not rubbish. Not never-ending trails of thoughts that go nowhere. Voices, real voices, that no longer have the means to communicate any other way but to find a channel still in this physical realm."

"What does that mean?" Annis could form her own conclusions, of course, but she didn't dare, not when they seemed to be entirely impossible even to her.

"It means, those who have crossed over sometimes find they've left things unsaid to those still living. And Floyd can hear them. Once upon a time, he could separate the spirits he heard within from those of us out here. But it was too strange, too frightening for people to accept who he was and what he could do. And so, doctors and treatments...and torture, meant to destroy the gift he had, ultimately only succeeded in destroying everything else. Floyd is still there, but he's within, where the voices are kind. Where there's safety in their love."

"So...the things he mumbles on about?"

"Aren't his words or thoughts at all. They're merely the messages of others, passing through him, unable to reach their destination because he's no longer in charge of steering his vessel." Poppy shook his head, sadness stealing away what little light his eyes still held.

"But some reached me," she whispered, slowly recalling the things he'd said and considering their meaning if he had not been the one to say them. "It was...Annis?"

Poppy nodded. "I suspect she's been here all along." His mouth curved gently. "The search for that letter turned our car upside down. Babe couldn't understand how they missed finding your old clothes. Wasn't until she went to check on Floyd early this morning that she understood."

Annis felt the pressure of a hundred tears welling in her eyes, but none were strong enough to fall. As she listened, her breath ceased to move through her lungs, but she was too captivated by his words to notice.

"Everything, your dress, the holey boots, the worn coat, right down to the ragged belt, all neatly folded and placed atop his night-stand, never bothered, never touched, because his car was the only one not searched." Poppy swiped at his eyes, reminding Annis just how much love he held for all those in his care. "Do you think she's still here? If I talk to him...do you think she'd answer?"

He met her gaze and held it, answering her before he said the words. "I think she said all she needed to. Don't you?"

Annis knew he was right. Guilt caught her, weighing her down for hoping she'd be there, just waiting. She'd want her to move on, to find peace. Now that Annis was truly safe, her namesake would have nothing left to hold her here. And Annis would find relief in that, someday soon.

She turned to face the window. The day beyond the dark inside her was beautiful. "A tragic irony," she whispered, taking in the glorious sun, who was oblivious to all the ugliness that transpired in her absence. "Were you surprised," Annis said, her voice still thready and thin, "when you saw Sawyer running to shield us?" He'd saved Fin too. Somehow it was easier for Annis to reconcile within her mind that Smalls had been willing to die for the wolf rather than for her.

"No."

She turned toward him, curious.

Poppy chuckled in the way he always did when things were obvious to him and invisible to others. "Sawyer Smalls is now and forever will be one of the most spectacular human beings I have ever had the privilege of knowing. People always thought of him as small, but truthfully, he was always larger than life in my eyes. He had more heart than any one person should have space to hold within them, and yet, a man with the smallest stature held a grander love inside him than any average-sized man might be capable of."

"Do you know the only time he was ever nice to me was that first day I showed up?" Annis said, laughing despite her heartache. "I thought he was so sweet, trying to make me feel comfortable when I was completely overwhelmed."

Poppy nodded. "You needed it then."

"I did."

"You got stronger fast."

It was true, in part because of Sawyer. He never coddled her, never took for granted that she was smart. And tough. He demanded it of her in every interaction. In a way, he'd taught her more about being herself than any lesson she'd been asked to learn by Poppy.

Poppy seemed to sense her trailing thoughts, because he cleared his throat and began one of his own out loud. "For some reason, people always do seem to place a great deal of value on the people who are nice and often overlook those who are kind, especially if kindness isn't shown in the manner they expect it ought to be."

"Nicely?"

"Precisely," he said. "It's an unfortunate reality, and one I've always found to be particularly odd and difficult to reconcile. Some of the most wonderful people I've known in my life were brash, at times, brutally honest, and nearly every last one of them would count themselves highly offended if referred to as nice. Most people tend to confuse niceness for kindness," Poppy continued, "and often forget that kindness and niceness are not mutually exclusive. They assume nice people are kind and forget those who have shown them kindness if they weren't nice while doing it. Truth is, nice is superficial. It's easy to be nice. Kindness takes effort. To show kindness you must be able to show mercy. Be willing to sacrifice, to compromise. Those who are kind cannot be selfish. Those who are nice, often are."

Sawyer wasn't the only one she thought of as she listened. So much of what he was saying was true about her Annis as well. She'd always been comfortable around Sawyer. Never shy or caught off guard by the way he tested her. Now that she could see, it was hard to understand that she'd ever been blind to it. The two were alike and had loved her similarly. It was no wonder she'd felt so at home, so much herself when engaged in banter with Sawyer.

"Don't you think it's strange, though, some of the kindest people having the roughest edges?" she asked.

"Not really," he said, stretching his back as he spoke, letting the sun wash over his face. "You choose to be nice in order for others to like you. When you choose to be kind, you get to like yourself. Not everyone sees value in the latter, and unfortunately, in my humble opinion, people often invest poorly by favoring the regard of others." He settled back down into his seat, letting his shoulders relax and meeting her eye to eye. "People come and go all throughout your life, but the one person you'll never escape is yourself. What you think of yourself will impact you far more in your time here on this earth than anyone else's opinion ever will. I suggest you see to it that it's a good thought. I assure you, Sawyer had no doubts about the man he was, and so had no doubts about the decisions he made. Right up to his last one."

"It's hard to think kind thoughts about yourself when so many people lost their lives on account of you."

"It's hard *not* to think kind thoughts of yourself when you are so greatly loved that others are willing to gift their lives on account of you." He patted her foot, which rested under the covers near him, and smiled at her. "Life is waiting. Don't waste a second of it."

He stood from the edge of the bed and left her to her thoughts. His hand was just clasping the door handle when Annis said his name.

"Poppy?"

He turned to look over his shoulder. "Yes, love?"

"The night you gave me an act, it was only because you'd run out of time. If it hadn't been for William and needing me to hide in plain sight, would you ever have put me in the show?" It had been nagging at her ever since he'd asked her those two questions that she'd waited months to hear, but she'd been afraid to ask his motivations until now. All of her worst fears had already materialized, and so a small thing like frustrating Poppy hardly seemed worth the worry anymore.

"Annis, love, I'm not the one who ran out of time. You did." He turned, resting his shoulder against the doorframe as he faced her properly again.

"All those months...I waited longer for you to ask me into the ring than anyone else here." She sat up straighter, running her hands through her disheveled hair as though clearing the tangled mess from her face would somehow clear her mind of the confusion she felt.

"I asked you into the ring the first night you were here. I daresay, you waited less than anyone, love, not the longest. And, as for that, there are those here who have been here far longer than you and still steer clear of the spotlight. Doesn't mean they always will." He crossed his arms over his chest and his left ankle over his right one, settling into the doorframe.

"No, you made me wait," she insisted. "I didn't mind, I knew I had dues to pay, Poppy, I just wondered if I was close. If you were giving any thought to asking me before you had no choice but to do it."

He sighed loudly, shaking his head as she stared down at the wooden slats at his feet. "You ever wonder why Jacob's not in the show?"

"The monkey?"

"The boy. The very hardworking, very charismatic, very dedicated and kind boy," he corrected.

"Goldilocks," she said. She'd always assumed he'd wanted it that way.

"Yes, Goldilocks." Poppy's familiar twitch shadowed the corner of his mouth. "Don't you suppose I could find better use for him than the handiwork he keeps busy with?"

"Why don't you?"

"He's not ready."

Annis kneaded at her blanket with her fists, frustrated by Poppy's refusal to even once give a straight answer. "Maybe he's just waiting for you to ask him, same as I was."

He shifted up straighter. "You didn't want me to ask any more than he does."

"I don't understand why you keep saying that. I was ready. I was waiting."

"Annis," he said calmly.

"Yes?"

"Who do you see when you look at Goldilocks?"

She shrugged. Not in carelessness, but because the answer was obvious. "Someone brilliant and charismatic, like you said. He's lovely just to look at, but then you get to know him, and there's so much grace in the way he holds himself. There's honor in him, a deep-seated knowing of right and wrong. He's chivalrous and humble. And he values honesty and loyalty above all else. He's like a knight without the armor."

"Precisely," Poppy agreed with her. "What do you think he sees in himself?"

Annis's mouth opened without hesitation, and then shut. The words she was about to speak registered inside her mind and she sighed, silently accepting the defeat she now understood was coming. "He sees a lost boy, with no home, no family, who never wants to be a bother or a burden. He sees someone who has to work twice as hard as everyone else, do twice the dirty work and half the complaining, just to be accepted, to be allowed to stay." She shook her head, her eyes glued to her hands in her lap. She twisted her fingers until they ached. It was the first time she'd acknowledged the painful delusions he lived within. "He doesn't even know how handsome he is, always hiding half his face under that shaggy hair."

"And he won't. Not until he's ready."

Annis slowly raised her gaze to meet his. She understood everything now. "Having an act, taking our place in the show...It was never about how the world sees us, was it?"

"No," he admitted. "It's about healing how you see yourselves."

"But..." she whispered, tears stealing her voice as they rose in her throat. "I *was* that pitiful girl. The pathetic little lamb. I know I was. It was only once I was here that I learned to be more, that I grew into more."

Hugh held her gaze, his confidence in her blazing from his eyes like a fire she could feel warming her skin. "Do you really believe a lamb could have survived what you did? Do you believe your beloved Annis would have sent a lamb out into the night to fend for herself? A lamb wouldn't be here today. A lamb wasn't here that day you showed up. We didn't change you. We didn't ask you to be anything other than what you already were. You were always the wolf, Annis. And everyone could see it. Except you."

Emotions crashed in on Annis from every direction as she watched Poppy exit the car. Thoughts and feelings collided inside her until all she could do was scream to let them out. Anger. Pain. Grief. Love. Courage. Truth. All exploded from her lungs and poured from her eyes as she sobbed into the pillow pressed to her chest. Eventually, the screams subsided. The tears dried up, and what remained carried on silently, unwinding inside her own head.

It would take weeks, maybe months, maybe every last second of her life, to sort through them all. She found she was alright with that. She began to feel comfortable with the tangled up bits of memories and feelings that still whirred within her. She'd piece them together someday. Until then, they had a home inside her, right along with a heart that felt grander than before, capable of holding more love and light than she might have imagined. She blamed Sawyer for that. And she made a silent promise to thank him for it every day.

MONTHS PASSED. SOMEWHERE along the way, the Brooks and Bennet family found their new normal. They moved forward by taking the memories and releasing the grief a little bit with every mile they traveled and every town they left behind.

The hardest part, logistically, was finding a suitable caregiver for the lions. For a long while, they all took it in turns to fill the void Sawyer had left, which each person falling back as someone new kept stepping forward. Annis had a hunch about who would take the job for keeps.

As with everyone, Goldilocks had changed in the months since Sawyer's passing. It seemed to Annis as though confronting the tragic truth of life's brevity and fragility had made him more determined to be alive, to be present, to be seen. Goldilocks would soon be ready to take the ring for himself, and, if Annis was right, he would be the new Brooks and Bennet lion tamer.

"Any idea where we are?" Maude asked, stepping from the elephant cart with Edi, who swung her large trunk lazily back and forth as she walked at Maude's heels.

"No," Annis answered, tossing the last of her breakfast to Fin, who caught it in midair. "But I'm sure Sequoyah does."

"What's that I know?" he asked, coming up from behind her, surprising her with a kiss on the cheek.

"Our current location," she said, beaming back at him. It was still new to her, the way he showered her with affections beyond their previous handholding whenever he came around her, causing her to turn red and internally melt.

"Savannah."

Annis stopped short. "Savannah, Georgia?"

He nodded. "You had to have known we were headed this way?"

"I did." She tilted her head from shoulder to shoulder, unsure of how it all made her feel. "I just thought we were days out. Had hoped for weeks, to be perfectly honest."

"Your thinking's been all wonky since you two started all this kissy stuff, have you noticed?" Maude teased her.

"It has not." It absolutely had. Who could carry on rational thought when a man as beautiful as hers was smiling at her? Touching her skin. Holding her hand. And placing those soft lips so tenderly against her own.

"In any event," Maude went on. "Do you have plans to do anything in Savannah, now that you know you're here?" She arched her brow at Annis curiously, a slight skepticism showing through.

"I'm not sure." Annis placed her hand to her stomach. She suddenly regretted having had that second biscuit at breakfast. At least she'd given most of the third one to Fin. "I think I want to go to the house," she said quietly, wondering if hearing the words out loud would make them sound less crazy than they did inside her mind.

"I'll go with you," Sequoyah answered without hesitation, his hand sliding down her arm to meet her palm. "We can go this morning. I don't have much left to do. And Poppy will understand."

Maybe it wasn't crazy. Maybe it would be good, healing even, to go and say goodbye for good.

"You don't think anyone will be there, do you?" They hadn't seen any wanted posters of her since William had been shot down by the police. It seemed that without him as the driving force, the case had died—much like everyone involved in it.

"It's been months. Who would suspect you'd show up now? After all this time?" he reasoned. He was good at helping her mind align with more rational thoughts.

"So, we'll go," she said, confirming the plan to herself.

"We'll go," he agreed.

Less than an hour later, they were on horseback – Annis on Catori, the very mare she'd finally learned to ride on - taking the trails along the outskirts of town, headed for the Sanders' house.

The whole way there, Annis's heart sputtered about in her chest, seeming to threaten to quit one second and explode the next.

"Having second thoughts?" Sequoyah asked, as though reading her mind.

"No." It wasn't until he'd posed the question that she'd realized that wasn't it. She wanted to go. In fact, she felt more determined than ever to see the house. She wanted to take in all the material fortune William and her mother had felt so entitled to that they'd been willing to shred their own souls to attain it. Now neither of them ever would. Annis was certain she could draw some sick sense of satisfaction from seeing the abandoned mansion for herself.

She felt her chest tighten and her jaw clench as she thought about all that William had cost her, but her heartbeat gave up its erratic patterns, taking on a fast and fierce beat that her breath could hardly keep pace with.

"I want to see it," she said calmly. "I want to see what my mother and William saw. What they deemed more valuable than the lives of others. I want to see it. To see it and know that they'll never have it."

Sequoyah looked taken aback by her words. "You don't mean that."

She nodded. "Yes, I do. It's the only justice left for us."

His eyes narrowed. "There will never be justice for what they did, Annis. What they did, what he took, can't be undone or returned. There will never be justice. What you're looking for, you won't find at the house."

"You're wrong."

He laughed, but it was far from amusing. "Am I? About this? I'm surprised you of all people would say that to me."

Annis exhaled her frustrations loudly. "Why are you on about this? Don't you think this is hard enough as it is? If I have this one small thing to cling to that will ease the pain, why can't you let me have it?" she demanded, unable to grasp what his intentions were in picking a fight with her on this of all days.

"Because it won't ease the pain," he returned. The concern in his eyes reminded her he was always looking out for her, even if she didn't know she needed it. "You have to forgive them, Annis."

"I can't."

"Don't you see? If you don't forgive them…If you can't let this go, you don't let *them* go either. They'll be with you forever. You'll never be free. You'll never truly be…with me."

"Don't say that." It wasn't true. She was already with him. Her heart had been his from the moment she'd laid eyes on him. It didn't matter how broken she'd felt. She'd shared it, every last part of it, and he'd accepted it as it was. Until today.

"It's the truth, Annis. As long as you hold this inside you, it'll keep us apart. You'll never let me get any closer to you than you hold the grudge. It'll be an impenetrable barrier between us."

"Don't you see? That's the problem. I can't get past it from my side either. Every day, I live with the weight of what they did. Suffocated by it. Knowing you're there, on the other side, it's what gives me hope. It's the strength I need to keep carrying it. To keep pushing onward, even with this."

"No. It's not enough." He shook his head. "It's not the life I want for you. For us. A half-life, always tainted by the shadows of your past. You deserve more. We both do. I've given you every part of me, Annis. I want the same of you, if for no other reason than to set you free."

"I'll never be free of this."

"Yes, you will. Maybe we can't undo what they've done, but we can stop them from hurting you ever again. That's what forgiveness is, Annis. That's how to defeat them. That's how we win. You forgive them, and they lose all power. You refuse, and they'll torture you for the rest of your life. Long after they've taken their last breaths, they'll still be sucking you dry of yours."

"Could *you*? Could you ever forgive the people who murdered your family?"

"I have. I wouldn't be here today if I hadn't."

"I don't believe you."

"Yes, you do," he reminded her. "Because I've never given you reason not to." He turned away, looking out into the open green beyond the path they rode. "White men killed my family, Annis. And white men saved me. I wanted to hate them. I did hate them, for a long time, because it felt safer to do so. Safer to hate every white face I stood eye to eye with. And then, one day, I realized I was living isolated. Despite being taken care of and surrounded by love, I was still being robbed of my family. I couldn't forgive the men who had taken the first one, so I couldn't accept the men who had given me another. Once I understood...I changed my way of thinking. I let go. I forgave."

Annis rode in silence beside him. She reached out to take his hand and hold it in hers. She'd meant to give him comfort, but it was she who drew strength from him.

"It's not fair, you know," she mumbled under her breath after a long while. "You being raised by Poppy."

He turned his head toward her, surprise gleaming in his eyes. "I'm sorry?"

She shrugged, allowing a silly smirk to surface on her face. "How am I ever going to win any argument with you? It'll be impossible. I've got a lifetime of feeling foolish and making sheepish apologies ahead of me. It's not going to be an easy road. For either of us."

"Be easy for me," he said, squeezing her hand. "I'm good at forgiving."

She took his words at the depth they were meant and nodded solemnly. "I'll learn. I promise." Even as she said it, her intention to forgive took hold and the tightness in her chest dissipated. The cage she'd been living in creaked and stretched, and then pieces of it crumbled away. She found it easier to breathe with the load weighing down on her shoulders slowly lightening.

Sequoyah left her in silence to undo the mental web she'd weaved in her search for justice until, at last, they turned a bend and the mansion came into view.

"This is your home?" Sequoyah asked, his eyes wide. "This is where you grew up?"

She nodded, unable to speak. What William saw when he looked at this house was no longer of concern to her once she realized it was her home, her childhood, her past—and the last tie to those she'd loved, and lost, right along with those relics.

Slowing the horses to a walk, they came up the drive. The gate had been left open and the grounds unkept for months. Everything about the house felt abandoned, like just another ghost of the life she'd once known. Then, the front door opened, just as they were sliding down from the backs of their horses.

"Emmeline?" A man's voice called out, hesitation and disbelief encasing her name. "Is it you?"

Annis's first instinct was to shake her head, but the man coming toward her wasn't accusing in his question. His tone was hopeful.

"Mr. Charleston?" Annis recognized that the man who walked toward them was her father's attorney.

"It *is* you!" his eyes went wide, a smile of shock spreading over his face. "I had lost hope. After all that you've been through, all that happened..." he trailed off. "You can't imagine the guilt I've wrestled with after that letter was found. I'm just so relieved you're alive. You've come home!"

"Letter?" Annis couldn't make sense of anything the man was saying. "What letter?"

"Your housekeeper," he said, clearly dumbfounded by her ignorance. "Annis. She wrote a letter the night William killed your mother, a witness statement, giving a full account of all she'd been privy to over her time here. She even foretold her own death, Emmeline. Well, she suspected it anyway. But she was smart, she was. Placed the letter in the mailbox that night before he killed her. It was lost under another file for months." He shook his head, still visibly wracked with guilt over it all. "But you're here now. You're here, and the truth has surfaced. And all will be well in the nick of time."

"I'm sorry?" she still couldn't wrap her mind around what was happening. The only thing she was certain of was that things had not been well and that nothing had been sorted in the nick of time. Time had come and gone, and many a tragic moment right along with it. He simply hadn't been there to witness them.

"The house. Your inheritance. You've been missing so long and, given all that happened surrounding your absence, they were preparing to declare you dead so that the city could handle the state of your family's affairs moving forward." He turned back and forth between her and the house. "But you're here now. And you're of age. It's yours to claim. All of it."

Annis blinked, speechless. Finally, she understood the meaning of Floyd's words. The letter. Floyd had been threatening William, telling him his time would come, that the proof of his guilt would be found. If only Annis had understood that night. The things it might have changed. And Sawyer...

She shook her head, trying to clear the overwhelming clutter of her own thoughts, which had piled on top of each other. As they began to fall away, the more clearly she saw what was right in front of her. Her family home. She wasn't sure she wanted it. No, she was sure she didn't want it. The house she had come to say goodbye to, that much had not changed in light of this new information.

"What does he mean, what is he talking about?" Sequoyah asked quietly as time went on and Annis remained silent.

"I think he's saying I just became head of my family's shipping company." She gulped. It sounded absurd. "I own a fleet of ships. Seventeen, to be exact."

"Wh-what?" he stared back at her in disbelief. "What do you plan to do with them?"

She shrugged, staring out across the woods behind her house and remembering the night she ran toward them, certain she'd never look back. She'd been right to run. She'd found so much more beyond those trees than she ever could have dreamed. Maybe it was time to take another leap of faith, to cross new borders she never imagined she'd see the other side of.

"Think elephants get sea sick?" A small smile crept over Annis's mouth as the vision came into view within her mind's eye. A storm was brewing inside her, Annis could feel it stirring. And the world, it had better be ready.

THE END!

Acknowledgements

In a lot of ways, I'm not much unlike Annis from this story. I began the journey of writing her tale a very different woman from the one who's about to send the completed manuscript out into the world. And, just like Annis, I had a lovely circus of beautiful people guiding me along the way.

First and foremost, I want to thank my parents, who not only have always supported and embraced my desires to let my freak flag fly wild and free and upside down but have been the wind to make it dance sky-high in moments I needed it most. This story would not be what it is today, if it wasn't for them.

While I'm on that, this story wouldn't be at all, if it weren't for my mother. From the source of inspiration to completion, no aspect of this book would have come to be if it hadn't been for her. I hope she knows the depths of my gratitude, the words 'thank you' will never suffice.

My brilliant editor, Jaclyn DeVore. Magic brought us together. And magic was made once it did. It's as simple as that. And as profound. I've never had a more trusted partner in my writing endeavors, and I look forward to more exciting writing adventures together.

No book would be complete without a gorgeous cover, and thanks to Regina Wamba, this book has just that. The way she managed to capture the essence of Annis's tale is more than I could have hoped for and I can't wait to see this beauty in print!

Sending a book out into the world can be a scary thing. Having wonderful author friends willing to read your book first to take the edge off said fear, is awesome. So, thank you, S.A. Hussey and Debi Matlack for being those first eyes, for sharing those first thoughts, and catching those pesky typos that always slip through, no matter how many edits and proofreads are done.

Speaking of proofreads, I must mention the amazing Barb Piper, who comes through without fail in the last minutes, under pressure, regardless of how crazy my deadline, to proof my manuscripts. Thank you for enabling my 'best under pressure' operating style and always having my back in all things typos.

Zeke, I know you're waiting on that Beemer. I'm working on it.

Ella. My heart. My daily motivation. My proof of magic.

And you. The reader. No story would be complete, without an audience to join in and enjoy.

~ Karina

Did you love *The Wild in her Eyes*? Then you should read *Bittersweet* by K.S. Thomas!

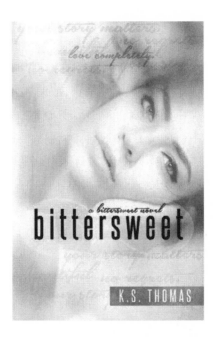

Esi is young, beautiful and smart. She's got it all...and then some, but it's not what you'd expect.

Seven years after fate has her colliding - literally - with the man of her dreams, the two finally find themselves walking down the aisle. The day couldn't be more perfect. For one shining moment in time, she has it all.

Then a tragic accident changes everything.

Getting married was supposed to be the final touch on their already blissful relationship, but after the car crash, nothing seems right anymore. Soon after they get home from the hospital, Esi discovers she's pregnant. However, after the extensive damages her heart has endured from the night of the traumatic wreck, this miracle of life brings with it the reality of death.

Now Esi and Carter both have to face facts. Someone might not survive.

While ever after may not be as happy as Esi has always hoped, she's learning to appreciate the beauty in strength and surviving, and finding that love, no matter how true or how complete, sometimes is simply *bittersweet*.

Read more at www.authorksthomas.com.

About the Author

The stereotypical writer through and through, I find hiding out alone in my office, cut off from society where I can pursue my obsessive compulsions in peace & carry on uninterrupted conversations with my imaginary friends while I sip coffee, to be all the rage.

I like people too.

The real ones.

But I'm shy and often awkward, so I don't show it well (unless you're my kid, then I'm like, hug central - but you're probably not so...).

If we meet - please don't hold this against me.

I should tell you, while my one, single, solitary novel may not show it, it's actually year seven in my publishing career, and I've just entered my third author life.

Previously, I've been a genre jumping story chaser, as well as a committed contemporary romance junky (our addictions may have crossed - I'm known as K.S. Thomas in those circles and you may find my long list of romantic fixes at www.authorksthomas.com).

This next life, I'm tackling as myself - Karina Giörtz. No pen name. No set genre. No game plan.

It's exciting.

And scary.

And I'm nervous.

But I'm told you need those...nerves. They let you know when you're growing, taking chances, becoming more. If you don't feel the rattle of your teeth between your jaws every now and again, you're not living right. Hell, you're probably not living at all.

Made in the USA
Middletown, DE
09 April 2019